W9-CJL-081

GOOD
BAD
WOMAN

A Frankie Richmond Mystery

GOOD
BAD
WOMAN

Elizabeth Woodcraft

KENSINGTON BOOKS
http://www.kensingtonbooks.com

This novel is entirely a work of fiction. The names, characters and incidents portrayed in it are the work of the author's imagination. Any resemblance to actual persons, living or dead, events or localities is entirely coincidental.

KENSINGTON BOOKS are published by

Kensington Publishing Corp.
850 Third Avenue
New York, NY 10022

Copyright © 2000 by Elizabeth Woodcraft. This edition is published in arrangement with Collins Crime, an imprint of HarperCollins, London.

All Kensington titles, imprints and distributed lines are available at special quantity discounts for bulk purchases for sales promotion, premiums, fundraising, educational or institutional use.

Special book excerpts or customized printings can also be created to fit specific needs. For details, write or phone the office of the Kensington Special Sales Manager: Kensington Publishing Corp., 850 Third Avenue, New York, NY 10022, Attn. Special Sales Department. Phone: 1-800-221-2647.

Kensington and the K logo Reg. U.S. Pat. & TM Off.

Library of Congress Card Catalogue Number: 2001099267
ISBN 0-7582-0258-X

First Printing: September 2002
10 9 8 7 6 5 4 3 2 1

Printed in the United States of America

To Caroline

ACKNOWLEDGMENTS

Many people have helped in the writing of this book including Peggy Perry, Marijke Woolsey, Dorothy Reinders and Maureen Hanscomb. I would like to thank in particular John Petherbridge and the class at City Lit; my agent Annette Green; Julia Wisdom, Anne O'Brien and the team at HarperCollins; and Val Wilmer for sharing some (!) of my taste in music and saying I should give it a go.

In the United States I would like to thank my editor John Scognamiglio and the Kensington Publishing Corp. And my very great thanks go to Sue Katz, Sarina Scialabba, Anne Block and Jean Smith for their help in the translation from English to American.

One

Wednesday Afternoon—Chambers

The phone on my desk rang. I licked my fingers, moved my cream cheese and tomato sandwich and picked up the receiver.

"Frankie, I know you said you wanted to do paperwork tomorrow, but Davidson's have just rung. Kay's got a quick in-and-out job for tomorrow morning that she wants you to do. She's faxing the papers through. It's at Highbury Corner Mags."

I groaned. A quick in-and-out at Highbury Corner Magistrates' Court was a contradiction in terms and Gavin, my clerk, knew that very well. Then again, if Kay Davidson wanted me in particular there might be something interesting in it.

"What is it?" I asked.

"Drunk and disorderly."

"Drunk and—Gavin! I'm meant to be doing those appeal papers in Morris. We're nearly out of time."

"She said it was important."

"Oh, what, important that someone regularly in the Court of Appeal should return to the magistrates' court?"

"Someone regularly where?"

"All right, someone who would like to be regularly in the Court of Appeal. Someone of nearly ten years call—"

"Who is charming and eager to help out a clerk in distress . . ." Gavin was playing the game in his gruff, cockney accent.

"Someone who has been at the Bar for nine years, and who may well be charming and eager to help out a clerk in distress but who has, it should be remembered, forgotten most of the crime she ever knew—you are saying it is important that she should do this case?" I asked.

"Yes," he said.

"Isn't there anyone else?" I wheedled. In the pause that followed I knew Gavin was pretending to look at the computer screen to see what everyone else in chambers was doing the next day. He liked Kay. If she had asked for me, he would make sure she got me.

"No," he said. "There's no one else."

"All right, Gavin, I will do it. But if I'm not out of court by half past eleven you will seriously regret it."

"You say the sweetest things," he said. I replaced the receiver and picked up my cup of tea.

My phone rang again. I spilled tea on my sandwich as I answered it.

Gavin said cheerfully, "I've got Kay on the line, to have a word about tomorrow."

"OK." I pushed the briefs on my desk out of the way of some insistent drips of tea and looked for something to make notes on. I found a piece of paper that looked suspiciously as if it had been on my desk for some time. I read "FR ring Dr. Henry" and a number with a Brighton area code, and promised myself I would do it as soon as I had spoken to Kay. Gavin put her through.

"Frankie, I'm sorry about this case."

Yeah, yeah, yeah, I thought, as I dabbed at the tea by the desk calendar.

"It's just that it's an old client of yours." She paused. "It's Saskia."

"Saskia! My God, Saskia."

I hadn't seen Saskia for at least five years. Tall, blonde,

lovely Saskia. She had large grey eyes and a wide friendly smile with perfect teeth. I'd represented her on several occasions when she'd been arrested after demonstrations. We'd had some good results, mainly due to that charming smile. She made you think of full fat milk and welfare orange juice, as my mom would say. She was in fact more a child of the seventies and eighties, rebelling against the Conservative government.

"What is Saskia doing being charged with drunk and disorderly? I would have thought a little marijuana was more her thing."

"I don't know. She rang me from the police station. She sounded in quite a state."

"What time was she arrested?" I began making notes.

"Half past two this afternoon."

"Half past two! Where?"

"Balls Pond Road. Outside the sofa factory."

"I can't believe this. What was she doing in Islington? I thought she lived in Manchester now."

"I don't know any more about that than you do. It was a very short phone call," Kay said. "The last I saw of her was at one of those women's sixties evenings at Camden Town Hall. That was years ago."

"Do you mean THE women's sixties evening, where you and I . . . ?"

"Yes."

I snorted. That must have been seven years ago, almost to the month. Kay and I had had our final, noisy, passionate argument at the back of the hall when she refused to dance to "Get Ready" by the Temptations. She said you couldn't dance to that beat, whereas anyone with half an ear for music . . . but don't get me started. Kay and I hadn't spoken to each other for nearly a year after that night, and since she was a criminal solicitor and I had stopped doing crime shortly after, we had rarely spoken since.

"What's in the brief then?" I said professionally.

"That's about it, actually."

"And I assume this is a freebie." I tried not to sound calculating.

"We'd never get Legal Aid for it." Did she breathe deeply before saying, "How about I take you out to supper to make up for it?"

"When?" I asked.

"When you like." She was expansive. "How about tonight?"

Mentally I surveyed the contents of my fridge. Olives and two-percent milk would test the powers of the best TV chef. I put majesty into my voice: "All right, where?"

"What do you want to eat?"

"Italian?" I ventured.

"There's a good Korean restaurant near here."

"I said Italian."

"I know you did."

I wondered who had stood her up. I could hear the olives calling me, pathetically, tragically. The milk, I knew, was sour.

"Chinese?" I was willing to compromise. I always had been. There was silence. "I don't want to eat Korean," I complained. "The only thing I like are those flowers carved out of carrots and turnips, and you can't eat those."

She sniffed.

"Think Italian," I continued. "Think of red wine and garlic and crusty bread and a cheerful companion. We can go to that place on Upper Street and you can drive me home after."

"I'll see you there at seven." I didn't like her resigned tone of voice. "I'll bring your brief," she added.

"And your happy face," I pleaded. I put the phone down and said, "Damn." I'd been so close to getting through a phone call with Kay without whining. I began dabbing White Out over the tea stains on the instructions to prepare Mrs. Morris's notice of appeal.

* * *

I always forget where Gino's is and I got off the bus at the wrong stop just as it began to rain. When I arrived at the restaurant I was very wet. And late. I was not cheerful.

As I opened the door, warmth, candlelight and the smell of garlic embraced me.

"Buona sera, signora," Gino bustled up, his hair a new alarming shade of aubergine. "Comment allez-vous? Very very wet, I see. Table for ... ?"

I looked round the room. Kay was late too.

"Two."

"And some vino tinto, signora? Asseyez-vous." He put me next to the huge open fireplace.

"Yes." I was puzzled. Kay was never late. I sat down, absently giving Gino my dripping coat. My long black jacket, bought expensively from Ede & Ravenscroft, suppliers of wigs and robes to the legal profession, was wet too. I took it off and hung it on the back of the chair. My trousers would have to stay where they were. It was my favorite court outfit, and I was pleased I was wearing it when Kay suggested going out. I always liked how I looked in it, slick but professional. Except that at the moment I looked slick like a wet rodent looks slick. And so much for my fabulous new haircut—my lowlights had slid into my highlights and they all looked just wet. In the back of the spoon I could see spikes of my long bangs sticking damply to my forehead.

Perhaps her car had broken down in the rain, although that was unlikely. She always had a new car; being a successful solicitor, it was a business car. I was still driving my ancient Renault. Not that I'm bitter, but she wouldn't have got where she is today without me. I was the one who sat up with her at nights testing her on criminal procedure and client/solicitor relations. Huh!

Perhaps she hadn't come because she'd had a better offer. She had done that to me before, but not for seven years, and she was meant to be bringing me my brief. Kay would never be unprofessional in that way, she'd never leave me without a brief. Although, as she had said, there was nothing in the brief. It would be merely a piece of white paper with a pink ribbon around it. My instructions would be: "Counsel will do her best."

The red wine came. I ordered some garlic bread. To hell with what it did to my stomach.

She didn't come.

It was eight o'clock. I didn't have my cell phone with me—I wondered whether I'd left it plugged into the charger—so Gino let me use the phone on the bar and I rang her office. The answering machine wasn't on. I thought about ringing my apartment to pick up my messages but I couldn't remember my secret code number. I rang Kay's home, she still lived in the small Victorian house in Stamford Hill which we had shared during our relationship, and left a concerned and only slightly irritated message. I ordered spaghetti à l'amatriciana and my clothes and my hair began to dry. The house red which Gino had poured solicitously into a large glass was soft and full and tasted almost as if I was in Italy. And as I sat, steaming gently by the fire, waiting for my pasta, I thought nostalgically back to me and Kay on our last vacation in a tent in Tuscany.

I had just passed my final exams—yes, OK, she had done her bit and had tested me on revenue and trusts—and she had just been taken on by a law center in North London. We were both very pleased with ourselves and bursting with success and ambition. The weather in Tuscany was glorious and we visited wonderful cities and ate fabulous food. Then, on our last night, as we walked back to the tent after a silent meal in a small restaurant, she told me our relationship was over. As I stumbled along the path trying to take in what she was saying, she told me she wanted her freedom. We both needed different things, she said, at this new time in our lives. We had had five good years and now we should move on. I assumed that she'd met someone she was attracted to at her interview.

Of course, the trouble with being on vacation in a tent is that you can't put physical distance between you. We crept into our individual sleeping bags, but by the first light of day we were in each other's arms for warmth. By the time we got to the airport we had reconciled, and we bought joint olive oil and sun-dried tomatoes in the duty-free shop. The relationship had limped along for another eighteen months until the night of the women's sixties party when she had gone home with a woman who probably thought "Green Onions" was something you threw out of your kitchen cabinet.

Gino brought me my pasta. "Everything OK, signora?" he asked, concern filling his soft, round face.

I probably would have burst into tears but I took a mouthful of my food and nearly choked on the chilli.

"Everything's fine, great," I said, breathing in.

I drank almost the whole bottle of wine. Kay had still not appeared and I was worried.

I asked Gino if he could bring the bill and check again whether anyone had rung me. He went to confer with the chef and brought over my damp coat and the bill with a sad shake of his head.

It was still raining and cars hissed by me as I walked back to the subway. I felt peculiar and it wasn't the effects of the alcohol or the mix of red wine, garlic bread and green salad. Upper Street was almost deserted and as I approached Highbury Corner, with the little alleyways leading off and the dark looming pub on the corner, the strangeness increased so that if anyone had asked me I would have said that I thought I was being followed. Just near the bus stop someone behind me coughed, but when I turned around there was no one there.

A taxi was passing on the other side of the street. I

shouted at it, gesticulating, and narrowly avoided being crushed by a number 19 bus as I ran across the road.

The driver had to go some way in the wrong direction before he could turn off for Stoke Newington and I was pleased. When we got to the house I asked him to wait until I'd got inside the front door before he drove off.

I walked into my ground-floor apartment and locked the door behind me. The timer had already turned on the lamp in the living room, filling the room with a pale light. Everything looked normal. The flashing red light of my answering machine on the floor, the *Guardian* draped over the couch where I had left it last night and a pile of papers marked "Return to solicitors NOW" waiting patiently on the old comfy armchair. A used wine glass, mine, and a half-drunk cup of tea, also mine, sat together on the dark wood coffee table, next to the remote control for the TV. Everything was normal.

I played my messages. My mom, laughing, leaving me her name and number like the machine had asked her to, just saying hello. Dr. Henry's secretary primly asking me to ring the doctor at my earliest convenience. And then Kay. Her voice was strained.

"Frankie, it's me. It's, em, a quarter to seven. I . . . I just went out of the office to get some cigarettes and when I got back the place had been burglarized. I've rung the police. I can't remember the name of the restaurant to ring you there. I'm sorry I shan't make it. Hope you get this in time. I'll . . . I'll speak to you."

There was a beep and then it was Kay again, sounding more relaxed. "You're still not home. Don't you ever take your cell phone with you?"

I silently answered an outraged "sometimes" as I noticed my phone in its smart black jacket sticking up sadly between the two cushions of the sofa.

"I hope you're having something nice to eat," the message went on, "and you haven't given yourself indigestion.

It's nine o'clock. The police took ages. I had to buy some more cigarettes. Ring me when you get in."

And finally Lena. Lena was my best friend.

"Hi, Fran. Just to remind you about tomorrow evening. The film starts at six forty. The reviews say it's absolutely amazing. Ring me soon. Night."

I really wanted to ring Lena, but I knew I ought to ring Kay because she had my brief.

She answered the phone immediately.

"They made such a mess of it," she said. "All my files everywhere. But no one else's. And they didn't even take any money. They scratched the cash box but didn't open it, or even take it, which they could have done."

"Perhaps they were baby burglars and didn't know what to do. Or perhaps it was an unhappy client who got community service when he'd really wanted forty days in jail."

"That's what the police said, that it might have been a client who'd got a bad result, but there's no one I can think of."

"What about my brief?" I interrupted her train of thought.

"Oh, I'm sorry . . . Can you make yourself a back sheet?"

"I suppose so. What name is Saskia using now? And what is she pleading?"

"Susan Baker. I think it's a straight guilty plea, unless she tells you something that makes you think you should fight it."

"Are you all right? Do you want me to come over?"

"I'm fine, fine."

"OK, I'll ring you tomorrow when I've finished."

I rang Lena.

"Hiya," she said, brightly. "How are you?"

I told her about my evening. Despite being in a traumatic relationship, which was more than I was, Lena's always good for a bit of advice, the telephone equivalent of a cup of cocoa. Not that I drink cocoa. But then, she regularly gives me advice that I ignore.

"Do you think she really was burglarized?" Lena asked. "You don't think she was . . . required elsewhere?"

"No, no. She was burglarized, you could tell from her voice. Anyway, how are you? Is the gorgeous Sophie accompanying us to the Screen on the Green tomorrow?"

"She might." Lena sounded doubtful. "We're not seeing quite so much of each other at the moment."

"Oh dear," I clucked.

Our conversation continued along the old comforting lines. I forgot about Dr. Henry and went to bed, clicking on a Motown cassette and drifting away as the Four Tops implored their woman to get out of their life and let them sleep at night.

Two

Thursday Morning— Highbury Corner

Highbury Corner Magistrates' Court was full of cigarette smoke and depressed young men. Susan Baker was listed as appearing in Court 5 and I made myself known to the usher, smiling so that we would be called on early. Saskia herself was in custody and I made my way down the concrete stairs to the cells to see the jailer.

"Have you got Miss Baker here?"

"Indeed we do, madam," he said cheerfully. "Just along there, past the nurse's room on your right."

I made my way along the dark corridor, past solid, locked cell doors, breathing in the smell of disinfectant on concrete. A woman asked me for a light. I could see her lips through the grated window in the door. I didn't have any matches. Each door had a small blackboard beside it. I stopped by the board with the word BAKER chalked in clumsy upper case letters. I peered through the grate.

"Saskia?" I asked into the gloom of the tiny cell.

"Frankie!" Saskia crept up to the door. Her face was a mess. Not so much peaches and cream as pork and beans.

"What *has* happened to you?" I looked at her in alarm.

"I'll tell you later," she said. "I'm going to get out, aren't I? Have you got your car here? Oh, Frankie, get me out." She was crying.

"OK. First of all, how did you come to be charged with drunk and disorderly? Were you?"

"No. But I'll have to say yes, won't I? Yes, say I was, say I was. Because I don't want to plead not guilty, I just want to get out. I will get out, won't I?"

"Yes, you will, whether you plead guilty or not guilty. If you plead guilty today you'll get out, with a fine probably. But you could fight it. They'd have to give you bail unless there's any serious reason why they shouldn't. Are you living in London now?"

"Yes . . . well, I was. Yes, yes, I am."

"Saskia, are you OK? Have you seen a doctor?"

"What? In here? You're joking. Look, Frankie, I'm just going to plead guilty to this. OK, I was on Balls Pond Road and I was singing, rather loudly. Things have been a bit tough recently. Then the cops came and we had a bit of a discussion about one thing and another. The only thing of any relevance was that they said I was singing flat. I knew I wasn't and the streetlight agreed with me. And I asked lots of people in the street what they thought. I don't think they like music in Balls Pond Road." This is just what she used to be like in those demonstration cases. Talking to streetlights! I could imagine how they would feel about that in Balls Pond Road. It was a busy road with huge trucks pounding along day and night, but it couldn't make up its mind whether it was a select residential area, with its large houses converted into expensive apartments, or a lively friendly place with high-rise public housing. Either way they would think she was drunk.

"Well," I said, trying to find the right tone, "was it protest music? Did it have Important words?"

I remembered her singing in court one day, years before, about the purpose behind one of the civil disobedience demonstrations she and her friends had done outside a movie theater that showed porn films. The song had about fourteen verses, but the magistrates were so shocked they listened to every line. Perhaps singing did mean she got her message across. I sighed. I felt old and cynical.

Now she looked at me disapprovingly, as if she knew I still ate meat and that I did not take my bottles and cans to the recycling bins.

"None of us can claim our music is important. Only history will tell whether it was."

"All right, what was it about?"

"That, Frankie, can only be told over a cup of coffee. You used to make lovely coffee. Are you still in the apartment with the Danish pastry shop across the road? Mmm, warm cherry." Saskia was obviously beginning to perk up, which I knew had nothing to do with my presence or any sense of confidence she had in my courtroom skills. It was because we were having something like a political argument.

"Saskia, were you drunk?"

"I don't know. Maybe. It was sunny and I was drunk on the crisp autumn air."

"Oh, for God's sake, Saskia, shut up for a minute," I snapped, momentarily losing my professional veneer.

She smiled at me, a shadow of her normal smile, canned pineapple and Cool Whip, but devastating just the same.

"Do you consider that your behavior was disorderly?"

"I don't know. What do you think?"

"I think the magistrates might."

"I'm pleading guilty, Frankie. I want to get out." She was desperate again. I was surprised. This woman had gone in and out of custody very regularly at the height of the demonstrations. She never agreed to be released on her own recognizance, she was always sent to jail.

"OK." She knew the score. I would follow her instructions.

It was five to ten. I went back upstairs and spoke to the man representing the Crown Prosecution Service, who looked about fourteen. He had a large pile of buff-colored files in front of him and was trying to talk to six barristers at once. I pushed myself to the front, hissing, "I'm a quickie, I'm a quickie," and got him to tell me what evidence the police were intending to give. Extraordinarily, their story was almost identical to my client's, except that they said she asked a traffic light whether she was singing flat. "Streetlight? Street furniture?" I suggested hopefully. We settled on "inanimate object" and I told him we would be pleading guilty. He seemed relieved.

The usher was bustling importantly at the back of the court, her black gown occasionally revealing flashes of a shocking pink dress. I pointed to the name of Baker on the list attached to her clipboard and told her that we were a five-minute job and we could be in and out before she had time to turn around. I thought I was being irresistible.

However it wasn't until twenty-five past eleven that I leapt to my feet as Saskia was escorted to the witness stand. "I represent Miss Baker this morning, madam."

They weren't used to drunks looking like Saskia or being represented. The charge was put to Saskia, she pleaded guilty and I had hardly finished repeating my name for the third time for the benefit of the very old magistrate on the left when the chairwoman said, "Miss Richmond, we were thinking of a twenty pound fine and ten pounds costs or one day. Do you wish to say anything?"

"No, madam."

"You may stand down, Miss Butcher."

"Baker," I corrected.

"Yes."

By being in custody overnight Saskia had served her one day in prison so she wouldn't have to pay the fine. She knew that and grinned at me as she walked out.

I bowed to the bench, picked up my *Guardian* and slid along the seat. A shifty-looking man in his mid thirties, wearing a shapeless brown jacket with the collar up, and holding a spiral notebook, approached me at the back of the courtroom.

"Miss Eh . . . ?"

"Yes?" I said pleasantly. I noticed that he bit his nails.

"Your client there, isn't she also known as Saskia Baron?"

"You'd better ask her."

"And how do you spell your name, Miss Eh . . . ?"

"Correctly," I said primly, and walked to the door of the court as he slid over to speak to the officer in the case. It was eleven thirty exactly.

Saskia appeared from the ladies' room and we walked out to my car, which was parked on a side street off Holloway Road. There was five minutes left on the meter.

"Did that journalist speak to you?" I asked her as she got into the car.

"What journalist?" she asked, clicking her seat belt into place.

"In the courtroom," I said as I slowly turned the car in the narrow street where I had parked. "He had pock-marked skin and was wearing brown shoes. There he is—" I watched him cross the road. "Why's he leaving at this time? He can't have finished work, it's too early. And I doubt your case is the scoop of the day, it's hardly front-page news."

As I waited for a large delivery van to squeeze past me, I saw the man get into the passenger seat of a dark sedan.

"Where?" Saskia twisted in her seat, as the car moved away in the opposite direction. "Where?" Her voice was loud and anxious.

"He's gone," I said, irritated that she hadn't seen him, concerned by her reaction. "Are you all right?" I asked her. I didn't tell her he'd had a driver.

Saskia sat with her head back and her eyes closed, as if

savoring her freedom. As we turned into Holloway Road I asked, "Do you want to run in and see Kay? Her office is just down here. You could wash up, then we could go somewhere nice for coffee. There are some good places on Church Street."

Saskia pulled down the sun visor and looked at her face in the mirror. "Oh my God, look at me," she said mournfully, touching her face with her fingertips. "My cheek, my eye—Frankie, I can't go out in public looking like this. Can we just go to your place? Would that be OK? I can't face seeing anyone. Perhaps I could have a bath or something . . ."

I looked at my watch. I could hear the appeal papers in Morris calling me. Rapidly I reorganized my timetable. "OK," I said, "OK." We drove past Kay's office and I touched her arm gently. "You don't look that bad."

She smiled at me gratefully. "You know, you haven't changed a bit," she said.

"What do you mean?" I asked.

"You're still . . . well, smart and crisp, all professional in your black clothes," she said. "I like your hair, is it different?"

"No." I looked at myself quickly in the rear-view mirror. "It's always been like this." It was short at the back and long at the front. "I've just had some blond streaks put in, to highlight the brown or something." I flicked my bangs back.

"Well, it's lovely to see you," she said. "It's like coming home."

At my apartment I ran a bath in my small white bathroom and found some green herbal essence which filled the room with something vaguely related to the smell of fields and trees as I poured it under the running tap. I put out two giant blue towels and an old clean shirt of mine and left her to it. In the kitchen I made coffee and took some apple strudel out of the freezer to put into the microwave on Saskia's reappearance.

I rang chambers and told Gavin I'd be in later.

"You've got a couple of messages," he said. "Can you *please* ring Dr. Henry. And someone called Hayman or Wayman rang—I can't read this, Jenna wrote it, she's a lovely girl, but her handwriting's terrible—anyway, I think it says it's not urgent and they'll ring back."

"Who is Dr. Henry?" I asked.

"I thought you knew," he said. "She said he'd ring you at home, he has your number."

"Who did?"

"The secretary. I thought it was personal." He gave me Dr. Henry's number again, reminded me of my appeal papers and rang off.

I dialed the number. "Dr. Henry's surgery," an efficient female voice said.

"Is Dr. Henry there?" I could hear Saskia singing something folksy in the bath.

"I am afraid Dr. Henry is in consultation at this moment. Could I ask you to call back later?"

"Well, no," I said. "Dr. Henry appears to be trying to contact me."

"What is this concerning?" The thin voice was guarded.

"I have no idea. My name is Frances Richmond."

"Oh, Miss Richmond," her tone was concerned, caring, "I'm afraid Dr. Henry is so busy right now, but I'll say that you called. I know that the doctor is very anxious to speak with you."

I thanked her and put the phone down as Saskia came in, smelling sweet and looking much better than I ever did in my grey denim shirt. Her blond hair stood up in wet spikes.

"Frankie, that was a life-saver. Mmm, something smells wonderful." She sat down at the kitchen table as I poured coffee into two cups. The autumn sun cut through the

French doors. Outside two late pink roses swayed in the wind. Saskia looked like a battered angel as her hair dried into soft pale layers.

The microwave pinged and I took out the strudel. I cut slices and put them on my blue and yellow Italian plates. "Now," I said, pulling out a chair, "we are going to do some serious talking."

She nibbled her strudel.

"First of all," I began, "where do those bruises come from?"

She picked up her cup and ran her fingers across the blue-painted rim. She took a mouthful of coffee. "Heaven."

"Yes?"

"Well . . ."

The phone rang in the living room.

"Frankie! You're in! I was going to leave a message on your machine."

"Lena, I'm a bit busy at the moment. Can I call you back?"

"Well, actually, sweetie, you can't—that's what I'm ringing about. I'm just off for three days to Paris."

"Paris!" I turned to raise my eyebrows at Saskia, to see her disappearing into the hall.

"Saskia!" I called and heard the front door click.

"Frankie? Frankie?"

"Look, Lena, I've got to go."

"I'm ringing just to say I'm going to Paris with Sophie."

"With Sophie? My God. I thought you two weren't talking to each other." I stretched the cord of the phone as far as I could and looked out of the large bay window. I banged on the glass as I saw Saskia heading toward Stoke Newington High Street.

"She rang last night after I spoke to you and said she was exhausted and—"

"Lena, I've got to go."

"You're not upset, are you?"

"No, no, have a lovely time, send me a postcard. Bye bye."

"It means I shan't be able to make the film."

"No problem. Bye."

"OK. Bye. I'm sorry. Bye."

I slammed down the phone and ran out of the house. At the corner of the road there was no sign of Saskia but a number 149 bus was sailing majestically toward Dalston. "Shit," I said and turned back to the apartment. "Shit," I said again as I realized I was locked out.

Three

Thursday Afternoon—Chambers

"**Y**ou look a bit cold, Frankie," Gavin said, as I walked into chambers an hour later. "You should have come out in a coat."

"I should have come out with my purse, keys and wallet and then I wouldn't have had to walk most of the way and been frozen half to death," I said stiffly. I had found a pound in my jacket pocket but I'd had to get off the bus at Liverpool Street. I had come into chambers because I kept a spare set of house keys in the drawer of my desk. I know most people have a good friend or neighbor who looks after a spare set of keys for moments such as this, but Lena lived in Finsbury Park, which was too far away, and I didn't know my neighbors very well.

There had been attempts, by my neighbors, when I first moved in to the apartment. The woman who lived in the top apartment invited me to a make-up party. It was shortly after my split with Kay, and I thought I could buy my way back to attractiveness and social success through cosmetic products. As it turned out, I spent the evening feeling bleak and out of place and signed a check for £27.50 for two small bottles of something green for my complexion. I hadn't spoken to them since.

I felt I could do with something green for my complexion now, particularly my nose, which I knew was red and glowing.

I thought that was the reason for Gavin's stunned look. "I didn't know you were coming in, so Marcus is having a meeting in your office." He was apologetic. "He's, eh, he's only just gone in."

I groaned. Marcus was famous for his two-hour conferences with clients.

"Think of it this way," Gavin said, "he's a sad guy and it's the only social life he's got." Marcus was a self-made upper class man. He had changed his voice, his education and his background to become more aristocratic than any of them.

"Think of it this way: I'm a sad woman," I said, thinking of the now cold cup of coffee and the congealing slice of apple strudel waiting to be eaten in my kitchen. "I am not Marcus's social secretary. This means I can't even get on with my appeal papers."

I slumped onto a chair.

"Jenna's just run out to pick up some books from the High Court," Gavin said. Jenna was the newest recruit in the clerks' room, our fourth junior clerk. "So you can sit there for a moment."

"Thank you," I said. There was a constant battle in the clerks' room between the clerks trying to retain their territory and barristers wanting to flop down in the secure and busy atmosphere of the center of chambers.

"I think Simon wanted to speak to you, actually." Gavin picked up the phone. "Simon, Frankie's in. Didn't you say you wanted a word? She looks as if she needs lunch . . . He's coming right down," he said to me.

"Gavin!"

My life was an open book to the clerks, but Gavin still persisted in trying to pair me off with men.

"I know you're, you know, That Way," Gavin had said to me in the pub one evening, "but I also see you as a very open-minded person." He had been drunk. "Now Simon, he's just the type of man you could do with."

"Does he dust? Does he clean? Would he have my dinner on the table when I got in?"

Gavin blinked at me.

"Well then, what's the point?" I said.

"No no, he's, he's, well, you're a bit of a thinker, aren't you? And Simon isn't. What, for you, could be more perfect? A lot of ladies do find him good looking, you know." Gavin had been looking at too many computer screens. "Plus, he's loaded."

Thinking of the pots of money I knew Simon had inherited only recently after the death of a doting grandmother, his regular private income and his part share in a farm, when he walked into the clerks' room, I said, "All right, Simon, you can take me out for lunch." I looked at his wide smile and his good teeth. He really was quite good looking in an old-fashioned way. If he paid more attention to his choice of tie, I thought, he'd be quite a catch for someone.

We went to the Café Rouge in Fetter Lane. As soon as we sat down Simon ordered a bottle of Bourgueuil.

"Is that just for you, or are we sharing it?" I asked as the waitress walked away.

"It's for both of us," Simon said. "Oh God, I'm sorry, I should have asked you. You know about wine, don't you?"

"I'm not sure that's the right answer, Simon. If I had been a man I assume, perhaps stupidly, that you would have asked me at least to agree to your choice."

"If you'd been a man like Marcus, who knows nothing about wine, I probably wouldn't," he said irritatingly. "But I concede your point. I forgot about your knowledge of wine, because you are a woman."

"Well, thank you for that," I said.

"Do you hate all men?" Simon asked.

"For God's sake, Simon, what a stupid thing to say. I work with you, don't I?"

The waiter came to ask if we were ready to order and we both asked for steak and fries, rare.

"But it's an interesting thought, isn't it? Lesbians . . ." I didn't like to think where this conversation might be going. "Have you ever thought of starting your own set?" Simon poured wine into my glass. "You could be head of the first women-only set."

"Are you trying to get rid of me?" I asked.

"Not at all. I like you being in chambers. It's an idea, though, isn't it?"

"I'm not sure what the point would be. It couldn't be all lesbians, there aren't enough of us at the bar." I had thought before about the possibility of striking out into the strange territory of an all women's set of chambers, with women clerks.

"And so," Simon said carefully, "some of the barristers would have boyfriends or husbands, and they might have boy children."

"Exactly, you couldn't keep men out." I tore a piece of bread in half, showering the table with flakes of crust. "You'd have male clients. Then there'd be the motorbike couriers, the mailman, the window cleaner."

The waiter placed our orders in front of us.

"And I know you'd be the last to say this, Simon, but women barristers are not necessarily any better, whatever that means, than men. They're not intrinsically more politically right on. Margaret Thatcher was a barrister. They're not kinder or gentler—but you don't want that in a barrister anyway." I stuffed fries into my mouth.

"They usually smell nicer."

"Simon," I said. "Barristers are barristers. Rich, posh, privileged."

"Are you?" he asked.

"I'm trying to make a political point. I'm not, as it happens, as you can tell perfectly well from my vowel sounds. And I'm not rich . . . well, not particularly. Certainly not at the moment, anyway."

"This lunch is on me," Simon said with concern.

"Thank you," I said.

We raised our glasses to each other. Simon said, "You don't really think I'm trying to get rid of you, do you?"

"No, Simon, I don't."

"Because that would be absurd. Because, you know, I really like you." His cheeks began to glow. "And if there ever came a time when you thought you wanted to, you know, try . . . try again, try with a man . . . you could always turn to me."

"Thank you, but no."

"No strings attached, just to see, you know."

"Simon, give me a break."

"Just a bit of practice?"

"Simon," I said, slowly swilling the contents of my glass, "if this were not expensive wine, I would pour it on your head now." I looked at his broad face and his eager blue eyes. "Just order two Armagnacs and we'll forget you said that."

"OK," he said. "Sorry. This is rather good wine, isn't it? I assume neither of us is in court this afternoon."

"I'm not," I said, still trying to assert a sense of annoyance.

"But if the system is so awful," Simon said, as we sat with large glasses of rich amber Armagnac, "isn't it going to corrupt you?" He gazed at me.

"It might, but not the way you want it to, Simon. Don't start that again."

"Well, let me cheer you up and tell you about my morning in front of His Honor Judge Swiffham till you regain your sense of justice and love for all humankind."

"A slight feeling of pity may be as good as you're going to get," I said. "We'd better have some coffee."

I ordered two espressos and Simon began his story. We were a few minutes in when I realized he was talking about the dreadful pornography case that he had been involved in for weeks, led by our head of chambers. Their client had been found guilty and had been sentenced this morning.

"And just as the judge was about to pass sentence, our client leapt up and shouted, 'Police corruption! Police corruption! I paid good money to keep out of court, and look at me now. How much are you supposed to pay?' "

"How much *are* you supposed to pay?"

"I don't know." Simon grinned. "But our client had obviously not paid enough. I didn't know anything about it, it hadn't been part of our case. But from something my client mumbled later in the cells, he paid something in the area of five thousand pounds. Not that he had anything to pay for, of course. His was an entirely above-board art bookshop. It was all a horrible misunderstanding. But I have to say, some of the officers in the case arrived at court in very nice cars."

"I suppose that's one of the perks of working in Soho."

"Yes. Although not all our shops—all right, so we had a string of them—were in Soho. One of them was in Camden."

"Why do you do cases like this?"

"It's the cab-rank rule, Frankie. If it comes in with my name on, in my area of work, I have to do it."

"Oh yes?" I said, thinking of barristers who return cases because there's not enough money on the brief.

"I don't have your politics," he said. "But, anyway, I thought you did this kind of work when you did crime."

"I represented prostitutes, not the jerks who live off them. Although I did once represent a woman charged with running a brothel. When she was acquitted, she gave me that china high-heel shoe on my table in chambers. But all of that's a million miles away from your case."

Somehow the story ended up involving hiccups, snoring

and bad language. It wasn't very funny but by the time we had finished the coffee, and against my better judgment, we were giggling like contestants in a game show. I felt sure enough time had passed for Marcus to have finished his conference so we got the check.

"He's still in your room," Gavin said mournfully as we walked into the clerks' room.

"Can I make a phone call from here?" I asked.

"Yeah, Jenna's desk's free, use her phone." As junior clerk, Jenna had to take her lunch very late or very early. She was still at lunch. I rang Kay and told her as coherently as I could about Saskia's court appearance, bruises and all.

"Oh no," Kay sighed. "Where is she now?"

"I don't know, she just skipped off while I was on the phone."

"What, at court?"

"No, in my apartment."

"In your apartment? God, Frankie, you never give up, do you?" Did she sound irritated? I was.

"I'm sorry," I said, "that's none of your business and, anyway, she just came to have a bath."

Kay shouted with laughter.

Normally, this is where I put the phone down, but I was seriously worried about Saskia.

"There was a guy at court with brown shoes," I said.

"Oh yes?" Kay said. "So it's true, brown is the new black."

I squeezed my eyes tight shut with frustration, then went on calmly: "He seemed very interested in Saskia."

"I'm assuming he wasn't a reporter, am I?"

"I thought he was at first, he looked the type: seedy, greedy, all those -eedy words." I reflected for a moment. "Not tweedy, I suppose." I remembered I was talking to my instructing solicitor. "But then he left court at the same time as us, about half past eleven, and was driven off in a sleek black car. Saskia didn't see him but she seemed quite shaken when I told her. What's going on?"

Kay was silent.

"Why was she so bruised, why was she so desperate to get out of the cells, and what was she doing in Balls Pond Road, of all places?"

"I don't know," Kay said.

"She's not involved in anything . . . iffy, is she? Nothing that could be connected to your break-in?"

Kay was silent, then said curtly, "Meet me tonight at the same place as last night."

"We didn't actually meet last night, if you remember."

"Seven o'clock all right?" Kay asked in a clipped voice.

"Yes," I said humbly.

As I put the phone down it occurred to me that I was quite tired and I needed to do something that would wake me up and keep me awake if I was going to make it through to the evening.

"I'm going to the movies," I announced.

"You going with, erm, you know?" Gavin leered.

"If you mean Simon, no, I'm not."

"Not what?" asked Simon, coming through the clerks' room to make himself some coffee. His blue and orange tie had something related to steak and fries on it.

"Not going to the movies with you."

"But why not? I love the cinema. *Apollo 13, James Bond, Toy Story.* Whatever. *Toy Story 2.*" Simon was eager, like a bouncy puppy. "We could share a tub of popcorn, although you probably like salted, don't you? We could have one each. Ice cream, coffee. What are we going to see?"

I looked at him. In court he was feared for his sharp wit and ruthless cross-examination. Around women he was a goofball.

"Something French and obscure."

"Oh, I'll take a rain check then," he said.

"Bye," said Gavin, shaking his head with disappointment.

I remembered my financial state. "Lend me twenty pounds, Simon."

"Is that enough?"

"It'll do," I said, snatching the old spare raincoat hanging behind the door in the clerk's room. I was on the landing outside chambers when I remembered my keys.

I went back into chambers. "Because the conference has been going on so long," Gavin said, "I'll go in and get them." It was a strict rule that conferences must not be disturbed. When he came out he handed me the small bunch of keys. "The things you've got in your top drawer," he remarked. "It could have been very embarrassing for Marcus."

"He could have said they were for his feminine side. Perhaps it might stop him having meetings in my room. He shouldn't look in the drawers of my desk anyway," I said, and swept out of chambers.

The film was French but light and had that comedy the French laugh at—people hiding in garbage cans and being loaded onto sanitation trucks by mistake, like Benny Hill with an accent—which I always forget about when I say I like French films. But I enjoyed myself being critical and feeling superior about the subtitles, which were too short, too vague, too late. The story of my life.

It was a quarter to six when I came out of the cinema and the air was less cold than it had been earlier. I was humming the film's catchy theme tune which hadn't yet become irritating and I decided to walk to the restaurant to meet Kay.

All I will say is, Brunswick Square to Kings Cross was easy enough, through the streets of high mansion blocks and large houses, past the turrets of St. Pancras station to the concrete flatness of Kings Cross, but the hill up to the Angel reminded me that I had done a lot of walking already that day and also notified me of all the spots where my shoes rubbed. At least it wasn't raining.

I felt irritable and ragged when I limped into Gino's.

"Signora," Gino bustled towards me, his face all concern, "you look a little fatigué. Come, sit down, asseyez-vous, and I bring you a bottle of vino tinto red, yes?"

The restaurant was empty and Gino guided me to a small, discreet table tucked behind a large Swiss cheese plant.

"I am expecting someone," I said defiantly, as he put down the bottle of wine and began removing the plate and silverware opposite me.

"Of course, yes, signora," he said, pretending to tidy them. "How long you will be waiting?"

It was ten to seven.

"Fifteen minutes," I said. I had £15 left from the £20 Simon had lent me. That meant, if absolutely necessary, if she didn't come, I could have the wine, an appetizer and just about enough for a cab home. I was worrying about the tip when Kay appeared.

I always do a double take when I haven't seen Kay for a while. She's tall, about five foot nine, and carries her weight well. She has dark hair and dark eyes, but it's her mouth that I'm drawn to. It is full and perfectly shaped and she does something which always makes her lips shine. She licks them. It works.

She leaned on the back of the empty chair opposite me. "May I?"

I smiled and she sat down. She was wearing a grey trouser suit, with a long draping jacket, it said Armani, it said Donna Karan, it said, successful solicitor. I realized my outfit today said Target, and the jacket was too tight across the shoulders. I poured her some wine and Gino hurried forward with a menu. I ordered a mushroom risotto and Kay ordered chicken.

I had warmed up, I was relaxed and it was good to see her.

"Saskia rang me," she announced. I sat forward in my chair. "She said she was OK and thank you very much and sorry she left without saying goodbye. Oh, and she said something about a grey shirt?" It was a question.

"She went off in my shirt. But did she say where she was? Did you ask her about the bruises?"

"Well, I couldn't really ask about the bruises because I didn't see them. And she didn't say where she was." She looked at my face. "And, no, I didn't ask her, either. To be honest, I didn't have the time for a chat." *Unlike you,* I read in her eyes. *I make time because I care,* I flashed back, silently. *Oh, please*! Her eyebrow twitched.

She shook out her napkin. "She did say something odd. She said, 'It's the singer not the song.' I wondered if she'd been flicking through your record collection."

"Did you ask her what she meant?"

She didn't bother to answer. "Sometimes I think Saskia says things just to be mysterious. It doesn't mean anything. What could it mean?"

I shook my head and shrugged my shoulders.

"There's nothing more you can do," she said sensibly. "Saskia's an adult. And she's pretty much told us to back off." She poured more wine in my glass and I tried to put my anxiety aside.

We had a pleasant evening. I talked about chambers, she talked about her office. Once we looked at each other as we were laughing about the elevators at Wood Green Court, and the possibility of going home together hovered in the air, but the moment passed.

In Kay's car at the end of the evening I concentrated on what Saskia could mean by that comment, "the singer not the song." It was true, she often said things for effect, she said it brought interest to people's lives. But there was something wrong, something not Saskia in all this.

As she dropped me off, Kay said, "Look, Saskia was a client, you represented her, the case is over. All you can do now is return the brief and forget about it. There's no Legal Aid for all this worrying, and your professional insurance probably doesn't cover you for it either. Knowing Saskia, she'll turn up in about two years' time, after another protest rally, and you'll be representing her on an assault police charge."

I looked at her.

"For God's sake," she said, "go to bed."

I went into the apartment and headed straight for the bathroom to run a bath to relax me so that I could sleep. I noticed that Saskia had carefully cleaned the bath, which is not my practice. I believe in self-cleaning baths like other people believe in fairies. My theory is self-cleaning ovens exist, so why not self-cleaning baths?

I undressed as the bath filled. I opened the clothes hamper to dispose of my underwear and noticed a blue shirt sheltering like a cuckoo in the nest of my dirty clothes.

I looked at it, uncomprehending, for three seconds then realized it was Saskia's.

I lifted it out of the hamper between thumb and forefinger as if it was a piece of china which might have fingerprints on it. It was a long-sleeve polo shirt with a pocket over the left breast.

I couldn't work out whether I felt like a detective or a thief as I considered slipping my fingers into the pocket to see what was in there. I knew that Saskia liked and trusted me so I decided I could assume the rights and even duties of a good friend. Also, if there was a tissue in there and I washed it, it would wreak havoc with my court things. I hooked the pocket open with my index finger and looked in. There was nothing but a crumpled-up turquoise and white wrapper, Orbit sugar-free gum. I was humming the advertising slogan as I pulled it out of the pocket and tossed it in the trash bin. I tried to picture Saskia chewing gum. It didn't fit, I had never seen Saskia chewing gum, so I scrabbled among the tissues and old toilet roll to retrieve the wrapper.

What was I expecting? Something dramatic, something helpful, a note that said, "I have moved and can now be reached at 0837-24391," perhaps. Perhaps an address. Perhaps something more sinister, a name, written in blood.

It didn't say anything like that. But it did say something: "7:30 Gino's F."

What? At first I thought I must have written it. I had just come from Gino's. How had that fact got into Saskia's pocket? I'd been with Kay. Had Kay written it? It wasn't Kay's writing. I tried to remember Saskia's handwriting.

"7:30 Gino's F."

What did it mean?

Automatically I got into the bath, washed and got out, no more relaxed than I had been five minutes earlier. I wandered into the living room in my dressing gown.

The answering machine light was flashing.

"Frankie, it's Gavin. It's eight thirty. Look, I'm sorry about this, but a new solicitor has just rung and needs someone to do a quick non-mol at Edmonton. You know I wouldn't normally ask you to do an injunction, but you live so close and she needs a bit of soft soap which I know you're good at."

"You taught me everything I know, Gavin," I said to the machine, and missed the last part of the message.

I played the tape again. "Client's name is Fiona Stevens, brief at court. Don't forget, Edmonton's a ten o'clock start. See you tomorrow."

I groaned, then groaned again. A non-molestation application at Edmonton County Court could take all day. The application itself would last ten minutes, the rest of the time would be spent waiting till the judge or the clerk decided which of the twenty or so cases in the list could go in.

This was so depressing. I shouldn't be doing cases like this, picking up my brief at Edmonton County Court on the morning of the hearing. I should be in the High Court, staggering under the weight of briefs which I'd received months before, for hearings which would last two or three weeks. What was the matter with my practice? Was it my solicitors? My clerks? Me?

I put on Sam and Dave singing, "Hold On, I'm Coming" and thought, "Well, hurry up then," and went to bed.

Four

Friday—Edmonton

Edmonton was everything I had dreaded and more. I left the house in good time, puzzling over the meaning of the sugar-free gum note, and was still abstractedly worrying about it at half past nine as I climbed the narrow stairs to the tiny Ladies Robing Room in the eaves of the brick courthouse. As I shrugged off my heavy dark grey overcoat I realized I had forgotten to put on my jacket. I considered my options. I was wearing a black T-shirt, which fortunately had long sleeves, but was rather short and a little faded. I had no options. I tied my black devoré scarf around my neck and hoped it looked deliberate.

"I'm in the case of Fiona Stevens," I told the new court clerk downstairs in the waiting area.

"Are you being represented this morning, Miss Stevens?" he asked me.

"I'm the barrister," I hissed.

We were there all day. Fiona Stevens needed an emergency injunction, without her ex-husband knowing, to protect her and the children. He had punched her the day before as she was leaving home to collect the children from school and had threatened to come back to her house and tear it apart one night while she was out with her new partner, a woman.

Before we could appear in front of the judge we had to

issue our application in the court office. But I had no papers, I couldn't issue anything. "Everything is in the file," the solicitor told me when I rang her, "the outdoor clerk picked it up last night." I had no outdoor clerk. "We tell our clerks to be there half an hour before the hearing," the solicitor said accusingly, "she'll be there somewhere," as if I was being stupid by failing to see her.

"Are you ready?" the court clerk asked me twice, and I said winningly, "Well, we haven't issued, but yes."

"Oh, no," he said. "I can't send you in before the judge without issuing. He'd have my guts for garters," and he laughed. I laughed too, in case I needed him later. My client went downstairs for a cigarette.

The solicitor's clerk arrived at quarter past eleven. She was late because she had washed her hair so it looked lovely and clean, but as she searched for the papers it became clear that she had been given the wrong file. She had to go back to the solicitor's office to collect the right one.

"I wouldn't mind," Fiona Stevens said as we sat outside the ladies' room, sipping bad coffee from beige plastic cups, waiting for the clerk to come back, "but he never wanted to go out with me, day or night. He used to like going out with his buddies or with his girlfriend, he'd get all dressed up, but he'd say, 'Who in their right mind would go out with you?' So I found someone who would, and he doesn't like it."

We left court at quarter past four with the injunction which would be served on Gary Stevens later that evening. When I got to my car, I was sorry I had snapped at the solicitor's clerk as the car wouldn't start and I had to ask her for a push. Humiliatingly, the client helped and then there was an uncomfortably quiet journey as I gave them a lift to Seven Sisters tube station.

My mental memo, which this morning had read, "Find Saskia," now read, "Find Saskia. Buy new car battery. Possibly buy new car."

I drove back to my apartment and rang my solicitor to tell her what had happened in court.

Gratifyingly she said, "The client was really pleased." But then she added, "She's got a large ancillary relief case coming up and she'd like you to do it."

Through gritted teeth I said, "Of course, I'd love to." I hate ancillary relief. Divorce work is bad enough with people being horrible to each other, but money matters seem to bring out the very worst in everybody. Compromise is usually the only answer because there's not much money and the legal costs are so high, but the parties feel that compromise is giving in, like losing, so they argue over who gets the lawn furniture and it goes to trial and the only winners are the lawyers. Then I thought of the car battery I needed. "Send me the papers," I said.

I rang chambers. Gavin was obviously distracted as he didn't even apologize for sending me to Edmonton. He said, "I've got you a five-day case in the High Court, starting two weeks from Monday. You're for the First Respondent, the mother. The solicitor wants a conference next Thursday. Brief's coming down to chambers early next week."

"Gavin, I love you," I said, thinking, *Perhaps I could get a new car, a green one.*

"I'm glad someone likes me," he said.

"Bad day?" I asked, thinking, *I could have four doors and a sun roof.*

"Your roommate Marcus sometimes has a very forthright way of expressing himself," he said, meaning Marcus had sworn at him for something which was doubtless Marcus's own fault. "Do you want your messages? Hang on . . ." Gavin put me on hold while he collected the messages from the message board. " 'Lesley Page,' " he read, " 'please ring back.' Do you want the number?"

I made a note, asking, "Is that a solicitor? Did they say what it was about?"

"I don't think it's a solicitor. That's a cell phone number isn't it?" Gavin said, "I've no idea what it's about, I didn't take the message."

"OK, fine. I don't suppose there's a message from Saskia?"

"Nothing here."

"Anything from Kay?"

"No."

"Are you sure?"

"Frankie, you're not starting all that nonsense again, are you?" Gavin asked. He liked Kay, but there had been two occasions when he had found me in tears in my room at the tail end of our relationship, and he had put my coat over my shoulders and taken me to the George and bought me drinks till I cheered up.

I rang the number he had given me for Lesley Page. A snooty voice told me it had not been possible to connect my call. Someone else who never switched on their cell phone. I put it out of my mind. People know where to find me.

I had a shower—the luxury of my bathroom is that I have a separate shower—and put on some black jeans and a loose black sweater. I put on my black suede boots. The reason I became a barrister is because I like black clothes.

I was going back to Gino's. F could be Frankie, but it could be Friday. It could of course be foolish, but I had no social life anyway. The weather was still cold and I wrapped my heavy overcoat around me as I walked out to my car, which started perfectly.

I got there at seven fifteen. The restaurant was empty except for Gino and a man in a white coat and a blue and white apron who I knew was the chef. They were sitting side by side at a table near the kitchen with a crossword between them.

"Signora, so lovely to see you. How many you are? A bottle of vino tinto red?"

"Gino," I said carefully, drawing him over to the bar

area, "I don't know if I'm staying and I don't know if I'm meeting anyone."

"Si, signora, yes, of course," he said with concern. "So you would like just a glass of red for the meanwhile and you sit at the bar, yes?"

I smiled at him gratefully and eased myself onto a stool. Gino bustled around behind the bar. I could see his grey roots as he bent his head to pour the glass of wine.

"Gino," I began slowly, "have you seen a woman with spiky blonde hair, taller than me, wearing . . . I don't know, possibly a rather nice grey denim shirt, in the last day or two?"

"I have seen you in the last day or two, signora. You didn't see her yourself?"

"No, I didn't. But then it might not be her I'm expecting," I murmured, partly to myself.

Gino placed the glass of wine in front of me with a flourish. "What are imitation germs?" he asked. "Five letters. P something S something something."

"Pests?" I suggested.

"It's paste," the chef growled. "It was imitation gems, not germs."

"Oh, you English," Gino twinkled and went to welcome some new arrivals.

I sat at the bar with my back to the restaurant watching in the reflection of the peach-tinted mirror as the restaurant began to fill up. I had almost finished my glass of wine when he walked in. It was the man with the brown shoes from the magistrates' court.

I watched Gino hurry over to him and greet him like an old friend, like he greeted everyone. He showed the man to a table and came back to the bar. The man looked at the clock on the wall which stood permanently at half past nine and then at his watch.

I checked my watch. It was seven twenty-five. Gino was popping the lid from a bottle of mineral water.

"Gino, has that man been in here before?" I asked casually, out of the corner of my mouth.

Gino threw me a look.

"Si, signora, he was here last night, about this time, and, maybe, the night before, I think." He creased his face in concentration. "He did not stay long. He too is waiting for someone. Is he waiting for you? Is it a Blind Date?" he asked eagerly.

"No, no," I said, shocked. "Not with those shoes."

Gino placed the mineral water in front of the man and hurried away to greet some newcomers. The man followed Gino with his eyes, then looked at his watch again.

In the subdued lighting of the restaurant, it was hard to get a clear picture of him in reverse. I noticed that the rosy sheen of the mirror made me look very well and I couldn't be sure whether the man was young and attractive, as it appeared in the reflection, or mean and nasty. I didn't want to turn around in case he recognized me. He took off his beige raincoat. He was wearing a grey sweater with a short zip at the neck. With tan shoes! Extraordinary.

Gino came back to the bar and opened two bottles of wine. He looked quizzically from me to the man but said nothing.

The man reached into the pocket of his raincoat and drew out a folded copy of the *Daily Telegraph*. I'm always surprised when people, especially people under forty, read the *Daily Telegraph*. All the news of a tabloid with the disadvantage of the size of a broadsheet.

What would Saskia be doing, knowing someone like that, I wondered.

He was reading the sports pages. Each time the door opened he half-closed the paper and looked up expectantly. It was ten to eight.

Gino had just poured me another glass of wine. "I'll charge you for the bottle," he said, pushing a packet of bread sticks under my nose, when the man began elaborately to fold the newspaper and gestured toward the bar for his bill.

"Gino, see if you can find out his name," I hissed, cramming three inches of bread stick into my mouth. I realized I hadn't eaten since breakfast. Edmonton didn't have much to offer if you didn't want to eat at McDonald's, and, as a gesture of solidarity with Saskia, I hadn't.

I watched Gino's dark head bobbing in conversation. A look of confusion passed over the man's face and then he drew out a credit card. Gino bounced back to the bar and spoke to me from the corner of his mouth as he fiddled with the clumsy machine.

"His name is P. J. Kramer," he murmured excitedly.

"He doesn't look old enough," I muttered back.

Gino's eyebrows rose. "P. J. Kramer," he enunciated slowly.

"I thought you said Billy J. Kramer," I said and snorted with laughter. Oh God, I was not sober. I shoved another bread stick into my mouth.

The man was putting on gloves.

Casually I shrugged into my coat and put a £10 note on the counter.

He was leaving the restaurant.

I slid off the stool and then froze as he stopped at the door, adjusting the newspaper in his pocket. He went out into the street, leaving the door of the restaurant open to the cold night air, and turned sharply left. I followed him and closed the door.

He was about five foot nine and skinny but looked strong. I wasn't sure what I was going to do. Physically, I knew I was no match for him. What was I doing even thinking about the possibility of physical confrontation? I am five foot five but slight. I once did a six-week self-defense course and I could probably still do the moves and the shouting, but any real possibility of a physical exchange was bound to end in tears. Mine. At best.

He was getting into a car; not the dark sedan but an old Ford. It was parked two cars away from mine, facing in the opposite direction. I shrugged down into my coat to hurry past him and jumped into my car. As his headlights came on, I fumbled with the key, turning it in the ignition. The engine whined in a tired unhappy way, like an exhausted wasp, then was silent. "Come on!" I pleaded, breathing deeply but casually, trying not to let my car know I was questioning its continued existence in the world. "Oh God," I muttered as the man started doing a U-turn. In Upper Street. He had to be mad. Or desperate. "I don't really want a new car," I whispered faithlessly to the dashboard as the Ford lurched unhappily backward and forward in the middle of two opposing lines of traffic. I turned the key again. The engine coughed and purred into life. Now what was I going to do?

I followed him. He drove to Highbury Corner, turned into Holloway Road toward Archway and then up Highgate Hill. Then a Pizza Hut moped rider overtook me and I lost sight of the Ford. I was looking around for the car when I turned and found myself staring him in the face. I hadn't noticed that he had pulled in to the side of the road, and now I was driving past him. He had parked outside the little house in Waterlow Park where on summer nights people have parties. But now it was dark and cold, cheerless and threatening and he seemed to be speaking angrily on a cell phone.

I drove on, casually slowing down, throwing anxious glances in my rear-view mirror. Headlights were coming up behind me and I couldn't make out if it was his car. As the lights drew closer I was dazzled and quickly looked away. Suddenly there was a bang and I shot forward. My seat belt clicked firmly and thrust me back. I could hear the revving of an engine very close behind me. Something large had made damaging, buckling contact with the back of my car. Automatically, I switched off my engine. I had no fear, just an enormous sense of fury and protectiveness for my small, unassuming car which had never hurt anyone. Certainly not since I'd had it, anyway. I unbuckled my seat belt, ready to jump out to look at my bumper and confront the bastard who had done this, when suddenly the door was wrenched open.

I was conscious of a narrow, pointed face with pockmarks and thin pale lips leaning toward me. I could smell garlic and something meaty, like pâté. A hand came around my neck and I was being dragged out of the car.

I was outraged, choking and gagging, repeating, "What? What?" and clawing at the hand. There was a swish of material and something came toward me very fast. It was a fist, which punched me hard in the right eye. As my head jerked back a thin, harsh voice hissed, "Just keep your fucking nose out of things," and something that sounded like, "Fucking lesbos—you're all the same," but perhaps I was just feeling sensitive. Then he threw me on the ground and my face landed in gravel. I lay still for a couple of seconds, hoping he would go away, but he was standing there moving back and forth on shoes that in the half-light looked suspiciously as if they might be brown. I stretched out my left arm and groped along the ground, trying to get my bearings, trying to find something to hold on to, when a foot landed in my stomach. The impact flung me against the edge of the open car door. I snaked my hand around until I felt the door compartment with the reassuring cassette tapes, then eased my forearm up to the arm rest and began to pull myself up, using the door as protection.

Somebody was breathing heavily, which could have been me, but when he coughed a laugh I knew it wasn't. "Got a bit of a headache, have we?"

As I stood up I smelled pâté breath from the other side of the door. I swayed slightly, my face and in particular my right eye were stinging.

As he advanced toward me I pulled the door quickly toward myself, then thrust it back hard against him. From his groan I guessed the edge of the door had hit the target. He bent forward and I came around the door. Raising my right knee and flipping my foot sharply, I kicked him very quickly between the legs. "That's for all the lesbos," I said. He staggered backward clutching his groin, and I contemplated doing it again, but decided to leave while I was ahead. As I slid behind the steering wheel I watched him in the rear-view mirror, limping over the gravel. I locked myself in with my elbow as a car door slammed behind me. There was a sound of violent revving and squealing into reverse, and I heard a car roar past me, but by then I had my head in my hands, leaning on the steering wheel, so I saw nothing.

Had that really happened? I'd been following a man and then he'd beaten me up? I hate that kind of clichéd situation. And keep my fucking nose out of what? Saskia? Kay? One of my other cases? Could Kramer have something to do with a family case of mine? Had he been hired by the husband of one of my clients? Most of the men in the cases I did would probably want to say that to me. The man in the case today might well have felt like that when he was served with the papers. Then I heard a car laboring up the hill. Was he coming back? Had he even gone? I lifted my head, conscious of a pounding pain behind my right eye. I turned the key in the ignition, prayed, and the car sparked into life. I jerked into first gear, pulled away from the curb and across the road in one movement and sped into Hornsey Lane. I wanted to get away from the place, away from the man, away from the pain as soon as possible. I put on a cassette of *Motown Greatest Hits*. The low cello introducing Brenda Holloway singing "Every Little Bit Hurts" seemed appropriate, the slow, deep notes solicitously filling the car, taking my mind off the throbbing in my head.

My mind was still scrambling over the events of the last few minutes. I was trying to remember all the details. Should I tell the police? Something niggling in the back of my mind said I shouldn't. What would I tell them? I saw him in court. "And then you were following him, madam? A man you say you've never met . . . I see. And then he assaulted you? Well, sounds like we've got a bit of a domestic here, madam." If I missed out the part about seeing him in court—and I was beginning to wonder if I had seen him, perhaps I'd just imagined that part—they'd probably say it was a road-rage incident. "Don't you worry, madam, we get a lot of this: attractive young lady in a small car, meandering slowly up the hill, gentleman behind gets a little bit impatient, a bit aggressive. Unfortunately that's the modern world of today. Perhaps you should try keeping up with the speed limit, madam." But it wasn't just road rage, he knew me, and that meant he might try it again. Surely I should at least get the assault on the record.

Then it came to me, the reason why I couldn't go to the police. I was drunk, that was why.

Brenda Holloway was wondering why her lover treated her so, when I had to stop the car and vomit in the gutter. It didn't last long, but it was a very intense experience. When I stood up I leaned on the railings of the viaduct and looked down at the traffic rushing along the Archway Road below and wondered if he was down there looking up at me. I shuddered and turned back to the car. As I opened the door, I glanced up at the sky which was clear and filled with stars and a crisp crescent moon. My eye hurt and my stomach ached.

I drove home carefully, wincing at every bump in the road. I was driving so slowly I worried I might be stopped, but it was still only nine thirty and the police obviously hadn't started looking out for Friday-night drunk drivers.

I went into the apartment, shut the door and considered who I could ring. I couldn't ring Lena because she was in

France, and I definitely couldn't ring Kay because she had very clearly warned me to leave well alone and I couldn't bear to hear the unspoken "I told you so" in her voice when she sighed, "Oh, Frankie." I did a mental run through my address book and realized there was no one I could ring at ten o'clock at night and say, "I've just been punched in the face, it hurts like hell, will you be nice to me?" Feeling alone and extremely sorry for myself, I fetched a glass of water from the kitchen and took two aspirin.

I trailed into the living room and put on the Four Tops, who said I could reach out and they'd be there.

And I wondered, as I so often had, if the idea was to reach out now while I was listening to the song, which would be fairly unproductive since I was quite obviously on my own, or if I should wait till I was at a really good party and then reach out and it would all fall into place. Except at parties you can never be sure how good the music will be. That's why I like sixties nights—they do both, play the song and it's usually a good party, so you can reach out without anxiety. Except, of course, the last one I'd been to, I'd reached out to Kay and she wouldn't dance. The Four Tops said I just had to look over my shoulder. You do that, of course, and you're doing the Hitch Hiker—not my favorite dance. It was time to go to bed.

Five

Saturday Morning—Church Street

I had forgotten to switch off my alarm. At seven thirty the voice of Sue MacGregor, joking with a sports reporter on Radio 4, brought me into consciousness—seven thirty on a Saturday. The sports reporter was giving the racing selections for the day: Loyal Boy in the three fifteen at Chepstow. It was seven thirty on a Saturday. I was disgusted. I needed a drink of water. I put the light on and looked blearily around my bedroom. My bedroom was fairly disgusting in its own right. Clothes everywhere, blobs of dust on my chest of drawers where I keep my hairbrush and my collection of small earrings for court and I could see a spider's web up in the corner above the bed. It was still dark. It was seven thirty.

Was this a sign? A message that if I got up now and cleaned the apartment then I could spend the rest of the day slobbing around?

I made a bargain with myself. If I did the vacuuming in half an hour I could have a blueberry muffin from the freezer for breakfast, back in bed.

"It's a deal," I said aloud and twisted out of bed. My whole body ached and my eye throbbed. For a moment I couldn't think why I felt so terrible but the memory came flooding back and filled me with despair and alarm and a nagging worry. Vacuuming therapy seemed as good an idea as any.

As I dragged the machine from its place at the back of the cupboard I greeted it like an old but distant friend. I clicked the *Motown Dance Party* cassette into my Walkman, slipped the Walkman into the pocket of my robe, switched on and started. I vacuumed, I dusted and I put bleach in the toilet. I was just wiping around the window frames, singing along with the Velvelettes, 'He Was Really Sayin' Somethin',' when I noticed the red light flashing on the answering machine. There had been no messages when I came in after my adventure the night before. Someone had rung me while I was cleaning. Yet another reason why housework is a bad idea. You clean, you miss phone calls. I rest my case.

I pressed the playback button. There was a long silence. "Shit," I shouted. "Shit, shit, shit."

I rang call retrieval and was told that the caller, who had rung twenty minutes earlier, had withheld their number.

Miserably I made my coffee, heated the blueberry muffin and went back to bed, but the muffin stuck to the roof of my mouth and the coffee grains floated to the top of the cup and niggled against my teeth. I hate missing phone calls. To take my mind off the frustration I began to worry at the quick crossword of the day before. Slowly I relaxed and had even got as far as referring to my Thesaurus when the phone rang.

I snatched it up and breathlessly said, "Hello?"

"Oh, Frankie, that was quick. I didn't even hear it ring."

It was my mom.

"Did you ring me about half an hour ago?" I asked.

"No," she said. "I wouldn't ring you that early on a Saturday." She explained that she had one or two Christmas presents she had to buy (it was October after all, she reminded me) and she wondered if she could come and stay.

I walked with the phone into the bathroom to brush my teeth. That's the effect she has on me.

I caught sight of my reflection in the mirror. I had a black eye. How would I explain that to my mother?

"I'm going out," I said desperately.

"That's all right, I've got a key."

"No, I mean tonight." It wasn't true, but something might come up. "I might be in really late."

"Don't worry, I'll make up the bed and switch on the TV and it'll be just like home."

I sighed. I don't know why I even bother to try. If my mom wants to come and stay, my mom will come and stay. I thought it best to wait and tell her about the black eye face to face. She'd only worry.

"I've got a black eye," I heard myself blurt out.

"A black eye? Why, whatever have you been doing?"

I looked at myself again and my mind went blank. "I walked into the door," I said. "The bedroom door," I explained, adding detail to make it sound true. "I switched off the hall light before I switched on the bedroom light and I forgot." I wasn't taken in, was she?

She sighed. "Well, as long as you don't have a friend who has one just like it."

"No, I don't," I said, thinking of the owner of the pockmarked face with its sly grin, unsullied by bruise or cut, but with hopefully fatal internal injuries. "I don't fight, Mom," I said, thinking, *Not very well anyway*.

"I'd hate to think it was in the genes," she said, obviously thinking of my father's uncle, who had a reputation for assaulting his women friends.

The consolation was she didn't think I was the victim. But then, which was worse? To be the victim or the aggressor?

"I don't think it's a genetic thing, Mom, I just have a black eye. It happens."

"Hmm," she said. "I'll see you later."

At least the house was tidy.

The phone rang again. It was Lena.

"Did you ring me about half an hour ago?" I asked.

"No," she said. "I wouldn't ring you that early on a Saturday."

"Where are you ringing from?" I asked. "I thought you were in Paris."

"I'm back. I came home early," she said, too brightly.

"Where's Sophie?"

"Oh, she's still there."

"Are we having coffee then?" I asked. "The Blue Legume in twenty minutes?"

"That would be great."

"I'll bring the brandy," I said and rang off before she burst into tears. She and Sophie, what a pair.

Slowly I put on some jeans and a faded black sweat-shirt. My muscles were creaking. I wondered if I had over-done it. Physical assault followed by housework, not a good combination. As I bent to lace up my Doc Martens my eye twinged, reminding me I should wear dark glasses. I went to the sunglasses shelf on my bookcase. In front of three volumes of *Stone's Justices' Manual* of 1992 and two volumes of *Rayden on Divorce* lay twelve pairs of sun-glasses, most purchased on vacation because of my habit of forgetting to pack the pair I bought last year.

After five minutes fussing in front of the mirror I had chosen a groovy round wire-rimmed pair that looked as if they came from the thirties and convinced myself that the black eye was scarcely visible. I nearly broke my neck going down the steps of my house because the lenses were so dark, but it was a bright sunny day and I got used to them.

I walked down to Church Street and found Lena already at a table in the gloom of the small café. I stopped in surprise. There was something about her that made me feel I was looking at a reflection of myself. She was wearing dark glasses, but then I realized she was also wearing an old jacket of mine which I had put out for a thrift store. It looked so good on her that I suddenly and intensely wanted it back, till I remembered it had never looked that good on me. With the great jacket and her thick black hair, caught back in a ponytail, you'd never have thought she was ten years older than I was.

"Frankie, darling, what has happened to your eye?" she exclaimed as she leaned over to kiss me. "Tell me in a minute," she said, picking up her large wallet from the table and heading to the counter to order the coffee. She had obviously considered who was more deserving of sympathy and had decided that, superficially at any rate, I was.

Lena and I had known each other for almost eight years. We'd been really friendly for seven, ever since the infamous sixties night, when I'd gone into the toilets to be tragic over Kay and, instead, found Lena grimacing into the mirror, swigging determinedly from a hip flask. Her on/off girlfriend, Sophie, had just danced past her, very obviously on with someone else.

"I wouldn't have minded," she had said through gritted teeth, her dark bangs flopping into her eyes, "but that other woman is wearing a shirt exactly like the one I put in a bag of stuff for Sophie to take to the thrift store. Bloody nerve." So we left the toilets together and danced all night long. We even danced the Twist, which is not something I normally do.

The day after that I rang her to see if she was OK.

"Do you want to go to the movies?" I asked. "Then we could go out for dinner and trash our girlfriends."

"Oh, Frankie, what a pal you are." She grinned down the phone. "That sounds great. What shall we go and see?"

We wanted a film with wit and women, which we felt were missing from our lives. There was a Cary Grant retrospective at a small cinema in Soho and we went to see *His Girl Friday,* to pick up a few tips on being suave and elegant, and then we went to Chez Gerard in Charlotte Street, for the prix fixe menu. As we sat spreading anchovy butter on French bread we shared our life histories.

They were remarkably similar. We had both grown up in public housing with parents who had wanted us to do better than they had.

My dad was an old Teddy Boy and my mom had had a beehive and wore American tan stockings, even on their wedding day. She and my dad went to the local dance hall together and jived to Bill Haley and Eddie Cochran. But when Tamla Motown came in in the sixties my mom swapped her allegiances and became a mod, while my dad naturally became a rocker. After that my mom went to dances with her girlfriends, and on the odd occasion she took me. I have no real memory of it but apparently once she took me to see Wilson Pickett at the town hall. She loved the big trumpet sound of "Midnight Hour" but Wilson Pickett was late and she only dared listen to two songs before running all the way home with me asleep in her arms. Perhaps that was the night the music seeped into my bloodstream.

By 1969 they were separated and Dad moved to an apartment around the corner. My mom trained to be a primary teacher while my dad carried on working in his car-repair workshop. I saw him regularly and there wasn't too much wrangling, not that there was much to wrangle about, but they both had solicitors and had to go to court a few times. I think it was the mystery of all the legal correspondence and the dressing up for the days in court that made me decide to study law.

I looked over at Lena as she smiled and chatted with the young man behind the counter. Lena had danced her way out of her humble beginnings, and eventually became a teacher of modern dance. You could tell by the way she moved. She was an inch shorter than me and her hair had one or two dashing streaks of grey. But the main difference between us was that she always made people feel that they were the most interesting person in the world. That's how she always knew what was going on. People told her everything.

"My darling, I thought I was feeling bad, but you look terrible," she said, putting two large creamy coffees down on the table. "I was going to suggest we go to that new bar this evening, the one that's just opened off the City Road. To cheer me up. But you might not want to go out, looking like that."

"I would love to go out," I said, ignoring the implications of her comments. "My mom's coming up."

"Are you sure?"

"Why? Ashamed to be seen out with me?"

She hesitated. "Of course not. It should be good. There's a band too."

"Oh God, you didn't say there was a band. They'll play modern music really loudly." My brain was clicking. "Oh, I don't know, I can't bear to stay in with my mom, not on a Saturday. What would it say about my life?" I took a small bottle of brandy from my inside pocket and held it up.

"Great," she said, and I poured a slug into her coffee. Then I lifted the bottle to my lips but thought better of it.

"Yes, do come," she went on. "But I will just say one thing. Those sunglasses are a little odd and they don't actually cover up the blue and purple bits. Are you going to tell me what happened, or am I going to have to drag it out of you?"

"It was a client." I didn't want to tell Lena, I felt there was a need for secrecy, confidentiality, discretion. Perhaps I'd been doing the job too long. She looked at me, amazed.

"A client hit you? Why, because you lost? I didn't realize clients got that unhappy with their barristers."

"Actually, it was the client's husband," I said wildly. "There was a bit of a commotion outside court. I don't really want to talk about it."

"What did the police say?"

"Well, I haven't actually told them because it was partly my fault."

"Frankie," she said sadly, "violence is never the victim's fault. Which court was this?"

"I shouldn't say any more." I sneaked back behind professionalism. "The case is ongoing."

Lena nodded sagely and I turned the conversation to safer matters. "What happened in Paris?"

Lena told me how they had arrived at the Gare du Nord and argued because Sophie had wanted to sit in cafés all day while Lena had wanted to visit as many museums as she could. Then things had got more personal and Lena had had to leave. "She called me a tourist!" Lena gasped.

I knew I could not afford to say, "Well, you were."

"What am I going to do with my mom?" I asked.

"She could come with us tonight."

"Lena!"

"Just a thought. What about Columbia Road tomorrow morning? She could buy some plants to take home."

We finished our coffee and wandered down Church Street, window shopping in the secondhand shops. It was hot and sunny and we were half looking for a new table for Lena's kitchen (she had just reorganized her apartment) but half looking for outfits for the evening. In a small shop selling pine furniture and altar cloths was a large cardboard box full of shoes. Most of them were the same style, dull black and gold slingbacks, but one pair had three-inch heels, sharply pointed toes and neat stud buttons up to the ankle.

"Perfect club wear!" Lena exclaimed.

"They're sevens," I said sadly, feeling like an ugly sister who knows that even if she sliced off the tips of her toes they would never fit. Not that I would ever have worn them, but they were such a bargain at £3. The pair! Lena on the other hand was bouncing with excitement since seven was exactly her size.

"Come on, Lena, you can't wear those. They're far too femme for you," I said.

Lena sighed, as if I was spoiling her fun. "As you and I have discussed on many occasions, Frankie, the headings Butch and Femme are merely a shorthand and superficial description of the myriad ways women express their sexuality. And clothes are the least helpful indicator of how a woman feels about herself. I have a leather jacket, you have a leather jacket, and we are sometimes described as butch, but then Kay has a leather jacket and Sophie has a leather jacket, and they are undoubtedly femme. What conclusions can we draw from that?"

"That we're all very boring people. But those are really femmy boots."

She tried them on and she couldn't walk in them so they went back in the box.

By the time we'd slipped into Fox's Wine Bar for a small glass of white wine and some haddock pâté and then gone into the book shop on High Street for something uplifting and topical to read and discuss, it was past four o'clock. It was time to prepare myself mentally for my mother's visit. I sauntered back home, thinking positive thoughts, planning a little more dishwashing and general tidying, and bought a small bunch of white and orange freesias to perfume a small part of my living room, in her honor.

As I turned into Amhurst Road I could see a taxi outside the house and a short bulky figure getting out. It was my mother in a large fake fur coat.

"What do you think?" she said, twirling in the street.

"It's astonishing," I said, paying the driver and picking up her two cases. "You're early."

"Freda next door was going into town and offered me a ride to the station. Anyway I thought it would be nice to have a bit of time with you—and your black eye—before your big night out."

Fortunately, for both our sakes, she didn't mention the eye again. Instead we spent two hours drinking tea while my mother brought me up to date on all my relatives who live near her in Colchester: two aunts and their husbands, and one unmarried uncle. Then I heard about the neighbors and the parents of old friends of mine who still lived nearby. By now we were on gin and tonic. When we got to the antics of the couple who were the vacation replacements for the people at the corner store, I left my mom to watch *Blind Date* while I went into the bathroom to prepare for the Queen of Sheba, as the club was known.

"Now don't you worry about me," she said, looking up from the *Guardian* TV page, as I slid my wallet into my inside jacket pocket and decided against wearing a coat. "There's not a lot on television tonight, but I'm sure I'll find something. Can you get Channel 5 here?"

"Not very well," I said, and pointed to the pile of Rock Hudson and Doris Day videos I had dug out from my collection specially for her.

"Oh, you know me," she said, "I can never work a video. I'll be all right, dear. Off you go and enjoy yourself." She patted my hand bravely and I stomped out of the house, rage and guilt steaming off my skin into the cold night air.

Six

Saturday Evening— The Queen of Sheba

Lena had rung to say she'd just remembered her car needed a new inspection sticker so we agreed we'd take my car and I'd pick her up from Finsbury Park. I honked as I drove past her house then double-parked a couple of doors down.

Through the rear-view mirror and in the light from the lamp-posts I saw her come out of her house and walk toward the car. She was wearing her long straight maroon coat, her hair was loose and shiny and she looked exotic and mysterious. My own efforts at glamor had been to change my round dark glasses to small rectangular ones, and to put on my charcoal grey Jigsaw suit with the bootleg trousers.

As Lena settled herself into the passenger seat she asked, "Where's your license plate?"

"What?"

"Where's the back license plate? You have no back license plate."

"Oh my God, it hasn't dropped off again. I thought that was just in summer, when it got hot. I stuck it on with some . . ." I tried to remember the name.

"Duct tape?" Lena asked brightly. "Well, it doesn't seem to have worked."

"It's dropped off," I said.

"Yes." Lena put on her best understanding voice. "Where do you think it dropped off?"

"I don't know. It could have happened anywhere." An idea was forming in my mind but I didn't want to deal with it. "It could have happened weeks ago, months ago, I never look at the back of my car."

"You would have been stopped by the police by now if it had been that long. Where have you been in the last day or two?"

"Here, there, you know."

"Did you hear anything?"

I looked at her.

"You know, when it dropped off?"

We were at Stoke Newington Green. I signaled and pulled into the side of the road, got out of the car and walked around to the back. Lena followed. There was no license plate.

I looked under the car, in case the license plate was hibernating underneath where the spare wheel should be.

"We could retrace your steps over the last twenty-four hours." Lena seemed to relish the prospect of a game of hunt the license plate. I ran my hand along the bumper. "We should organize this methodically. We could do it tomorrow morning. Frankie? Frankie, what is it?"

"Look at that," I said, "not a mark on the rest of the car. You wouldn't even think it had been bashed."

"Bashed?" Lena said uncertainly.

I took a deep breath and decided to come clean. "Last night someone banged into the back of the car and then came around and punched me in the face."

"What? Your client's husband?"

"Yes . . . no. Let's get back in the car." We settled back into our seats and I switched off the lights. "It wasn't my client's husband."

"Who was it then?"

"I don't know, someone called P. J. Kramer."

"Billy J. Kramer?"

"No, P. J. Kramer. I don't know who he is, he's been following me. And I—well, I've been following him." I was fiddling with the ignition key.

Lena scrunched around in her seat to face me. "I don't understand."

"Nor do I."

Her face was creased with such anxiety it was contagious and with a jerk I started the car. "Don't do that," Lena said.

I switched off the engine.

"Now explain."

"I don't know what to say," I began. "Did I tell you I represented Saskia the other day?"

"You never tell me the names of the people you represent," she said, regretfully. "But Saskia . . . How is she? Why does she need a family lawyer? She hasn't had children, has she?"

"Let's just say I represented her, but there was a man at court who seemed interested in her. Then she disappeared. I thought she might be at Gino's last night. She wasn't but he was, so I followed him and he ended up banging into the back of the car and punching me in the eye."

"Did you tell the police?"

"I was drunk, I couldn't tell them. And anyway, it didn't seem right to get the police in. It's all just hunches on my part."

"A punch is not a hunch."

"No, but in a way it was my own fault."

"Because—why? Don't tell me, you were driving *really* provocatively. Frankie, I told you there is never an excuse for violence."

"Don't lecture me, Lena," I said. "I just have to think now what I'm going to do."

"You could go and see if the license plate is there, where it happened."

"But that means going back . . ."

"Well, you've got to, because if the license plate is there and you don't find it, he will and then he'll be able to find you."

"Oh God."

But in the end it wasn't him who found me—it was the police. But I'm getting ahead of myself.

When I told Lena where it had happened we agreed that there was no point going all that way back up to Highgate, especially since we were both looking so glamorous for our evening out. As we drove down toward Old Street, we assured each other that there were two possibilities. If we went to Waterlow Park and the license plate was gone, there would be nothing we could do, but it would ruin our evening. And if it was still up there, lying in the road, it was unlikely to be stolen while we, along with most of the population of London, were out having a good time.

At Old Street roundabout I was still trying to convince myself that all this had a logic and was true. When we found a parking space right outside the club I knew we had made the right decision.

The club was still quite empty. "This is one of the good things about being older," Lena said. "We arrive early and so we get a seat. Youth doesn't arrive, on principle, till it's standing room only." I wasn't sure I liked being included in her comments about age. I felt I should do something childish and petulant to highlight our age difference, but I couldn't think of anything, so I sulked.

The room was dark and small, about the size of a living room that's a good size for a party. Tables formed a semi-circle around a raised dais, each table boasting a flickering night-light. We chose a small table near the front and I went to the bar to order a bottle of California Chardonnay. Already the room was beginning to fill up with women who looked the same age as me and Lena, who took all the tables. As I sat down again I was feeling old on my own account, but it meant I could stop sulking. Lena poured the wine. It was chilled and fruity and I began to relax.

Lena knew someone involved in the management of the club so she explained, "When there's no act the stage is where the dancing happens." But a small neat woman in a tux stepped into the spotlight on the stage and announced that tonight there was an act, a singer. I was disappointed, I had got used to the idea of a loud band and dancing so I could forget all the things that wouldn't leave my mind: Saskia and my black eye and my unreliable car and my lack of work.

When the act stepped onto the stage half an hour later the club was almost full. She looked tired, in her late thirties or early forties, and had thick coarse blonde hair. She wore a black beaded sheath which accentuated her full figure, and her black patent high-heel shoes highlighted her good legs. She tapped the microphone and I could see her hand trembling as she adjusted the height of the stand. The piano, her only accompaniment, began to play softly. She coughed and missed her entrance.

My heart sank. Had I left my warm friendly apartment with a good night's TV for this? I remembered I had also left my mother and sat forward, willing the singer to do well.

She sang "Cry Me a River." Her voice was soft and smoky. The longing and loss in her voice touched me and I guessed most of the people in the room. Everyone was silent, no glasses tinkled, no money rattled in the register at the bar. Everyone was transfixed by the beauty she brought to the song. As she sighed the last notes and hung her head in conclusion, the place erupted with applause. She looked genuinely surprised and pleased, smiling and bowing, holding her hands pressed together between her knees.

She sang "Funny Valentine," "Georgia," "Me and Mrs.

Jones" and all those sleepy, sexy songs that make you miss everything you thought you had but didn't, or thought you wanted but couldn't.

At the end of the set women were whistling and whooping and the MC, leaping back onto the stage from her position on a stool at the side, had trouble quieting them down. "Margo will be back in half an hour," she said, and there was a smattering of applause before people drifted to the bar. A jazz trumpet began sobbing softly through the PA system.

I went to the bar to order another bottle of wine. When I got back to the table it was empty. I knew where Lena would be: standing at the side of the stage talking to the singer. I wasn't surprised. Lena was an old performer, she'd been a dancer and was very good at telling other artists how much she liked their work. Sometimes, as I did then, I sat and watched the recipients melt with pleasure beneath the warmth of her sweet praise. Margo smiled, looking down, frowning slightly with a deprecatory expression. Then Lena gestured toward our table and Margo smiled over at me and I nodded in reply. Lena was explaining something and Margo looked at her watch. Lena wrinkled her nose and patted Margo's arm. Margo turned and went backstage and Lena returned to the table. "She's going to join us for a drink," she said, pulling over an empty chair from the next table. "At first she said she wouldn't but I convinced her that there would only be serious intellectual conversation and dry white wine at our table so she relented. I think she might even have a small interest in you. She said she'd heard of you when I mentioned your name." She raised her eyebrows at me and I raised mine back.

Feeling pleased with myself, I sauntered to the bar and called to the bartender who was waiting as a glass filled with beer. "Wineglass," I mouthed. "For the singer." Across the heads of the crowd, she passed me a glass and gave me a wink. The stud in her nose flashed.

I had just sat down when Margo came to the table, moving worriedly through the crowd, smiling occasionally at people who said hello. She was wearing another dress, red, short and tight, with high red sparkling shoes. I felt confident that the Jigsaw suit was good. She sat down and Lena introduced us.

"You're a barrister," Margo said. I nodded. Sometimes it turns people on that you're a barrister and I was happy with that.

"And you're a wonderful singer," I said, pouring wine into her glass. "How long have you been singing?"

"Not long," she said. "A year or so. Are you a wonderful barrister?"

"Oh, the easy ones first. I don't know if I'm wonderful, but I think I'm quite good and I fight hard. Why? Do you need a barrister?" I hoped she didn't, since a professional relationship might interfere with the relationship I had in mind.

"Maybe. Don't we all sometimes?"

"I suppose so, possibly, mmm."

Lena said, "I'm just going to talk to . . ." and slipped away.

I was looking at Margo's almond-shaped eyes. There were lines at the corners and her mascara was slightly smudged, but they were the deepest blue I had ever seen.

"Why are you wearing dark glasses?" she asked me.

"I have a black eye," I said. "It's a long story."

"Take them off."

Reluctantly I removed the glasses. She raised her hand and gently smoothed her fingertips over the bruise. Her hand was cool. "You can hardly see it," she murmured, kindly. "Don't put them back on. You have lovely eyes. I like brown eyes."

"How did you come to be singing here tonight?" I asked. I watched her mouth as she spoke about knowing the bartender who was a friend of the manager and the band they'd booked having let them down and the manager having rung her friend who had rung her. She spoke softly and slowly and her full red-stained lips formed the words hypnotically. I had to stop myself licking my own lips.

She looked at me watching her and smiled. For a moment neither of us spoke. She looked at her watch.

"I've got five minutes. I need to get some fresh air before I go back on stage," she said. "Do you want to come outside while I have a smoke?"

We walked to the side of the stage and she led me out through a fire door into the chill dark air. We were in an alley, with high brick walls on either side. The narrow rectangle of the sky was clear and there were some stars. "Can we see the Plough from here, do you think?" I asked her.

She leaned against one wall and took a pack of Camel cigarettes from the small bag on her wrist.

I don't like smoking—I don't like the smell of smoke, I dislike the sight of an ashtray filled with squashed cigarette butts, I hate it when people smoke in the non-smoking compartments of trains, but now I was standing in a dark alley next to a woman with a cigarette in her hand. And at that moment all I wanted in the world was to slip my hand in my pocket, pull out a silver lighter and flick it open to light her cigarette. But I didn't have a silver lighter, or any lighter at all, and she lit her own cigarette with a match which she waved out with a snap of her wrist.

She rubbed one arm with the other.

"Are you cold?" I asked, "Do you want my jacket?" I started to take it off.

"No, no," she said. "You'll get cold too."

I leaned against the opposite wall and watched her as

she smoked, inhaling deeply, creasing her eyes against the smoke. "It always feels so good, up there on stage," she began, looking down the alley. "It's such a buzz." She shook her head and inhaled again. "It's so different from the rest of my life. I feel like a different person, a stranger. And tonight there's you. I don't know what's happening. I've never spoken to a barrister before." She looked me straight in the eye. "I didn't know barristers could be lesbians."

"Barristers can be anything," I said. "It's not who we are, it's what we say that counts. I suppose it matters sometimes . . ." I could feel myself getting boring, but I couldn't stop. "Sometimes you don't get the briefs. But that's usually because you're a woman, not because of who you sleep with."

"How long have you been a barrister?"

"Ten years."

"Ten years is a long time. What would my life be like if I'd started doing this ten years ago?"

"I don't know, what was your life like ten years ago?"

"Well, ten years ago it wasn't bad, it just got worse as time went by." She shook her head again, then looked up. "What did you say about the Plough?"

We both gazed up at the sky. I took a step forward and could feel her close to me. I ran my hand down her arm and felt her shudder. We looked at each other and I took another step toward her and put an arm across her shoulders, watching her face to check her reaction.

She was an inch or two shorter than I and she looked up at me with her head on one side. I pushed her gently back against the wall and put my hands on either side of her head. She slid her arms around my waist and closed her eyes.

She felt soft and ripe in my arms. I bent my face into her hair and smelled perfume and cigarette smoke. She raised her eyelids and looked at me while I put my hand against her cheek. It felt like peach down. I tilted her face to mine and kissed her. Her lips were as soft and full as they had looked in the club, and now they parted slightly. I slid my tongue between her teeth and in the warm dark wetness of her mouth her tongue touched mine.

I pulled her closer and felt the curves beneath her dress all the way down my body. She moved her arms up around my neck, sliding her hands into my hair, pulling my mouth closer into hers.

As we drew apart she smiled at me. She licked her lips. "I feel like a stranger in paradise," she said. "You're a good kisser."

"It takes two to tango," I said.

"I've always been fond of dancing," she murmured, and pulled my head down.

After five minutes or perhaps ten she looked at her watch. "Oh God, I've got to go back on."

"What time do you finish?" I asked and then remembered my mother. "I'd like to see you afterward, go for a drink, invite you home with me, but my mother is staying. She came up to do Christmas shopping."

"Don't talk to me about Christmas," she said. "It's OK, I'd like to invite you home with me, but I can't."

"Another time," we said together.

I took out my wallet and gave her my card, writing my home number on the back. I wrote her number on the reverse of another and slid it back into my wallet.

She walked slowly onto the stage for her last set. She sang "One Fine Day" in her soft, husky voice of honeyed gold. And I thought that I certainly wanted her for my girl.

As the room erupted with whooping and cheering, Margo was gazing at the back of the room. I turned and saw Saskia.

And she did look remarkable. She was wearing my grey shirt, which looked stained and crumpled, and, I noticed with some concern, torn along one of the sleeves. Her hair was flat, which made her look subdued, crushed. The bruising on her face wasn't so visible. But her expression as she stood staring into the room was bleak and desperate.

I stood up abruptly and pushed my chair back. I was torn between staying to applaud and smile at Margo and going to speak to Saskia. I patted my wallet which contained Margo's phone number and turned toward the back of the club.

The crowd seemed to have swollen. Everyone was on their feet now, clapping and whistling, stamping their approval, pressing toward the stage. I pushed my way to the back, stepping on toes, knocking elbows, shouting, "Sorry, excuse me, sorry, sorry, excuse me." When I got to the back of the room, Saskia was gone.

I went through to the small lobby and out into the street. It was narrow and dark, lined with cars. There was no sign of her. I walked around to the side of the building and looked down the alley, which was lit by a solitary light, beaming over the fire doors that Margo and I had come out of an hour before. She wasn't there. I walked back to the front of the club and stood looking around for two minutes.

Had she seen me? Had she come to see me? How would she know I would be there?

The door to the club banged open and people began to spill out on to the street. Lena came over to me. "What are you doing out here, sweetie? But more importantly, tell me about Margo. Shall I make my own way home, or can we journey together?"

"I have no plans," I said. "Let's find the car."

Seven

Sunday—Columbia Road

At half past seven there was a tap on my bedroom door. "Cup of tea?" my mom said brightly and came into the room.

I had been dreaming. I rarely dream of the people I want to but in this one I'd been dancing with Margo, moving slowly around to a sensual rhythm, holding her in my arms, feeling the softness of her body, smelling the sweet rose perfume and cigarette smoke in her hair.

I sat up crossly. "Mom, I didn't get in till three o'clock."

"You said we had to get to Columbia Road early to miss the crowds."

"Yes, but I didn't say the middle of the night."

"Ah, now, talking of the middle of the night, before I forget, about midnight a friend of yours rang. I can't remember if she said her name. Ssss—"

"Saskia?"

"Mmmm, perhaps. I'm sure she told me, and I was going to write it down, but she said there was no message. I told her where you were anyway."

"And did you know where I was?"

"I heard you talking on the phone to Lena. If you said 'the Queen of Sheba' once, you must have said it ten times during the conversation. Did she find you?"

"Yes," I said, "in a manner of speaking." I yawned. My

throat was raw and my head was not happy. I didn't know if that was the alcohol or the black eye. I tried to remember how much I had had to drink the night before. I'd had too much to drive and there had been the very scary experience of Lena driving us home, meandering slowly through the streets of the city. "I'm better when I've got my glasses on," she had said.

"Drink your tea, it's getting cold," my mother reminded me.

I sat up obediently.

"Now there is something I wanted to talk to you about," she said, settling herself on the edge of my bed. I moved over to make room for her.

I waited.

"Have you heard of Dr. Henry?"

"That name rings a bell," I said.

"He said he'd ring you."

"Oh yes," I said, "he has rung me. I tried to ring him back. Is he a friend of yours?"

"Well. . ." My mother smiled coyly. "In a funny sort of way, I suppose he is. I met him at a drinks party at Audrey's a month or so ago." Audrey was my mother's oldest friend, from her schooldays. "I know in this day and age a woman ought to be able to simply ring a man and ask him to the theater, but I've never felt happy doing that. So I found a sort of excuse."

"What do you mean? What kind of a doctor is he?"

"He's a surgeon, a plastic surgeon."

"So, what, you've been ringing him up asking about thigh reduction? I thought you were proud of your firm thighs. I thought it was the one thing I had to thank you for."

"Don't be unnecessary, Frankie. No, it was a nose job, actually."

"You don't need a nose job. You've got a really nice nose."

"Well, it wasn't for me," she said slowly, looking at my face.

I started to laugh. My mother wanted me to have a nose job because she was hot for the doctor.

"It doesn't have to be a nose job, I just thought you might like that," she said. "It could be collagen in your lips, that would be nice. Or possibly," she hesitated, "breast enhancement."

"For God's sake, Mother."

"I'd pay."

"Mom, are you desperate or what? I can't tell you how shocked I am. You are going to ring this man and tell him very clearly that I love my nose and all those body parts you mentioned, and I want none of them changed."

"I wonder if he does things with black eyes," she murmured.

"Mother! I am very happy with my body and I don't even want a sniff of a plastic surgeon in my life. If you want to go out with him, ask him, just ask him. Or at least have the decency to go under the surgeon's knife yourself."

"He is very attractive," she said.

We drove silently to Columbia Road and I made her buy me bagels and coffee for breakfast. As we wandered through the market I began to relent. I knew she was lonely and had been for a long time. She's a very nice woman and it made me angry that she still felt the need to engage in subterfuge to catch a man. We bought two bunches of deep red and white chrysanthemums, and two small pots of early Christmas bulbs for Freda next door, and Mom said she was weighed down and would have to do the rest of her Christmas shopping in Colchester. By the time I put her and her case and bags of flowers into the train at Liverpool Street I was sorry to see her go.

"I tell you what," I said, "why don't I ask him out for you?"

"Oh, Frankie, you can't," she said. "Have you got his number?"

"Yes, I have, and I shall ring him tomorrow and tell him there's a perfectly formed woman in Colchester who would like to go and see *The Return of Martin Guerre* with him, to discuss whether he did it by plastic surgery."

She giggled with pleasure. "I have no pride," she said. "Do it if you must."

As I walked away from the platform and went into W. H. Smith's to buy the *Observer* I realized that my headache wasn't just a hangover, I was getting a cold.

I rang Lena and we went to Hampstead to see a re-vamped copy of *Bringing Up Baby*. I had to go out halfway through the film to buy a packet of tissues and by the end my nose was streaming.

"You should go home and have a hot toddy," Lena said.

"Would hot whisky have the same effect?" I sniffed. "I don't think I've got the other ingredients."

Lena ordered me to stop the car at the corner of her street while she went into the Italian shop and came back with three lemons and a jar of honey.

"Go to bed," she said, thrusting them on to the seat, "I'll walk from here."

It was only seven o'clock when I turned into Amhurst Road. My head was aching and I was sneezing every thirty seconds. A car drove away from outside my house just as I was slowing down to a crawl, looking for a parking space. It's like a small but precious gift when you can park outside your own home in London. I switched off the engine and the voice of Paul McCartney singing "I Saw Her Standing There" disappeared abruptly. Out of the corner of my eye I noticed something that I knew was significant, but I was so busy concentrating on turning the car key the right way up to lock the door, smooth side up for driver's door, smooth side down for passenger door, that I didn't think.

As I walked up the steps to the front door I looked over at my bay window, the half-drawn white blinds gleaming in the darkness. In the darkness—that was it, the window was dark. It shouldn't have been dark, the lamp on the timer in the living room didn't go off till one o'clock.

"Bloody long-life bloody light bulbs," I muttered, juggling the bag of lemons and honey, scrabbling in my pocket for the key.

The door swung open and I stepped into the hall. I lifted my hand to press the communal timer switch and sneezed at the same time. The bag fell from my hand and lemons and honey escaped across the floor. As I picked them up in the silence I could hear the timer switch wheezing its way slowly out again. I was shoving the jar of honey back into the bag when the timer gave a final sigh and the light went out and I realized my front door was open.

Tentatively I pushed the door and slid my hand around the door frame to switch on the light in my hall. As light flooded into the living room, it was clear the room was empty. It was also completely untidy. Papers strewn on the floor, newspaper tossed on the sofa, cups knocked over on the carpet. Or was that just how I'd left it before I went out?

I went over to my table. The desk drawers were open and the papers in them looked messy. That could mean anything.

Then I saw it, in the middle of the desk, on top of my laptop: a card. It said, "Make love, not sausages."

"Saskia!" I said. "Saskia?" I walked through into the kitchen and switched on the light. "Saskia?" The kitchen was empty. "Saskia?" I walked back through to the bedroom and opened the door. The bed was empty.

I looked down at the card in my hand. I turned it over.

On the back were the words, "It was too easy to get into your apartment, you should do something about security," written in a small, tight hand as if she was anxious about what she was writing. And so she should be, breaking into people's homes.

I walked back into the living room, wondering whether I should ring Kay, or even the police about Saskia's visit. I immediately rejected the option of the police. Burglary of domestic premises was a serious offence. Not that it was burglary. It was Saskia. But the police might look at it differently. And I was more than happy that Saskia should come into my home at any hour of the night or day, to have a bath, help herself to a bowl of ice cream from the freezer, or even something more substantial. I just wish she'd stayed. I needed to talk to her.

The more realistic option was Kay. I looked at my watch. Quarter past seven. She wouldn't want me to trouble her at seven o'clock on a Sunday evening. I'd think about it again in the morning.

I put on Marvin Gaye singing "Ain't that Peculiar," then moved the newspapers from the sofa and sat down. I thought about how Marvin Gaye died, shot by his father. Lovely voice, lovely rhythm, who would have thought danger was so close to home?

Eight

Monday Morning—Paperwork

I had taken Lena's advice. I had made myself some hot toddy and I was in bed by nine o'clock, but when I woke up in the morning I had developed a real, heavy, tight-chest, aching-limbs, blocked-red-nose, boxes-of-tissues cold. I rang chambers.

"Gavin, I don't want to overstate things, but I feel like death. If I feel like this tomorrow, I don't think I'm going to be able to do that directions appointment at the Principal Registry."

"OK, I'll put Iotha on standby."

I sneezed and put the phone down.

I didn't have the energy to get dressed. I put on a large pair of socks and tied my robe tightly. I got out a jigsaw puzzle I'd been given three Christmases ago and settled down to an enjoyable day of suffering and sloth. I completely forgot about Dr. Henry.

The jigsaw was really good, with lots of hard bits which seemed indistinguishable from each other till you had gazed at them for ten minutes, and then they slipped easily into place. And there was an old black-and-white movie with Fred and Ginger to look forward to in the afternoon.

At lunchtime I switched on the TV to catch the news. I'd missed the national news but I got the local. There was a story about litter and something about bicycles. Then a blurred photo appeared of a youngish, thin man's face. I gazed at it, blowing my nose, scarcely even thinking, *There's something in this image. Something I should take note of.* Then it dawned on me, it was him. I was sure it was him. P. J. Kramer. He was dead. His body had been found on the edge of Waterlow Park. His death was being treated as suspicious.

I hoped small animals had burrowed into his body or at the very least chewed his hair into an unattractive style. Perhaps that was uncharitable of me. After all, I hardly knew him and all he had done to me was to ram the back of my car, punch me in the eye and kick me in the stomach.

The news story referred to him as Kevin Latimer. I wondered who the credit card belonged to, who P. J. Kramer was. Was it an alias? Was it stolen? Perversely, I thought of that song, "Ain't that lovin' you, baby, and you don't even know my name." We'd had a very intense relationship but he was a stranger to me. Of course, I hadn't loved him. And he probably did in fact know my name, from talking to the police at court.

He was described as a thirty-four-year-old financial adviser. I stopped chewing my baked beans on toast to ask the television to do me a favor.

An anxious windswept reporter stood at the edge of the park and interviewed the detective in charge of the murder investigation. The detective looked about the same age as me, far too young to be a detective, certainly too young to be able to afford that well-cut suit. He told the reporter that Latimer had been stabbed three times, two superficial wounds and the fatal injury on the left side of his chest, late on Friday night or early Saturday morning. The police were of the opinion that he had been killed at or near the spot where he had been found. From the evidence it appeared that he had gone there voluntarily.

I was stunned. When I had last seen Kramer, Latimer,

whoever he was, he was heading away from Waterlow Park at great speed. Why had he gone back? Was it for my license plate? Had he realized that the license plate had fallen off and I might use that fact as evidence when I brought an assault charge against him? Had he crept back late at night grubbing around in the gutter for my plate? What if I had gone back at the same time? I shivered at how close I'd come to a murder. It might have been me. Had he tucked the license plate neatly under his arm like car salesmen who drive cars to remote parts of the UK using trade plates and then hitch lifts home carrying the plates as evidence of their good character? Was he lying there with my license plate beside him when they found him? A man of good character with someone else's credit card.

There was no mention of license plates on the TV report. I wondered if I should ring the police and tell them what had happened.

I decided I'd watch the Fred and Ginger movie and then make up my mind.

But just as the girls were flying down to Rio, bravely standing on the wings of the old plane in their skimpy outfits, and I was turning up the thermostat to protect my health and theirs, the phone rang. At first I thought it was part of the film and I only just picked up the receiver in time to stop the answering machine from springing into action.

"Hello," I said, sounding nasal and not well.

There was silence.

"Hello?"

There was the sound of breathing.

"Hello? Hello?"

The phone was replaced at the other end.

The flying girls were laughing and shaking their hair, which looked remarkably unmessy after what they'd been through, when the phone rang again.

"Hello? Hello?"

"Frankie?" The woman's voice was a cracked whisper.

"Yes?" I said, softly, not to frighten her away.

"Frankie?"

"Saskia?" I said, doubtfully, hopefully.

"Oh, Frankie, what can I do?"

"What's the matter?" I could feel an enormous sneeze twitching my nasal passages and I averted my head and exploded into the room. When I turned back to the receiver, apologizing, blaming my cold, Saskia had gone. I rang call retrieval and was not surprised to be told that the caller had withheld her number.

"Saskia, what's going on?" I said to the phone. "Call me back, call me back."

I would not let the phone out of my sight. I took it to the kitchen when I made myself a hot whisky with lemon, I took it over to the thermostat when I started to expire from the heat and had to turn it down, and I took it to the toilet. She didn't ring.

Something told me I should not ring the police. I felt I knew too much, but not enough to tell them about Saskia. Any of the little bits of information I had would only make things look very suspicious for her. And what were those little bits of information? The dead man had been in the courtroom at her hearing. He was in the restaurant when I was looking for her. What was I worried about?

"What do you want us to make of that, Miss Richmond?" I could imagine the smooth-looking police officer saying to me. "I'm more interested in your black eye and the license plate, belonging to your car, upon which the corpse was lying. Have you considered the possibility," he would say, "that it has nothing to do with your friend Saskia, but rather a lot to do with you?"

At five o'clock I rang in to chambers for my messages. No one had rung me and Iotha was booked to do my directions appointment the next day. I quickly put the phone down in case Saskia rang again and thought about getting "Call Waiting" so that I would know if someone was trying to get through while I was speaking to someone else. I felt too ill to think where that would come on my Memo of Things to Do. I concentrated mindlessly on the jigsaw. I was doing the sky. It was all the same blue. I began to feel terrible. My head felt like the drum in a primary school band, pounding and jumping with artless energy. My limbs felt as if I had been carrying enough suitcases for a three-week vacation. And my nose looked like those red plastic things you can buy for your car during Comic Relief. Perhaps plastic surgery was something I should seriously consider.

I made another cup of hot whisky and planned an evening of soap watching. The phone was silent. I watched *Coronation Street, EastEnders,* and then a video from the Friday before. By half past nine I was in bed, asleep.

I was woken by my door bell, ringing and ringing in a continuous brutal note. I looked at the clock. It was two thirty in the morning. Two thirty. My heart was pounding and my stomach filled with adrenaline as the bell continued to sound. Subconsciously I was aware of my head, which felt as if a big bag of cotton wool had been shoved through one temple and out the other side, and my throat felt dry and sticky. I sat up, my eyes sliding around the room as if someone might have already got in. Slowly I climbed out of bed and took my robe off the hook on the back of the bedroom door and slipped it on. Then I put on my Doc Marten shoes. They felt cold and hard, and looked, I knew, ridiculous but gave me a sense of being in control. At least I could kick someone if necessary. I moved through the apartment, switching on lights and flicking on the radio, so that any intruder would know I was awake and had company, even if it was only the BBC. And if the person ringing the bell was Saskia she would find a warm friendly welcome from all of us.

I opened the door to my apartment and looked along the hall to the main front door of the house. Through the frosted glass I could see large shapes. It wasn't Saskia.

"Frances Richmond? Frances Richmond? Open the door! It's the police."

I looked through the spy-hole. They were right. It was the police.

Nine

Tuesday Morning—Stoke Newington Police Station

Kay said, "What on earth are you doing here?"

"I knew you felt awful sending me to Highbury Corner magistrates court, and I knew you wanted to do something to repay me. So I thought I'd ask you to come down to Stoke Newington police station in the middle of the night."

"The next time you get yourself arrested for murder I would appreciate it if you could do it at some time other than three in the morning."

"I'll bear that in mind but, strange to say, I wasn't consulted about the timetable for all of this. Anyway, you always said you were a morning person. In fact, you said that was one reason our relationship failed."

"Shut up, Frankie."

She looked tired and she had forgotten to comb her hair. I on the other hand had been awake a little longer and had run a brush through my own locks. We were both wearing jeans, but mine were on top of my pajamas.

"Have you said anything yet?"

"No. I told them I was a barrister and I wanted a solicitor immediately because this was such a ludicrous charge. They didn't say anything else and just put me in a cell."

Two of them had escorted me into a small, brightly lit cell with sour yellow walls and a dirty gray concrete floor.

There was a stained mattress and a thin smelly blanket on a bench, a toilet and an overwhelming smell of disinfectant.

"We'll try as hard as we can to rouse your solicitor," the slick, well-dressed officer said. I recognized him from the television. He didn't look much better in the flesh. "Of course, Miss Davidson is a very busy solicitor, she may be out protecting the weak and fighting injustice at another police station. You could be here a little while."

"I'll try and make the place a bit homey then," I said, and began to unfold the blanket as they closed the cell door. "See you later, guys," I called. As the door clanged shut and I heard the key turned in the lock, I sank down on to the mattress with a sense of desolation. Along the corridor someone was banging relentlessly on a door. Someone else was crying out, "I need a doctor, I need a doctor," in a voice filled with fear and loneliness. I knew how they felt.

I drew my knees up under my chin and replayed the events of Friday evening in my mind. The restaurant, the drive, the park. I had been there. I had had physical contact with him. I had been drunk. What had happened? I began to wonder if I had killed Kevin Latimer.

"You said that?" Kay asked me. "About it being a ludicrous charge?"

"Yes. Why, what's wrong with that? I was being firm and assertive."

She sighed. "They're not going to like you because you're a woman on a charge like this, they're not going to like you because you're a barrister, and really not like you if you're a pompous idiot." She sat down opposite me and opened a blue counsel's notebook. The interview room, where they had brought me when Kay arrived, was a slight improvement on the cell. It didn't have the soft furnishings the cell had, just a table and three hard chairs, but neither did it have the pervasive odor of disinfectant.

"Who is this man you're supposed to have killed? I'm not going to ask you if you did it, but I am assuming that you didn't."

I knew she would never ask me that, but I could tell her. "You assume right. I didn't murder him. I didn't kill him at all, so it's not manslaughter either. I don't know anything about him, I don't know his name or who he is, and I hardly even know him."

"Hardly?"

"He beat me up."

"Which is why your eye is that attractive shade of yellow. Of course. When was this?"

"On Friday night."

"What time on Friday night?"

"About nine o'clock."

"And at the moment the police are saying he was killed some time on Friday night. I see."

"I went straight home afterward. After he beat me up, I mean."

"Can you prove that?"

"I don't know." I thought back. "Well, Gino saw me leave the restaurant."

"You were at Gino's?"

"Yes. He came in, this Latimer guy, and ordered some mineral water and then he left and I followed him out."

"You followed him out." Her tone was incredulous.

"Yes, but please don't repeat everything I say because, when you say it, it sounds as if I was behaving really stupidly." I sniffed and silently she handed me a tissue.

"Was there any particular reason why you followed him out?" she said icily.

"Because I thought he had something to do with Saskia. He was the guy at court on Thursday, with the tan shoes."

"And, just by pure coincidence, you saw him in the restaurant?"

"Yes. Well, not exactly coincidence."

"Was Saskia there?"

"No, but I thought she might be. I'd found a chewing-gum wrapper with the word Gino's and a time written on it. I thought you might be meeting her."

"Me? And if I was, you thought you'd come along and make it a threesome? Oh God, this means I'm involved too. I may not be able to represent you."

"Don't say that. You're not involved, it was just an idea. Look, I didn't really think you'd be there. I don't know what I thought. I suppose I felt that she might come, and I was worried about her."

"But instead he came, had a drink and left. And you followed him out . . . ?"

"Yes." I told her as much as I could remember, including the words he had hissed at me.

"And now he is dead, having been murdered in Waterlow Park on the very same evening," Kay said. "And I was going to ask why on earth the police should think of you."

"Ah well, that was my license plate," I said helpfully.

"Oh yes, they mentioned that. Dare I ask . . . ?"

"It must have dropped off when he bashed the car."

If we hadn't been sitting in a police station I knew she would have exploded with some comment like, "Why don't you just go straight to jail and save us all the trouble and expense of a trial?" But one of the first rules of speaking to someone in custody is, as far as possible, to keep up morale. "When did you notice it was gone?"

"Saturday evening."

"And they've only arrested you now? They would have found out your details almost immediately."

"Perhaps nobody would answer the phone at the motor vehicle department. You get that a lot. Remember that time I lost my log-book?"

"I think the police have a direct line. What are they up to?"

The expression on her face alarmed me. "What do you mean?"

"Nothing, nothing. It's probably just part of their investigation procedure."

"Everyone was probably off-duty till tonight."

"Yes," she said absently. "Did anyone see him hit you?"

"I have no idea. I got out of there as quickly as I could."

"And did you tell anyone about all of this?"

"You mean the police? No. I didn't tell anyone. Except Lena on Saturday."

"Was there anyone at home when you got in on Friday, after he'd punched you?"

"No."

"Did you ring anyone?"

"No. And don't give me that face, I specifically thought about ringing you, just to tell someone, but I knew you'd be like this if I told you what had happened."

"I'm like this, as you put it," she enunciated clearly, "because you appear to have behaved extraordinarily stupidly and are now facing a murder charge without an alibi. I would not have been like this if you had rung me on Friday evening."

She would, but I didn't want to argue with her. She was angry with me because I was messing up the case before we'd even started. I have clients like that all the time. You have a wonderful case, a clutch of winning points, you've trashed the opposition, the judge is on your side, and then your client goes into the witness box and gives evidence. And you lose the case. Of course, looking at my situation, we didn't have a wonderful case and as far as I could see no winning points except for the fact that I was a barrister. And against that I was a working class lesbian barrister.

"Plus, I was probably drunk. Well, I was drunk," I blurted out, desperate to confess everything. "I was certainly over the limit." I sneezed and pulled a soggy shredding tissue from my sleeve. Kay handed me another dry one. "I feel like shit," I said.

"Do you want a coffee or something?" Kay rang the bell and when the officer came she asked for two coffees.

"Madam, this is a police station, not a café."

Kay was calm and crisp, she didn't smile and she didn't get angry. We got the coffee. It came in Styrofoam cups and it wasn't hot, it wasn't even coffee really, but it was something to hold and to think about. For a few minutes we were silent.

"So there is absolutely no possibility that they have any forensic evidence which connects you with this murder."

"I can't think how they would have. Unless he picked up fibers from my car when he punched me."

"You watch too much American police soap."

"Cop shows," I corrected.

She ignored me. "They want to search your apartment. Is there any reason why they shouldn't?"

"No."

"No drugs or anything?"

"Advil and Nyquil," I said.

She rang the bell and we all went back to my apartment in a police car. Kay and I and a policewoman sat in the back, and the police officer in the smart suit, who had arrested me, whose name Kay informed me was DCI Fletcher, and another, younger, policeman sat in the front. It was four in the morning but there were cars on the road. Their headlights lit up the interior of our car as they swished by us. I found myself humming "Rainy Night in Georgia" in time with the windshield wipers. Sometimes it does feel like it's raining all over the world. At my end of Amhurst Road no lights were on in any of the apartments and I was relieved that no one saw us arrive.

The police officers went through all my belongings, groping through the clothes in my closet, opening the drawers with my underwear in, upending the plastic bags full of postcards and papers. I was sure they had all just been eating fish and chips and were using my things to wipe their greasy fingers on, leaving stains and marks on everything they touched.

The woman officer at least had the grace to look anxious as she asked DCI Fletcher if she should search the bathroom. Fletcher said, "Yes, Barbara," with a "but of course" smile. When she lifted Saskia's top from the dirty laundry basket I walked into the kitchen to get a glass of water. I heard Fletcher saying, "Go on, get on with it."

"Where are my manners?" I called. "Does anybody want a cup of tea?" I moved into the living room.

Fletcher was squatting beside my record collection flipping through my LPs. "I take mine white with no sugar," he said. "But I don't want anything fancy, no Earl Grey or Lapsang Souchong."

"Officer, you won't find anything incriminating in my apartment, particularly not Earl Grey. Nor will you find sun-dried tomatoes or coriander."

In a sing-song voice, through gritted teeth, Kay murmured, "Shut up." Then, smiling, she said aloud, "Go and make the tea."

"DC Rowland, could you accompany Miss Richmond to the kitchen?" Fletcher had already turned back to my stack of LPs.

"You stay here and watch him with them," I muttered to Kay.

"*What We Did on Our Holidays* by Fairport Convention!" Fletcher was holding the LP cover. I could see he was impressed. And rightly so, it hadn't been an easy record to come by. I had found it in a shop in Soho one Saturday afternoon when I'd missed the beginning of a film and was wandering in Chinatown, cross with myself. Now I wanted to stay and bask in Fletcher's enthusiasm. I wondered if there were trade-off possibilities: "I give you the record, you drop the charge."

"How long is it since I heard 'Meet on the Ledge'?" he said, shaking his head.

"I don't know," I said, lingering.

"Kitchen," Kay said.

"I never heard her sing," he said. "She died before my time."

"I saw her," I said.

"You must have been young."

"Thank you," I said. "I was about twelve."

"Was she good?" he said, with longing.

"People said she wasn't as good as she had been, but she was pretty good."

Fletcher carried the album over to my bulky black stereo system where I occasionally played my original 45s and LPs.

How could a person who likes early Fairport Convention be all bad? I thought. Then I remembered all the relationships in my life which had started so wonderfully when people had enthused about my record collection, and then died when they walked off with my best albums. And he was a police officer. He could quite easily be all bad. Not that I'm prejudiced.

Fletcher took the record out of the cover as if it was a fragile piece of Ming porcelain. Carefully he switched on the power and lifted the arm. I slunk out of the room.

Standing in the kitchen I could hear Sandy Denny's voice powering out the song. Fairport Convention were part of my growing-up period. I never stopped liking Soul and Motown but I had to try other things, listen to other sounds, so that I knew that the early sixties were the best, and it wasn't just something I had been told. But Sandy Denny could make you wonder, with her cut-your-heart-in-two voice.

I crossed back to the living room and stuck my head in the door. "Could you turn it down a bit? Remember my neighbors," I said.

"Won't be your neighbors for long, will they?" He grinned. "Not if I get my evil way."

Kay ostentatiously made a note of what he'd said.

"Oh, come on," he said in an injured tone. "Can't you take a joke?"

"Say something funny and we will," I said.

"Kitchen!" Kay said. "I have to write down what you say as well."

"And these are not my best lines," I said. "Sorry, all, I have to go."

DC Rowland was leaning against the work surface next to the sink with his arms folded. He was one of those people with dark auburn hair with that fresh-faced, slightly tanned looking complexion as if they live a healthy outdoor life. And then on top of that there's the ruddy tinge, that looks like a permanent blush that implies that they are too innocent for this world and need to be protected. I hate people like that because I always answer that call and while I'm busy trying to wrap them in cotton wool to keep them safe, they smile their sad uneasy smile and then bite me on the arm. Every time.

I took some mugs out of the cupboard. He was watching me. I noticed that my hands were shaking. "Are you sure you don't want to look in these before I destroy any evidence by dissolving it in hot water?"

He held up his hands and smiled, a slow blush creeping up his neck on to his cheeks. "I'm sorry about this," he said in a soft northern accent.

"So am I."

"We've . . ."

". . . already looked," we finished together.

"And the fridge?" I asked.

"Yeah. Sorry."

"I bet when you joined the police force you never thought you'd be inspecting groceries."

"There's worse jobs," he said. "If I'd stayed up north I'd still be stacking the shelves, not investigating them."

I looked at his loose frame. He had a good physique under the navy fleece and jeans. "You've come a long way," I said.

His cheeks flamed. We both stared at the kettle as I filled it.

"It's a good job being a police officer," he said.

"Arresting innocent people and then playing their records?"

"A lot of them aren't innocent. You want protection from all those criminals, don't you?"

"Of course I do, but it's how and why." I was struggling to fit the plug into the socket. I hoped he didn't think that was a sign of guilt. "He knows I did not do this."

"What do you mean?" he said. "Look, you were seen talking to Latimer at court—giving him the brush off, and we found your license plate with his body—that gives us reason to arrest."

"All right," I said. "But it doesn't make any sense at all. Why on earth would I kill him?" I was glad that Kay was in the other room with her notepad. I just hoped she was making sure Fletcher didn't steal my entire seventies collection. It was small but it was good.

"Who knows? You've got a bit of a black eye, haven't you? Where did that come from?"

I gripped the handle of the kettle to stop my hand flying to my face to protect my eye, cover the bruise.

"Does anyone take sugar?" I asked, pouring boiling water into the mugs.

"Eh, Barbara does, I think, but not me," he said.

"Do you like it then?" I asked. "The life of a policeman? Why did you come to London anyway?"

"Better training. If you're London trained you can go anywhere."

"As a police officer."

"Yeah, but Fletch put me up for university. That's unusual these days. The force paid for me to go, I loved it."

"So why did you come back to the police?" I pulled sodden tea bags out of the mugs.

"Because I owed it to them. They had faith in me. Especially Fletch. I can't imagine doing anything else." His eyes darkened and I thought he was going to cry.

"But what's his problem?" I said. "Why me? Has he got a thing about women?"

"Oh, he likes women."

"Yeah?"

"I suppose you'd say women are his Achilles heel."

"Would I? Are they? That's not a lot of use to me." I might let him have Fairport Convention but I wasn't putting on lipstick for anyone. "Are you married?" I asked, "Do you have a partner? Dependants?" I meant did he have responsibilities that meant he had to stay in the job, but he misunderstood me.

"It's difficult to meet people in this kind of work," he said. "A lot of people react like you do and don't look behind the uniform."

"Well, you have just arrested me for nothing," I said, fighting the impulse to say, I'll be your friend.

"I've made some friends down here," he said. "Perhaps not what you'd call friends. People I can talk to."

"Friends are good," I said. "Hang on to them." I was thinking, This guy isn't going to last five minutes.

"They've been very good to me," he repeated. He nodded his head toward the living room. "He's been good to me." Fletcher had changed the record and put on Jefferson Airplane, Grace Slick was demanding to know if I needed someone to love.

"Well, I suppose he's got good taste in music," I said.

"He's a bit of a music buff, actually." He laughed. "His searches aren't normally as long as this."

"You mean if all I had was Barry Manilow or muzak we'd have been out of here ages ago?"

"Probably."

"Damn my good taste." His smile was accompanied by an anxious flush of rose. "Aren't there rules in PACE about this?" I asked, groping into my memories of criminal law. I took the milk out of the fridge.

"I don't think the Police and Criminal Evidence Act specifically refers to musical accompaniments to a search." He was looking around the room. "Although if you get a good lawyer they'll probably get the evidence we find excluded on that basis."

"There is no evidence!"

"Whatever you say," he said blandly. He was a police officer again with his conciliatory tone. I wondered if they taught them that at the police academy. "Have you got a tray?" he asked.

As he bent to pick up the tray, I saw that the blush touched even the back of his neck. I said, "Don't let him get you into any trouble."

A smile flashed across his face. "I could say the same to you," he said, and walked quickly out of the room leaving me to carry in the tray.

In the living room, Fletcher was tipping up my Santana LP, giving it a little shake. Out clicked a small square of plastic. I stared at it, transfixed. "What's this then?" he said, picking it up from the floor.

"Well, I don't know, but I assume you do."

I looked at Kay. Her face was expressionless, but her eyes were shocked.

"Are you accusing me of planting evidence?" Fletcher asked mildly, standing up, brushing the knees of his trousers. "Ask your brief, she was here all the time."

Kay said nothing.

They took away the clothes I had been wearing on the Friday evening and three rather old Kitchen Devil knives of varying sizes. And the credit card.

P. J. Kramer's credit card.

Back at the station Kay and I returned to the interview room.

She waited till we were left alone. "So how did that get there?"

"I have no idea," I said. "He must have slipped it in while you weren't watching."

"I was watching him all the time," she said. "He didn't put it in there."

"Do you think they know whose card it is?"

"Well, it depends. If Latimer used the name Kramer as an alias they'll know that already. If it was just a stolen card, they'll soon find that out. Whatever happens, you've been found with a credit card which is not yours, in your possession."

"In a Santana LP," I pointed out.

"Good forensic point," she said. "We'll use that at the trial. 'Members of the jury, how could anyone say she possessed that credit card? It was found in a seventies LP and you know she's never really liked seventies music.' You should have given me all those records when we split up. But no, the integrity of your record collection came first." I felt Kay was losing her veneer of professionalism, I was in bigger trouble than I thought.

"Have I got to tell them that I know it was his credit card?"

"It's up to you," she said, rubbing her hand across her face. "Pros and cons. If you tell them, you inextricably link yourself to Latimer right now. If you don't, they'll find out and wonder why you didn't say anything."

"So that's a yes."

"I think so. But how on earth did it get in there?"

"It could have got in there last night," I said, quietly.

"Meaning?"

"My apartment was broken into last night."

"And you of course immediately rang the police."

"It was Saskia," I said. "So, no, I didn't."

"Have you mentioned her name to them at all?"

"Do you think I should?"

"Yes, I do. I think you should tell them everything, including Saskia. Everything. Otherwise there's a big question mark over your association with Latimer, how you came to know him. They know nothing, so they suspect the worst. Saskia makes your connection to him innocent. Well, more innocent. You've got to tell them everything, you have nothing to hide. You've got to tell them about Saskia." She saw the expression on my face. "Saskia is a big girl. She can look after herself. They'll have to know about her one way or the other. The police already know the kind of person she is, the kind of life she leads, obviously, from years ago. We'll be mentioning her name in any defense statement we make, if they decide to actually charge you." She fixed me with a piercing expression. "There isn't anything I should know, is there? You haven't slept with her in the last forty-eight hours, for example?"

"No," I said. "Why, have you?"

"Frankie, shut your mouth." She was making notes. "Are you like this in court?"

"No."

"Well, pretend you're in court."

I hadn't told Kay about seeing Saskia at the club or the phone call from the day before. I hadn't mentioned the note that Saskia had left for me, mainly because it was an adverse comment on my home security and I knew what Kay would say about that. None of it seemed relevant in the light of this new development. Saskia had left a credit card in my flat. A credit card which had brought me considerably closer to a murder charge. How could she have done this to me? But then, perhaps she hadn't "done it to me"—perhaps she'd been desperate to get rid of the card and my house had seemed a safe house to her.

Kay rang the bell and leaned against the wall looking at her watch as we waited. "It's six o'clock," she said. "Are you up to this?"

I nodded.

The door swung open. "My client is ready to be interviewed," Kay said.

Ten

Tuesday Afternoon

Igot out at half past two in the afternoon, on police bail.
I had told the police everything I had told Kay and I
thought the interview was going well till we got to the end.

"Of course, you know what would help you enormously, Frances . . ." DCI Fletcher made a great show of
hitting the off button on the tape recorder and picking up
his papers and patting them into shape.

I looked at him. "I assume you're going to tell me."

"What would help you enormously would be if you
could tell us where Susan—or should that be Saskia?—is
at the present time."

"If I knew that, none of this would have happened."

"None of what?" he said quickly, hoping to catch me
out at the last moment.

"Oh, come on, officer," I said, "you know what I mean."
I paused and prayed he had never been cross-examined by
me in the old days when I did crime. They don't like to be
humiliated for lack of truthfulness or over-zealousness in
pursuing their police functions. I didn't have any memory
of him, but then I never remembered any of them. I
thought I was probably safe enough with DCI Fletcher. He
looked fresh and almost new. How could he afford an
Armani suit like that? I knew I couldn't. Perhaps I was in
the wrong job.

"My client has told you everything she knows about Miss Baron," Kay said sharply.

The officer looked at me and smiled. "I would love to say I believe that, Frances, but do you know, I don't."

I set my mouth in an "oh really?" expression and returned his gaze. I heard Kay grinding her teeth.

Grudgingly, he told me that they would send the papers to the Crown Prosecution Service and that I was to return to the police station in ten days' time. I sneezed.

"I'll drive you home," Kay said, handing me more clean tissues as my house keys and my watch were returned to me by the custody sergeant.

We walked out together into the car park of the police station. It was raining, a light damp drizzle. Her car felt comfortable and safe. The windshield wipers worked quietly and efficiently as we drove up High Street.

Hopefully I said, "Ten days is significant, isn't it? Doesn't it mean I'm almost off the hook? If they really thought I did it, wouldn't they want me back sooner, say, in a week? Although, I suppose, if I was completely out of the frame, they'd just hedge their bets and want me back in a month."

"You're not well, are you?" Kay said. "None of that is true, necessarily. Now it depends on what the CPS think. I have to say though, your friend Fletcher could have pushed harder to stop you having bail. The custody sergeant was all for charging you there and then. Fletcher must like you, he probably recognizes a kindred spirit, you're both bullshitters." We were in a line of traffic near Church Street.

"It's probably our shared interest in music."

"I think you're more use to him out on the street," she said.

"What do you know about Fletcher?" I asked. "Have you met him before?"

"His name rings a bell," she said. "I'm trying to remember. It'll come back to me." She looked in the rear-view mirror as we edged forward. "I wonder where Saskia is," she said.

"She rang me," I began.

"What? Who?"

"Saskia rang me. Yesterday, at lunchtime. And I saw her at the club on Saturday. But I didn't talk to her. It was just for a second. She was wearing the shirt I lent her."

Kay put her head on the steering wheel. "Was I supposed to divine this? Were you going to tell me about this at any point? How could you not tell me? I don't know, it could be material evidence that you have kept from the police. It would certainly firm up your defense. Look, just because you are out on bail does not mean you are out of the woods. You should have told me. How can I advise you properly if you don't tell me everything?"

"Should we go back and tell them?" I suggested.

"Of course we can't go back and tell them. The custody sergeant will probably book you for attempting to pervert the course of justice and remove bail. He's not a bad guy, I've got a lot of time for him, but he doesn't like to be messed about." She was silent while the traffic moved off. As we drove across Rectory Road she said, in a more friendly tone of voice, "So what did Saskia say when she rang?"

"Nothing. She just said, 'Oh, Frankie, what can I do?' I said, 'Saskia, what's going on?' and then she rang off. And there was no number."

"Oh God."

"Is it bad?"

"Well, I think we're going to have find Saskia pretty quickly because you are in big, big trouble."

I still hadn't told her about Saskia's note. I reckoned I didn't need to tell her, certainly not straight away. I had ten days to sort things out.

However, other things started happening which took up my time.

When I got in the light on my answering machine was flashing. There were two messages. Gavin telling me that a long-running case of mine had blown up. Mr. Break-speare, the violent father of two children, had breached an injunction not to assault his wife and at 10:30 A.M. in the morning in the Royal Courts of Justice there was to be an application to commit him to prison. I wrote "Launder collarette" on the back of my hand, while the machine beeped for my second message.

"Frankie?" The soft husky voice sent a shiver through my body. "Frankie? It's Margo. I know it's a bit soon to be ringing. I know the etiquette is to wait about a week, but, well, I had such a great time on Saturday, I want to see you sooner. Ring me?"

I looked at the machine in disbelief. Margo was gorgeous. She must know that. Why was she ringing me in such a desperate way? She didn't have to do that. I would have rung her—probably later that day. I realized with pleasure that she had obviously enjoyed Saturday as much as I had.

I wanted to ring her straight away but first I had to ring chambers. Gavin asked me whether I would be fit for court the next day. I made a non-committal noise. He said it looked like Mr. Breakspeare had really blown it this time. Gavin had obviously been reading the instructions, so it must have been a quiet day. When the phones don't ring the clerks amuse themselves by reading the briefs. I said I'd do it.

"Do you want your messages?" Gavin asked. He went to fetch them. "A DCI Fletcher rang about ten minutes ago. He said there was no message, he would just wait to hear from you."

"Yes," I said.

"And there's one here from Dr. Henry returning your call."

"Oh no." Dr. Henry had gone completely from my mind. I wrote "Dr H—Mom" on the pad by the phone.

"Are you all right, Frankie?" Gavin asked.

"It's just this cold," I said, sniffing, conscious that I didn't sound as ill as I ought to, having returned a brief.

"No, I don't mean that." He sounded concerned. "That police officer, DCI what's-his-name, sounded a bit anxious about you."

"Did he? You see, Gavin, I'm a person of eclectic taste." I was still buzzing from the message from Margo. "I have friends everywhere. I like to think I have them in the clerks' room, and I also have them in the police station."

"If you say so. You're not in any trouble, are you?"

I hesitated. Your clerk should be privy to your inner-most thoughts and the deepest recesses of your private life in case it is ever necessary for things to be explained to the Professional Conduct Committee of the Bar Council, but I was worried about chambers' gossip. Sometimes the clerks' room is like the editorial office of *Hello!* magazine and *Crimewatch UK* rolled into one, as the clerks and whichever barristers are wandering through swap gentle innuendo or outright blatant hearsay about other members of chambers. And sometimes I join in.

I could just imagine Gavin and Jenna and Scott, the fees clerk, and Malik, the diary clerk and Jayne, the practice manager, having their half past nine cup of coffee while Jenna opened the mail and Scott distributed the Legal Aid checks, caringly discussing my arrest for murder. And then a solicitor would ring and Gavin would pick up the phone while he finished his sentence: ". . . and anyway, who would have thought Frankie would have had a knife sharp enough to peel a potato, let alone commit a murder? Good morning, 17 KBW, Gavin speaking."

And then it would be all around the Solicitor's Family Law Association and they'd pass it on to all the clerks in the Temple and then my mom would somehow find out. Quickly I decided I would tell them if and only if I was charged.

"I'm fine," I said.

He hesitated. "I'll just say, keep in touch." He cleared his throat. "Two other things: the brief in the ancillary proceedings for Stevens has come in and they want an advice."

"Oh no."

"And did I give you the Rachel Hayman message?"

I made a note of her number, then he said, "Your listing tomorrow is Court 43, you're in front of His Honor Judge Goodge. Second on at ten thirty. I'll messenger the papers over to you now."

Still putting off the pleasure of ringing Margo, I dialed Dr. Henry's number. His receptionist told me that he was free and put me straight through.

Saying hello, his voice was deep and hearty and did not inspire me with confidence. I thought of the money he must earn from cutting people up to make them fit some image which they thought made them more socially acceptable.

"Dr. Henry." I tried to make my voice sound friendly for my mother's sake.

"Miss Richmond, your mother spoke to me about you and was quite insistent that I ring you."

"Dr. Henry, I have to tell you, I don't want any plastic surgery."

I thought he might say, "Not even a little bit?" but instead he said, "I am so relieved to hear you say that. I think your mother may have misunderstood what my line of work actually is. I deal mainly with burn victims and people who have had radical surgery, usually for cancer."

Now his voice was sounding deep and reliable and I imagined that he was slim with silver hair and twinkling blue eyes, just right for my mother.

So I asked him out for her and he said yes with real pleasure in his voice.

Eleven

Tuesday Evening

I rang Margo. Well, OK, let me explain exactly how it went. I poured myself a glass of wine. It was four o'clock, and in my book that is the cocktail hour, and I needed, deserved even, a cocktail. Then I rang her.

All right, I had a bath first, with the glass of wine in the bathroom, with a few candles. I brought in a loudspeaker and put on a CD of Marvin Gaye singing slow smoochy songs. I wanted to get in the mood.

Twenty minutes later, I was clean and sparkling, dressed in fresh clothes, clean jeans and a black sweater, and smelling of Ô de Lancôme. And then I rang her.

The phone rang for a long time.

Finally she answered. "Hello?" She sounded stressed, even irritated.

"Margo?"

"Oh . . . Frankie, hello." The honey of her voice poured over me.

"Is this a good time?"

"Mm," she said, absently.

We had a short, stilted conversation and I could hear her putting her hand over the mouthpiece to speak to someone else in the room. We made an arrangement to meet at quarter to eleven at the Queen of Sheba.

As I put the phone down I felt uneasy and I couldn't

work out why. Perhaps it was just youthful anticipation. Perhaps it was the small matter of a threatened murder charge hanging over my head. Marvin Gaye began to sing "Can I Get a Witness?" but as the answer was clearly no at the moment, I put on the Elgins singing "Heaven Must Have Sent You," and danced around the living-room floor.

At eight thirty the doorbell rang. My heart leapt. I imagined all sorts of people, Latimer, oh no, it couldn't be him, Saskia, DCI Fletcher. It was a messenger. Stiffly, with leather-gloved hands he passed me a large envelope, which obviously contained my brief, and then a clipboard with a grimy piece of paper attached, to sign.

I went back indoors and took a collarette out of my wig tin. A collarette is the female and, some would say, feminine version of a collar, to be worn with a wig and gown. A strip of white cotton circles the neck, attached by Velcro. Two small rectangles of white cotton hang down at the front. They're meant to be crisp and snowy white, which they always are on TV series. Mine seem to get grey and grubby just sitting in the tin. It's probably the proximity of my wig, which I have never cleaned in all my years at the bar. In family work, most hearings are in chambers, which means that the public aren't allowed in, and so you don't need a wig or a gown, but an application to commit someone to prison for breach of an injunction is regarded as so serious that it's one of the few occasions when the public are permitted in to court and that you therefore need to dress up for.

I ran water in the sink in the bathroom, added laundry detergent and left the collarette to soak.

I ripped open the envelope and a jumble of papers spilled on to the floor. I looked at it with despair. It would take me ages just to sort it out, let alone read the new documents and check that everything was there in the right form.

It took me forty-five minutes just to put the brief in order. Forty-five minutes. For a committal you reckon an hour's preparation at most, because you already know the story, you just need to know which parts of the original order he has actually broken, make sure the solicitor has set everything out properly in one short document and work out some cutting cross-examination. However, I was sitting on the floor surrounded by the current application, old applications going back three years, orders that had been made years before that and something that looked like a love letter from someone in prison who was completely unconnected with the case. I made myself a cup of coffee which I forgot to drink as I picked through the statements of the parties, an affidavit of service and copies of all the phone messages my solicitor had ever received.

I read it all doggedly, probably more assiduously because I knew I had to be finished by ten forty-five.

On our evidence there were four flagrant breaches of the order we had obtained only three weeks before. Doubtless Mr. Breakspeare would deny everything and say he was outside the house of his ex-wife at three in the morning with a bread knife because he knew she loved toast for breakfast and he was just there waiting to slice it for her.

My instructions told me that Mr. Breakspeare would be represented on the application. That was a relief or he'd be cross-examining my client in the witness box for hours, demanding that she admit that he had always been a good father to the children, reminding her that he'd looked after them when she'd gone to the hospital after that time he stabbed her.

It was almost twenty to eleven when I finally tied the pink ribbon back around the brief. I felt the satisfaction I always feel when I'm on top of the case and the brief is all in order, but I was nervous about going to the club, I was surprised how nervous. And I'd be lucky to get there in ten minutes.

I laced up my brown ankle boots, put on my tan suede jacket, put a handful of tissues and my wallet in my jeans pocket and left.

The car coughed into life after a stern talking to. The traffic was busy as I drove south into Dalston, people dashing to pubs for a drink before closing time, gangs of young kids hanging out, cars stopping to chat with them, and then it was a clear run down to Shoreditch. I pulled up outside the club at ten forty-seven, feeling very pleased with myself.

The street was deserted. Pages of the *Sun* drifted along the pavement, rising and falling to a silent rhythm. She had said she would be at the club at quarter to eleven, there was no need for me to come in, outside would be fine. There would be people around. I waited till eleven o'clock. No one left or entered the club, no cars drove up, or even by. I got out of the car and walked up to the door of the club. I looked to see if there was a message, a note, a piece of scribbled graffiti, "Frankie, we are in Joe's Café, see you there." There was nothing, except a scrap of orange peel in the corner of the small porch. For the second time that day I felt desolate. I needed her to be there. I hadn't realized how much I wanted to feel her affection, her appreciation, her softness.

I pushed the door and it swung open. There was no one at the desk at the entrance so I walked straight in. Some piano music that sounded like Keith Jarrett was playing. There were about five women at the bar, who all turned slightly to look at me. I didn't know any of them. Behind the bar, standing on a step-ladder doing something mechanical with a light fixture, was the same woman who had been serving on Saturday.

She came down the steps immediately. "Some Australian Chardonnay?" she asked with a pleasant smile. She was young and chunky and now I noticed that as well as the stud in her nose she had about twelve rings in her left ear and something that looked like a bolt in her right eyebrow.

"No thanks," I said. I looked around the room. "You're quiet tonight."

"Tuesdays are always slow," she said. She hesitated. "Are you meeting someone?"

"No, no one in particular," I said. "I was just passing. Thought I'd have a look in, see if anyone was around."

"OK," she said. "Margo hasn't been in all night."

I smiled with embarrassment. Had it been that obvious? I looked at my watch. It was five past eleven. "Goodnight," I said and left.

I felt I was spending my life waiting for people who didn't turn up. Was I being stood up? Was I doomed to live my life as I had in my adolescence and in my relationship with Kay? It didn't feel like that, but that was probably because I didn't want it to feel like that.

I got back in the car and pushed a tape into the machine. Fontella Bass began to sing "Rescue Me." A heavy bass guitar and a loud brass section accompanied me and Fontella most of the way to Balls Pond Road. I had almost forgotten why I had gone out and then the Chiffons started "One Fine Day" and I thought of Margo and wished she'd been there and thought how it could have been. She'd have smiled and got in the car, and I would have driven her home and then we'd have kissed. I remembered her soft lips and all sorts of images filled my mind. But she hadn't been there and there was just me in the car and I realized I was driving without my lights on.

At home the light on my answering machine was flashing mockingly. My answering machine had more success with women than I did.

It was a message from Margo. In a soft, breathy voice she explained that she'd got her dates mixed up and there was something else she'd had to do. She'd tried to call me earlier but my telephone was busy. "Liar," I moaned. No one had rung me all night. Would I forgive her, she asked, and make another date?

"We'll see," I told the machine.

Twelve

Wednesday—Royal Courts of Justice

"Good morning, Miss Richmond," Mr. Breakspeare said to me grandly as I arrived outside Court 43 at ten past ten. I had just been congratulating myself on arriving in time for a civilized twenty-minute conference with my client and counsel for the other side and now it was obvious that Mr. Breakspeare had fired his lawyers. My heart sank. This meant I had to talk to him to see if we could come to any agreement before we went into court.

My client sat behind a table in one of the glass recesses in the corridor outside courts 43 to 46. She gave me a weary smile as I threw on my wig and gown and I noticed that my collarette trick hadn't worked. As I had staggered into the bathroom at ten past nine after sleeping through the alarm the collarette was still on the side of the sink where I had left it when I brushed my teeth last night. As I really couldn't face wearing a wet collarette, not in October anyway, and I didn't have time to iron it dry, I had put on the grubby one which was waiting patiently at the bottom of the wig tin. I had hoped the creases would fall out with the heat of my body and the pressure of my coat. My hopes were not realized.

Reluctantly I went to the next alcove where Mr. Breakspeare was lurking. He was short with thick pebble glasses and was wearing the green Barbour jacket he wore every time he came to court. "We have nothing to say to each other, Miss Richmond," he said with a smirk. I wondered if it was the collarette or the fading yellow bruise around my eye. "I shall say everything I have to say to the judge." With relief I slid back to my client. Although coming to court was always a strain for her she looked better every time I saw her, her eyes sparkled and her hair shone. Today she looked smart in a turquoise cotton suit which she told me proudly she had bought for two pounds from a thrift store. But it was a cold day and she didn't have a coat.

I walked over to the door of the court to look at the list as Brenda, the usher, with her bright pink lipstick and black gown, bustled out. "Oh, it's you, Miss Richmond," she said. "You've got a piece of work there." She looked over at Mr. Breakspeare. "He's already tried to see the judge on his own."

Brenda was about forty with auburn hair. I thought my job got depressing but at least I could go to the movies in the afternoon. She had to stay there all day every day listening to stories of unhappy marriages. I looked at her left hand. She had three chunky gold rings on the third finger. "Are you ready to come in?" she asked. "Two of the judge's other matters have settled and one's been transferred back to the judge it was reserved to in the first place. It shouldn't have been on our list at all."

Mr. Breakspeare asked for an adjournment to enable him to obtain legal representation. An adjournment would enable me to go home to bed with two aspirin. But I objected. I won and the committal hearing began.

My client gave her evidence first. She stood still and straight in the witness box as she described how he had danced in the street in the middle of the night, brandishing the knife, shouting that she was a slut and a whore. Before we came into court she had promised herself she would not let him see her cry but when she described how the curtains of the neighbors' windows twitched, and how one or two came out into the street in their robes, a tear slid down her cheek. Mr. Breakspeare questioned her about her child care, the cost of her clothes, her care of the garden. I objected. His Honor Judge Goodge was one of the old school. He thought you should let a man ask anything he wanted so that he could get it all out of his system and would have no grounds for appeal. My client began to shiver and her hair seemed to droop.

Then it was Mr. Breakspeare's turn. He sprang energetically into the witness box. His evidence was that he had the knife for self-protection, his wife being known for her violent tendencies, and he had shouted slut and whore because it was true and he could not be sent to prison for telling the truth, could he?

Portentously the judge said, "I find the case against you proved overwhelmingly, Mr. Breakspeare, and I commit you to prison for a period of twenty-eight days . . ."

I heard my client sigh with relief.

". . . suspended for a year."

Mr. Breakspeare left court with the smirk he had worn at half past ten.

I was back in the Temple at ten to one. I walked up the stairs to chambers, composing the letter to *Family Law* which I knew I would never write, about the inappropriate way domestic violence cases were dealt with in our courts today with outmoded procedures and dinosaur judges. I was wondering whether the word "dinosaur" was a bit strong or just a cliché when I saw Anthony Garforth, my head of chambers, on the landing outside the clerks' room. Damn. I rarely saw Tony and spent as little time as possible in his company. But bumping into him like this was a sign, it meant I had to tell him. It was a task I didn't relish.

Tony leered at me. "Francesca, how I would love to invite you to a delicious lunch where we could while away two happy hours considering life and all its imperfections, but sadly I must spend an hour in the dull company of Mr. Justice Dangerfield. Another day, another time, my dear, and then I will show you the magic of the Orient—and I'm not talking about the Temple Tandoori." He laughed at his joke and made to continue down the stairs.

I put my hand on his arm. "Actually, Tony, there is something important that I ought to talk to you about."

He looked flustered and I felt rather sorry for him. He was nearly sixty, had only recently taken silk after thirty-three years at the bar and was desperate to become a judge. A lunch date with Mr. Justice Dangerfield was a coup for him and he didn't need me to decide that today was the day I wanted to seriously engage him about something. And he didn't even know what it was.

"It will only take a minute or two," I said, "I can walk to the Wig and Pen with you." I knew this was Tony's favorite lunching venue. I had once eaten there with him and Simon, in the dark wood-paneled room, with stunningly white tablecloths and heavy silver cutlery. Tony was leading Simon in their obscenity case which had involved chambers being full of porn magazines. Tony was trying to prove to me that Simon and he, particularly he, were good guys really. Over sausage and mashed potatoes Tony had had difficulty dividing his time flirting with me, justifying doing the case and casually nodding hello to anyone in the room over sixty, which was practically everyone except Simon and me, so we finished eating long before he did and then filled in the time drinking red wine from the club's well-stocked cellar. I had felt sure that in some way I was morally compromised by being there, or by drinking the wine, but after two glasses I had stopped trying to figure it out.

Now, as we walked briskly up Middle Temple Lane, with Tony saluting graciously the young women and old men who passed us, I explained my dilemma. It came out more baldly than I intended.

"Tony, I've been arrested for murder."

"What?!"

I repeated what I had said while, I could see, his career at the bar flashed before his eyes. All those boring people he'd had to suck up to, all the years of humiliating rejections as he tried to take silk, all wasted, all for nothing, farewell the judgeliness, farewell the knighthood. A member of his chambers had been charged with murder, the shame, the pity of it.

"All right!" I broke into his train of thought, "I've only been arrested, and I didn't, repeat didn't, do it."

"Oh, Frances." He sighed. "I'm sure you didn't. But what are you doing here? Are you a fugitive from justice? Have you escaped from your shackles to prove your innocence?"

"Tony, you watched too much *Boyd QC* in your youth. I've got police bail."

"Oh." He nodded indiscriminately at one of Middle Temple's security guards. "Well, how has all this occurred? Was it some terrible lesbian brawl, with torn clothing and scratching with long red nails? Is that a black eye, Frankie?"

"Perhaps you just read too much of the literature you spend your time defending in court." Tony had gone straight on to represent another pornographer charged under the Obscene Publications Act. "It was a man," I went on, "he was stabbed. He was found with the license plate from my car next to his body."

We stepped through the heavy gates into Fleet Street and were hit by the noise from the traffic roaring past. Cabs chugged to a halt picking up barristers going to the West End for their lunch, exuding clouds of diesel exhaust. I looked up at Tony. The nostrils of his aquiline nose were pulsating with despair. In his youth he must have been very good looking and considered quite a catch. His third wife, whom he had married two years before, was a lovely woman of thirty-five. "Your license plate?" he repeated, looking around to see whether anyone was listening. Two tourists in matching pink sweats, nodding their heads up and down between a map and the street, caught his eye and asked how to get to St. Paul's Cathedral. "I don't know," he said, while I directed them to a number 15 bus.

"It's a long story," I continued. "Just remember I didn't do it. And I've only been arrested. I haven't been charged and I am therefore innocent, as you would say to your jury, since I have not been proven guilty. So I'm intending to carry on working."

"Is that wise?" he asked anxiously.

"That's really what I want you to tell me. But the other thing is, I haven't told anyone else in chambers."

"Quite so, quite so. Do you have a good solicitor?" he asked me, and I was touched that he was able to think about my welfare, when my very existence was such a problem for him.

"Yes," I said, "Kay Davidson."

"Oh good," he said. "Lovely girl, lovely girl. You'll do very well with her. What about counsel?"

"Tony, I haven't been charged yet," I reminded him, "which means there cannot, as yet, be a trial. I am hoping it won't get that far."

"Yes, yes, good, good. Oh well, here we are." We stood outside the yellow frosted window panes of the Wig and Pen, while he wondered how he could best dispense with my presence without an unseemly display of rudeness or relief. Suddenly I didn't want to be left on my own.

He pulled open the heavy door. "Perhaps very low-key work," he mumbled.

"All my work is low key," I said, bitterly.

"Oh, Frances," he said, and disappeared into the dark hallway.

I stood on the street for a moment wondering if I had sufficiently impressed on him the need for confidentiality, but consoled myself that his fear of infamy and shame would probably keep him quiet. I felt alone and almost afraid, in a vague, stomach grinding kind of way.

I wondered if there was a chance that Lena was free for lunch. I went to a payphone to call her. As I dialed her number I looked at the adverts, dozens of them, urging, cajoling, demanding that men ring up for a good time. The one advert aimed at women was for cheaper car insurance. I thought about my license plate. Would I get it back from the police? Would I get stopped by the police for not having one? Could I claim for a new one on my insurance?

After several minutes I was informed curtly that Lena was teaching a class over the lunch break.

I was considering whether to go and buy a copy of *Private Eye* from the newsstand opposite the Royal Courts, to cheer myself up, when I saw the broad smile of Simon advancing in my direction.

"Frankie, mon brave! How are you?"

"Strangely, Simon, all the better for seeing you. Do you feel like lunch?"

His face fell. "What a terrible day to ask me that question. I'm on my way to Ebury Bridge Road, for a hopeless application before the tribunal. Quite an interesting legal point, though."

"I take it that's a no, then," I said.

"Do you need some money for a sandwich?"

"Oh God, I still owe you that twenty pounds."

"Don't worry about it. Are you all right?" he asked with concern.

I was touched. "Simon, why haven't you got a girlfriend?"

He looked down at the gold chain spanning his waist-coat. He nodded his head thoughtfully. "I don't know," he said, looking up with a smile. "I don't think I've met the right girl yet. Or rather, I've met the right girl, it's just that she . . ." He flashed his eyes at me.

"Oh, piss off, Simon," I said.

"That's why I like you, Frankie," he said, "it's your en-dearing down-to-earth approach to life. Ah, here comes a number eleven, I'm off. See you later."

"Not if I see you first," I called, as he leapt onto the platform.

He turned and blew me a kiss.

Smiling, I walked back to chambers. As I emptied my mailbox of memos and back copies of *Counsel,* the bar's in-house magazine, I told Gavin to keep me out of court for the next couple of weeks as I would be doing paper-work and was unavailable for public appearances. Unless it was the Court of Appeal or somewhere higher, I added.

"When we say paperwork, we mean the Morris papers, don't we?" Gavin asked.

"Oh my God!" I had forgotten. "Yes, yes, of course," I said naturally. "Of course. Yes, yes, we do."

"Might I suggest that you take the opportunity of a free afternoon to finish off the grounds?"

I looked at him doubtfully.

"Start it . . . ?" he ventured. "Do the research?"

"Yes, yes, yes."

"And then you can dash off that ancillary relief advice."

"Of course."

"And you haven't forgotten about the chambers' meet-ing tonight. . ."

"I have completely forgotten. I've even forgotten what you just said."

Gavin ignored me. "Chambers' rent is on the agenda," he said. "Marcus wants an increase in the flat rate." Chambers expenses came in two parts, a flat rate which everyone paid and then a percentage of earnings. I didn't like the flat rate, because it penalized people who were not earning a lot. Like me.

It isn't done to criticize fellow barristers to the clerks, so I didn't ask Gavin to confirm that Marcus had only recently received an enormous check for his part in a three-month trial at which he was last on the indictment and had therefore had to ask only about four questions. He had strutted around chambers for days, holding the check ostentatiously in one hand and asking anyone who passed how much luxury sedans were costing these days. I'd said, "I thought the blue ones were more expensive than the silver ones, but the green ones went faster."

Now I just said to Gavin, "Presumably he wants chambers to pay for another painting for his room."

"I think he's after a marble fireplace."

"For God's sake," I said. "Although, as he's so fond of having conferences in my room, perhaps he'll argue for a fireplace for me."

"So you'll be supporting the rent increase?" Gavin asked.

"Gavin, I have no money to pay my own rent, my mortgage that is, let alone that of chambers. I know it's chambers' rent which pays the pathetic salaries of the clerks"—I knew Gavin earned much more than I did but I was trying to win my point—"and much as I want you to be even more highly paid . . ."

"Well, if you would do crime . . ." Gavin began.

"I told you, I am not doing crime, thank you, no matter how much money that would bring me."

"Tell me again why you don't do crime."

"Because the cases they want to send someone like me are the rapes and the sexual abuse of young children," I recited, "so that the jury say, 'He can't be all that bad, she likes him and she's a woman.' "

He sighed. "It makes sense when you say it, but I can't hold it in my head longer than about five minutes."

"And I am particularly not doing crime, since my recent criminal experience has caused me so much grief."

"I won't ask you what you mean." Gavin's reply made me think he knew exactly what I meant. I wondered if he'd been talking to Kay. He looked at me. "Are you all right?"

"And why shouldn't I be?" I raised my eyebrows.

"Good question," he said, and I wanted desperately to tell him everything. He seemed the only person in chambers who really cared about me as a person, not me as a rather inappropriate sex object. Even if his interest really was financial, since how much work I brought into chambers affected his percentage, it seemed pure and uncluttered and I wanted to throw myself at him, sobbing, and confess all.

"Gavin," I began.

"Mmm?"

The phone rang and he leaned across his desk to answer it.

"Nothing," I said, and mouthing, "I'm going to the library," I left the room.

Thirteen

Wednesday Evening—Chambers

On the large round table in the library were volumes of *Family Law, Family Law Reports, Family Court Reporter* and *Current Law*. I was looking up an authority which I was sure existed but none of the law reports seemed to have heard of it. Without this precedent my Morris appeal had no chance of success. I had read it somewhere, but I couldn't remember the name of the case or the date. I thought it began with T or possibly M, but then that's what most family cases are called, "In re T (a minor)," "M *v* M, number 2," "Re T and M (minors) (contact)." Our chambers' library was better than some, but our *Times Law Reports* only ran from 1993 and some of the other reports we simply didn't carry.

Ignoring the possibility that I had read the story in the *People's* "They Did What?!" column, I was considering the tedious prospect of walking over to my Inn Library or even to the Bar Library in the Royal Courts to do a fuller investigation. All barristers have to be a member of an Inn (mine is Inner Temple) and each Inn has a library for its members. The Bar Library is for all barristers, but it's farther away. And I hate going to my Inn Library, because it means I have to rub shoulders with other barristers and young people who are about to become barristers and I am reminded of the kind of people barristers so often are.

Upper class, privileged people with posh voices who have had very expensive educations. When the phone rang I hoped for two seconds it was a pupil eager to do extra work who would be glad of the opportunity to get out of chambers to go to another library for me.

But Jenna said, "It's Lena Johnson for you, Frankie."

"Lena?" I was surprised. She rarely rang me at work.

"Frankie, I'm ringing you to ask if you fancy going out to dinner."

"When?"

"Tonight." This was even rarer. She had never done this. "We could go to Mezzo in Soho."

"You won't get a reservation at this stage, will you?"

"I reserved it last week. For . . . someone else."

"Sophie?"

"No."

I was silent.

"A friend, Nicky, it's her birthday, but apparently she's had a better offer, so I've got a reservation that I don't want to waste."

I looked at the books on the table and breathed a sigh of relief.

"I've got a chambers meeting," I said, "but that should finish at about seven thirty."

"That's OK," she said. "I've got a Street Life meeting first." Lena was involved with a group of women, prostitutes, residents and councilors, trying to deal with the issues of prostitution in Finsbury Park. "The table's reserved for eight fifteen," she said.

It was two thirty, and the chambers meeting was due to start at six. I had just over three hours to finish my research and do a first draft of the appeal. I always work better when I have a deadline and even better when I have something pleasant to look forward to afterwards.

I went along to the clerks' room. "I'm off to Inner Temple Library," I announced.

"I thought that's where you'd gone already," Jenna said. "A message just came in for you." She went over to the message station, pulled out the small blue slip and handed it to me.

" 'If we don't hear from you we shall simply go ahead at the appropriate moment,' " I read. "Oh my God," I wailed, "what does that mean? Who's it from?"

My mind went through all the possibilities. It sounded like a note from kidnappers. Had it happened then, had she been kidnapped? I must have missed the first note which probably said something like, "We have Saskia. Put a large amount of money in a blue barrister's bag and leave it in a trash can at Temple subway station or else." That message had got lost presumably because someone had written it down wrongly or put it in Marcus's mailbox, so I only received the second message, which was just a threat.

Jenna's initials were in the margin. She took the note from me and squinted at it. "Does the part that says 'Message from Rachel Hayman' mean anything?"

No wonder Gavin liked her, she was smart and sensible. Whereas I was getting too jittery for my own good.

"I have to go and make some calls," I said, and left the room.

I rang the number for Rachel Hayman but was told primly that there was no one there called Hayman, could I mean Wayman? I agreed I could and that I would wait, and soon a cheerful voice informed me that I was speaking to Rachel Wayman.

"You left me a message?" I began cautiously.

"Yes, I'm from *Family Law Documents*. John Michaelson spoke to me about your Court of Appeal case."

"What Court of Appeal case?"

"Em . . . Morris?"

"But that hasn't happened yet."

"We may want to report it. John Michaelson mentioned

that in the court below you argued your point in a rather interesting way, concerning reasons for refusing contact."

"Oh, did he?" I said. John Michaelson had also threatened to report me to the Legal Aid Board for arguing that point, saying I was wasting public funds by running my case in that way.

"It's an interesting point that a lot of judges have been saying they want to cover."

Just my luck, I thought. My one chance of fame and success and I'm about to be charged with murder.

"Do you have a copy of your skeleton argument?" She was referring to the document which forms the basis of the argument put forward at the hearing. The barrister has to produce it a few days before the hearing.

"I will have," I said slowly. "You know we haven't issued any proceedings yet."

"Ah, I was led to believe matters were perhaps a little more advanced. As you know, we have been running a series of articles on neglect as a part of domestic violence, and I really wanted to grab you first."

"Really?" I made a mental note: Read back copies of *Family Law Documents*. They were in a pile in the bathroom.

"OK, I'll send you my skeleton, very soon," I said, adding to my mental list: finish grounds of appeal; issue appeal; do more research; prepare skeleton. That shouldn't take too long.

I found the case in Inner Temple Library. It was called "Re R" and was reported in the *New Law Journal*. The *NLJ* appears weekly and is taken by most solicitors' firms and for some snobbish reason, is rarely read by barristers. The copy I wanted was out. I hunted around the tables tucked in between the shelves till I discovered someone reading it as if it was a newspaper, leaning back in his chair, with his legs crossed. I was about to ask if I could see it, feeling confident in my priority of claim since I assumed the person reading it was a solicitor. Then I noticed the tell-tale pink ribbon draped over his pile of papers which marked him out quite clearly as a barrister. I waited till he left the room. Perhaps, I thought, it's just me who doesn't read the *NLJ* because I presume it's for solicitors. Perhaps I was turning into, or maybe I already was, a snobbish barrister. How could I be a snob? I was a good working class girl. I wanted to call the librarian "buddy" to prove my working class credentials but I couldn't bring myself to do it, and I just mumbled politely, on equal terms, that I would like to photocopy the page, please. She was very kind and spoke to me as if I was a student so I wasn't sure if I'd got my point across.

I was feeling very bad about myself. I really needed to see Lena.

The case notes were short and didn't say exactly what I wanted but I could use some of the judgment to get my appeal off the ground. When I got back to chambers I had the very best intentions to start drafting my particulars, but other professional duties conspired against me: messages from two solicitors to ring them back, tidying my inbox, speaking to Gavin about my fees and tidying the paperclips on my desk and suddenly it was five past six and too late to start anything properly.

The clerks' room had filled with barristers. Several people had glasses of wine in their hands. This boded ill for the brevity and sensibleness of the chambers' meeting.

"What's the wine for?" I whispered to Jenna.

"Marcus got a check today for the House of Lords case he did in February. He's bought three bottles of wine."

And a car with electric windows and a built in CD, probably.

"Good evening," I said to Marcus, who had just noticed my arrival. In an unexpectedly friendly gesture he was holding out a glass of something the shade of a urine sample. "Thank you, no," I said. I couldn't risk it. If I drink at chambers' meetings I say stupid things and make references to Tamla Motown which no one understands and then I shout at people and I can see them wondering what I'm like in court.

"Well done," I said to him. "Did you win that case?"

"Actually, no," he said grandly, his high forehead creased with pride. "But then I was being led." His QC had presented the case, and the word was that Marcus's job had been to do the photocopying. I knew he didn't really want to engage with me, but he was bursting with news to tell. "*Appeal Cases* have just rung to ensure they spell my name correctly."

"Good to get the important things sorted out first," I said.

"Don't mock it till you've tried it, Frankie," he said. "Don't worry, your day will come. Although, who knows when?"

Marcus was always rude to me. Perhaps I was a bit too close to his origins for comfort. Perhaps he'd had one too many conferences in my room and decided he didn't like the decor. I did have an old poster on the wall that said, "Women who seek equality lack ambition," but it was very tastefully done.

Simon appeared in the doorway of the clerks' room. He gave me a wide smile.

"How did you get on?" I asked.

"Surprisingly, we won."

"Well done," I said.

"The meeting will start in five minutes," he called, and people began to pick up their briefs and bags and straggle up to the library.

There were only eight people around the table, I calculated. We needed ten for a quorum. This meeting might end really quickly.

Marcus was watching me. "Before you say anything, I would like to remind you that if no one challenges the quoracy, then we can carry on."

For the moment I ignored him and sank into one of the broken chairs at the edge of the table. It was one of the chairs which had been passed around most of the rooms in chambers, getting gradually more decrepit, and had now come to the library to find everlasting life. I found myself sinking almost to the floor and pulled myself forward, trying to find a way to balance on the frame. I was about to ask Simon to formally count the number of tenants present at the meeting so that we could all go home, when he said, "Ah, here are Tony and Iotha. You'll have to get yourselves seats, I'm afraid."

Things were getting worse, now that Tony had appeared, which he rarely did. Not only was the meeting now quorate, but as head of chambers he would chair the meeting instead of Simon. Tony was a hopeless chair. The meeting could go on all night.

Marcus was passing around a typewritten document. It was very thick and as my copy plopped in front of me I read the title: "Why we need to alter the rent arrangements."

"I thought we were discussing an increase in the flat rate, not a change to the arrangements," I said. There was always a small faction in chambers who wanted an increase of the fixed monthly fee, the theory being that the high earners would pay proportionately less and therefore be less likely to leave chambers for another set where the rent was lower. However, a quick glance at Marcus's document showed that he wanted our contributions to consist solely of a simple lump sum every month with no percentage. His check today must have been huge. The new car probably had leather seats. "I'm sure if people had known that you were proposing to alter the whole basis of chambers' expenses, more of them would have come tonight. Why wasn't this document circulated earlier?"

"Through the chair, through the chair, you didn't make your comments through the chair," Marcus crowed.

Several people groaned. "If it's going to be that sort of a meeting," said Vanya, a young bouncy woman who had been given a tenancy two months before, "I'm leaving at seven."

"You can't go, we have a lot more wine to get through." Marcus picked up a half-full bottle from the floor and pushed it toward her.

The meeting ended at twenty to eight and the number 23 bus got me to Oxford Street with twenty minutes to spare. I ducked guiltily into HMV's rock and easy listening department. With nothing specific to look for, I renewed my ten-year search for "She's About a Mover" by the Sir Douglas Quintet. It would be nice to be able to give it to my mom for Christmas. She'd never seen the group perform live, but had loved the song. She sang the words to me as a lullaby when I was small and then I had walked on her treasured copy of the single and broken it when I was celebrating winning a tenancy in my first set of chambers.

It was ten past eight when I turned into Wardour Street and I arrived at Mezzo at twenty past, pink and damp. I had been to the restaurant once before when I had taken my mom out for a meal, but as I stepped in through the huge glass door I was still unprepared for the pale floor and the high ceiling and the chrome attachments and the people who worked there. They all seemed to have gone to sliding school, they were slipping and sliding, greeting people, checking the diary, indicating the sweeping staircase down to the body of the restaurant, all at an angle of forty-five degrees. In the restaurant it was the same thing, they all seemed to walk with a permanent list, as if they had been employed for their ability to move with the camber of the floor.

Lena was already at the table, reading the paper. She is one of the few people I know who don't make me feel bad at arriving late. She had ordered us both a gin and tonic, which was long and sharp and had lots of ice.

"What did you buy?" she asked.

I looked at her blankly.

"I assume that's why you're a little flushed. You were lured into a music store and forgot the time."

"Lena! I am a professional barrister. I have come straight from chambers."

"Via?"

"Via HMV, but you'd hardly know. There was nothing there I wanted."

"They still don't have Sir Douglas Quintet then?"

"No." The waiter brought us the short menu, leaning from the waist.

"How was your meeting?" she asked me.

"Boring," I said, "but ultimately successful. How was yours?"

"As ever, we needed a lawyer." Lena had been trying to get me involved since the group began in '96. It was so long since I'd done crime, that I'd suggested she ask Kay. Apparently Kay had gone along, but after a few meetings she left the group and I never asked why.

"Oh, Lena," I said, as I always did. "Don't ask me. Especially not now." I took a deep breath and as briefly as possible I told her about my arrest, only stopping when the waiter sashayed up and took our order.

"Why didn't you ring me?" Lena complained.

"I had one phone call and much as I would have liked to hear your voice, I felt the situation demanded a solicitor."

"But think of the comfort I could have brought you. I'd have brought a flask of coffee with an almost unnoticeable dash of brandy and a change of clothing, and within a few minutes, and the minimum of accessories, I could have made your cell look modern without being cold. I could have left some leaflets there too, about prison reform."

"It wasn't a prison, it was a police station."

"Same difference," she said.

The waiter slid two plates of food in front of us.

"I suppose you rang the dreaded Kay."

"I had to. She was good. She did all the right things."

"Hmm." Lena stabbed arugula leaves and shavings of parmesan cheese. "But this means now you have first-hand experience of crime you could join the group. OK, OK, just a joke. But are you saying that if we had gone and picked up the license plate on Saturday, none of this would have happened?"

"Don't say that Lena, I can't bear to think about it." I thought about it, chewing a mouthful of sardine. "Probably we'd have bumped into the police and both been arrested. We might even have discovered the body."

"Well, that really would have spoiled our evening," Lena said. "But what are you going to do?"

"The only thing I can do is find Saskia."

"Where does she live?"

"The answer to that question is so depressing that I think we should change the subject."

We tried Sophie as a topic, but she had tragic overtones too, and I didn't even mention Margo, so we discussed the other diners in the restaurant. I was just pouring the last drops of the house red into Lena's glass, when she said, "What's the etiquette about relationships with people in groups you're in?"

"I thought that was the reason people joined groups, to develop a social life."

"You might, but some people join because of their political beliefs."

"OK."

"So? Can you get together with someone in your group?"

"Are we talking hypothetically?"

"Mmm, maybe."

"I don't see why not."

"What if it's an abuse of power?"

"Who's got the power, you or the other person?"

"Well, if—*if*—we were talking about me, it would probably be me."

"Don't ask me, what do I know about morality? I usually check whether it's banned by the Bar's Professional Code of Conduct and if it isn't, I do it. Just be as good as you can, I suppose."

She swirled the wine in her glass.

"Are you going to tell me any more?"

"Not at the moment. I've got a lot to think about."

As we sat side by side on the 73 bus home Lena said she would ask around about Saskia. Lena was once known as the North London Gazette for her ability to garner in and disseminate information among the women's community.

"But be discreet." I was anxious about the gossip that might ensue.

"Well, if you want," Lena said, "but discretion may not be your best weapon at this stage. Other people aren't always discreet. By the way, how's Margo?"

"Don't ask," I said.

"She doesn't seem to be making you very happy," she said. "Maybe it's not the best thing for you, especially not at the moment."

Normally Lena was very positive about new developments in my social life. Perhaps she was more worried about me than I was. That was worrying.

I let myself into the apartment with a heavy heart. I felt I should be doing something, to prove my innocence, to find Saskia, but I didn't know what to do or where to start.

I went into the bathroom and ran a bath. Things weren't going how they should at all. Not at all.

Fourteen

Thursday Afternoon

Iwas on the 76 bus going into chambers, gazing out of the window, trying to spot Saskia. When we got to Old Street, and near the club, I started looking for Margo, even though it was one o'clock in the afternoon. I wondered what adjective the silent people on the bus would use to describe me, if asked. Tragic? pathetic? sad? Pathetic, probably. But part of me was excited that for once I had a decent case to prepare.

Gavin had rung me half an hour earlier, waking me from a deep sleep. "I'm just reminding you about your conference this afternoon."

"My what?!"

"Your conference in Laydon. The brief's just come in and I should tell you that it's about four inches thick."

"Is this the case you told me about where I'm for the mother? When was the conference booked in?"

Gavin consulted his computer screen. "It was booked in about a week ago. The hearing's on Monday week, as you no doubt remember. It's your new High Court practice. Five days, to be precise."

"I had forgotten my life is looking up. What's it about?"

"It's dad's application for residence and/or contact." He had opened the brief and was reading the instructions: "One child, history of violence, parties separated three years ago, da de da, child has behavior problems, possible medical cause . . . mother's got some history of psychiatric difficulties. Although," he read on, "that seems to be based on a short history of prostitution. And depression. Might be some domestic violence with the new partner. Child is represented by the Official Solicitor. Your solicitors are Walton & Co., someone called Bridget Devine. She hasn't used chambers before. She seems a bit inexperienced and you'll have to hold her hand."

"Four inches, you say."

"Loads of reports. What have we got here? Social workers, a psychiatrist and something that looks like a consultant pediatrician."

It sounded like a wonderful, meaty case. With my luck, of course, by the time the hearing came up, I would have been charged and bail refused, and I would have to return the brief. I wondered if I was under a professional duty to tell my solicitor of the possibility.

"What time's the conference?"

"Three thirty. And your solicitor in Morris called asking when the Grounds of Appeal will be ready."

"Soon," I said. "Very soon."

The brief was thick, more like six inches, organized neatly, in two three-ring binders, divided into helpful sections. I liked the solicitor already. I was halfway through the psychiatrist's report when Jenna buzzed me to say that the conference would start an hour late because the client had gone to see her sister. It was useful to have the extra time but I was concerned about the client's attitude.

When she did arrive she told me that she didn't want to fight the case, she was fed up with court hearings, meetings with her lawyers. It was her ex-husband who wanted contact, but her life was under the spotlight, the things she did, the people she knew. He was the one who'd forced her into prostitution, but no one seemed to care about that. If he was so crazy about the kid, he could have him, he could bring him up, take him to all the doctor's appointments, all the hospitals, on all those buses, with all the changes.

If she gave the child up without a fight I would lose the best case I'd had in ages. But it wasn't just that which made me try to change her mind. I did have a duty to the child. All her statements said that her ex-husband was hopeless with the boy, unreliable and inattentive. I spent a long time trying to find out why she was so depressed. Was it really her choice to give up the child?

Then I spent a little time trying to convince her that children were wonderful and that she would miss the sound of his little voice around the house. When she turned and asked me if I had children and did I know what it was like, I decided it was time to end the conference.

I walked slowly across Fleet Street at six o'clock, thinking about children, and what they were like, but Saskia kept popping into my head. An image of Saskia with children. Were they hers? A woman she knew? I remembered tears and driving someone somewhere. I remembered the traffic circle at Archway. Where was she? What was going on?

I was watching one of my favorite episodes of *NYPD Blue*. I will never cease to admire Jimmy Smits. I need to know where he got his clothes, I could do with some interesting greys in my closet. The phone rang. I stopped the video and Chris Tarrant's face appeared on the TV screen.

When I picked up the receiver there was silence.

"Hello?" I said gently.

There was a large intake of breath as if someone was about to speak. Then silence.

"Hello?" I said again.

"Oh, hello," said Lena. "Sorry, I thought I heard the man upstairs loitering outside. I'm just ringing in case you'd forgotten."

I scrabbled through my recent memory. "I obviously have," I said after a few seconds.

"As I got off the bus last night you said you'd come around and pick up some used clothes."

"Did I? When did I say I would come?"

"Tonight. About half an hour ago."

"Was I coming for supper?" I said cautiously.

"No, just to get the clothes."

"Do I have to?" I moaned. "I've just got to such a good bit in *NYPD Blue.*"

"Is that back on?" Lena asked. "I'm sorry to spoil your fun, but you'd better come." She sighed. "I've got something to tell you."

Fifteen

Late Thursday Evening— Finsbury Park

Half an hour later I was knocking on Lena's door. Lena lived in a small co-op apartment on a wide, busy road in Finsbury Park. She had lived there for ten years. She loved her apartment, which she kept as neat as a magazine photo and whose walls she covered with Berber rugs and the windows with velvet curtains.

She opened the door herself rather than buzzing me in, and she greeted me absentmindedly. She was in the hallway with one of the upstairs tenants, who was awkwardly holding an old and large vacuum cleaner. I knew from Lena's stories that this man, who was a retired businessman, knocked on Lena's door late at night, at six in the morning and at weekends, complaining about the position of the trash cans in the front garden, the noise of Lena's music and the Government's plans to get rid of the House of Lords.

Lena was saying to him, "Any other time, of course, I wouldn't be making a fuss about you leaving the vacuum cleaner down here. It's just that I have only this minute put the phone down on my daughter-in-law who is going through rather a bad time with Roger—you remember, my son, the architect—and she wants to come and stay, and of course with the twins I shall need the room out here for the stroller."

"Is this her?" he asked suspiciously. He was wearing a striped shirt and a thin creased navy blue tie.

"Oh no, this is my friend Frankie, the QC."

He turned and walked up the stairs, banging the vacuum against the walls as he went.

We went into Lena's apartment and into her small narrow kitchen with a new pine table. "Since when have I been a QC?"

"About as long as I've had a son."

"And how long's that?"

"Since my husband died." She filled the kettle.

"Your husband?" I asked.

"Yes," she said, "it was very sad, he was killed in a skiing accident."

I started to laugh. This was all complete fantasy. "But you don't like heights."

"That's the tragedy of it. It was all so, so pointless." Calmly she spooned coffee into a small Greek coffee pot.

"Did you get any insurance?"

"No, because the check he had used to pay the premium had bounced, so there was no pay-out. I didn't mind for myself, it was Roger."

"Your son."

"The architect. Yes. He had to bartend to pay his way through college." Carefully she poured water into the long-handled pot and the warm smell of coffee filled the kitchen. "That's where he met Vicky," she said, rifling through the silverware drawer and taking out a tea strainer. "She was drinking harmlessly with friends in the pub one night, and having difficulty getting rid of the Salvation Army, and he fell for her vulnerable blue eyes. And her enormous breasts."

"Lena!"

"I know," she said. "I'm appalled by him too."

She carried the coffee and two small cups into the neat living room which was lit by two ivory-colored lamps. I sat in the brocade-covered armchair, while Lena put the tray on a low table and settled onto the sofa.

"Sometimes it's the only way I can deal with Arthur Upstairs. I thought if there was a strong young man in my life, I wouldn't have to waste so much time asserting myself as a strong older woman. Unfortunately, I was right and it has actually made things better. He doesn't knock late at night now."

"How long have you had this family?"

"Quite a long time, a year or so."

"Wouldn't it have been easier to make a complaint about him knocking and coming down?"

"I did think of that, but he's not that bad, just irritating."

"What does he make of all your women friends?"

"Oh, that's my Women's Circle. Knitting, dressmaking, recipes—you know." As if to demonstrate, she balanced the strainer on a cup and poured out thick black coffee.

"Do you think he notices that you never cook?"

"Well, I like to think that when Sophie and I throw saucepans around, he imagines we're being creative in the kitchen."

We were back in the real world. "Is everything OK with Sophie now?"

Lena said nothing. She and Sophie were such a strange combination. Even they didn't understand it.

They'd met in Basingstoke as teenagers, in a restaurant where they both had casual jobs. Together they had moved to London and Lena had become a dancer and, when the dancing was slow, a teacher of English as a Foreign Language, and finally a dance teacher. Sophie was a few years younger than Lena, but she had become an ultra whizz hairdresser, first with Sassoon and then with Trevor Sorbie. They'd been together and apart, on and off, for more than twenty years. They'd had other partners and Sophie had once had a fling with a man, who, unfortunately for me, liked Tamla Motown, so when Lena and I discussed it I couldn't say he was all bad.

They were well suited—Sophie's fair, Lena's dark, they're the same height and they both like doughnuts. They've been to the States on holiday several times to pursue their shared interest. It must be something to do with their catering background.

But they argue. Lena calls me late at night, alternately raging and panicking down the phone, and I tut and say "hmm" and wait till they get back together again.

"What's the problem? She's always had little things with other people, hasn't she?"

"Yeah, but something's changed. It could be me, I suppose."

"Why, what have you done?" I sipped my coffee.

"It may be nothing."

"Is this to do with the person whose birthday it was yesterday?" I asked.

She looked sheepish. "I can't bear to talk about it at the moment . . . Oh, all right. She's in the group. She's a prostitute. She's got a wonderful voice and she's taller than I am."

"That can be exciting," I said.

"Yes, she's just so—so interesting. She's done stuff."

I looked at her.

"She's been totally open with me about her past. She had a relationship with a married man who was a sort of pimp and also, I think, something nasty and short with someone else, although she hasn't said much about that. And a girlfriend that lasted four years. The rest has just been work and meaningless." Lena took a mouthful of coffee. "Like you."

"Sorry?"

"Clients. You don't call your clients friends, just because you know their life story. And before you ask, her health is good and it's safe sex all the way down the line.

Regular tests. In fact she doesn't work much now, mainly clipping. That's where—"

"I know what clipping is," I said. I had represented quite a few women charged with promising a man heaven in fifteen minutes' time, arranging to meet him somewhere, and then never turning up. It always seemed a little hard on the punter. "What do you think about clipping?"

"Don't you charge for cases that never go to court?" Lena asked.

"Oh, touché," I said.

"And she has a diamond in one of her teeth."

"Is that compatible with dental hygiene?" I asked.

"It's compatible with me," Lena said. "Anyway, there's this other thing . . ."

I looked at her.

"The thing I mentioned on the phone."

I looked at her.

"You know your friend Saskia?"

"Yes, I know my friend Saskia."

"I saw her two nights ago." She began pouring more coffee into her cup.

"Two? Wh-wh . . . And you didn't ring me immediately? And you didn't even mention it last night?"

"I know, I'm sorry, I forgot."

"Lena!" I felt the earth move under the brocade-covered armchair. It could have been the subway, but my sense of shock and bewilderment was intense. "Where was this? Where?"

"In the Glass Bar."

It was a women's bar, just by Euston Station, two rooms, one on top of the other. There were sofas and bowls of peanuts on small tables, and in winter a real fire. I was annoyed at Lena just for having gone there without me.

"Did you talk to her?"

"No."

"Who was she with? Was she on her own?"

"I don't think so."

"Who was she with?"

She hesitated. "Your singing friend."

"Margo?"

"Yes."

My stomach lurched. "So?"

Lena hesitated. "They looked quite friendly."

"What do you mean?" I asked coldly.

"I'm just the messenger," she said. "Don't take it out on me." She looked at me till I had tilted my lips at her in an attempt at a smile. "They looked quite friendly. Nothing dramatic, just . . . close."

"Oh God," I said, "Oh God. Shit, shit, shit."

Sixteen

Thursday Night/Friday Morning

It was ten o'clock when I left Lena's apartment. After the coffee and to ward off all bad feelings, mine, not hers, we had finished off a bottle of Chardonnay Lena had found in the bottom of her fridge.

I wove my way back down Green Lanes, past the late-night Turkish cafés and the swirling orange lights of the cab offices, listening to Betty Everett's complaint that "It's Getting Mighty Crowded," and, unusually, the traffic did nothing unexpected and there was no call for unseemly behavior from me or any other road user.

I lugged the black garbage bag of old clothes that Lena had given me out of the back seat and rested it on the sidewalk. While I locked the car door I wondered why I'd taken it. There was never anything in her bags I wanted, it was usually stuff of mine that she'd filched from my bags and then decided she didn't like. The bag was full and banged against my jeans as I dragged it into the house. I propped it up against the cupboard in the hall, went into the kitchen and made a cup of tea.

Picking up the small section of the *Guardian* from the kitchen table, I moved into the living room to start the crossword, to ease my mind. I flicked the video on and Jimmy Smits smoldered into view. I took a mouthful of tea. Then I noticed the answering machine flashing.

Margo had left me a message. "I'll be in the pub next to the club at half past ten if you want to see me."

That was all. "What am I meant to do with that?" I asked the machine. "The person I thought I was getting close to has been getting close to someone who broke into my flat and got me into really bad trouble, and now the person I thought I was getting close to rings me up and asks me out. Just like that." I didn't want to go.

Not at all.

It was a small pub with one or two locals drinking alone. They briefly flicked their eyes in my direction as I walked in, but their attention slid back to the large TV screen which dominated the room.

Margo was squashed into a corner at the end of a long empty plush-covered bench. She was smaller than I remembered, wearing a grey raincoat which she hugged tightly around her. A glass of something that looked like whisky sat on the table in front of her.

Of course I was ready to forgive her before we even met. I was so pleased to see her that all the comments I might have made—What's going on? What's your game?—never crossed my mind.

I didn't care what was going on, or what game she was playing. She was here.

She looked ill, pale, tired. Her hair was sticking out in thick tufts. She looked older than she had in the club. I stepped around two tables of men playing dominoes and stood in front of her, smiling foolishly.

"Thank you for coming," she said.

"Pleasure," I said. "Have you been at the club?"

"Sort of."

What did that mean? Had she been at the club or not? Had she been there with Saskia? "Do you want another drink?" I asked.

She shook her head. There were dark grey grooves

under her eyes and her lips were pale. "Do you want to go?" I asked.

She nodded and swallowed her drink in one gulp. As she stood up I remembered her perfume. She was shorter than before, wearing jeans and desert boots. She picked up a black bucket-shaped bag and moved ahead of me to the door. Her hand was on the handle when she dropped her arm and stepped back, waiting for me to pass her and pull open the heavy door.

As I moved in front of her she slid her hand into the back pocket of my jeans and pulled me back. "Is there anyone in the street?"

I looked out, up and down. "No."

"Any cars?"

"Only mine. Why?" I felt as if she'd stepped into my nightmare.

"Let's get into the car first." She eased her hand out of my jeans although I had felt quite happy with it there, and we walked the ten yards in silence. I was thinking, *I'm the one who should be feeling paranoid and anxious. It's unlikely that you have been arrested for murder. And I haven't been smooching around with anybody else.* Had I? I did a quick check. No. The moral upper hand was mine for once.

As I stood on the pavement unlocking the passenger door for Margo I could see through the window that the car was a mess, with old newspapers and pink brief ribbon all over the floor. I leaned in to clear away the two small empty water bottles and the tangerine which unaccountably lay on the passenger seat. But Margo pushed me away and slid into the car. I moved around to the other side of the car, got in, revved the engine and we drove away.

I drove west, through the Barbican, then turned left toward Moorgate. As we approached Liverpool Street station I said, "Where am I going?"

"Nowhere, anywhere," she said.

I drove back toward Old Street, then south into City Road. As we approached Moorgate again I said, "I'm going in a circle."

She said nothing so I stopped outside Marks & Spencer's.

We sat in silence for a few minutes then she said, "Do you mind if I smoke?" She pushed in the lighter in my dashboard, then dug into her bag and pulled out a packet of Camels. She took out a cigarette and lit it with my silver lighter, but somehow it didn't make the right click, or perhaps I could tell it wasn't real silver. I'd lost the feeling.

"So why did we creep out of the pub?" I asked.

"I'd better take you home," she said.

We drove in silence except for her brief direction to the projects off Essex Road. She told me where to park and then led me up two flights of stairs. Watching her small feet in the neat desert boots walk slowly up the stained concrete steps and along the gloomy landing, I wondered what her life was—carrying kids up the stairs, staggering with a stroller, avoiding trouble, a bit like my mom's had been. By the time she had turned two heavy keys and opened the front door I had forgiven her for everything that had happened and anything else that might happen in the future. As I walked behind her down the dark, narrow hall in the cramped apartment I wanted to tell her everything was my fault.

She snapped on the overhead light in the living room and the first thing I was aware of was how bare and brown it was. Pale brown walls, worn brown furniture and a small brown rug on bare floor tiles. In one corner of the room was an incongruously pink plastic box. It was full of toys, Lego, board games, dolls with their legs sticking out at random angles. On a brown dresser were four framed photographs. In the silence of our arrival I walked across the room to study them. One photo was a sleepy

Margo in what looked like a hospital bed, holding a baby in one arm and a toddler on the pillow with the other. Two were formal school photographs, each frame containing a portrait of a blonde little girl, with a formal smile and a maroon sweatshirt. The last was a picture of Margo and the girls in a field, bundled up in coats, blonde hair blowing in their eyes, laughing at the photographer.

She gestured me into a large brown armchair, then without taking off her coat, she took two small chunky glasses and a bottle of whisky from the dresser and poured us both a drink. She handed me a glass, and shrugging off her coat, sank onto the sofa. She took a large swallow of whisky. Still she said nothing.

"You didn't tell me you had kids," I said, in a tone which contained an accusation.

"Perhaps I forgot I had them," she said.

"How old are they?" I said.

"Shelley's six and Carley's eight."

She shifted in her seat. She was wearing a buttoned up soft pink cardigan that revealed her throat. The skin was white and looked soft and warm.

Although I had already done it that night at the club, my eyes grazed her left hand.

"I was married," she said, following my glance. She took a mouthful of whisky and leaned her head back with her eyes closed. "Sometimes he was lovely." She shook her head gently. "Sometimes when we danced I felt we were really close. But you can't dance through life, can you?"

I was considering that when she said, "My decree absolute comes through in two weeks." She laughed bitterly. "The relationship ended years ago, really. For me, anyway. For me, it ended the night I had Shelley. He just wasn't there. He was out somewhere, causing trouble. He came to the hospital the next morning and said, 'So it wasn't a boy, then,' and left." She jerked her head toward the dresser. "A nurse took that photo. He actually left—where are we now? October, isn't it?—eight months ago." She stood up and walked around the room, smoking. "Oh, and he had another woman, who rang up now and again to remind me she was there."

"Where are the kids now?" I asked.

"What? Well, they're not here, obviously. Or are you worried that I've been out enjoying myself and left them all alone?"

I wondered if she had seen that question in my face, or if she was used to people thinking that about a single woman with children. "It's OK," she said, in a tone more friendly than I deserved. "They're with my sister, till Sunday." She took a swallow of whisky. "He wasn't a bad man," she went on. She saw the expression on my face. "Well, not really. Although he is the reason the apartment's so bare. He came in one Thursday after I'd taken the kids to school. I always do my shopping on a Thursday. He knew that. He cleared the place out. The furniture, the carpet, the TV, the washing machine. Left me the bed though." She laughed again and poured herself some more whisky. I shook my head as she held the bottle toward me.

"I assume from that he doesn't give you any money for the kids?"

"Oh no, never any money. But then, he lost his job, didn't he?"

"What did he do?"

"He worked for the local government. I'm sorry, I shouldn't be going on about this."

"It's OK," I said. It was rather like being at work, but I was enjoying listening to her voice, watching the way she moved her hands, her throat as she swallowed.

"He had a thing about environmental health. He enjoyed getting people in trouble, you know, reporting them for keeping too many pets, and things like not putting their garbage in the right place. It wasn't even his department. It's a joke. He was happy enough to leave us in this dump."

She looked around the room. "I just want you to know, this isn't my choice. A friend of my sister's gave me the couch. The rug I got at a garage sale. The walls are my fault, though, they're brown because I smoke. I suppose at least it matches."

I laughed.

She walked behind the armchair and put a hand tentatively on my head and began to stroke my hair. I sat still, not knowing what to do, then I stretched my hand back and took hold of her wrist. I drew her around to face me and pulled her onto my lap.

I knew there was something I meant to ask her but just at that moment I couldn't remember what it was.

"Are the children coming back tonight?" I said, instead.

"I told you," she murmured, running the knuckles of her hand slowly down my cheek, "they're at their auntie's."

I gazed at her face. I looked at the lines, the fatigue, the pale softness of her skin. I could smell the rose of her perfume. I ran my hand up the sleeve of her cardigan to her shoulder. I felt the pulse throbbing warmly at her throat, then put my hand on the nape of her neck and drew her face toward mine.

Her full lips parted and I slid my tongue into her mouth.

"Do you like dancing?" she said, pulling away from me.

"Uh, yes," I said.

She stood up and walked over to a small cassette player. She pressed a button and the first notes of Esther Phillips' harsh pleading voice singing the Beatles' song, "And I Love Her," softly filled the room. She clicked the light switch so that the room was lit only by a diagonal line of light from the hall.

She moved back to the chair and held her hands out to me, pulling me up. At first we danced an inch apart, not touching. Then I slid my arm round her waist and she moved her body into mine. As we danced I could hear her breathing the words, everything and tenderly.

I stopped moving, and we looked at each other. I drew her face toward mine. As we kissed, moving gently in time to the music, I undid the buttons of her cardigan.

"We could go somewhere more comfortable," she murmured, kissing my ear, as I ran my hand over the lace covering her soft full breast.

She led me to the dark bedroom and pulled me down onto the comforter.

Seventeen

Early Friday Morning

I woke up with a start. Her clock radio said it was two o'clock and with a jolt I remembered what I wanted to ask her. "Where does Saskia come into all this?" I asked her sleeping back.

"What? What?" She turned to face me.

"Saskia. Where does she fit in?"

"I don't know," she mumbled.

"But you know Saskia," I prompted.

She sighed and leaned over to switch on a small lamp on an upturned box beside the low bed. She bent her arm back and dragged her pillow up against the wall, then heaved her body into a sitting position. She took a cigarette from the packet next to the lamp, lit it with a match, and inhaled deeply. In the silent night I could hear the crackle of the paper burning. She let out a stream of smoke.

I lay flat, pulling the comforter up to my armpits, and waited.

"Do you know the first time I slept with a woman?"

I waited.

"About six months ago. I met Saskia and a friend of hers at a fair, in Clissold Park. They were giving out leaflets or something, at an Animal Liberation booth. We got talking, the kids did really. There were lots of pictures in the booth of animals in experiments and the kids got upset. Saskia and her friend Ash—you know, the woman behind the bar at the club—"

"With the studs."

"They were really good with the kids, talked to them in a way they could understand. The kids thought she was great."

I snorted.

"We went and had an ice cream. Then the kids wanted her to come home to tea and one thing led to another. She stayed the night, the couch was uncomfortable."

I groaned.

"I'd never been with a woman before but she was so lovely. I don't know, I was lonely, I'd been on my own for a long time. But it wasn't just that. I loved it—you know, sex with a woman." She put her hand to her throat. She smiled. "It felt so natural."

I didn't know whether I was pleased about that or not. If you have sex with a woman who has never done it with a woman before there's always a risk she won't like it or be frightened of what she's doing. At least Margo had got beyond that stage. But I'd already worked that out for myself.

"Anyway, he found out, I don't know how, some gossip from neighbors, or one of his buddies, I don't know. But there was hell to pay. He couldn't stand it. I couldn't have done anything worse as far as he was concerned. It hit him right in his manhood. He blamed everything on Saskia, me becoming a lesbian, his bad luck, losing his job." She sighed. "From his point of view I suppose it was a case of all the bitterness and frustration about his life bubbling up . . ." She lit another cigarette. The spark of the match was reflected in the long thin mirror at the end of the bed. I looked at the shadowy reflection of Margo, alone, smoking, the tip of her cigarette glowing red. "I rang you up, actually," she said.

"When?"

"A week or so ago."

"Was that before or after we met?"

"Actually it was before."

"Did you speak to me?" I had no memory of any conversation with her, but it wasn't impossible. From time to time women or their friends ring me because they've heard on the grapevine, usually somehow through Lena, who I am and the kind of cases I do. I was reluctant to start discussing a legal problem at this point. It's like being asked about a person's gallstones if you're a doctor at a dinner party.

"They said you were in court. I left a message."

"Oh well, I never got it. Unless you're a member of a solicitors' firm or you pretended to be. Raising my hopes by promising me a huge brief."

She laughed, stubbing out her cigarette. "No, but I did use my real name. My maiden name. It's Lesley Page."

"Oh?"

"Margo's just my stage name, but I prefer it. If you don't like your life, change your name. Do you like it? Margo? Is it all right?"

"I think it's great," I said, impressed. "I couldn't have spoken to you anyway, when you rang, not if you wanted me to represent you. You have to go through a solicitor."

"You're talking to me now." She turned toward me, leaning on her elbow, and ran her finger along my hip bone and down my thigh.

"I think that effectively counts me out of representing you. Is the problem sorted out?" I asked. "I could give you advice, but that's all."

"Give me some advice then." She leaned over and spoke softly into my ear. "Tell me what I should do to give you the best time you ever had."

Moaning, I inclined my head to hers, raising my shoulder in pleasure. Then I remembered why I had woken her up. "Why?" I asked, jerking away.

She moved her head back, slightly. "Do you mean, why should you tell me, or why should I want to give you the best time you ever had?" As she spoke she moved her mouth toward my face and I could feel her breath on my cheek.

My body yearned toward her but my head gave me another pressing direction. "Why?" I hissed. "Why are you doing any of this? Excuse me, but I don't like being used." I pulled the comforter back and groped for my clothes.

"What?"

"You and Saskia. You have a relationship, then you have a bit of a problem so you go to the club and pick me up. A couple of nights later you stand me up to meet Saskia, and then tonight . . . this happens." I struggled into my sweater. I felt sick.

"I don't understand," she said. "Saskia's in a lot of trouble."

"You can say that again. Look, I don't know what your game is, I just don't want any part of it."

"Frankie!" She sat up in bed.

"Is it all a big joke, or was it just to get cheap legal advice?" I pulled on my jeans.

"Frankie! Are you drunk?"

"Oh shut up," I said.

"Shut up?"

"Yes, shut up," I repeated, thinking, if this is the best a barrister can do under pressure maybe it's not surprising my practice is in a mess. "Just leave me alone," I said, shrugging off her hand as she followed me out of the bedroom. I played for time in the living room, looking for keys which I knew were in the pocket of my jeans, thinking if she comes over and puts her arms around me and whispers in my ear again, perhaps I'll adjourn the rest of this discussion till the morning. But she remained standing in the doorway of the bedroom, watching me lace my boots.

I didn't look at her as I snatched my jacket from the hook in the hall. I knew how lovely she would look, sleepy and tousled and soft and I didn't want to regret what I was doing any more than I already did. I left the apartment.

I tried to slam the door to show my annoyance without making so much noise I'd wake the neighbors. I lurched along the landing and almost fell down the stairs.

I could hardly walk straight, let alone think straight, I was so overwhelmed with outrage and bitterness. It was all just to get around me, just for Saskia. I was bitter because everything she and I had said and done had meant nothing to her, and outraged that she thought she had to come on to me, so that I would, what, help her fight a lesbian custody case? Help Saskia out?

I walked down to the garage, where I had left the car. As I unlocked the door I looked up to Margo's apartment. I saw a light go off in a room I calculated was her bedroom and the apartment was in darkness. The sky was clear and full of stars. There was scarcely a sound of traffic from Essex Road. The place didn't look bad in this light, but after a few seconds the graffiti and burst bags of trash and old sofa cushions became visible. What kind of life did Margo and her kids have, living here? Not much of one, I suspected. Perhaps that was why she had leapt at Saskia and then gone for me. Perhaps she should grab the chance of any happiness and comfort she could get, whenever it came along.

I got in the car. Aggressively I revved the engine and it roared into life only to die instantly away. I tried again and again, but it wouldn't start. Five minutes later I accepted it had probably flooded, so I switched on the radio to Capital Gold, hunched into my seat and closed my eyes, to wait the twenty minutes or so I knew it would take for the car to have even a hope of starting.

The sounds of gunfire, the first notes of "Shotgun" by Junior Walker on the radio, made me open my eyes. The clock showed that it was three thirty. I had drifted off to sleep. I stretched and flexed my stiff shoulder muscles, leaning forward to start the car, automatically looking in the rear-view mirror.

A figure was approaching the steps to Margo's building from the direction of the street. The bulb in the streetlight had gone, or been shot out, and I couldn't make out who it was, probably some other poor resident who'd been out trying to have a good time before coming home to this depressing place. But something about the shape of the large coat, the rolling walk, reminded me of someone. Who was it? The figure passed out of sight on to the stairs.

I looked around. There was no one else about. Quietly I opened my door and got out of the car. I could see Margo's apartment. A shadow moved along the landing and I heard a soft knock. A light appeared in the window I had noticed before, and a few seconds later the front door opened and the figure disappeared inside.

Who on earth was that? Was it Saskia? Was Margo safe? It didn't look as if someone had rushed inside, it was as if they had been expected. Should I stay or should I go home? As I watched the apartment another light went on, in the room I thought was the living room. It stayed on.

Her private life was nothing to do with me, I told myself, especially not now. I got back in the car, turned the key and irritatingly the ignition roared into life. As I drove home Kim Weston's rich voice informed me that we all have to feel heartache at some point, and right now, she was feeling hers.

In the apartment I was too tired to respond to the flashing light of the answering machine and I went into the bedroom, pulled off my boots, jeans and sweater and fell into bed for the second time that night. I hardly had time to think how lonely it felt before I fell asleep.

Eighteen

Friday Lunchtime

I dreamed I was driving around with guns firing and bells ringing. It was my doorbell. It was midday and Fedex was ringing with a package for someone in the upstairs apartment. My head felt like it had passed the night on the very newest and largest of Blackpool's roller coasters. Had I been drunk? Or perhaps this was how I always felt, regardless of whether I'd been drunk or not. Sobering thought.

I padded around the flat in my pajamas, looking for painkillers, having alternate flashes of Margo and her sweet body and her revelations about Saskia and wanting legal advice from me. I stood at the sink, gulping down aspirin, going hot and cold.

The light on the answering machine was flashing from the night before. I could hardly bring myself to listen to it, wondering what new disaster might befall me. In spite of myself the voice made me melt with pleasure. It was Margo.

"Frankie, I don't know what to say. I don't know what you think about me and . . . the other person, but I think you may have misunderstood me. I don't know, I seem to have mishandled this whole thing. Call me when you get this." The machine said she had rung at 2:53 A.M.

I played the message again and swayed to the sound of

her smoky voice. I didn't know what to do. She had obviously left the message before her visitor arrived last night. If I hadn't seen the visitor I might have rung straight back, but I had. I didn't feel ready to handle all of that.

I tried to concentrate. I would settle down to the Morris papers, I thought piously, as I arranged myself at my desk. Get at least some part of my life in order. Do my work. Be a professional. I looked over at my bag in the corner of the living room. My work bag. It was large and black, made of some sort of nylon material, with nylon canvas handles and a long shoulder strap. I get through about three bags a year. Some would say this is because I always buy such cheap ones, but I say if you buy quality, you buy weight. And I don't want to carry a heavy bag as well as heavy contents. People usually stop arguing at this point, usually because they can't be bothered.

The bag was gaping open, its zip already starting to go, with the two briefs containing unfinished paperwork glaring accusingly at me. I flicked my eyes over the desk calendar; I had at least five days left on the Morris case before time ran out and the Stevens brief just needed advice which I could give at any time. Probably better before Christmas, but I had ages.

"Don't look at me like that," I said with a sneer to the snivelling pink bows in the bag. "I'm going out." They stared at me. "It's Friday," I said, "I stand almost charged with murder, my last month's billing figures were ludicrously low, and someone I thought liked me is messing around with someone who may well be the person who should be charged with murder. OK, I will put you on my desk. But that's it."

With my forearm I swept aside the mess of papers on the table. As I was heaving the Morris papers out of my bag a small crunch of paper fell from under the pink ribbon. It was the sugar-free gum wrapper. I began humming the tune as I smoothed it out: "7:30 Gino's F." I picked out the card from Saskia which had become part of the pile of papers on the edge of the table. I stared at them both, thinking, *These things should be with Kay.* I stared harder. "Gino's" was the only word to compare. I squinted at the words "get into" on the card, trying to ignore the extraneous letters. It didn't look like the same writing. But it was only one word. It really didn't look the same. But what did I know? Sometimes I couldn't get my own signature to look the same as the one on my credit card. But then perhaps Saskia hadn't written on the gum wrapper. I felt the need to speak to Kay. She ought to be doing this kind of worrying, not me. That was her job. I rang her number.

The receptionist said that Kay was in a meeting and was taking no calls. She thoughtfully suggested I speak to Kay's voice-mail. I didn't know where to start. I could have said, "I have an important chewing-gum wrapper, which proves . . . which proves . . . that I didn't go out looking for Latimer." It sounded stupid even to me. But perhaps I should have said it. She might have thought it was really important and rung me straight back, arranged to meet me straight away to see this vital part of my defense, and a lot of trouble might have been saved. But I didn't, I just left my name.

Because, you see, I rang Margo. Don't ask me why I did that. Perhaps I wanted to carry on the argument. Perhaps I needed to see someone I had just slept with. Perhaps because she was the only person I knew who wouldn't be at work.

She was surprised to hear from me. "Coffee? Emm, OK. OK. Where? There's nowhere around here."

"We could go somewhere on Church Street."

"I could get a seventy-three."

"I'll meet you where the bus turns on to High Street."

I didn't let myself even think that she might be reluctant or have other people on her mind.

"OK, see you in about half an hour," she said. "I'm glad you rang."

Although the sky was blue, small spits of rain were trying to make the sidewalk wet. I threw on my raincoat and decided to walk down High Street to the restaurant. I shuddered as I walked past Stoke Newington police station, all windows and concrete, set back from the edge of the road, as if it was diffident about its place in the world. I remembered the smell of the cell and the sound of policemen's voices in the night. I really would have to speak to Kay soon.

Margo was getting off the bus as I crossed at the lights on Church Street and I waited for her as she threaded her way back through the drunks spilling over from Abney Park Cemetery. She was wearing a black jacket and jeans, pulling the jacket tightly around her. A feeling of fond concern came over me. She never looked as if she wore enough clothes.

"It's so cold. It wasn't like this when I came out of the apartment." She shivered and tucked her arm through mine for the last few feet of the journey.

The Blue Legume was almost full and I realized it was nearly lunchtime. I bought two coffees and threaded my way back around the tables to where Margo was sitting. She lifted her jacket off the seat she had saved for me. As she turned her head, for a moment I thought it was Saskia, the blonde hair, the easy smile.

But Margo was different; where Saskia would have been jumping up and winding her arms around me, Margo gave me a small nod of thanks as I placed the coffee in front of her. She looked tired, her tight blue shirt highlighting the shadows under her eyes.

"So how are you?" I began stiffly.

"Fine," she said. "You look nice."

I was wearing my black sweater over black jeans, with my black button boots. "Thank you," I said. Perhaps this was not a good idea. Perhaps I was feeling too raw.

"Do you ever feel you've wasted your life, Frankie?" She raised her eyelids from her cup and gazed at me with her deep blue eyes. "No, of course not," she answered herself. "You've got your work, haven't you? All those cases, fighting the good fight."

A grumbling sense of guilt about my appeal papers kept me silent.

"Why is my life so crappy?" she said, staring at her coffee.

"What's the matter?" I asked. "Are you in trouble?"

"I've been in trouble since the day I was born."

It sounded like the first line to a song. I didn't want to hear what she might be going to say. "Do you mean the divorce?"

"I should never have got married. What's it done for me? Nothing but heartache."

"You've got lovely children."

"How would you know?"

I sat back in my seat.

"I didn't need to get married to have kids. But it's not just that." She shuddered. "I don't want to talk about it." She pulled a cigarette from a packet on the table and bent her head as she lit it.

We talked about the froth on the coffee and the people coming and gradually going in the coffee shop until it was empty except for us and the girl with a sensible ponytail behind the counter. It was half past two and time to go.

The rain was an insistent drizzle when we came out and Margo looked down at her jacket. "This isn't mine," she said, anxiously.

Whose is it? I wanted to ask. Saskia's? "Take my raincoat," I offered. "This is a really old sweater."

"Are you sure?" she asked. I took off the coat and she slipped it over her shoulders.

"We don't have to walk to a car service office," I said, "we could ring one from here. Give me the coat back another time."

"No, the fresh air's nice," she said. "Let's make a dash for it."

Despite the rain there was a surprising number of people about and on High Street we dodged on and off the sidewalk, jumping over small puddles, breathing in to let strollers go past, stopping when a big gang of girls filled the whole sidewalk and cars were swishing by in the road.

I heard Margo say, "What!" Then her head twisted down and she said, "Your coat."

On the left sleeve of my coat a large dark stain was moving down her arm. It looked like oil—cooking oil or car oil.

"Something's happened to my arm," she said. "I think I've been bloody stabbed."

Everything around me was silent, I could scarcely take in what she was saying. "What? Who by? How?" My eyes raked the street. I saw a gang of girls, women with strollers, old men with bags of shopping, I saw navy raincoats, brown coats, black jackets, grey, purple, green. I saw nothing.

"Someone banged my arm." She staggered.

"I'm sorry. I'm so sorry," I said.

"Why? It's not your fault," Margo grimaced. "Is it?"

"No," I said. "How could it be?" Thinking, *A client? A client's husband? How would they find me? Latimer? He's dead.* "Why would they stab you anyway?" I said aloud.

"I dunno. I'm wearing your coat?" she said, shortly. "Oh, for God's sake! It's nothing to do with you. It's just happened."

We were near the bookshop. "Let's go in there," I said. "I'll call an ambulance and the police."

"What for? It's not that bad," she said, surprising me.

"You've been hurt," I said, opening my arms, trying to

encircle her, without touching her, to protect her from anything else.

The woman in the bookshop ushered us into the back of the shop and gently led Margo to a chair. As the two of them bent over Margo's arm I watched Margo's blonde head looking up at the bookseller. As the two women spoke softly to each other, I thought of the other possibility. Saskia. She looked like Saskia.

Nineteen

Friday Night

I told the woman in the shop I'd drive Margo to the hospital as it would be quicker and I dashed home and got my car. Margo sat quietly all the way to St. Bartholomew's Hospital as I tried to avoid potholes and wild cornering.

She was seen almost immediately at Bart's but they decided to keep her in overnight. "Don't come and visit me," she said and I couldn't argue with that.

Miserably I drove away. I wondered if my negative feelings had somehow played a part in what had just happened. I drove to the Temple and parked at a meter in a road just off the Embankment.

The thing about going into chambers is, people rarely look at you closely, they're all wrapped up in their own problems.

Gavin scarcely looked up from his computer. "Hi, Frankie," he said.

Jenna said, "There's a couple of messages for you, I've just taken one." She was scribbling onto a square of blue paper and then held it out to me. "Are you all right?"

Her tone made Gavin look up. "You look like shit," he said.

"Thanks."

"If a clerk can't be honest, the relationship isn't working."

"That's such rubbish, Gavin. You spend your whole life lying. To solicitors, to barristers, to courts."

"And the above statement is a lie," said Gavin.

"I don't care what it is," Jenna said. "Do you want a cup of tea?"

"Yes, please," I said, and sank into her chair as she moved over to the kitchen.

"Do you want to talk about it, or shall I carry on as usual?"

"I wouldn't know what to say," I said, "so why don't you just talk?"

"Do you want to do some personal injury?" Gavin asked, his hands hovering over an open brief.

"Not really," I said. It occurred to me that in the scheme of things I could be considered as having already done it. Margo could sue me for injury she had suffered as a result of my breach of a duty of care. I hadn't protected her when I should have. "It's paperwork basically, isn't it?" I said. "I don't need any more paperwork."

"Perhaps if you had a bit more paperwork you'd do the paperwork you had."

"And the above statement is balls," I said, "if I may use a legal term."

"The solicitors have been on me again."

"It's nearly finished," I sighed.

Jenna gave me the tea. I went to stand up but she told me to stay where I was, because she had to check the Crown Court warned lists anyway.

"Paperwork can be a nice little earner," Gavin said, "if you get yourself into a routine. People always say how nicely you draft pleadings."

"Hmm." This was good for the soul.

"And if you don't want this brief, I'll probably have to give it to Marcus," he said neutrally.

I almost rose to the bait, but I knew I couldn't do it, then his phone rang and he picked it up.

I looked at my messages. They were both from Kay.

"By the way—" Gavin put his hand over the mouthpiece—"have you endorsed your Breakspeare brief? The solicitors want the papers back."

I made a face at him.

"Frankie, if you don't endorse your briefs when you finish a case, I can't bill the solicitors, and if I don't bill the solicitors you don't get paid." He turned back to his phone call.

I walked to my room, feeling grey and gritty. I endorsed my Breakspeare brief, I didn't want Gavin grumbling at me on top of everything else. Carefully I wrote on the back sheet what had happened in court and then precisely how long the hearing took, how much time I had spent in conference, and how long we had waited. As I tried to remember how much time I had spent preparing the case I thought of that night, my excitement as I read through the papers, anticipating an evening with Margo, and how she'd stood me up to be with Saskia, and now she was in the hospital with stitches in her arm.

I drew a dark loop through the names on the front of the brief and rang Kay. "Will you have dinner with me tonight?" I asked.

"Is this for business or pleasure?"

"A bit of both."

"You know our relationship's over, don't you?"

"Strangely, Kay," I said, "that is the least of my worries."

"Well, I do need to talk to you. Where do you want to go?"

I thought for a moment. "Nowhere really." I couldn't have Kay being stabbed, even though on some subliminal level I often wished for that. "Do you want to come around to mine? I could cook. In fact, I'd like to cook." It might take my mind off things.

"Do I get a choice between spaghetti bolognese and shepherd's pie?"

"Oh no," I said, "it will be a big surprise." To both of us. "Since you and I separated I have obtained two new cookbooks."

"That's impressive. Just remember that I don't eat raw onion or cucumber."

"Damn," I said, "and I have this wonderful recipe for cucumber à l'oignon. I'll just have to save that for someone who really appreciates food. That's what I need, isn't it, a woman who understands good food. But who can cook as well."

"Do you think the pursuit of sex will ever stop being your driving force?" she asked. "We'll just have a version of meat and two veg, if that's all right with you. And I'll bring some wine. In the meantime, perhaps you should have a cold shower."

"Great," I said.

I put the phone down and then immediately rang a florist in Stoke Newington and ordered a large bunch of flowers with a lot of pink roses to be sent to Margo in the hospital. I told them to write "Sorry" on the card.

As I dropped the finished Breakspeare brief into the clerks' room, Gavin said, "We're going for a drink later. Do you want to come? Simon's coming."

I laughed. "That's so nice, Gavin. I wish it was that easy." If I could just become another person, I thought, for whom the last few days had produced nothing more worrying than the problems of getting to court on time and going out for a drink with someone romantic from chambers.

My feelings must have been showing on my face because as I pulled open the door to the clerks' room he called, "Take care."

Depression settled on my shoulders like a car coat. I could still smell Margo on my hands, I could feel her skin, taste her lips. See the blood on her arm, the rip in my coat.

I felt stupid about last night and guilty about lunchtime, but deep down, underneath it all, I had a horrible feeling that I was right, and she was taking me for a ride.

In Dalston I parked on a rough patch of ground called a car park and trailed into Sainsbury's. Listlessly I threw an eggplant, some zucchini and a parsnip into my basket. By the time I arrived at the checkout the addition of a bottle of Brown Brothers dessert wine and a roll of black garbage bags meant I had spent just enough to be awarded a token giving me a penny off every gallon of petrol I bought at a Sainsbury's petrol station in the next two weeks.

I thought about what to cook. I was beginning to look forward to Kay coming to the apartment. I hadn't cooked a proper meal in a long time and it was true that I had some cookbooks that had some interesting recipes.

The Rolling Stones were reminding me "You Can't Always Get What You Want" when Kay arrived.

"Love the music," she shouted as I let her in, "but what's that smell?"

I ran back into the kitchen. My deep-fried root vegetable chips were filling the room with smoke. I switched off the gas, then switched off the cassette.

"Don't tell me, you saw the recipe on a TV show," she said. "You should get out more."

"I've been getting out a bit too much," I said, opening the claret she had brought.

"What, or should I say who, is it this time?" She took glasses out of the cabinet.

"A woman called Margo, a friend of Saskia's."

"An animal person?"

"Don't think so."

"I don't know her," she said.

"Yes, well, she got stabbed this afternoon." I poured wine carefully into her glass and realized I was on the verge of tears.

"How?"

"I don't know. One minute we were walking up Stoke Newington High Street discussing seafood, the next . . ."

"You were with her when she got stabbed? What is it about you at the moment?"

"Don't."

"Who did it?"

"I didn't see."

"What did you do? Was she badly hurt?"

"We went into the bookshop and Margo took my coat off . . ."

"I won't ask," Kay muttered.

". . . and there wasn't much of a wound, so we left before the police arrived. I took her to Barts and they gave her a couple of stitches."

"What did the police say?"

"I haven't told them."

"The hospital will."

"I gave the hospital a false name."

Kay pulled out a chair and sat down. "You never cease to amaze me. You are the most law-abiding, play-it-by-the-rules person I know, you won't even post a letter if the stamp's on upside down, and you haven't told the police. What does—what's-her-name?—Margo say to all that?"

"She said she didn't particularly want to wait for the police, and I should say what I thought best. I said we were Cathy McGowan and Teresa McGonagle."

"Who are . . . ?"

"Stars from *Ready Steady Go.*"

"Frankie, this is getting so serious. I can't believe you gave a false name to the hospital and didn't tell the police."

"What's the point? It was probably some kid out of his head on smack or glue. They'll never find who did it."

"That's not the point."

"Why should I give my name?"

"I don't know—because it's your civic duty or something. But also, this is too much of a coincidence. It's all getting out of hand." She sat down, wearily.

"So who am I going to tell? DCI Fletcher? I don't think so. He'd love it, wouldn't he? He'd probably charge me with stabbing her myself."

"The hospital might think you did."

"Oh, for God's sake! But . . ." I took a deep breath, "I am a bit worried about . . . well, I have a sort of couple of theories. There are two other possibilities apart from the smackhead."

Kay put down her glass and looked at me.

"She—Margo—was wearing my coat, so she might have looked like me. She is a bit shorter than me, not much though—a couple of inches. I can't remember what shoes she was wearing. I don't know if it was really noticeable."

"And the other possibility?" Kay cut in.

"She looks a bit like Saskia, especially from behind."

"OK, but, who would want to stab Saskia? Or you, for that matter? Apart from irritated ex-lovers?" We shared the dream. "How do these theories work, then?"

"If the stabbing has something to do with the death of Latimer, then it's quite scary either way."

"Why would someone involved with Latimer's death have a go at you? You're the person who stands to take the blame, to take the heat off them."

"I don't know, a warning or something. But then, it could be to do with Saskia. Although I thought with Latimer's death her troubles might be over. The problem seemed to be between the two of them. I mean, it did cross my mind for half a second that maybe Saskia was involved with his death, although I can't think how someone who has Saskia's principles about animals could conceive of killing a person. But now it seems like there's someone out there who wants to get her. Or at least send a message to her."

"That's a very well worked out theory for someone who thinks this was most likely a random street stabbing."

"Yes. It probably was a random street stabbing. This is just in case it isn't."

"Did they take anything?"

"No."

"So, no motive, which would make it a really random attack. There really is very little random street violence." She pushed her chair back from the table. "Frankie, you've got to tell someone."

"Who? Do you think I can trust the police? Don't you think it's weird that I haven't been stopped for driving without a license plate? Doesn't that make you think they're all in it?"

"That's coincidence, you're just paranoid. Although Fletcher might be bad news. That's what I was going to tell you, his name crops up in three or four cases where we've taken action against the police for false arrest and malicious prosecution."

"How involved?"

"Nothing specific against him. Just his name appears every now and again."

"And now his name's cropping up in my case. Great. So, who can I tell?"

She thought. "That custody sergeant at Stoke Newington, he's a pretty straight guy, I've got a lot of time for him. You could tell him." She walked over to the phone and began pressing numbers. "I'll find out when he's next on duty and we can both go."

"What about Rowland?"

"Fletcher's sidekick? I don't know anything about him."

"No, why don't I tell him?"

"Why would you?"

"He knows I didn't do it. He apologized to me that night in the kitchen."

"What? In specific terms?"

"Almost."

"He was probably apologizing for rearranging the perfect symmetry of the pile of three-year-old *Guardians* in the middle of your living-room floor."

"No, it was more than that, you could tell. He seems like a nice guy. He was really upset at what was going on."

"If you're going to tell him, you might as well tell Fletcher. He'll tell Fletcher whatever you say to him."

"I don't think I could bear to sit in the same room as Fletcher. Do I have to tell anyone? It's not a car accident, it's not as if I'm legally obliged to report it . . . am I? It's not even my injury to report."

She wasn't listening. "My sergeant or your Rowland?"

"Rowland."

She spoke into the receiver.

"He's in on Sunday. We'll go down together in the morning. And it may not be your injury, but you're the one with a problem."

I knew that. I had hoped that no one else thought it was true. I scooped the charred remains of the root vegetable chips on to a sheet of paper towel.

"We're not eating those," Kay said. "You might as well throw them in the trash."

As I scrunched the chips into a ball she asked grimly, "Have you cooked anything?"

"I thought we'd have smoked mackerel and salad." I had an aging packet of smoked mackerel in my fridge.

"Apart from the fact I can't bear mackerel, and you're offering me a cold meal and it is a very cold day, the menu does not sound like a meticulously planned and executed dinner party experience."

"With bread," I said.

"Why don't we get takeout?" she suggested. "I could

ring the Eleganza and order, what, some pancake rolls and pork and noodles and Chinese greens?"

She knew me so well. "The comfort of ex-girlfriends?"

"There has to be something we can retrieve from that painful experience." She went to the phone again.

Thirty minutes later my small kitchen table was covered with a pot of jasmine tea, an almost empty bottle of red wine and foil containers of fragrant Chinese food. As a concession to my beleaguered state, Kay said we didn't have to eat with the wooden chopsticks which had been tucked into the bag with the food.

As we unfolded the edges of the containers from the lids, I said, "Saskia left me a card that night."

"You mean when she did the burglarizing?"

"Visiting," I said, putting a pancake roll in my mouth. I went into the living room to find it. "And she didn't take anything," I called.

"No," Kay commented, "she left you a small token of her respect." She wiped her fingers and took the card from me. She looked at it intently. "She's obviously right about the security angle." You see, I knew she'd say something like that. She was frowning at the message. "Are you sure this is her writing?"

"Aren't you?"

"I don't know. I'll take it to the office and see if I can find something with her writing on, to compare them." She slipped the card into her jacket pocket.

I took a mouthful of jasmine tea and scalded my mouth. "And Lena actually saw Saskia."

"When? Where?"

"On Tuesday at the Glass Bar."

"Why don't you tell me these things?"

"I only found out yesterday and I rang you today but you were in a meeting. And here I am now telling you." I realized with a shock that I was almost whining. I felt so guilty about everything. I wondered if guilt could actually eat you up from the inside, like the Ebola virus.

"Did Lena speak to her? Do you know where she is?"

"No. No to both."

"You've got to get hold of her, Frankie. I'm sorry, but you've got to put loyalty, friendship, past professional relationships, whatever it is, to one side. If she did deliberately break into your apartment and maliciously leave that credit card, she's not only important to your case, she's also trouble with a capital T."

"I know how to spell trouble," I said.

"But I'm not sure you'd recognize it if it punched you in the face."

"It did."

She sighed. "If you mean Latimer, the fact is, his death is not the end of your troubles. Because even if you get off the murder, there's the credit card. Handling a stolen credit card would be fairly disastrous for you, I would have thought, both legally and professionally. Dishonesty; breach of trust . . ." She looked at my face. "I'm sorry."

"It's OK," I said. "I've been thinking about alternative jobs for a little while anyway."

"How long?"

"About three days. I was thinking I could run away to London and start a new life."

"You're in London already. This is your life."

"Damn."

"But we must have something more to say to the police. We have less than a week."

"OK, OK, OK. I've told you everything, there's nothing more to say."

"All right, let me tell you something. It's not much: someone in the office has been rooting around. Latimer wasn't a financial adviser. In fact, he was a bit of a lowlife, no fixed abode, no formal employment."

"He owned a car."

"Lots of people own cars. Unlikely as it seems, you own a car."

"Are you saying I'm a lowlife?"

"It's not for me to judge. You're my client."

I looked at her hopelessly. "Can we talk about something else?"

"On the basis that at midday on Sunday you and I will meet to go and see DC Rowland to discuss your case, yes, we can talk about something different."

We talked about her new office decorations (bright) and the new pupil in chambers (also bright), whether Lena and Sophie would make honest women of each other and live together (outlook not bright), and the situation in the former Yugoslavia (cloudy and grey). At quarter to twelve I asked her if she would like to hear a new version of "Where Did Our Love Go?" by Donnie Elbert, which I had discovered on a cassette in a thrift shop in Bromley. She said this seemed to her to be a sign that she should be going home and, warning me to be ready at the door at noon on Sunday, she left.

I put the cassette on anyway and listened to the track, lying on the sofa, staring at the ceiling. As I was listening to it for the fourth time it occurred to me my neighbors might not think it was as good as I did so I went to bed.

Twenty

Saturday Morning

I woke up as the phone was ringing. I lay there as it stopped and my answering machine voice asked the caller to leave their name and number. My mother began to speak.

I picked up the receiver, throwing a resentful glance at the clock. It was eight thirty.

"Did I wake you up? How's your eye?"

"It would be better if it got more sleep."

"The reason I'm ringing you so very early on a Saturday . . ." she hesitated and I couldn't bring myself to fill in the gap ". . . is because I have a date tonight. With Alan."

I could hear her smiling down the phone and, as years of training kicked in, I knew what I had to ask. "Alan who?" I grunted.

Ignoring my tone, she replied, "Alan Henry. He rang and asked me out and we're going to a show tonight. Isn't that nice?"

It did seem rather nice, so I dragged myself into a sitting position and wished once again that automatic coffee makers worked like they ought to, at the flick of a switch, without any of the preparation and dishwashing which was actually involved. But then, I didn't have one, so the issue didn't really arise.

"So," I said, "the great Dr. Henry has come through."

"And I do need somewhere to get ready. Whether I shall need somewhere to sleep I can't say." She laughed girlishly.

"Mom! It's far too early for that kind of talk. What time will you be here?"

"About three."

"Can you make it four?"

"Well, it might be four, if the train is late. That's why I'm saying three."

I groaned and said goodbye. I put my head under the pillow and went back to sleep.

Until Lena rang. "Look this is a long shot but it might be the answer to your problems. What are you doing this afternoon?"

"Nothing?"

"Do you want to take part in a protest?"

"What kind?"

"A shopping protest."

"But I love shopping."

"Yes, yes, this is why it's such a good protest. You enjoy the shopping part, but you make a sound political point at the same time."

"Go on."

"You fill your shopping cart with goods containing animal products, where the animals have been reared under terrible conditions, and then leave the full cart at the checkout."

"But I buy those products myself, I eat them, I enjoy them. I can't pretend I have a major repugnance if every other day I take them into my own home."

"You only buy them because that's all there is. You do try to buy organic, don't you, Frankie?"

"Yes, I do. Although, as you know, my food shopping usually consists of a few packets of ready-prepared entrées and a bunch of parsley to throw over it for the personal touch."

She was silent.

"So what do you want? Have I got to give up meat for

the duration?" I said. 'Do I have to wear a T-shirt that says 'Animal rights are human rights'?"

"No, just be there. Fill a cart. It's an action—it's to get publicity, to make journalists ask questions."

"Oh yes, and if a journalist asks me a question, what do I say? 'Well, I'm someone who's about to be charged with murder . . . No, you're right, not much respect for life there. And actually, yes, I do hate cats.' "

"You're only possibly going to be charged with murder. And you don't hate cats, you're just being extreme."

"Huh."

"Will you come?"

"Yes, yes, I'll come. But when do I do my own shopping? I can hardly say, 'This half of the cart is a protest, but I'll keep the tea and ginger cookies, thank you.' "

"You'll have to work that out for yourself." I knew Lena was wondering whether all this was worth it.

"We're not going to get arrested, are we? Maybe I shouldn't come. Who's organizing this, anyway?"

"Someone from the Street Life group told me about it. I think it's a coalition of animal groups. It's bound to be peaceful. And I'm definitely not planning on being arrested. I have a hot date for tonight which I am not missing for anyone."

"And this someone from the Street Life group, could it be *the* someone?"

"No."

"Will she be there?"

"Maybe." She laughed that laugh that people have when they're having a good time in a new relationship. I couldn't blame her, but I didn't need to hear it just at the moment.

"OK, tell me the rest later. Just remind me, why am I doing this?"

"Because your missing friend Saskia might be there," she said.

I rolled out of bed.

I wanted a bath. As I passed the mirror I looked at my eye. It was almost impossible to tell that I had been punched. I could hardly remember it at all, so much had happened since then.

I put oil in the bath water and took Beryl Bainbridge's latest novel in with me, and it was nearly two o'clock when I gathered together some plastic bags to go up the street for the protest.

I was very low on gas, but I had my Sainsbury's voucher and all the petrol stations I passed were not Sainsbury's and very expensive. As I parked in the supermarket car lot I hoped I would remember to buy some petrol before I got stranded somewhere. As I was halfway through writing the word "petrol" on the back of my hand, I put the pen down. It occurred to me I shouldn't have driven here, it probably created the wrong ecological atmosphere, but if the going got rough I wanted to make a speedy exit.

There didn't seem to be any unusual activity as I walked toward the store: no banners, no shouting, no police. Perhaps that meant I had missed the demonstration. That was a relief, it was crazy for me to even think about doing this. What would Kay say? I'd just do my shopping. I pulled a cart out from the line and moved into the vegetable section. I made myself stop in front of the lettuces. I thought about my position. The way I shopped really reflected my life. Pre-cooked food and no lettuce. I didn't know what it meant but it seemed important. I had to make some changes. I had to live properly, especially during this period of enforced rest. I took vegetables off the shelves. I left my cart by the bananas, I would think about bananas in a minute, now I needed passion fruit. When I came back with a bag of plums, my cart had disappeared.

I found it at the meat counter. It was definitely my cart, I saw the packet of arugula and the bag of organic carrots. There was also a packet of noodles, which weren't mine, but which I thought I might as well keep. And now that I was at the meat counter I could look for something substantial. Noticing what I thought was a special offer, I picked up a chicken with a yellow sticker over the price. I had to read the thick black letters twice before I realized what they meant. WARNING: THIS PACKAGE CONTAINS THE DECAYING CARCASS OF A SMALL TORTURED BIRD.

I wondered who had stuck that on. So much for a peaceful protest. This sticker was teetering on the verge of criminal damage. I was glad I'd missed it.

A little silver-haired old lady wearing a beige jacket walked over to my cart and put a proprietorial hand on it. She began to push it away, staring at the shelves of chicken thighs and breasts. She had a yellow sheet of paper in her hand and as I watched she peeled off a square and pressed it on to a bird in the corn-fed chicken section.

I hurried after her. "I think this is my cart," I said, then added, "I'm part of the protest too."

She started, then, looking me up and down, simpered, "Would you mind saying that again? I have a little hearing problem." She toyed with her right ear, looking at me innocently through her large, clear glasses.

"It's all right," I mouthed, "I'm not a store detective or security."

"No, perhaps not," she said, "not in those boots." I was wearing my cowboy boots; their pointed toes had started to curl upward. "Of course, you could be very deeply undercover. But I can't hear what you're saying anyway."

She took a step away from me.

"But it is my cart," I said. "I need it for the action." I noticed someone in an unattractive brown outfit with gold braid on the shoulders, hovering uncertainly at the top of our aisle. I grabbed her arm and she looked down at my hand as if it was covered with non-organic manure.

"I think there may be a store detective watching us at this very moment."

Her expression was blank. "I don't know what you're talking about."

The man was approaching. "Come on, Gran," I said jovially, "we'll miss our bus."

Together we wheeled the trolley past the man in the brown polyester. At the end of the aisle I looked back and saw him standing watching us with his arms folded.

"I'm a lawyer," I said. "I'm meant to be taking part in the action, but I think we may have to give it a miss. It looks like they've already got our number."

We passed Lena, who was taking the opportunity to pile her cart with all the things she would love to buy but knew she shouldn't—exotic desserts and jars of chicken stock and large packs of veal. "Hi, Frankie," she said softly.

"Are you Frankie, the lawyer?" my companion asked. "I imagined you taller."

"You know who I am?"

"Oh, yes," she said. "I think I've got your phone number somewhere."

"Who gave you that?"

We were approaching the checkout. Several young people with suspiciously full carts were standing looking casually at the racks of camera film and sewing thread. "Look," I said, "I don't know about you, but I can't really afford to be caught with someone who might have been committing criminal damage. You don't fancy a cup of tea, do you?"

"A cup of tea would be lovely," she said gratefully. "I think you're right, Saturday's not the best time for guerrilla shopping."

I left my cart where it was—I didn't feel close to it and it had obviously felt no loyalty to me—and we left the store.

We crossed the main road and walked to a small cafe in a group of shops while my companion introduced herself: "I'm Delia."

In the café she sat at a table near the window while I ordered us two cups of tea and a plate of toast.

I carried the tray to the table. She had taken off her jacket to reveal a small handknitted lavender cardigan, buttoned to the neck. She looked neat and twinkly. We talked about animal rights protests and she told me about Julian and Sheila, two activists I had represented years before in my criminal days. They were married now and had a child.

"Did they give you my number?" I asked.

She had been involved in the campaign for a long time, she said. She rescued dogs who were treated cruelly by their owners. We talked about veal exportation and factory farming.

"So who gave you my number?"

She put her hand into a voluminous cloth bag and rooted around. She drew out an old envelope. "Do you know that handwriting?" She pointed to figures written hurriedly by the stamp.

"I'm not sure," I said, "but that's not my phone number."

"Oh, isn't it?" she asked. "Then who are you?" I could see her replaying our whole conversation, from the moment I had found her with my cart to our intense discussion about the iniquity of foie gras. She was weighing me up. I groped in my pocket for a business card to prove who I was. I pulled out a handful of pink ribbon. It would have to do. I began to unravel it, winding it around my fingers.

"I'm Frankie, I'm a barrister."

"Well, why would I have your number? Barristers are no good to me in a police station, are they?"

"No, you need a solicitor. That's probably a solicitor's number. In fact, isn't it Kay's number?"

She looked at the number again. "Yes, of course that's who it is—Kay. But you're not Kay."

"No, I'm Frankie, I'm the barrister. Who gave you that number? Was it Saskia?" I said.

For a second she stopped sipping her tea and sat motionless.

"Do you know Saskia?"

"Why?" she asked quietly. "Why do you ask me that?"

"I represented her last week, I think she's in trouble. I need to find her."

She put the thick white cup carefully back in the saucer.

As the silence lengthened I said, "I'm in a bit of trouble too, which is another reason I need to see her. But basically I just have to speak to her. Do you know where she is?"

"You know Kay?"

"Yes."

"You do cases for her?"

"Yes," I reminded her, "that's how I know Julian and Sheila. I represented them in the big demo of 1992. We got acquitted."

She looked me up and down. "She's in a safe house."

I swallowed. I hadn't really expected that Delia knew Saskia, let alone knew where she was.

"Why is she in a safe house?"

"I understand she has received threats."

"Who from?"

"I don't know." She was toying with a corner of toast. "I don't know." I was losing her.

"Where is the safe house?" I asked urgently.

She was silent.

"Please," I said.

"I can't tell you, because then it wouldn't be a safe house."

"Can you contact her? You could tell her I need to see her. Then, if she was prepared to see me, you could let me know."

"I have no way of contacting her," she said. "There's no

phone there, and I have no direct contact with her my-self."

"Does she ever leave the house?" I asked.

"She's not meant to. It's not really safe for her to do that."

I wondered if Delia knew she'd been out of the house on Tuesday, visiting my possible girlfriend. "How does she get food?"

"We have a rota, every two or three days."

"Could I write her a message or something? Put it in the food parcel?"

"That's not really my area," she said. "Is it truly ur-gent?"

I considered my options. I had a week to prove my in-nocence, before I had to return to the police station.

"Well, I . . . we've got a few days," I said, "so it's fairly urgent."

"I'm not sure you'd even want to go there. It's quite grim."

"Perhaps I could take her a vacuum or an electric blan-ket or something."

She laughed, a small gurgling sound. "She'd probably be very grateful for that."

She took a mouthful of tea and seemed to settle herself. Speaking into her cup she told me the address but asked me not to write it down. "I'd better go now," she said.

I looked at my watch. It was twenty to three. "Oh God," I said, "so had I."

I left her walking toward Tottenham and hurried back to the supermarket. I had bought no food. There was a po-lice van almost blocking the exit to the car park. I couldn't bear to even look in the store. I just hoped Lena was be-having herself. I slid into my car and drove on to the hill and down, and I was at home in the apartment at five to three.

My mother arrived on the dot of three o'clock. "Say what you like," she said, "I don't think the trains were ever so reliable and good before privatization."

"Tell that to the *Guardian* readers of the West Country," I said, taking her bag, which was worryingly large. "How long are you staying?" I asked, as I hung the fake fur coat in the closet in the hall.

She simpered. "I don't know. That depends on the good doctor." I could have slapped her. I was surrounded by them. Her, Lena. There is nothing worse than someone who is lucky in love when you're not.

We had a cup of tea and she told me about their whirlwind courtship, via phone and e-mail.

"We don't have all the time in the world," she said, as I looked at her with concern. He had been to visit her in Colchester, which had gone very well. "He was very decorous," she said meaningfully, not wanting to embarrass me. For which I was grateful. This was to be their first date on his territory.

"Could I have a martini?" she asked me suddenly. It was ten past four.

As I groped to the back of the cabinet for a dusty bottle of vermouth, she said, "Can we talk about sex? Safe sex. How long do you have to do it for?"

"I don't know," I said cautiously, wiping the bottle with a kitchen towel. "Depends who you're with. I'm not sure of our context here. Is this a theoretical discussion?"

"So far. But I'm right to be thinking about it, aren't I?"

"Yes, I . . . yes." I put ice into two glasses. It crackled as the gin hit it. "I'm assuming this has nothing to do with having children."

Mom snorted, so I knew I had one less thing to worry about.

"It's just that it could be a bit of a problem if we . . . get carried away. All the fiddling about you have to do."

"That's the whole point of it. To stop you getting carried away and doing something foolish." I poured a dash of vermouth into the glasses and handed her her drink. "Is this a serious conversation, Mom? Are you really asking me?"

"Who else do I have to ask?"

"OK. When did you last have a sexual relationship with someone?" I asked.

"About twenty years ago."

I hadn't known that. I wasn't sure if I wanted to know any more. "How many men have you slept with? In your whole life?"

"Well, two. Not counting Alan. Who I haven't slept with yet."

"What about Alan?"

"He slept with a few women before he got married, but he assures me he was faithful to his wife and they were married for thirty years."

"And since then?"

"He says he hasn't slept with anyone since she died. That was two years ago."

"Advice wise, to be on the incredibly safe side, I suppose I should say safe sex until you both go for a test and then if you're both clear of everything you can go wild. But is it going to last that long? I mean, is the relationship worth the hassle of going through all the tests?"

"I hope so," she said, and gave a funny little smile. "I do hope so. I really quite like him."

The room was suddenly filled with birdsong and sunshine and I had a lump in my throat. I obviously hadn't been getting enough sleep. "That's fantastic," I said. "How does he feel?"

"He says he feels the same."

"Just don't scare him off," I advised her.

At six o'clock I gave her a ride to Highbury Corner subway station. As I watched her walking into the station, all fake fur and excitement, I envied her.

I went home and put a pre-packaged duck à l'orange with spinach into the microwave and put on a CD of the Shangri-Las. You'd be surprised how listening to "Give Him a Great Big Kiss" played really loud can cheer a person up. So I rang Lena, who of course was out on her hot date, and I played it down the phone to her answering machine. In case she needed cheering up, or even if she didn't.

She's good bad but she's not evil.

Twenty-one

Sunday

I could hear my mother snoring gently in the living room. I crept past the door into the kitchen and began making coffee. It was one of those cold crisp sunny October mornings where a person might be putting on a big thick sweater, perhaps navy, perhaps cream, and polishing some stout, well-worn boots and planning a long walk in the country. I am not that person and I stood looking out at the garden, the wet grass, the blackened plants, the last leaves hanging limply on the oak tree, and was pleased the kitchen was warm and cozy and the coffee fresh and strong.

I knocked on the living-room door and popped my head around. My mother sat up guiltily. She was not alone. A silver-haired head lay sleeping on a pillow beside her. How had this happened? How did my mother get lucky when my life was such a mess?

"Morning," I said. "So that's two cups of coffee?"

"Yes please," my mother whispered, her face so pink and her expression so happy that I felt like the "uptight" part of "Everything's Alright," but I don't think she noticed.

I took in the coffee on a tray with some croissants.

"I'm just going to make some phone calls," I said.

"Does that mean, keep the noise down, or don't come out?"

"Both." I closed the living-room door and from the kitchen rang Margo's number. I had looked up the address that Delia had given me for Saskia and it was in Walthamstow, not the kind of place that I normally go. I would have to bite the bullet and ask Margo. She might well know how to get in touch with Saskia, given their . . . closeness, then I could avoid having to make the trip. That was my only reason for ringing her number. And, of course, to find out if she was OK. Believe me. Any kind of relationship between us was impossible—not only did she have a thing going with Saskia, but I'd got her stabbed. I didn't feel we had much of a future. I was just ringing her for the purpose of pursuing every avenue to find Saskia.

The phone rang and rang. There was no answer.

I rang the hospital. She was still there but I couldn't speak to her on this number. I was told the number of a phone which would be taken to her bedside in a minute or two.

I rang again. By the time she whispered hello I was really feeling tense. But even I couldn't deny the pleasure in her voice as she replied to my hello. I wanted to be crisp and efficient, but I found myself smiling. Obviously being with someone when they're stabbed is a really intimate experience. I said, "What are you doing still there?"

"The wound looked funny, and since I didn't have the girls I said I'd stay an extra night."

"But are you all right?"

"Yes, I'm just about to leave now."

"Who's picking you up?"

"I'm getting a cab."

"Stay there," I said. "I'm coming to get you."

As I walked into the ward I grinned with pleasure. She was sitting on the edge of her bed, her hair was brushed

back from her face and she had make-up on—red lipstick
and something dark around her eyes. She was wearing her
long grey raincoat, which she held tightly around herself. I
had a split-second fantasy that she wasn't wearing anything underneath.

She smiled in return.

"You look nice," I said, as I leaned over to kiss her.

"So do you."

I wasn't sure that my jeans and sweatshirt merited even
that level of compliment, but perhaps she was being more
spiritual.

"Are you ready to go?" I asked.

"They're just waiting for the doctor to sign me out."

I sat down in the chair beside the bed, next to the bedside table upon which stood a dull plastic water jug, a box
of orange juice and an extravagant bunch of pink roses,
cornflowers and white carnations in a grey cut-glass vase.

"Does your arm hurt?" I asked. "Can I see it?"

She shrugged off her coat to reveal her baby blue cardigan and a tight black skirt. I wondered who had brought
her clothes. "My sister brought me this stuff, last night,"
she said, watching my eyes. She undid the buttons of her
cardigan and slid it off her left shoulder. The top of her
arm was tightly wrapped in a neat bandage. I stretched out
my hand and she instinctively shrank away. Unhappily I
put my hand back in my lap.

"Margo, I'm so sorry about you being stabbed, but I
have to ask you about Saskia."

"I thought you might say that," she said carefully, but-
toning her cardigan. "What do you want to know?"

"My friend Lena saw you with her the other night. She
said you looked . . . well, friendly."

"You have spies, do you?" She eased her coat back on
over her shoulders.

"No, she told me because she's my friend and she doesn't
want me to get caught up in complicated situations."

"Saskia's in a lot of trouble," she said. She looked around the ward. "God, I could kill for a cigarette." She groped in her bag. "Gum?" She held out a green packet of Wrigley's.

I shook my head. "What kind of trouble do you think she's in?"

She unwrapped a stick of chewing gum and folded it into her mouth. "I can't say."

"You've got to tell me."

"Why? I should have thought you're the last person I should tell, you being her lawyer and everything. Aren't you meant to tell the police everything you know?"

I sighed. "Only in the context of a trial, and then only if she wants me to, and my only other duty is not to mislead the court," I recited.

She gazed at me.

"If you don't want to tell me what it's about, do you at least know where she is?"

"No."

Can you get in touch with her?"

"No."

"Are you sure?"

"Frankie! Don't ask me that. Trust me."

"Trust you to what?"

"Just trust me."

"What do you mean?"

"I just want this to be clear. I've made too many mistakes, I don't want any misunderstandings between us." She pulled a cigarette packet from her pocket and began to turn it between her fingers. "I don't want to be tied down."

"I didn't get you stabbed to tie you down," I protested.

"You didn't get me stabbed. Did you?"

"No."

"I just mean, I suppose my independence is an important thing to me. That's what you learn when you get married. Especially when you have children. And my children come first above everything."

"Yes."

She smiled. "Are you still with me?"

A nurse came up to the bed. "Doctor says you can go," she said with a bright smile. "Just make an appointment with your internist for the stitches to come out in a week's time."

I picked up the small bag of Margo's things. "Do you want the flowers?" I asked.

"Oh." She wrinkled her nose.

"Didn't you like them?"

"Are they from you?" Who did she think they were from? Who else would write "Sorry"?

"Yes," I said.

"Oh, well, yeah then."

I wrapped the stems in some tissues and we walked to the elevator in silence. When we got outside she lit a cigarette.

"Do you believe the other side of love is pain?" she asked.

I looked at her arm. "I don't know."

"I think that's the name of the game," she said dreamily. I wondered if the hospital had given her too much painkiller. She drew deeply on her cigarette. "But I'll just say again, no, I don't know where Saskia is." She breathed smoke down her nose. "I want to find her as much as you do."

I believed her. I smelled her perfume of roses and peppermint and cigarettes and I touched her face as she got in the car. I believed her, even if she did talk in song lyrics. I drove quickly to her building. As I pulled up in her bleak, windy car park, I looked at my watch.

It was quarter to twelve. "Oh God," I groaned. "I've got to go. Look, look, I've got to find Saskia, she's mixed up with a man called Kevin Latimer," I said. How could I keep something like that from her, after everything I'd put her through. "He's dead."

"I know he's dead," she said. She was clicking the nails of her thumb and little finger of the hand in which she held her cigarette. "I've known almost since it happened," she said, click, click, click.

I sat silently while my mouth made the shape of words I couldn't decide on using. Why? How? What? Finally I said, "Who is he? Does he have something to do with you?"

She was silent, sitting very still. Then she inhaled. She breathed out smoke. "He was my husband."

"Kevin Latimer was your husband? Does Saskia know this?"

"Oh yes," she laughed, a short mirthless bark. "She knows. There wasn't a lot of love lost between them. How did you work out the connection between him and Saskia? Did she tell you?"

"Saskia didn't tell me anything. It sort of grew on me. He was following her."

"Yes, that was his idea of fun."

It was ten to twelve. I knew I had to go and I wanted to go. I wanted to get away from this conversation and all the implications it raised. I leaned across her to open the car door but she caught my arm and held me there, my face level with hers. She breathed the smell of cigarettes into my mouth as she said, "I know there's a lot of shit around, but I really do want to give this as good a go as I can."

"So do I," I said reluctantly, and if it hadn't been Kay that I was meeting, at that moment I would have offered to carry her bag up the stairs. "Ring me if you hear from her," I said.

"And if I don't?"

"Ring me anyway."

Twenty-two

Sunday Midday

At five to twelve I screeched into Amhurst Road and saw Kay leaning against the door at the top of the steps to my house, looking unusually casual. I hooted as I drove past her to find a parking space. I assumed we'd go in her car.

"We're walking," she said, as I moved toward the passenger door of her shiny new vehicle. "It's a two-minute walk. Where have you been and why do you smell so disgusting?"

"I have been making enquiries which I hope will prove useful to my case. Just like you asked me to," I told her, as we stood at the crossing on High Street. "Cigarettes were smoked."

"I wish I felt that you were taking this seriously," she said. She was carrying a newspaper and wearing chinos and a denim jacket.

"Well, am I casual enough?" I asked, looking down at my sweatshirt, which I'd found in Lena's bag of clothes.

"Very funny, but actually it's important. This is a low-key, fancy-seeing-you-here kind of appointment." Unexpectedly she led me past the police station and turned into a pub a few doors down. "Just behave," she said, before I could open my mouth.

The clock behind the bar said twelve o'clock exactly as we entered. It could have been twelve midnight; the room was dark and the pink bulbs gleaming dimly from the ceiling did little to lighten the scene. The pub had recently been redecorated and was now one large room with American-style booths lining the walls and small dark wood tables in the middle. We walked over to the bar. Two minutes later the doors opened and five or six men walked in. Kay groaned. "There weren't meant to be quite so many," she said, scarcely moving her lips as she paid for our drinks. They were obviously police officers, even though they were not in the navy uniform with helmets tucked under their arms. They were all wearing zip-up bomber jackets in various shades of mauve, magenta and maroon. As we walked through them to a dark alcove I glanced at them, all young, all brash. I thought I recognized Rowland, but when I looked again they all appeared the same.

As a group the men walked to the bar, joking loudly, swearing, banging on the bar. I assumed this was the relief of the end of a shift. They ordered drinks and all stood waiting for them, as if it would be unmasculine to go and find a table and sit down. They were served with large glasses of beer and after some jokes about whose round it was and who was and who wasn't a tight wad, they moved en masse across the room. They walked without a second glance past our table where we sat nursing two glasses of mineral water, which Kay had bought on the basis I was not to be trusted with alcohol.

One of the men separated from the group and moved across to us. Away from the group you could see his distinguishing features. Dark hair, anxious look. In the gloom you couldn't see his blush, which was something.

"I can't stop long," he said, holding his head stiffly, obviously desperate to turn and look to see if anyone was watching. "When we've finished, I'll stay here while you leave. Don't look at them. They'll just think you're my contacts."

"Don't they recognize us?" I asked.

"They didn't see you," he said. "What did you want to talk to me about?" He kept swallowing. I had a sudden strong feeling that he didn't know what he was doing. Oh God, perhaps Kay had been right. I wanted to say, "Can we swap you for an older model?" Perhaps he was just nervous because he wasn't with Fletcher. Maybe Fletcher would flip if he knew. When he knew.

As he picked up his glass I noticed the dark shadows around his eyes.

"Something else has happened and I need to know what you think about it."

Kay had not told him the reason I wanted to see him and I explained about Margo being stabbed in the street.

"Oh," he said with a sigh. "We got a call in about that."

"Who from?" I asked.

"The bookshop manager. She told us you'd gone to the hospital, but she wasn't sure where." He coughed. "She couldn't give us any names."

"So?"

"We found the hospital—Barts, wasn't it?—and they said they'd had a stabbing. Different names though."

"Well, now you know it was me, and a woman who looks like Saskia . . . Susan Baker. Who definitely wasn't Saskia," I assured him.

"Why did you give false names? Why did you not tell us straight away?"

"Come on, think of the trouble I'm in, how could I have told you?"

"Is that what they call a rhetorical question?" he asked, shifting in his seat, sounding like a police officer in the witness box.

"Frankly, yes," I said sharply.

· "All right, you two," Kay interrupted. "She knows she should have rung the police."

"DCI Fletcher is very suspicious about you and Saskia." Rowland licked his lips. "I shouldn't tell you this, but he doesn't like Saskia. She got a friend of his into a lot of trouble."

I looked at Kay, who shrugged at me. She knew no more about it than I did.

"So how does that affect me?"

He swallowed. "I don't know this Saskia, but Fletch is very interested in her."

"So it would be a good idea if I could bring her to the police station?"

They both stared at me.

"Do you know where she is?" Rowland's face was changing color. Did he think he'd win a prize from Fletcher if he cracked this?

"No," I said truculently. "How would I?"

"All I'm saying is, be careful."

"He thinks Saskia did it, doesn't he?" I ventured.

"I don't know."

"And if he can't get Saskia, he'll have me. That's it, isn't it?"

"I cannot comment on that." He looked from me to Kay. He took a mouthful of beer and spilled some on the table as he put the glass down. "I'd be a bit worried about my legal career if I were you," he said recklessly.

My career, about which I feign such irritation and couldn't-care-lessness, suddenly seemed desirable, fulfilling and useful. I didn't want to lose it. I wanted it to flourish and develop. I wanted to see my name in the law reports. And I'd just bought a new suit which I hadn't worn yet. My career couldn't be over.

"I'd better get back to the others," he said, and picked

up his dripping glass. "See you next week." Even his ears were flushed.

I took a last mouthful of mineral water. It was warm and had gone flat and the slice of lemon slapped against my nose. I was trying to remember something he had said.

Twenty-three

Sunday Lunch

"Do you know where she is?" Kay demanded when we were a safe distance away.

"I don't know."

"I am your lawyer. You can trust me. You have to trust me."

"I know. What did you think of Rowland?"

"He seemed a bit jumpy to me. All that twitching and blushing."

"That's just his coloring," I said. "He's quite sweet, don't you think?"

She was silent.

"But are we really talking about Fletcher trying to frame me? I can't believe it."

"Why not? My young black male clients would believe it."

I don't know what I had expected of the meeting with Rowland, but as I watched Kay drive away in her lovely car, I realized I felt worse than I had before. Fletcher obviously had something on Saskia, and if he couldn't have her he'd happily accept me as substitute. If I saved myself by finding Saskia for them, then I was dropping her in three feet of inorganic material. Nevertheless I had to find Saskia to sort out this credit card thing. When I found her we could think of the next step together.

But first I had to do something with my mother.

As I walked back into the apartment I smelled the warm, meaty fragrance of a Sunday roast. Mom was in the kitchen standing at the stove, stirring gravy in a pan. The man I assumed was Alan Henry sat at the table, nursing a small glass of something that looked like sherry. He had a long, interesting face and they were both laughing at something he was saying.

"Thank goodness," Mom said as I walked in. "Alan, this is my daughter, the brilliant barrister, and Frankie, this is Alan . . ."

"The brilliant plastic surgeon," I said.

"Would you like a sherry?" my mother asked me.

"I don't think I've got any," I said.

"You have now. Alan and I did some shopping, and now we are going to have lunch." She put on an oven mitt, which I vaguely recognized as being mine, and lifted three plates out of the oven.

Mechanically I went to the drawer and took out knives and forks, as I had always done at home on Sundays.

"How do you know how to cook a roast?" I asked my mom.

"I usually read the label on the plastic wrap it comes in," she said. "Now, Alan, will you carve?"

"Unless anybody else wants to," he said.

I looked at him blankly. I knew I should be leaping to do it, but, sometimes I feel I have too much else to do.

"Why don't you open the wine?" he said.

I was ravenous. We all ate too much and Alan told a risqué joke involving plastic surgery, a severed finger and a packet of frozen peas. I looked at my mom to see her reaction but she was laughing with real amusement. Then we all moved into the living room to watch a bad black-and-white movie with Lana Turner. Alan and my mother sat next to each other on the sofa and occasionally held hands.

At five o'clock I got up to switch on the lamps and close the curtains. Mom said she had to go and Alan said he would drive her to the station. As my mother shrugged into her ludicrous fur coat and I watched Alan tenderly tuck her scarf neatly around her neck, I was filled with regret. They looked so happy and secure as they drove away, and the apartment felt so empty and lonely, that the prospect of what I had to do seemed doubly scary and stupid.

Twenty-four

Sunday Evening

Delia had given me clear directions. She had said Saskia was staying in a grim place. What she hadn't said was that the grim place was on a derelict plot of land, overlooked by the back of three high-rise blocks on one side and an industrial site on another. The third side of the triangle was a narrow access road, above which hummed the M11. In fact, I knew this place, although I had never been to it before. It was a piece of waste ground which groups of travelers were allowed to park their trailers on. Tonight it was clear the travelers had moved on. The place was deserted.

The car crept along the access road reluctantly, the wind straining to push it back where it came from. I was driving slowly because of the number of potholes. The whole area seemed empty. I couldn't see anywhere that Saskia might conceivably be staying. In fact, I couldn't see anything. I stopped the car and wound down the window for a clearer view. I don't clean the windows in my car any more than I clean the windows in my house. A cold blast of air whipped into the car and I could hear the moan of electrical wires, as I strained to look across the inky dark stretch of land. A few very high lamp-posts around the edges shed a dry orange light over small patches of the scrubby ground, enough to show me hillocks of dry mud and stones and small ravines filled with pools of some sheeny liquid, stagnant water or gasoline.

At the far side, which looked about two hundred miles away, but was probably only a few hundred yards, where the wall surrounding the tower blocks met the fence protecting the industrial site, I could make out a pinprick of light. It had to be the trailer. What I couldn't see was any obvious way to get there. How was I going to get there? The access road, I could see, ran out before it reached the tower blocks. There were no other roads. The ground looked like a picture of the moon, rocky, hazardous and dark. The car would never make it.

There was one obvious way—to strike out boldly straight across the field. On foot. In the dark. On my own.

"You are joking," I told myself aloud. I answered myself that if Saskia could do it, then, probably, so could I. I was wearing sensible shoes. In my suede jacket and jeans I could even be mistaken for a short man. I told myself that more attacks happen in the home, the attacks that happen on the street are usually in built-up areas, and there was nowhere for an attacker to hide in this barren place. And anyway, I had the cell phone.

I looked down at my trusty friend, lying in its little black leather case on the passenger seat beside me. For once, I had remembered to bring it. At least with the phone I would never be completely out of touch with the real world. I switched it on and tried to remember what it meant if there were only two lines to the arrow head, instead of five.

I turned the heater on full blast to warm myself up before I began the long trek. I wished I'd brought a thermos or a hip flask. Or a Saint Bernard. Or anyone called Bernard. Even Bernard Manning. No, not even in this crisis would I want to rely on Bernard Manning. I closed my

eyes, hoping that when I opened them I would be somewhere else, at home in bed, or at someone else's home in
their bed—Margo's, for example. "Oh don't get started on
that!" I shouted to myself. "Get out of the car!"

I opened the door and had it almost blown out of my
hand. Immediately I stepped into a puddle and discovered,
as I felt damp, cold liquid oozing over my toes, that my
boots were the sort the manufacturers don't guarantee
against bad weather. Maybe when all this is over, I told
myself, I'll change my life and sit quietly in a tidy office,
practicing consumer law and writing to the *You and Yours*
show about the meaning of the term "fit for the purpose."
I did not feel fit for the purpose.

I finally slammed the door shut and turned toward the
prick of light. I had gone about two yards when I realized
I had forgotten the phone. As I wrenched open the car
door I had a sense of movement on the other side of the
car. I leaned across the seat, picked up the phone, then,
holding it as if it were a weapon, I looked under the car for
legs. There were four. A thin, wild-looking cat was backing away from me under the front wheel. I jumped back. I
hate it when my instincts are right, it's so unsettling. But
because they're not always right, I never know which ones
to trust.

I zipped my jacket as high as it would go and, ignoring
the damp socks rubbing against my toes, I hunched forward to begin my journey. "Why did I come out?" I wondered, stumbling over patches of wiry grass. "Why did I
come out on this cold, dark, night, to this cold dark desolate place when I could have been sitting at home in front
of the fire, watching repeats of *ER* or *3rd Rock from the
Sun*, sipping a gin and tonic while mindlessly pressing
handfuls of chips into my mouth? Why did I come out on
my own, when I could have asked Lena, or even Kay, to

come with me? Why did I come in the dark?" These questions were, I felt, better answered at another time.

I began to sing "House of the Rising Sun" to focus myself. The wind whipped the words away so it became a test of skill to time the song between gusts.

As I half tripped for the third time I wondered how Saskia could live in this place. She must be really desperate—but why? What was she afraid of?

I heard a shout, two and three shouts. Lonely and harsh, like peacocks. I couldn't make out where the shouts came from, but I told myself it was kids from the tower blocks, out playing, when they should have been indoors in the warm, doing homework. Although I knew from my cases that they were probably safer playing outside than being at home.

I pressed on. I'd been walking for about ten minutes. I was in the middle of the site now, so it would have taken just as long to get back to the car as to get to the trailer.

The wind kept blowing and I gave up singing. I wasn't impressing anyone and I was straining my vocal cords, which were the tools of my trade. Then the rain began, just a drizzle at first, bouncing around with the wind, but gradually it came more persistently and there was hail stinging my face. By the time I arrived at the trailer I was soaked.

There were no steps so I reached up to knock on the door. Nothing happened. I knocked again.

A voice which seemed to come from the door itself called "Who is it?"

"It's Frankie," I shouted, "Frankie Richmond. Your barrister."

There was a rattle of keys and bolts sliding back. The door opened out toward me and I stepped back as warm, rosy light spilled on to the mud around me. Saskia held her hand out to me and pulled me up into the small, untidy room.

Before Saskia had handed me a towel and I had un-zipped my jacket, I realized she was not alone. Sitting on a narrow bench at the far end of the caravan, hugging her-self and nervously tapping her foot, was Margo.

Twenty-five

Sunday Night—The Trailer

The three of us looked at each other.

"How did you get here?" I asked Margo.

"Not the same way as you, obviously," she said.

That was self-evident. She was wearing small, strappy shoes which were clean of mud and a dry short skirt with a light v-necked top. I couldn't see her bandage. Her hair was dry and bouncy. She looked fabulous. In her hand she was holding a glass of wine. It was half-empty.

"How did *you* get here?" she asked, looking me up and down.

My jacket was soaked, which I knew wasn't good for suede. My socks were squelching and as I followed Margo's gaze I realized I was creating an indoor water feature on the floor of the trailer.

As if to highlight the difference in our physical states, Margo neatly slipped off her shoes and curled her feet up on the narrow bench seat. She looked like a warm, comfortable cat. A small gas fire popped happily by her side. I was torn between wanting to go over and pet her and wanting to knock her head off.

"Exactly how," she said, reading my thoughts, "is this my fault?"

"For a start, you said you didn't know where Saskia was."

"I didn't exactly, until this evening. And from what you said, you didn't know either."

"Well, you two obviously know each other," Saskia said. She sounded nervous. And so she should. She had a lot of questions to answer. Unfortunately I couldn't remember what they were. I wanted to be warm and dry and curl up with my head in Margo's lap.

"What are you doing here?" I asked Saskia. "How are you? Where did you go that day after you left my apartment?"

"I can't remember," she said vaguely. Her eyes were pink and swollen. I wondered if she had just woken up or if they had had an argument. I wondered what it was about. I wondered if one of them had just finished with the other.

"Do you want some wine?" Saskia asked shyly. "I'm afraid it's only Valpolicella."

"I'd rather have a cup of tea."

"Tea? Since when did you drink tea in preference to wine?" Margo snorted.

"When I need my wits about me," I said primly.

"Are you sulking?" she asked, laughing.

"You can just shut up," I said. "I'm wet and you're not. How *did* you get here?"

"I was driven here."

"Where did you park?"

"Just behind the trailer."

We were having a parking conversation. In a trailer in the middle of a field in the middle of nowhere in a raging storm, with a dead man between us all, we were having a parking conversation. Any second now we would start exchanging the names of roads. I couldn't stop myself. "Did you come on the A12?"

"We took the service road off the M11."

"You mean there's a way to drive right up to the back of this trailer?"

She nodded.

I was so irritated I forgot to worry about whether she'd been having an affair with Saskia and who had driven the car she had come in.

Saskia was being busy in a small tan kitchen area. The brown and orange curtains at the window beside her waved gently in a draught. I shivered.

"Do you take sugar?" Saskia called.

I wished I did, I felt I needed the comfort of something sweet. "No."

She handed me a mug of steaming hot, deep orange tea. "Saskia," I said, "you're a life-saver."

"Give me your jacket," she said. "Do you want to take off any other clothes? I've got a big sweater here."

I looked around reluctantly for somewhere to put my warm, comforting cup of tea. Margo moved some official-looking papers on a small table to make space. I pulled my soaking sweatshirt over my head and Saskia handed me a large fluffy red sweater.

"Do you need another towel?" she asked. "And I must remember to give you back the shirt you lent me . . ." she looked around her ". . . if I can find it." The place really was a mess. Blankets and clothes lay in heaps on the floor.

"Exactly how far do you two go back?" asked Margo.

Which of us was she jealous of, I wondered. Perhaps she was just irritated because I had broken up a pleasant evening. Perhaps she'd gone at me having seen me with wet hair. Or perhaps it was the sweater.

"We've known each other quite a long time," I said shortly, conscious of the need for client confidentiality. My relationship with Saskia consisted mainly of me representing her in court. It was up to her if she wanted to tell people how we knew each other. I was the lawyer. It wasn't for me to tell them. "Saskia, I do need to talk to you. In private."

"You can talk in front of Margo," she said. "We have no secrets."

"I'd really rather not," I said. What I had to say involved both of us in something very serious. The fact that Latimer was Margo's husband made the need for discretion seem even more important. I wasn't sure exactly who I was protecting, myself, Saskia or even Margo, but it didn't seem right for Margo to hear it.

Margo started to sing softly, "You Don't Know Like I Know" by Sam and Dave. Then Saskia joined in. Their voices fell into the harmonies, and I felt like an unimportant triangle player at the back of the auditorium. Perhaps they weren't having an affair, they were just a singing duo snatching a few moments of rehearsal. Like the Everly Brothers or the Pet Shop Boys.

They stopped singing and smiled at each other.

I shook my head so that they were sprayed with drops from my hair. There was silence.

"Would you like me to step outside for a few minutes?" Margo put her head on one side and raised her eyebrows. She was mocking me.

"In a perfect world, if the sun was shining and there was a beach outside and an azure sea, then I probably would ask you to slip out for a moment or two. But given you're not wearing a wet suit, I won't ask that of you." We glowered at each other.

"It's OK, honestly," Saskia said. "Margo probably knows what it is you're going to say." She paused and pulled me under the green light of the gas lamp. "Is that a black eye?"

"It was," I said. I noticed that the bruising on her face had disappeared. "That's part of it. Look, Saskia, if I made you swear on everything you hold good and dear . . ."

"Friends don't swear," she said.

I had forgotten she was a Quaker.

"OK," I said, "if I beseech you with every fiber of my being . . ."

"Ain't too proud to beg," Margo hummed.

Before they could start singing again, I said, ". . . will you assure me, so that I can go home happy, that you will go and see Kay tomorrow morning? It really is very important to me."

Saskia looked from me to Margo. "I don't like to leave the trailer during the day. Why don't you tell me now?"

"Will you go to see Kay?" She'd have to see her anyway, to make a statement or an affidavit. It occurred to me now she might not go if I told her everything I knew, especially the part about the credit card.

"Is it really that important?"

"Yes," I said.

"Oh, Frankie, you look so serious and caring." She put her arms around me and kissed me on my cheek. "All right, I'll go."

"Thank you," I said. "Are you all right here? It's a bit deserted, isn't it?"

"It's fine. Some of the kids throw stones now and again, but it's OK." She yawned a deep, exhausted, impossible yawn.

"Well," I took a deep breath, "I'd better be off." I looked over at Margo, willing her to say something to stop me. She was gazing at Saskia.

"Are you sure?" Saskia asked with little concern. She yawned again, too tired even to put her hand in front of her mouth.

"Yup," I said, draining the last of my tea. "You look wrecked. You should go to bed."

"Your jacket's still wet," Saskia said, holding it out to me.

"Don't worry," I said, "my vest is waterproof."

She hugged me. "Will you be there tomorrow?" she asked, opening the door of the trailer. The wind caught the door and it crashed against the side of the trailer.

"Probably not," I said. "I have to finish some paperwork."

"Have a good time," Margo called.

"Thank you," I shouted. "You'd better get back inside," I said to Saskia. "You will go tomorrow, won't you?"

"I will," she said, struggling with the door. I jumped boldly into the darkness and as I reached the ground the door slammed shut and I heard the bolts being slid home. I was on my own again in the dark, wet wasteland.

Twenty-six

Sunday Night

I set off cursing myself for my stupidity. I could have sat quietly in the trailer, getting dry and warm, making myself an integral part of the group, making them appreciate my presence. We could have smiled and laughed, even hugged a little. I could have asked Margo to come back with me. Saskia would have driven us to my car, if she could have kept her eyes open long enough. Or Margo and I could have taken this bracing walk together on our own. Then we could have, could have . . .

I had been walking for what seemed a very long time, muttering and cursing, watching for potholes, feeling wetter and colder than ever, when I realized I was walking in the wrong direction. Instead of being on my right, the towers were behind me. I'd been so busy being cross and trying, pointlessly, to protect my boots that I had walked in a circle. I was almost at the trailer again. And then, as I turned to walk in the right direction, I realized I had a stone in my shoe. You might think that my general physical condition was so distressing that a stone in my shoe would have been a small passing irritation. You would be wrong. It was just under the ball of my right foot, exactly where you put pressure as you make a step. I walked a few more steps then stopped to unlace my boot. I shook the boot and laced it back up and began my journey again.

The stone greeted my instep with the warmth of an old friend. It was in my sock.

I was about to express my thoughts to the dark rumbling skies, when I sensed rather than saw the man behind me, looming out of the darkness like a small tree. I hoped I looked as shadowy as he did, but I feared he had been watching me ever since I left the trailer. A cloud slid across the moon as an instinct made me turn toward a clump of bushes. I ducked down, hidden by the scratchy brambles, and watched with satisfaction as the man looked around in some consternation. Of course, I told myself sternly, he was probably out walking his dog and doubtless any minute now a cold damp nose would push itself into my hand and a friendly pooch would introduce himself to me. Or a pit bull would bite my ear off. After a few seconds I realized that the only cold damp nose was mine.

The man began calling, softly at first so that I could hardly hear him, then more forcefully. "Margo? Margo!" This must be the person who had driven Margo to the trailer. What on earth was he doing walking around this cold barren field? Having a pee, I told myself, and hoped he hadn't relieved himself where I was crouching. I wondered who he was and why Margo had brought him all the way here only to leave him outside. Did Saskia know him? Did he pose a threat to her? As Saskia's lawyer, more or less, it was my duty to warn her.

My hand was in my pocket, switching on my cell phone, when I asked myself who I intended to phone, and what exactly I intended to say. Before I had resolved that dilemma—I had no number for Saskia, and it was far too complicated to explain to Lena, which left Kay . . . with all that that entailed—the phone made a beep to tell me it was on, and then another beep, which meant the battery had failed.

At the same time my heart stopped as the man called

out, "Get back in the car!" He ran toward the bushes, heading straight for me, and I clutched the phone—if I couldn't use it to summon help then I could use it to do damage to an ankle. But he carried on, apparently without seeing me, tripping and stumbling as I had done, back toward the trailer. I noticed he was holding a bottle. It looked like a bottle of spirits. Whisky, or possibly brandy, I thought wistfully. Perhaps I had just let my spiritual St. Bernard pass me by. Perhaps not. I started worrying that he might be drinking and driving—oh no—with Margo in the car, then I stopped myself.

I heard Margo's voice calling, "Jack? Jack? Where are you?"

I felt I should stand up and help them out. "Jack, Margo's over there. Margo, Jack would like you to get back in the car."

Then Margo's voice called, "What are you doing out there? Hurry up, let's get going."

I knew she wasn't talking to me, and I felt a wave of bitterness that she hadn't shown me a little of that concern as I was getting ready to leave.

"Where are you?" I heard him call to her. "I thought you were over here. Get back in the car!"

She must have guessed that he had seen me, but she obviously didn't want him to know I was there, or who I was, any more than I did, and so I froze in my uncomfortable position, rather than leaping out, as of course I normally would have done in that situation, with a big hello. "Are you coming?" she bawled at him. "Hurry up!"

"Give me a chance in this wind. Just get back in the car! I won't be long."

She shouted something else but her words were swept away.

After five minutes which seemed like two hours I thought it was probably safe to get up and I made my way, stiff, cold and wet, back to my car. I made sure I was heading in the right direction walking toward the lights on the freeway.

Who was he? Was he the person I had seen going into her building at two o'clock in the morning? What had she said about her reason for coming here? Nothing, I realized. Why was she here? Did she wish Saskia harm?

I turned to look back at the trailer, a small flickering light. Flickering? It shouldn't be flickering. It should be a still, barely visible dot of light. It shouldn't be flickering. Something was wrong. I began running back, jumping through puddles, tripping over weeds, my heart banging against my chest, my lungs wheezing desperately.

As I approached the trailer I could see the fire through the curtains at the back window.

I ran up to the door and pointlessly turned the handle. Saskia had locked it firmly behind me, and I assumed she had locked it again after Margo had gone. I banged on the door, calling "Saskia! Saskia!" The sound of flames crackling and things shifting in the trailer was eerie. Smoke was leaking out of a hole in the window at the front. There was a smell and I wondered if it was the gas. Frantically I banged harder. The door was warm under my fist.

Another voice joined me, screaming "Saskia!" It was Margo, beside me at the door, pulling desperately at the door handle. "Why doesn't it open?" she yelled. "What's happened to her? Why doesn't she come out?"

"I'll go in!" I shouted as a gesture, sure she would stop me.

Instead, she shrieked, "What about the gas canister? Everything's gas in there."

"Where is it?"

"I don't know."

"Where's your boyfriend?"

"He's gone to get help."

"For God's sake," I said, "didn't he have a cell phone?"

"He said he couldn't get a signal."

I leaned down and saw the gas canister in a puddle by one of the trailer wheels to my left. Quickly I slipped under the trailer and moved crabwise over to the canister. It came to me that her friend Jack had read the same articles I had, that you shouldn't dive in to a raging torrent to save a drowning person, you should look around for a long stick. Fortunately, this was not a raging torrent, because there were no sticks around that I could see. In fact, I couldn't see at all, I could only hear the flames crackling above me. The floor at this end wasn't hot yet. I groped for the top of the canister. When I found the round notched plastic top I knew what to do. At last those dreadful summer vacations in Clacton were paying off, just like my mom had said they would. The top was wet, slippery and stiff. My hands were cold and wouldn't bend. I pushed and pulled, all the time hearing the flames above me and Margo pounding on the door, howling Saskia's name.

Suddenly the top gave and I felt rather than heard the hiss as the gas pipe closed. Now I had to get the canister out and away from the heat which was beginning to warm the back of my neck. The canister was heavy, obviously almost full. I leaned against it and knocked it over, looking around for the best way to roll it out. The front of the trailer was closer but there were great lumps of rock and puddles in the way, which threatened to be deep and marshy. The side where Margo was now crouching watching me was farther by about a foot but it looked a clearer path. I crawled around to the other side of the canister and put the full weight of my shoulder against it. It rocked, then slid back into a puddle. I pushed again, using my hands, arms, shoulders. Nothing happened. I turned my back to the canister and stretched my legs out in front of me. I planted my feet against two small tussocks of grass so that now I was almost sitting on the ground, and put the small of my back against the canister, straining against its leaden weight. It moved a centimeter, then bumped against a rock and stopped, then moved some more, and again. My right foot slipped away from the clump of grass and I sat down on a sharp stone and the canister seemed to roll on to my back.

"Are you all right?" Margo called. "Hurry! You must hurry!"

"I know," I shouted back. I moved my foot into position once more and heaved. I could feel the muscles in my shoulders straining, unused to this unnatural exercise. And I could feel the stone in my boot. But more than anything I was aware of the increasing warmth above me. I squeezed my face up and forced myself back into the canister. It moved again and again. And again. And then I was out standing up straight, rolling the canister away from the trailer, gulping down the fresh cold air, then coughing with the smoke from the far window.

Margo had resumed her position at the door, pounding and wailing. It was raining heavily and her skirt was sticking to her legs.

There was still no sign of Saskia. "She was so tired," Margo cried.

"I'm going in!" I shouted to Margo, as she leaned against the door with her arms outstretched, sobbing Saskia's name. I looked around for a stone, dipped down under the trailer again and picked up one of the large heavy pieces of brick I had stumbled against earlier. I held it above my head with both hands, took aim and threw it through the window. The window cracked and I punched pieces of plastic into the trailer. "Help me up!" I called, checking that my jacket was fully zipped up.

Margo unpeeled herself from the door and came toward me.

"Take your coat off!" I shouted. I helped her pull off the short leather jacket and threw it over the fragments of sharp plastic in the window frame. "Put your hands together!"

I grabbed hold of the window frame and put a foot in the stirrup she made me. Painfully I pulled myself up to the level of the frame. "Push!" I bawled. "Where the fuck's that boyfriend of yours?"

"I told you."

"How could you just let him go?" I couldn't believe that she would assume I would come back and do what I appeared to be in the middle of doing now.

"He said it would be safer than him jumping into the trailer."

"Oh great." As Margo pushed me up I looked through the window. I could see nothing but smoke. I swung myself forward into the room. I thought her friend Jack was probably right, but I wanted to prove that I was better than that. For God's sake. "I just want you to know," I called, "this is not the sort of thing I normally do, so don't expect me to do it again." I didn't want her getting any ideas.

"Shut up and get in," she shouted.

"Don't tell me to shut up," I said, and fell into the trailer and onto Saskia.

She was lying on the bench seat under a thin comforter. As I tipped onto her and down on to the floor she did not stir. The whole place was full of smoke, and the acrid smell of melting plastic from the far end of the room caught the back of my throat. "Saskia, Saskia!" I hissed, roughly shaking her body.

Margo's voice rose from outside the window. "Is she there? Have you found her?"

"She's here," I called.

"Is she all right?" Margo shouted. "She must have fallen asleep as soon as I left."

"Well, she's unconscious now. Where's the key?" I

started to cough and snatched up the towel which was still lying where I had left it on the table, and wrapped it around my face. My arms ached from moving the gas canister.

"I don't know. I think she keeps it in the door."

With difficulty I pulled Saskia into a sitting position. She was heavy and I realized she was at least as big as I was. I threw a desperate look around the trailer. The door was invisible because of the smoke and the sound of burning was everywhere. How was I going to get her out of the trailer? It would take me forever to drag her across the floor even if the key was there. There was a sudden roar and flames leapt at the edge of the table, from the direction of the door, catching the pile of clothes and papers. The window was the only way. With my arm I banged out more of the plastic. I tried to think of every episode of *London's Burning* that I had ever seen. I lifted Saskia's right arm and wrapped it around my shoulder and, kneeling on the bench, heaved her up toward the window.

Margo's face was almost on a level with us. "I found a milk crate," she said. As she saw Saskia's face she cried out, "Here, let me take her! I can take her."

I didn't know whether to get out, join Margo on the crate and pull, or stay there and push. Then Margo leapt in the air and caught hold of Saskia's shirt and began pulling. I crouched on the bench and pushed, and between us we pushed and pulled Saskia out of the trailer window till she collapsed with Margo onto the mud of the field.

I climbed onto the window frame and jumped down onto the crate. I banged my shin and looked over to Margo for some sympathy and a bit of gratitude and admiration, but she was cradling Saskia's head in her lap, sobbing at her. "What is going on? What is going on?" She looked up at me. "It must have been kids from those apartments, mustn't it? Some young kids, with nothing better to do . . . ?"

"I don't know," I said. I had seen no kids. "We should get her away from the trailer."

Carefully, Margo slipped her arms under Saskia's shoulders and I took her legs. Together we stumbled a few feet across the mud and puddles and laid her on a patch of grass.

"Is she coming around?" I asked. "We should probably give her CPR." While I was trying to remember how you did it, Margo shuffled backward, gently cradled Saskia's head onto the ground and began to breathe into her mouth.

We crouched in a tableau of wet silence, the burning trailer like a huge campfire beside us, when through the roar of the flames and the howling of the wind came the sound of a siren. A minute later an ambulance appeared beside the trailer. "About time," I muttered to no one in particular. "Where did he go to get them? Brighton?"

Two paramedics, in their dark coats with the luminous yellow strips, lumbered across with bags of equipment. As they knelt professionally beside Saskia, a fire engine arrived and firefighters tipped out of the vehicle calling instructions to each other.

I stood watching the men and women of the emergency services calmly and efficiently deal with the situation. I noticed people looking out of the windows of the tower blocks.

Margo was leaning protectively over Saskia while speaking to the paramedics. I crouched down beside her. "The police will be here soon," I murmured into her right ear, "I think I'll go. You can give them my name if you have to, but I really don't want to see them now."

"OK," Margo said, without asking me what I meant. As I set off back to my car, I felt as bereft as I had before, only this time I ached as if I'd just been put through a workout by a bad fitness instructor. My legs and arms were trembling from exertion. On top of that I was wet, dirty, smoky and probably committing an offense, attempting to pervert the course of justice by leaving the scene. But I was worried how it would look if the police found me and Saskia together at an "incident." Would they think I had caused the fire? Would they think we were in something together? I just wanted to get home.

Had she caused it herself? Fallen asleep with the gas on? But what about that hole in the window in the kitchen? Someone could have put something through that. That's what had happened. Someone had done this deliberately. Someone. I couldn't bring myself to think that it was the person Margo had brought with her. I didn't want to think that about Margo.

As I switched on the ignition and turned the car bumpily around I heard a sound like an animal yowling. I wondered if I had run over the thin cat I'd seen earlier. I didn't care. I looked over toward the trailer, now a mass of bright lights and activity. A siren wailed and I assumed from the passage of a flashing blue light that the ambulance was taking Saskia away. For the moment anyway, she was safe.

I drove away feeling increasingly miserable. I had learned nothing that was any use to me. I still didn't know what Saskia's part in any of it was. It was quite clear that she wouldn't be going to see Kay now, having so thoughtlessly got herself taken to the hospital. And somehow my personal life—if you could describe my so-called relationship with Margo as a personal life—had become tangled up with the small problem of a threatened murder charge which was still hanging over my head.

It was two o'clock in the morning as I drove across the reservoir at Ferry Lane. The wind had dropped and the rain had slowed to a steady drizzle. For once the windshield wipers on my car were working perfectly. I could see the lamplights of three or four fishermen hoping to catch something in the quiet of the night.

I switched on the tape player and listened to "This Old Heart of Mine" by the Isley Brothers. Their hearts had been broken a thousand times. She was here for the day and gone for the week. It was the story of my life. Then I realized I was part of the Tamla Motown mystery and that was some small comfort.

Twenty-seven

Monday

When I got in I went to bed and fell asleep but I kept dreaming about fires and women howling in the night, then I would wake up and find it was me.

When the alarm finally woke me I felt dreadful. My head was throbbing and my body ached. I felt filthy and as I turned over to switch on the lamp I could tell that the sheets were filthy. I was covered in soot and I smelled of melted plastic and fire and mud and something else I couldn't name. I'd gone to bed with my clothes on. I never do that. It's the only rule I have about how I live. I was relieved that I had at least taken my boots off, but the bedroom floor was covered in mud.

I rolled out of bed and staggered into the bathroom. I was shocked by my reflection in the mirror. My face was streaked with soot, and my bangs were frizzy. That was the other smell. Singed hair. I lifted up a clump from above my left eye. What was I going to do now? I thought perhaps I could get a perm, make it all match. Curls can knock years off your age. A perm, mmm . . . It struck me that worrying about my hair after all that had happened last night clearly meant I was in denial. A perm, I mean.

Sadly I picked up a pair of scissors and began to cut off the worst bits while I considered what I had to do. It was all getting out of hand. I should ring Kay. I looked at the clock by the bath. It was seven thirty. Kay would still be at home.

I was halfway across my bangs and my arms ached too much to carry on.

Oh God, could I face a conversation with Kay in this state?

I dragged myself into the kitchen spitting out small curls of singed hair and put the kettle on, then went back into the bathroom and switched on the shower. I was just struggling out of my mud-encrusted jeans when the phone rang. I hopped into the living room, as I heard the kettle click off, and picked up the receiver. It was Kay.

"Where are you?" I said.

"In the office," she said smugly. "I've got to do some paperwork before I go to court. Not like you barristers who don't have to do anything before half past ten."

I ignored her. I knew she wanted me to. "I saw Saskia last night."

"Ah," she said, with something like respect in her voice. "You went there?"

"The way you say that implies you might know where I went."

"The trailer," she said.

"How did you know?!" I shouted, trying to pull off the second trouser leg. I couldn't even sit down, the couch would be ruined.

"She rang me, sometime yesterday morning. There was a message when I got back from seeing you."

"Thank you for not sharing," I said bitterly. "All that way, I went all that way, and you knew where she was all the time. Well, maybe it was a good thing I did go. There was a fire. Or do you know about that too?"

"What do you mean?" she asked.

"I was leaving the place when it burst into flames."

"What about Saskia? Where was she? Is she all right?"

"Yes, she's OK, and surprisingly," I enunciated clearly,

"so am I. I dragged her out of the trailer. She was unconscious."

"Where is she now?"

"In the hospital, I assume. I left when the ambulance arrived."

"Not another scene of crime that you have fled from. Frankie, you are useless."

"And a very good morning to you too."

"What did you go there for? Why didn't you ring me first?"

"I told her to come and see you to make a statement. Why are you ringing me, anyway?"

"I want you to go to court for me this morning."

Her nerve impressed me. "If you remember," I said, "last time I went to court for you, I ended up being arrested for murder."

"I don't think those two things are as closely connected as you seem to believe. Anyway, I just rang Gavin on his cell phone and he said you were the only person available."

"Oh did he?" I asked, adding him to my "Must Kill" list, which now read: ~~P. J. Kramer;~~ Gavin.

"It's a remand, it'll be a fight in a month or so, which you can do if you want to, but this morning it's just a first appearance, for pleas and directions."

"Where?"

"Highbury Mags."

"That night all those years ago when we broke up, didn't I say I would never speak to you again? How has this happened? Not two weeks ago I appeared in that very court building for you and look at me now."

"Pull yourself together. Consider this as shock therapy. Have you had any coffee this morning?"

"No."

"OK, you go and have your shower and your breakfast, indulge yourself, have some white toast, and I'll ring you back in fifteen minutes."

Intimacy between counsel and solicitors can go too far. "Who's it for?" I asked grumpily.

"A really nice woman. Delia, Delia Phelps."

"When I have had my shower and my coffee, I will remember who she is," I said stiffly and ended the call.

As I washed my hair, small bits of plastic from the window and lumps of oil from the bottom of the trailer fell at my feet. It came to me who Delia was.

I dressed in a short black jacket and wide black trousers, had my coffee and some granola to prove that Kay didn't know me as well as she thought, and went back to the phone.

"What is Delia charged with?" I started.

"Section thirty-eight of the Public Order Act 1996."

"Which is . . . ?"

"Making it appear that foods have been tampered with," Kay said. "To be precise, chicken in a supermarket last Monday. Don't ask me to explain how."

"Oh, let me tell you," I said. "She puts little sticky yellow things that say this bird has been tortured onto the plastic wrapping."

"You've seen her work then?"

"I have."

"So that's why she was leaving me messages all day yesterday saying she wants you to represent her," Kay complained. "Oh, dear, maybe you'll have to be a witness."

"Reluctant as I am to say this," I said, "I saw her on Saturday afternoon. The Monday heist, as I believe you people in the criminal world call it, is something I know nothing about. OK. You say Gavin knows you're asking me to do this?"

"He does."

"Funny, I remember distinctly saying to him, 'Only the Court of Appeal and above.' Or is this the House of Lords sitting at Highbury?"

"Yes, something like that. Are you sure you're up to this?"

I thought about it. It would be £50. "Yes," I said.

"I'll fax through the papers to you now, and then you can ring me if anything isn't clear."

"Send me a copy of the section she's charged under," I said. "This is all new to me."

"There's also an article from the *Guardian*," she said, "about someone who fought this kind of case. I'll fax you that too."

As the papers slid out of the fax machine I scanned them quickly then folded them in half and tied an old piece of pink ribbon around them.

I was late. I spent ages driving to Sainsbury's for gas and then I had to drive around and around the streets looking for somewhere to park. I parked so far away from the court building, I might as well have left the car at home.

I was crossing the road by the side of the court at ten twenty-five when a large shiny bottle green late-model car pulled in to a disabled parking place. Something made me check the windshield to see if there was a sticker or any orange sign to indicate some problem on the part of the driver. There was nothing to see.

I stood and watched as a tall man, wearing a good, well-fitting, dark grey suit, swung out of the car. It was Marcus. "So you're disabled, then?" I called across the road to him.

"Very much so," he called back.

"Perhaps I could get a traffic officer to give you some help." I looked around—where are they when you need them?

He turned away from me as he swung a large expensive black bag out of the back of the car.

Two minutes after my arrival on the second-floor landing outside Courts 1 to 5, it became clear that Marcus was prosecuting my case. He must have really irritated Gavin to have been sent on this one. Delia was nowhere to be seen.

"No client?" he asked me with a smirk, as I fretted outside Court 4.

"How long will your case be?" The usher had appeared, staring at her list through half-moon glasses.

"Five minutes maximum," I said. "It's just a remand."

"Well," Marcus drawled, "if the defendant fails to appear, I shall have to request that bail is revoked and a warrant for her arrest issued. So we could be here for some time. Perhaps twenty minutes ... half an hour." Telling the usher we were going to be half an hour was probably putting us at the end of the list. And spelling out what he was proposing to do in court was all for my benefit, to wind me up, put me off balance, but in a way it was quite helpful because it reminded me of the procedure which I had forgotten. I was about to say thank you when he turned to me. "Nice hair," he snorted and walked off to the small glass room used by the Crown Prosecution Service.

I had been right after all. He was just a jerk. But where was Delia? In the unlikely event that we were called on, she would be in real trouble. I felt I was becoming a positive danger for my clients. Once I had a hand in their case they disappeared. At least Saskia had waited till *after* her court appearance.

At ten thirty-five Delia stepped blinking out of the elevator, calmly tucking a bag of bread crusts back into her large cloth shoulder bag.

"Delia!" I said with a frown, walking across to her.

"Hello, dear. I am pleased to see you. I did so want you to represent me." She sighed with contentment and my irritation dissolved. "Am I late? Did I make you worry? There were so many birds to feed." She brushed crumbs from her jacket. "I got quite carried away."

I took Delia back down the corridor to Court 5. Outside there were some empty seats where we could discuss the case. I rapped on the window of the CPS room as I passed and mouthed to Marcus that my client had arrived. We were about to sit down and I was slipping the pink ribbon off the papers and on to my wrist, when my heart quickened as I saw DCI Fletcher emerge from Court 1 and begin walking down the long hall in our direction.

I sensed rather than saw the glint of handcuffs and felt rather than heard the rustle of a charge sheet. This was it, then. They had found new evidence, something bloodstained with my fingerprints on it. Then I shook myself. I hadn't even been there. I didn't do it. Anyway, how on earth could his being here be remotely connected to me? Even if he had heard that Margo had been stabbed and I had been with her, and that there had been a fire at the trailer and I had been with Saskia, how would he have known that I would be here today? I convinced myself his presence had nothing to do with me, and even if it had, what the hell? I put a sneer on my face as I took Delia's arm and we walked toward him.

We passed Courts 5 and 4. He passed Courts 2 and 3.

"DCI Fletcher, what a lovely surprise."

His hair looked terrible, lank and greasy, his shirt was creased and grubby. He didn't look like the man who had leered and oozed his way around the interview room when he was questioning me last Tuesday. As I spoke he started and stared at me as if I were a ghost and he was afraid of ghosts. He struggled with the expression on his face, looking as if he was about to burst into tears, then, without a word, he turned on his heel and walked swiftly back the way he had come. As he passed the CPS room I saw him lift a limp arm in greeting. Then he disappeared back into Court 1. I couldn't think what he would be doing in there. I knew from my perusal of the lists that Court 1 dealt with all the overnight remands, the drunks, the prostitutes, the young men fighting outside pubs—quick matters, mostly pleas of guilty that would not tax the magistrates or the lawyers. Surely not the place for someone as high-flying as DCI Fletcher.

It almost seemed as if he had been distressed by seeing me. As if my presence in the building worried him in some deep and painful way. I wished he'd felt like that at Stoke Newington police station. For a moment I thought of going to look through the small window in the door of Court 1 and making faces at him, but my sense of duty to my current client made me sit down quietly, open my blue notebook and begin to ask her questions.

By eleven o'clock I had taken all the instructions which Delia needed to give me and we were discussing birds. I don't know a lot about birds, except that I rarely see them in my garden, so Delia was doing most of the talking. Suddenly DCI Fletcher reappeared from Court 1. He threw an anxious look in my direction then strode rapidly toward the stairs and disappeared.

Delia interrupted my train of thought. "And how is your little one?'

"Sorry?" I asked.

"Your little friend at home?"

I smiled anxiously at her.

"Your pet. You know, that really was the reason I trusted you enough to tell you—what I told you on Saturday, because you were writing notes to yourself about your animal. On your hand.'

"Ahhh," I said. "Yes, yes." I wished Lena, who was also pet-less, was with us. I could almost hear her describing a world of lolling labradors and Alpo and the people you meet in the park when you go out for walks. I thought hard and found myself talking about mice, since I know some people keep them as pets and I sometimes see them in my kitchen.

At ten to twelve we were called on. The single stipendiary magistrate sat looking bored. The charge was put and Delia pleaded not guilty in a small, sweet voice. She smiled at the magistrate.

I rose to my feet. "I wish to make a submission at this point." I was almost as surprised as everybody else was. "It is a submission that this case should be dismissed now. The papers which I have seen show no evidence that my client intended to cause alarm and anxiety in the general public."

"That is all very interesting, Miss, er, Richmond, but isn't that point better brought out in evidence or submissions at the trial?" the magistrate said. I heard Marcus snorting.

"This case is now about to be set down for a hearing," I plowed on. "Solicitors will have to do preparatory work, interview witnesses, make inquiries and instruct counsel. Counsel will appear at the final hearing. This will all be a burden on the taxpayer."

"I hear what you say, Miss Richmond, and I share your concerns, but the CPS brings the case, these are not matters for the court."

"The case will take up valuable court time," I continued. "My learned friend, who, I understand, suffers from a disability, will be put to anxiety and stress."

"A disability? Mr. Erdridge?"

"I don't know what my learned friend is talking about," Marcus said with a smile, rising to his feet. "I am perfectly fit."

"That is not what my learned friend said to me as he parked his car in the disabled parking space outside court this morning," I said, and sat down firmly. When a judge is sitting and there are lawyers in court there should always be at least one standing, unless the judge indicates otherwise. Marcus was forced to stay on his feet.

"Mr. Erdridge?" the magistrate said.

"Where I parked my car can have no bearing on this case."

"Of course not," said the magistrate. "But, out of interest, is your car parked in a disabled parking space?"

"It may be."

"Do the proprietors have a view on whether or not this case is prosecuted?" the magistrate went on, looking down at his papers.

"I don't know."

"I seem to remember that the last time a similar case came before this court, the supermarket chain itself was reported as saying that the decision to prosecute had been taken by the police. I am concerned about the expenditure of public money on such a case, with such a defendant." I could feel Delia looking older and sweeter behind me, with every word he said. "Do you have a CPS representative, Mr. Erdridge?"

Marcus looked desperately around the courtroom.

The magistrate shuffled his papers. "I will rise to give you time to take instructions from the CPS and possibly even the supermarket as to whether they really wish to continue with this matter."

Ten minutes later Marcus told the magistrate that the CPS did not wish to proceed with the case.

"Very well," said the magistrate, "if you really feel that is the right course. I will record a verdict of not guilty."

Marcus strode out of court without looking at me.

As I began the long trek back to my car, I gained only a very small amount of pleasure from seeing the shiny green car with a ticket on its windshield and a clamp on its front wheel being attached to an old, dirty tow-truck and being driven away.

Twenty-eight

Monday Afternoon

I went home and rang chambers.
"I've finished at Highbury," I told Gavin.
"When are you going back?"
"It was thrown out."
"Well done," he said. "I told you, Frankie, you could have a nice little practice in crime. You've got a feel for it and you could earn yourself some reasonable dough."
"Gavin, I did nothing remotely criminal this morning."
"There's a lot of solicitors who would brief you tomorrow if you'd do crime. Angus Nichol often asks me if you've definitely given it all up. He's always had a soft spot for you."
"Huh," I said, feeling a small glow of pleasure that some people wanted me. Even if they were tired criminal hacks who brushed their hair across their bald patches.
"Look," he said, and I could hear him rifling through the papers on his desk, "I've got a lovely little murder here you could do."
"I'm more than well suited in that area," I told him. If he understood, he didn't say anything.
"All right then, how about a week at the Bailey, possession with intent to supply, no? Ten days' armed robbery at Inner London? You could get yourself a new car. Or at least some new shoes."

"What's wrong with my shoes?" I looked down at the tired suede loafers I was wearing.

"Nothing, just think about it."

"I've thought, and—no."

"All right. Well, you've got no messages and so far you're clear for tomorrow."

"OK, Gavin, I'll speak to you later."

I put the phone down and it rang immediately. When I picked it up no one spoke. I couldn't be bothered to ring call retrieval. I figured I knew where everyone was, everyone that I needed to know about.

In the kitchen, as I made myself beans on toast and a cup of tea, I wished I did more shopping. I was just considering how I could make a rotten pear and a dry tangerine into a delicious and nourishing fruit salad when the phone rang again.

It was Kay.

"Have you read your *Guardian* this morning?"

"I only just bought it on the way home from court, I haven't had a chance."

"Turn to page five."

I picked up the paper from the end of the sofa where I had thrown it. I scanned the Home News page. "Bicycle proposal causes snarl-up in council chamber?" I read out. "Puma spotted on Bodmin Moor? Llama spotted in Stoke Newington?"

"Stop making it up and look at the bottom of the page."

In the bottom left-hand corner was a short article, entitled "Police suicide rates reach all-time high."

"What am I supposed to say? Aah?"

"Read the article."

"Why?" I let my eyes run over the lines. "Unfortunately I know that this isn't about DCI Fletcher," I said, "because I saw him at court this morning. He seemed a little distressed to see me. He hasn't been told to stop harassing me and drop the case, by any chance? Been gently shown the error of his ways?"

She ignored me. "Read the article. It wasn't Fletcher . . . Read the article."

At the end of a description of a recent study into suicide where the police came out tops, was a paragraph saying that a young police officer, DC Ian Rowland, from a North London station had been found dead in his car the night before.

"Oh my God."

"The station's apparently very concerned," Kay said. "It wasn't expected at all. He was quite a high flier."

"Yes, he went through my vegetable rack with skill and dexterity and an obvious enthusiasm for the job. Do you think we drove him to it when we saw him on Sunday?"

"Did you say something to him that I didn't hear?"

"No."

"Then I don't think we drove him to it."

"Oh, what did he have to go and kill himself for?" I wailed. "Now it's just me and Fletcher."

"Was I ever aware that you had such a sensitive side?" Kay asked.

"No, you loved me for my swashbuckling approach to life. And my love of birds. Which was doubtless why you sent me to represent Delia this morning."

"What happened?" she asked.

I gave her a modest description of my personal victory and when I felt I had retrieved my place in her heart I asked whether she had heard from Saskia.

"No. I'm not even sure which hospital she's in. I rang a few of the local ones but no one had any record."

"Which of her names did you give?"

"I tried as many as I knew and also gave them the circumstances. But no one seemed to have heard of her or the fire."

"Oh God," I said. "I've got to find her, just to find out why I can't find her. I don't think she was involved, she can't have been, but she does seem to be doing everything she can to avoid me."

"Setting fire to her own trailer seems a little extreme as an avoidance tactic, even for someone as wild as Saskia," Kay said. "Is there anyone else who might know where she is? Did you ask Delia?"

I hadn't, because it's not good practice to discuss your own possible criminal charges with your client and she hadn't mentioned having heard anything about the fire. She hadn't even commented on my hair. "No."

"Well, let's hope she gets in touch with one of us shortly," Kay said. "There's not much time."

She didn't need to say that. As I put down the phone depression snuggled around me like a security blanket and the beans and the tea were cold. I didn't feel much like eating anyway and I scraped the beans into the trash. It was three o'clock.

I rang Lena. Her answering machine was on, Abdullah Ibrahim playing heart-rending piano chords. "Lena, give me a call," I said. "I feel like shit."

She rang me half an hour later. I was standing looking out of the window. "What's up?" she asked, her voice full of concern.

"Oh, Lena, this is all so terrible. Everyone around me is having their life threatened. Nothing's been happening to you, has it?"

"Apart from very nice things, no. You sound awful. Do you want me to come around? I could give you half an hour now or, let's see . . . dinner—oh, I've got a meeting of my Street Life group."

"How long will that take?"

"Hard to say, there's a new element who are complaining about the prostitutes. The women need a bit of support. I should be able to make it by seven thirty."

"How about the Russian restaurant on High Street? My treat?"

"But I'm meant to be giving you the support."

"You give the support, I'll give the money."

"You're on. By the way," she said, "do the Shangri-Las still make records?"

"I don't think so."

"Thank God."

Twenty-nine

Monday Evening

I took an empty table by the window and ordered two vodkas, one for me, the house vodka, and one for Lena, Smirnoff. After two minutes mine was finished and Lena hadn't arrived, so I drank hers by way of a taste test. Then I ordered two more, one cherry and one lemon. Which I drank. In view of my personal circumstances, in particular my collapsing legal career, I thought if she didn't come I would just work my way, sensibly and methodically, through their vodka menu and then write it up. And I would be well on my way to starting a new life as a restaurant critic.

"The room was small, with only five tables, each covered by a red-and-white checked tablecloth and bearing a flickering, dripping red candle. The service, by young men with thick moustaches, was friendly and efficient. The vodkas . . ."

"Frankie!" Lena was leaning over the table to kiss me. "Am I that late?" There were four glasses on the table. Three of them were empty. She didn't know the half of it. The waiter had removed the first round. "I'm sorry I'm late." She was flushed and breathless. "I had to give a lift to a woman from the meeting." She paused. "Nicky, you know, *Nicky*—I've mentioned her."

"You have."

"I dropped her off near the police station."

"Ah."

"I asked her if she was in any trouble. I mean, taking a working woman to a police station doesn't seem right."

"No," I said.

"She said, '*I'm* not in any trouble,' and I wondered what poor idiot was." She was shrugging off her leather jacket and gesturing to the waiter at the same time. She hung the jacket on the back of a chair.

"Anyone who says they're not in trouble outside a police station usually is," I said.

"Do you think so? Oh, sorry, you probably know more about that than I do." She pulled out the chair and sat down. She ordered a vodka for herself and none for me. She gave me a piercing look. "You should get Sophie to do something with your hair," she said.

The waiter placed a basket of bread on the table and Lena put in a request for a large carafe of tap water.

"Tell me some more about Nicky," I said, not feeling ready to share my latest news.

"There's not a lot to tell," she said coyly. "Janet, who runs the Street Life group, as far as it can be run, the one who told me about the demo—which by the way went very well, got quite a lot of coverage and no arrests. Anyway, she said that Nicky's dangerous, a bit of a heart-breaker, but honestly"—she laughed that irritating, intimate laugh again—"I don't know if we'll get that far, not if she carries on wearing those outfits."

"Am I meant to ask what you mean?" I had a slight headache.

"Well, would you wear a fleece shirt with Capri pants?"

"I would never wear Capri pants," I said, "but that's just me. And she probably needs the fleece to keep warm at work."

"Of course." Lena was delighted.

"Whatever, you're very chirpy about it," I said. "Unless you had alcohol or other substances at the meeting?"

She grinned. "Oh no, we're very serious. However. . ." She put her hand back in her backpack and produced a red pen and a very small notepad which she put on the table. "Tonight," she said grandly, "I am a woman with a purpose."

"And does the notebook play a part in this?"

"It does." She cleared her throat as if she was about to deliver a prepared speech. "It seems to me that you are going through something of a crisis in your life at the moment and the way you are attempting to deal with it is through wine, women and song. Rather unsuccessfully," she added.

"Song?"

"Song. I was thinking of Margo, actually, or have you forgotten her?"

"No." A sudden image of Margo in the tight red dress, breathing "Me and Mrs. Jones" into the microphone, made my attention drift.

". . . flow chart for you," Lena was saying.

"What?"

"We could set out all the things that have happened in a clear, organized way and see what patterns emerge."

Her notepad was 3 x 5.

"And what's the purpose of all this?"

"Think of my notebook as a computer. Into which I shall put all the information we have, and out of which will come the answer."

"You don't know much about computers, do you?"

"Trust me," she said. "How many headings do you think we need?" She pulled a blue pen out of her jacket pocket. "I'd say two."

"What kind of headings do you mean?" Everything was a little unclear.

"The death of Kevin Latimer, that's one heading." She wrote *Latimer* on the top left-hand side of the page and drew a line down the middle. "And the stabbing of Margo is the other one." She wrote *Margo* on the top right half. Then, writing the words *Police View* in the margin, she said, "What do the police think?"

I hesitated. "Let's see what we think first," I said.

Lena turned the page, drew a line down the middle and wrote *Our Theories* in the margin.

"Perhaps we should write down the facts as we know them."

Lena started another page.

"Before you draw any lines," I said, "there may or may not be a third heading. Or, come to think of it, a fourth. Or a fifth."

Lena shuddered but said nothing. Her pen was poised above the paper.

"Last night I went to a trailer . . ." I swallowed. "Saskia was staying there and there was a fire. Saskia was in the trailer."

Lena's eyes widened. "Is she all right?"

"I think so."

"Where is she? What happened?"

"I don't know," I said. "Kay's dealing with that. Let's get back to the computer."

She drew three lines. "And there's your black eye as well," she said. "And the break-in at Kay's office." She sighed. "This is hopeless. I think the computer is about to explode."

"Crash," I said, and took a large mouthful of water. "We don't know that any of them are connected," I said hopefully.

"Of course not, that's what we're trying to deduce. But, Frankie, knowing your social calendar as I do, I must say you haven't had this much excitement in your life since you and Kay had a stand-up argument in B&Q over the color for your living-room walls."

"Let me just explain that B&Q thing," I said.

"I know, I know," she said. "You and pastels."

"They make me bilious."

"I know."

"Pale green is not a color I could live with. Of course, the trouble was, Lena," my head slid into my hands, "I was not a person Kay could live with."

"Now you're getting maudlin," she said. "Concentrate!" She clicked her fingers sharply under my nose. "Strange and unusual things are going on at the moment," she said patiently.

"Margo," I said, nodding my head, "is certainly unusual. For me. She's gorgeous and she seems to be attracted to me."

"What is her involvement in all of this?" Lena was picking up small pieces of bread and nibbling them. "Because, if you think about it, when Saskia said, 'the singer not the song,' she could have meant Margo. The singer."

"Oh no, no," I groaned. "Oh God, I might as well tell you: Margo was married to Latimer."

Lena stared at me. "This is all getting a bit too close for comfort."

"She told me on Sunday, when I was driving her home from the hospital. After she'd been stabbed. After she'd had lunch with me. Before I left Saskia in a burning trailer. Oh God, do you think I should taste that bread before you do, in case something's been done to it?"

"Like what?"

"I don't know, it could have been sprinkled with rat poison or injected with arsenic."

"Let's inject this conversation with a touch of reality here," Lena said, putting her piece down. "Is it true? Is she lying?"

"Why would she lie?"

"Attention seeking."

"In the middle of a murder investigation?"

"That's exactly when people do it."

"I honestly don't think so," I said. But what did I know? "Margo said she thought the fire in the trailer was kids, but I didn't see any."

"She sounds a bit desperate. What's her game? What's she got to hide? Oh, Frankie"—she looked at me with concern—"I don't think you should have any more to do with her. I'm worried."

"But she was the one who got stabbed. If that's part of her game, she's playing by dangerous rules."

"Even more reason why you should steer clear of her."

"OK, all right, yes," I said.

"Plus she just seems to make you unhappy."

"Not all the time," I said. "Can we change the subject now?" I took a long drink of water. "Kay seems to think I'm in real trouble with DCI Fletcher. Or at least, she wants me to think that I am. So that I take it seriously."

"Is she giving you a hard time again?" Lena wrote something in the book and turned back a few pages. "Shall I ring her up and speak to her?"

"I'll take a rain check," I said. "I may have to cash it if she really drives me crazy."

"Is that everything?"

"You want everything? DC Rowland, who I spoke to yesterday, has just committed suicide."

"Oh, oh, oh," she said in three different tones of voice. "Well, that absolutely can't have anything to do with you. Can it?"

"He was a bit edgy when I spoke to him, but I thought that was just the color of his hair."

"Bad hair dye? Oh, sorry, I didn't mean to say that."

"No, it's red, and he blushes—blushed. Always looked worried. I thought he was afraid of Fletcher."

"Does Fletcher know you were at the trailer?"

"I don't think so. How would he?"

"The other one, the dead one, could have told him . . ."

"I didn't tell him."

"Did he follow you?"

"I don't think so. He didn't know I was going."

"They could have been watching your apartment."

"They'd have had to wait for ages while we had dinner and watched the film and everything." Surely they hadn't done that. "Of course, the best way to find out what DCI Fletcher knows would be to ask him personally," I said, as I realized that DCI Fletcher was walking down High Street toward the restaurant. "And he's obviously got the same taste in women as you," I went on as he firmly guided a woman past some drunks ambling the other way. "Capri pants," I mused, "were they ever really fashionable?"

"That's Nicky!" Lena sprang up from her seat. "Is that Fletcher? What on earth is she doing with him? Are they coming in here?"

The couple walked past the window of the restaurant, two feet away from us, as we stood and stared. Lena pressed her face hard against the window to follow their progress as they walked on and out of sight. "Can I go out there?" she asked me. Her face had gone white.

"No, you can't."

She sat down again. "She has to talk to police officers," she said carefully, almost to herself. "It's part of the job. It's got nothing to do with your mess."

"Thank you," I said. "Does she go to court much?"

"A bit. Why?"

"He was at the magistrates' this morning. I wondered what he was doing there."

"She's a prostitute. They get a hard time from the police."

"Perhaps we should write that down too," I said. "DCI Fletcher snatching other people's love interest. Now you see what I'm up against. Do you think she'll be all right?"

"Yeah, she's tough. She's the toughest woman I know."

"Hmm," I said.

"You should hear her at meetings. She's a really good mediator. Tonight she made a deal with the tenants about the elevators in one of the buildings. Everyone agreed to try and use them as elevators, not bedrooms or bathrooms." She shook her head, remembering the meeting. "She's so good, and the diamond in her tooth flashes." She drew a breath. "Is Fletcher just behaving like a police officer or is he a real bastard?"

"He likes seventies music, I don't know what you can draw from that."

"You like the Shangri-Las," she said accusingly.

"I like the lyrics and the orchestration."

"Why is there no volume control on my answering machine?" she asked. "Anyway, I like some seventies music. David Bowie in his early period." She liked the mime.

"I wouldn't have said Bowie was Fletcher's cup of tea, but, even if he was, I'm not sure that makes him a lovable, friendly guy."

"Nicky obviously thinks he is," she said and snorted. "I'm going to need a bigger book." She flicked the pages. "I can't keep writing 'turn back to page three', 'continued on page six'."

"That notebook probably isn't the most efficient way to do this job, although I'm extremely grateful that you are doing it. But then, Lena, you're an artist, not a flow chart maker."

She smiled. "But I'm not a bad flow chart maker, am I?" She held out the book for my inspection. It looked like something by Paul Klee, all lines and circles.

"No." Sometimes I really enjoyed being with Lena.

An hour later, after we had eaten caviar on black bread and drunk one more small vodka, Lena's notebook was almost full and we had aired the main issues arising from the events of the last ten days. Then we gossiped about the people in her Street Life group, with a lot of references to Nicky, which Lena enjoyed, and I told her about my morning in court, with a few references to Marcus, which I enjoyed. Lena said it was important to maintain morale through such a depressing exercise.

"So, all right," she said, stifling a yawn, "here are your tasks. You and Margo have got to do some serious talking. You need to find out (one) about Saskia and Margo, (two) who stabbed Margo, (three) about Margo and her friend Jack, and (four) find out who killed Latimer."

"Oh, but isn't there anything else I can do?" I said.

"No, I think that's everything."

"And just remind me what you'll be doing?"

"Keeping notes. Polishing the computer." She rubbed the cover of the notebook. "I can't even ask Nicky about Fletcher—well, not tonight, she doesn't like me to ring her when she's working."

"That sounds like an old married couple," I said. "Exactly how long has this been going on?"

"Long enough. Frankie, she's fabulous."

"Is she?" I said, hoping it was true, not believing it, feeling old and skeptical.

"I know you're thinking, 'Does she have relationships with police officers?' "

"I don't think I am." I was thinking about going to bed. I forced my eyelids to stay open. "I suppose I'm wondering, with her job, if she's too cynical about sex and love to have a relationship."

"Oh, but she's quite romantic. She does nice things, she gives me flowers and leaves sweet messages on my machine, quiet messages."

"I get your point," I said. "But maybe that is the question—does she have relationships with police officers?"

"I think she's had one with Fletcher. But I thought it was over," she added worriedly.

"In her job, doesn't she just have to be tough and gruff,

lean and mean, and all other kinds of fairly negative adjectives that rhyme?" I said, trying to be reassuring.

"Like sexy and reckless?" Lena asked. "That's dissonance."

"I don't think I can keep up this level of witty banter." But it sounded like "winter batter." "Oh God," I groaned, "what's happening to me?" I rocked my head on to the table.

"You need a good night's sleep," Lena said, with concern. "You've got to look after yourself."

Speaking through my arms, I said, "Why has this happened to me? What have I done wrong? Have I made wrong life choices? Should I have stayed in Colchester? Surely not. Was it food? I know I should have eaten proper breakfasts. I should have had yogurt in my life. A regular lifestyle. Exercise."

"We could all do with that. But, it's not too late to start," Lena paused. "Why don't you come swimming with me tomorrow?"

I raised my head. Lena and I hadn't been swimming since we cruised an evening class for lady intermediates three years before. "Where?"

"Highbury. We can do two or three lengths and get lots of positive endorphins whizzing around our bodies, then go to the caff and have a slap-up breakfast."

"Egg, sausage and beans," I said dreamily. "All right, what time?"

"Seven thirty." She looked at me with concern. "Are you sure you're up to this?"

I sat up straight. "Of course!"

Thirty

Later Monday Evening

I walked back to the apartment as briskly as I could, anxious to get to bed. The rain was still falling and the streets were emptying. When I got home I had one message.

It was Margo. "Frankie, ring me. Doesn't matter how late it is."

It was ten to eleven. Lena's advice echoed in my head. I rang Margo. We had a brisk, business-like conversation.

"Saskia's fine," she said. "She's somewhere in Essex—where is Broomfield?—and she's coming out of the hospital tomorrow. She's fine, just smoke inhalation. Although the trailer's a write-off. Will you come around?" she said. "Now?"

I was up, the apartment was cold, the car was just outside. I drank a long glass of water, clipped the other half of my bangs, went back outside and drove to her apartment.

I knocked on the door with some trepidation. What kind of meeting would this be? I remembered her anguish as she howled Saskia's name the night before. Would we talk about Saskia? What they were to each other? Where I came in the scheme of things? That could be fairly depressing. And even if we didn't talk about Saskia, what if the children were in the apartment? That would pretty much write off the chance of anything else happening. Anything wild and wonderful.

As soon as she opened the door I knew things would go well. She was wearing a figure-hugging black dress and high black mules and she smelled like she had just come out of an expensive bath. She stood waiting as I ran my eyes over her body. "Like what you see?" she asked. She had on bright red lipstick and her blonde hair was spiky with gel. She looked amazing. I love women who love their own bodies.

"Yes," I said.

She took my hand. "The kids are at their nan's for the night. So we have the place to ourselves."

With a lurch my stomach realized she was leading me straight into the bedroom. I blinked in the dim light. There were candles dotted around the room, their effect doubled by the mirror leaning against the wall at the end of the bed. "Night-lights," she said.

"Night-lights last all night. Are we going to be here a long time?" I asked.

"That depends on you, doesn't it?"

"Does it?"

By the bed were two glasses and a bottle of something that looked like champagne. "Cava," she said, following my glance.

"Does that put more or less pressure on me to drink it out of your shoe?" I asked.

"You might not get much with these." She sat on the bed and swung her leg up. The mule dangled delicately on the scarlet nails of her toes.

"Let's give it a try," I said.

Skilfully she unwound the foil and wire holding the cork in place and the bottle opened with a small pop and a wisp of smoke. Silently she poured the Cava into two glasses. "To us," she said.

I raised an eyebrow. "To us?" I repeated.

If she heard the question in my voice she ignored it. She slipped off the mules, saying "We'll get to those later," and curled onto the dark cotton cover on the bed. "Do you want to make love to me?" she asked.

"I always want to make love to you," I sighed.

"It didn't feel like that last night."

"Strange as it may seem," I said, sitting on the end of the bed, "even last night, when I was crawling into a burning trailer and I wanted to shout at you for being there and for caring so much about Saskia, I did, underneath it all, want to make love to you."

She stood up. "Help me with this," she said. She turned her back to me and I reached up and unzipped her dress. Delicately she slipped it off her shoulders, shimmied it over her hips and down to her feet, then stepped out of it, like a rich, full-bodied Venus. She was wearing red lace underwear. Her legs were bare. I reached for the back of her neck and pulled her down onto the bed.

An hour or so later when we had finished most of the Cava and other sensual things, she looked at her watch. "I must go and buy some cigarettes," she said.

"Oh, don't go," I moaned. "Make today the day you start giving up the habit."

"No, no, I must . . . must have a cigarette." She pushed back the comforter and slid her legs out. I ran a finger down her back. "Mmm" she sighed.

"I tell you what," I said, "why don't I go and make us a cup of tea? And then we can both go out for the cigarettes together."

"OK," she said, leaning across to kiss me softly on the mouth. I smelled her rose perfume.

As she moved back under the comforter I pushed it away on my side and shivered out of bed. I threw on a T-shirt and tiptoed across the bare floor into the kitchen. I clicked the switch and a fluorescent light flickered into life.

It was a small kitchen with neat white cabinets around

the walls. On the work surface was a kettle and a tin I assumed would hold tea bags. On a small gate-leg table was Margo's bucket-shaped handbag. On top of the bag was an unopened pack of cigarettes. "Fantastic," I said aloud. I made the tea and put the two mugs on a tray. I put the pack of cigarettes on the tray next to the mugs, to show her that a midnight dash was totally unnecessary. I looked around for a box of matches to provide her with a complete service and so that she wouldn't have to get out of bed again. I pulled open drawers and found kitchen towels, silverware, plastic bags and no matches. And then I saw the photo.

I pulled it out of the drawer. I love other people's photos. I stared at the picture of two women. It was a photo of Saskia and Margo, Saskia's arm was round Margo's shoulders. The photo looked old. Saskia was younger, her hair the short combat style it had been when I first met her. On the back was written "1993." Six years ago.

Was it childish of me to be jealous of that photo? Infuriated by Margo, again. She hadn't told me she had known Saskia for that long. In the photo they looked so warm, so affectionate, so fond of each other.

What was going on? There was something in the photo, something I had seen in Margo's face last night, something primal, basic, essential.

And why had she said she needed to go out in the middle of the night to buy cigarettes when she already had a full pack? Who would choose to go out on a night like this? A nicotine addict, perhaps, but this addict had a full pack in the house and addicts always know how much stuff they have left.

I'd had enough. I walked into the bedroom.

"Just tell me," I said, "just tell me what your relationship is with Saskia."

She looked at me wearily, her face soft and shadowy in the flickering light of the candles. "I'm her mom."

Thirty-one

Monday Night/Tuesday Morning

Slowly she got out of bed and put on a dark terry cloth robe. She guided me back into the kitchen. Without looking at each other we sat down at the table under the harsh fluorescent light, facing each other across the tray with the cooling cups of tea. The deep navy of the robe made her look clear and definite.

"You're her mom . . ." I repeated. I was doing all kinds of calculations.

"I had her when I was very young," she said, partially reading my mind.

More importantly, I was trying to remember if I had ever slept with Saskia. I didn't think so, since it is never a good idea or even professional to sleep with clients, but there had been a night after one of the hearings when we had won and Saskia was no longer my client, and we had all gone out and got completely wasted and I missed my train home and I couldn't remember, as I stood staring at Margo, where I had slept that night.

"You've never slept with her," she said. "I asked her specifically."

"But your first lesbian experience," I said carefully, "who was that with again?"

"Ash, I told you."

"Ash? The woman in the bar?"

"Yes, Ash, the bartender, electrician and all-round handy person."

"With the studs?"

"Mmm, yes," she said, with rather too much pleasure in her voice.

"You mean if I could put up shelves or had a stud in my nose, I might have more luck?"

"In your tongue," she said.

"Oh." I said. "Oh."

"But, you don't need more luck, do you?" She smiled at me.

"Don't I?" I smiled back.

"No." She gave the word three syllables.

I looked at her.

"I'd say your position has been guaranteed by your own special talents and skill."

"Oh yes?" I said. The conversation was heading back to my favorite topic. But we had business to discuss. Reluctantly I made myself think about Latimer. "Oh my God," I said. "If you're Saskia's mom, that means Kevin was Saskia's dad!" He looked too young, too thin, too mean.

"No, no, Saskia's dad went long ago. Kevin was the girls' dad."

There were too many relationships here for my liking. I wasn't sure if the close tie between Saskia and Latimer made it more or less likely that she would kill him. Patricide is not common. A young woman on her own kills her stepfather? Not likely. But now a new nightmare was coming to me. Maybe Lena was right, maybe Margo *was* involved in Latimer's death. Margo and Saskia.

"Do you know who killed him?" she asked me in a flat tone. She reached for a bowl of sugar and put two heaping teaspoons into her mug and stirred it. I didn't know she took sugar in her tea.

"I wish I did. At the moment the police seem to think it was me."

"Why would you kill him?" she asked. She didn't express surprise, she didn't ask me why on earth the police might think so, how I even knew him, or if I knew him at all.

"My motive would appear to be that he beat me up the other night," I said. "And when his body was found in Waterlow Park, he was hugging my car license plate."

"Did you do it?" she asked, almost hopefully.

"Don't you start!"

"I wouldn't hold it against you."

"That's a comfort," I said, "but not a legal defense. I didn't kill him. But it may interest you to know that I have been arrested and am helping the police with their inquiries." I felt myself on the verge of tears. I knew I was tired but there was something else. Her responses weren't right.

"That's terrible," she said flatly.

"I know it is. Do you know who did it? Or who might have done it?"

"I've got some ideas." She took a mouthful of tea then said, "This is cold." She walked over to a cabinet and took out a new half-bottle of whisky and two tumblers. She poured two large shots and pushed one toward me. "To the life ever after," she said, raising her glass.

I sat still while she swallowed the whisky and poured herself another.

"Is that why you came to the trailer?" she asked. "You think Saskia's got something to do with it?"

We stared at each other in silence, then she said, "Don't tell me you think *I've* got something to do with it?"

"I don't think anything, I don't know anything," I said. "It's just a mess."

She took a deep breath, like a sigh, as if she was about

to say something. And then the phone on the wall jangled. She shuddered, then leaned across the table to pick up the receiver. "Hello?" she said uncertainly. "Yes? . . . Oh no . . . When? . . . Why? . . . No, no, I haven't heard anything." She replaced the receiver, raised her glass and poured the whisky down her throat. Her voice was unsteady as she said, "That was the hospital. Saskia left about two hours ago. They wanted to know if she was here."

"She's determined not to meet up with Kay," I said lightly, but Margo's face was tense and grey. She hugged her empty glass into her stomach. "Saskia didn't do it, did she?" I asked quietly.

"For God's sake!" she roared at me. A strange expression slid across her face, fear, despair and something almost sly. Then she whispered, "I—I don't know. Anything's possible. But why has she left the hospital? They didn't know whether she'd gone on her own or if someone was with her. Do you think she really is trying to avoid making a statement? Do you think she's got something to hide?"

"I don't know. I don't feel I know anything about Saskia."

"Why would she just disappear? She's not well enough to leave the hospital."

"I'm sure there's a simple explanation," I said. "Don't worry. Anyway, why would she kill him?"

"She'd have a load of reasons, from when we all lived together as a family—you must see it all the time in your job."

I looked at her, not wanting to assume anything.

"She was twelve when we got together. I didn't realize. She always tried to protect me, protect the girls. For years. She took a lot of abuse—physical, shouting. And he never stopped, even after we separated. The last time was a couple of weeks ago. He came steaming in here one morning." She was looking straight ahead, her glass still cradled against her waist. "I wasn't here, I was taking the kids to school, I just got back for the end of it. They were in here, he was holding her by the throat, up against the table, screaming at her that she was a pervert and she was molesting his kids, which couldn't be further from the truth. They really love her. Then he belted her so hard, a punch to the face, she was trying to shield herself, and I was shouting, 'I'm calling the police,' and he says, 'Go on then, go on. I've got friends, don't forget. You'll lose those kids as soon as you like.' And I knew what he meant, and that he meant it. Then Saskia said she knew what he'd been doing so we'd see, but she tripped on the chair and fell on the floor and he was kicking her and I was dragging him off. It was terrible. I'll never forget it. Then he told her to get out. She said to me, 'I'll only go if you want me to.' Her eye was all puffed up, so I made him let me wash her face." Tears dribbled down her cheeks.

"She had to leave, it was the only way to calm him down. I didn't dare call the police. She said to me, 'Will you be all right?' and I knew I would be, so she left. He left about thirty seconds later. That was the last I saw of him. But he'd really worried me, saying that about the kids. I started to ask around, I rang up that Lesbian Line, and I got your name."

"Did you?" I said. "It obviously didn't do you any good."

Margo was shaking her head from side to side, her hand over her face.

"That still doesn't mean she killed him," I said. "There's nowhere near as much murder of abusing bastards as there should be." I pulled a tissue out of my pocket and handed it to her. "And Saskia wouldn't have tried to drop me in it by putting my license plate with the body." Or leaving his credit card in my record collection.

"Did she know it was your license plate? She could have . . . done it, then just seen the plate there, and, I don't know, tucked it into his arms, to give herself a bit of time, to take the heat off. What was your license plate doing there anyway?"

"He bashed into my car. He must have picked it up."

"Oh yes, he'd love that. Keep it in case it came in useful, to make trouble or something." She groped for the pack of cigarettes on the tray.

"But Saskia can't have killed him. Look, you said last night that you thought it was kids from those apartments who set fire to the trailer? But you don't really think that, do you?"

She was scratching at the cellophane.

"Doesn't it seem likely that it's tied up with all of this?" I went on. "It's too much of a coincidence. And you being stabbed."

"That could have happened to anyone."

"Anyone who looked like Saskia from the back." Or her mom, I thought.

"Oh God," she said, and unsteadily put a cigarette in her mouth and struck a match. "You mean, if someone else started that fire, it could be the same person who killed Kevin. And who stabbed me."

I did mean that, but as it turned out I was wrong.

She lit the cigarette and inhaled deeply. "But that means someone deliberately tried to kill Saskia. And if they didn't kill her last night, perhaps they're out there now looking for her," she said slowly. She began worrying her throat with her hand. "Perhaps they've found her. But perhaps it means she didn't kill him," she whispered, almost to herself. "Why would they want to harm her?"

"Maybe it's just that Saskia knows something she shouldn't know," I said. "I mean, why had Kevin been following her? He was following her around in the last few days before he died. And me too," I added.

"Oh, that's nothing. He got pleasure out of stalking

her." Margo ignored the part about me. "He always hated Saskia."

"Who else might have killed him?" I interrupted her. "Who had a motive?"

She coughed with laughter. "Lots of people. Me, for a start. All those people he pissed off when he was working in the licensing department. But that was years ago." She stubbed out her cigarette and reached for the pack.

"Why were you going out just now?" I asked as she lit another. "All that nonsense about needing cigarettes."

"I wanted to make some calls. I had to ring the hospital. I didn't want you to know I was so worried about her. I thought you might decide to leave if you knew I was her mom." She blew smoke up to the ceiling. "Being someone's mom makes you sound about sixty-five."

"How old are you?"

"Not sixty-five," she said.

"Anyone would have been worried," I said. "I was worried."

"You wouldn't have gone out at two o'clock in the morning to ring the hospital."

"Maybe not," I said. "But anyway, your age isn't important. Except that I like a woman with experience. And I very definitely like you." Even as I said it, I wasn't sure if that was true. Desire, lust, even love seemed more apt to describe what I felt.

I moved my chair around to her side of the table and put my arm around her. She leaned her head against my shoulder and I breathed in the scent of her: soap and sex and cigarettes and whisky.

"They kicked him out of the job, in the end," she said, not looking at me.

"You said," I replied. "Why, what did he do? I thought local authority jobs were the safest you could get."

"He was involved in so much . . . stuff. It was his own

stupid fault, but he was very bitter about it all. He blamed Saskia. He thought she'd snitched on him." She was relaxing into my arm and I was beginning to think we might be able to move back into the bedroom to take advantage of the night-lights when she stiffened and said, "But where is she now?" She sat up straight. "I've got to make another phone call. I'll do it in the other room. I won't be long. Hang on, I'll get you something to pass the time." She left the kitchen and returned with a photo album. "Here, see what she was like when she was growing up. Me too."

She walked into the living room. Idly I flipped through the album, looking at baby Saskia and her sweet young mother, squinting into the sun in all the usual places. Saskia in a stroller, on Margo's hip, with friends at a birthday party. Then I heard Margo's voice rise in anguish, "We had a deal!"

Silently I closed the album and stood up. I moved along the corridor. Margo was hissing, "And you had better have a bloody good explanation!" She slammed the phone down and was in the hall before I could move back.

"I was just coming to say goodbye," I said. "I've got to get up early. I'm going swimming with Lena."

She stared at me as if she didn't recognize me. "OK," she said, "OK."

"Is there anything you want me to do about Saskia?"

"No . . . no thanks."

I dipped back into the bedroom while she stood silently in the doorway. I threw on my clothes, slipped my feet into my loafers, and grabbed my jacket. I brushed past Margo. "Bye," I said. We moved our heads toward each other and I grazed her cheek with my lips.

I ran down the steps and out into the night. I felt so bleak and confused about what I'd heard that I switched the radio on to a Dutch station and drove home not recognizing a single piece of music they played.

Thirty-two

Tuesday Morning

Lena was already waiting outside the pool as I parked my car at a meter that I wouldn't have to pay for because it was too early. She looked as dreadful as I felt, but she was smiling.

"It's closed," she said. "The pool's shut. Let's go and have breakfast."

I got back to the apartment feeling virtuous because I'd tried to go swimming, and satisfied by the plate of fried bread, tomatoes and scrambled egg I had eaten.

On the door mat was a letter from the bank. I allowed myself two seconds of hope that they were telling me I had wrongly added up the checks I had paid in three weeks ago and instead of £1,500 the true figure was £15,000. In fact they were simply informing me of what I already knew, that I had exceeded my overdraft and hadn't asked them. In a cloud of disappointment I took the letter into the shower with me. I had never realized how fast a good shower can dissolve a piece of thick writing paper. I just had time to realize that they were inviting me to make an appointment to discuss my financial affairs before the shreds of paper dissolved down the drain.

Before making the call I dressed in court clothes, switched on my computer and spread the Morris papers across my desk, so I could tell the bank manager with confidence that I was in the middle of a big Court of Appeal case which would bring in a tidy sum. I wouldn't tell him that on the few occasions when I had previously tried to go to the Court of Appeal I had rarely got past the initial application for leave to appeal and as a result only ever earned about £100. Although this is not bad money, as Lena would say, for not even going to court, I felt the bank manager would want more.

As I read through the papers my spirits began to rise. This case might well earn me a lot of money. There was more to it than I had thought. The downside, I realized, as I gazed at the remaining three inches of documents that I had yet to read, was that I was going to have to do more work than just quoting "Re R." I would have to go back to the library, possibly look at text books, even refer to ancient parliamentary debates. I groaned. It was overwhelming.

I decided I needed fresh air so I went out and bought a *Guardian*. Then I bought some parma ham and a piece of roquefort at the delicatessen. The sun was shining and there was no wind and it was the right time for coffee, so I strolled into Church Street to the Blue Legume. I sipped the coffee through the creamy froth, skimming the paper. Mother and two children found dead, father's body found, police not looking for anybody else. TV viewing habits, the average person watches twenty-eight hours a week. Think how much they must miss. And an article on police corruption caused by poverty, written by a journalist I had once met at a party who had talked to me as if I was a very interesting person till he realized I wasn't Helena Kennedy.

When I got back to the apartment it was lunchtime. I needed to speak to someone, to ring someone, to have human contact. I didn't think the bank manager would be able to satisfy those needs so I rang chambers.

Jenna answered. "Hello!" she said in her bright voice. "How are you?"

"I'm fine," I said, surprised. The clerks never engaged in this level of friendliness.

"Do you want to speak to Gavin?" she asked.

She put me through. "Gavin," I said, "is Jenna always this cheerful?"

"Yeah," he said, pleased. "I told you, we've made an excellent choice, for once."

"Well," I said, "she does seem very nice."

"She's nice and quick," he said. "She picks things up really fast. I was just about to ring you, actually."

"Does this mean that a check has come in? A big, juicy check?"

"There is a check here for you."

"Gavin, you're wonderful."

"It's for sixty pounds."

"Sixty pounds," I said in disgust. "That's no good to me. I need zeros, lots of zeros. What was it for, anyway?"

"Something you did ages ago," Gavin told me. "But that wasn't what I wanted to say. I was going to remind you about the management committee meeting tonight."

"Oh no," I said, realizing I had no other social engagement to justify my non-attendance. "I think my cold might be coming back," I sniffed. "I'm not sure how I shall be feeling this evening. What's on the agenda?"

"The chambers' Christmas party. To be or not to be."

"Ah," I said. We had this discussion every year. And every year we decided that we absolutely had to have one.

"And complaints from solicitors about late paperwork."

"Oh God."

"You can comfort yourself that you're not the only one," Gavin said. "The meeting's in the library at five thirty. See you later." He put the phone down without waiting for a reply.

I walked into the kitchen, put together a ham and cheese sandwich, made a pot of strong coffee, and carried it all on a tray into the living room. I poured a cup of coffee and sat and looked at the screen of my laptop.

PARTICULARS OF APPEAL

In granting staying contact of the children to the father the judge erred in that he gave no or insufficient weight to the following matters:

i. The violence which the father had regularly used against the mother for the five years of their relationship which had resulted in her being admitted to the hospital on one occasion;

ii. By his own choice the father had not had direct contact with the children for more than four years;

iii. The father had not exercised indirect contact: Christmas or birthday cards or gifts to Kylie since he had left home, but had sent Tristan regular checks, all in excess of £50, which meant that Kylie felt unloved and unwanted and allowed Tristan to assert male superiority.

I crossed out the word "male"

iv. In the period between June 1993 and September 1994 when the father was exercising contact there were many difficulties:
  a. he failed to turn up on several occasions;
  b. on one occasion when he did attend he knocked Tristan over playing football and blamed it on Kylie; and
  c. on every occasion persistently questioned the children about the mother's social life.

I read through what I had written so far. I thought about Margo and her life with Latimer. Had it been like this? Violence, disappointment, frustration. Was I missing something? Was there some clue in these particulars? I took a swig of coffee and narrowed my eyes. No, no message was coming through. I wondered if I needed an eye exam. I wondered if my cold really was coming back.

I put on a Temptations LP, opened the *Guardian* supplement and started the crossword.

At half past four I changed into black jeans and a charcoal grey sweater, touched my bangs with hair gel and drove into chambers. In the street next to chambers I found a meter with an hour left on the clock.

Simon was on the landing outside chambers. "The meeting's about to start," he said.

"I've just got to get some papers," I said. He turned away.

"Simon," I said. He paused. "What's that new term the police use for framing?"

"Noble cause corruption, you mean? 'It was filthy work but someone had to do it.' "

When I did crime there was no public acknowledgment that the police gave creative evidence, but privately the excuse was that since the job of the police was to rid the streets of crime, where there wasn't enough evidence to convict an obvious villain they'd make some up. Sometimes you could catch them out very nicely, especially on the finer details, the details they hadn't gone into when they'd made up their notes in the cafeteria.

"So now they've got a term for it, does that make it acceptable?"

"No, no, I think there's been something of a purge in the Metropolitan police. Rooting out bad officers, moving them into Traffic. Gilding the lily's all rather passé now. Very eighties. Oh, yes, far less opportunity for that rip-roaring kind of defense cross-examination now than when you were doing crime. With notable exceptions, of course." Simon's voice echoed in the bare stairwell.

"Just my luck."

"What's this all about? This doesn't usually come up in your family cases, does it?"

"No, I'm just trying out some ideas."

"Are you writing an article for a learned journal?"

"Simon, you know I'm not that kind of girl."

"So?"

"I can't really talk about it."

"Famous client?"

"Not really. A bit personal."

His face creased with concern. "A trouble shared?"

He was a man of status, wealth, some power. Perhaps that was why I was asking him. He might be just the person I needed to tell. I drew a breath but Iotha and Vanya came up the stairs, swinging their bags against their legs, laughing.

"People are arriving for the meeting," I said. "I'll see you in a minute."

I went into my room, threw some papers into my bag, switched off the light and walked up the flight of stairs leading to the library. While we waited for the other members of the Management Committee to gather I looked for a copy of the *White Book,* the practitioner's guide to procedure in the civil courts. It would tell me how to organize my Court of Appeal case. I intended to place it prominently in front of me during the meeting to show that I was on the job, in case embarrassing confessions about the current state of my paperwork were prised from me. By the time I had found the relevant volume the other five members of the group had appeared.

Simon chaired the meeting, there was no alcohol and it was finished in forty-five minutes. Simon threw me occasional concerned glances but I wouldn't catch his eye. We decided that the clerks should note in people's weekly planners how long they had had a particular piece of paperwork. "So, for example," I said, "my diary might say, 'Morris papers, two weeks to go.' " Gavin coughed loudly. "Or whatever," I finished.

We also decided that we would have a Christmas party and invite partners and a small group of our most loyal solicitors. Either way this would come to about four hundred people. We formed a party committee which I declined to join and pleading another engagement (with a video of *Homicide—Life on the Streets*), I slipped away from the meeting and out into the cold starry night.

Thirty-three

Wednesday Lunchtime

It was lunchtime and the air was grey and heavy with the threat of rain. My car was parked two doors down from the apartment, facing in the wrong direction and suddenly boxed in between two large vans. It took me five minutes to get out onto Kingsland Road. The car clock said one o'clock. I had just missed *You and Yours* on Radio 4, for which I was grateful. I plugged the cell phone into the cigarette lighter and put on Capital Gold. Foreigner were singing "Urgent."

I had been having a late breakfast in the kitchen, waiting for a piece of toast to pop up from the toaster, when the phone rang. I had slept from ten o'clock last night through to eleven this morning and still felt leaden and tired. Not working was bad for me. Everything was bad for me. My relationship with the police, my relationship with Margo, the contents of my fridge. My heart was racing as I snatched up the receiver. I hoped it was Margo.

It was Saskia.

"I'm in a phone booth. I've got to tell someone . . . Can you meet me?"

"When?"

"Now?"

I thought about the Morris papers. They seemed like old, dull friends, to whom I owed the allegiance born of a long relationship. I cast that allegiance aside. If they were true friends they'd understand.

"OK," I said. "Where are you?"

"In the pub next to the club."

"The Qu—?"

She interrupted me. "Yes, yes, yes."

I looked at my watch. It was ten to one. The lunchtime rush hour. "Give me ten, maybe fifteen minutes," I said. "I'm on my way."

"Hurry."

At last she was going to tell me what she'd done, or not done, who was pursuing her, why the police were so very interested in her and finally, how the credit card got into my seventies collection.

As I replaced the receiver I felt I should prepare myself for this. I picked up my cell phone and switched it on, only to hear it beep that the battery was flat. I would charge it in the car. I looked in my work bag for a spare notebook. At the bottom was a tangle of red ribbon, some paperclips and an old message saying "Ring Rachel Wayman" but no notebook. The notebook nestling in the Morris brief was full. A sudden inspiration made me rummage in the bottom drawer of my desk and drag out my old Dictaphone. At the back of the drawer was a box of batteries. I checked that there was a tape in the Dictaphone before wrestling two batteries out of the plastic covering. I noticed two grubby business cards which I slipped into my pocket on the basis that I might need proof of my identity. I still dream of being challenged about my age in pubs. And finally I thought about telling someone where I was going.

Pathetically, I rang Margo's number. There was no answer. I wondered where she was. Perhaps she was out keeping her boyfriend happy. Perhaps she'd changed her regime and was doing her shopping. The phone rang more than ten times and I cursed the people who have no answering machine. I could have said something witty and cryptic, like, "Stop in the name of love."

There was no time for more attempts. I snatched up my denim jacket, reminding myself I had to take my suede jacket to the cleaner, and shoved the cell phone and the Dictaphone into my inside pockets. I was just locking the door of the apartment when the phone rang again.

Kay didn't say hello, just, "I have received something very interesting." Her voice was quiet and precise. "You'd better come to my office."

"What? What is it?" I stared blankly at the car keys in my hand. "My God, is it something that helps my case? Does it vindicate me?"

She paused. "I don't want to talk about it over the phone. But it may have something to do with your friend Jack Fletcher. Do you want to come now?"

"Can I come this afternoon?" I said. "I'm just going to meet our mutual friend."

"Where?" She was shocked. "Will you be all right? I can't come. I have a two o'clock appointment and I have no way of contacting the client to put him off."

"It's OK," I said, my meeting with Saskia suddenly feeling less like a big adventure than a rather tragic lonely mission.

"Just take really good care," she said. And that I did not want to hear.

There was a thick yellow line on the road outside the club which I had noticed only subliminally on my earlier visits. The road had no meters. I drove around three streets and found a parking space. I put in a pound which bought us forty minutes. I had no other change. I realized I had no other money. It was quarter past one.

The pub was full of music and people, city workers and regulars. I wasn't sure if I recognized any of them but everyone looked healthy and rosy from the orange lamps which threw a warm glow onto the tables. I hoped some of it would rub off on me. The TV was on, but something was wrong. I couldn't think what it was but it made me feel I was in the wrong place at the wrong time. Then I realized, the person on the TV screen was gyrating to a tune with a different rhythm from the music coming out of the loud speakers. And Saskia was nowhere around. I hovered uneasily near the bar. A man of about fifty with a jovial manner and a toupee asked me what I would like to drink. I said I was thinking and hoped Saskia would appear and would have money.

I looked around the room, craning over the heads of the drinkers, and noticed the door to the toilets which was open a crack. As I watched, the crack slowly widened and Saskia's head appeared in the space, looking cautiously about her. When she caught sight of me her eyes widened and she looked around the room again. Then she beckoned me over with a slight movement of her head.

Trying to look like someone who needed to use the loo, but who hadn't come into the pub solely for that purpose, I strolled casually through the crowd to the now closed door.

I pushed it open and was in a small corridor with a pile of cardboard boxes and a bicycle and a smell of air freshener. There were two doors, one saying gents, the other ladies, and Saskia bobbing behind a large beer barrel.

"Did anyone follow you in?" she whispered.

"I don't think so," I said. "Should you be out of bed? You look terrible."

She seemed to have lost weight, her face was drawn and her hair looked too long and flat. She needed more help than an orange bulb could give her. She was wearing a green cardigan and some large, faded blue sweatsuit bottoms.

"I'm in such trouble," she said, "I couldn't stay in the hospital."

My stomach contracted. "What do you want to do?" I said. "Stay here? I haven't got any money for a drink, I'm afraid."

"Nor have I."

"We could drive around in the car."

"Oh God," she moaned. "I don't know. Will we be safe, in the open?"

"We'll be OK in the car," I said. "If worse comes to worst we can accelerate out of danger." As long as they're driving an ancient wreck, I added to myself.

We couldn't get out of the pub without walking back through the room. "Just keep close to me," I said, like I say to clients who are afraid of meeting their violent ex-partners. Of course at court there are other people around whose job it is to defend you if something terrible happens. Here the only person who might conceivably consider that his duty was mein host. I wondered what he would do if a crisis occurred. But he was nowhere to be seen; probably searching through his record collection to find another tune to play that would bear no relation to the picture on the TV screen.

At the door Saskia was so close behind me we were like spoons in a drawer. I felt I'd been here before. I wondered if this pub had that effect on all women or if it was just members of this particular family. She felt very different from her mother, taller, thinner, no smell of cigarette smoke. We slid out into the street and moved quickly through the gloomy narrow roads of warehouses and scrapyards to the car.

As I switched on the ignition the first notes of "Running Scared" by Roy Orbison boomed through the speakers and I snapped it off.

I found myself following the same route that I had taken

that night with Margo. Now it was busier, full of taxis and large trucks. "Where have you been?" I asked.

Saskia sat silent.

"Your mom's been really worried about you."

"So you've worked out that relationship," she said. "I've been around, staying with friends, here and there. Trying to lie low." She pulled a small plastic bottle of water from her pocket and took a mouthful.

I was swearing at someone for cutting me off at the lights near Moorgate Station when she said, "You know about me and Kevin?"

"What do you mean?" I asked cautiously.

"Kevin, Lesley—Margo's ex."

"Yes. What?"

"He set me up, you know. He got me arrested that day, after he beat me up. He hated me."

"Margo told me."

"He was always following me around, poking about in my life. He couldn't leave me alone. Reporting me to the school. He even got my friends in trouble. Him and his spooky friends in the police. That was on the top of the other stuff." She was almost breathless with the effort of speaking.

I kept my eyes on the road.

"She thought when she left him it would stop. But it didn't. He'd come back, hassling her, demanding to see the girls. It was just to wind her up. Then he'd start shouting, slap Margo around a bit. The girls got upset."

She didn't need to tell me all this. I knew he was bad news. I wondered if she was preparing me for something terrible that she'd done.

"You were there once."

"Me?"

"You were driving by. We were waiting for the bus. I was taking the girls swimming to get them out of the house. You took us up to Archway."

I didn't know what to say. "Did you have a nice time?"

"Yes, thanks. So it's funny, really, how upset I was when I saw him killed."

"Oh!" Although I'd been expecting something like this, I nearly collided with a messenger. This was it, then.

"I went to see him. That night. He drinks in a pub near the park, I knew he'd be there. I wanted to give him shit in front of his pathetic pals for what he'd done. Show him up, cause a fuss. Do you mind me telling you all this?"

"No, no," I said. "Do you mind if I record it? For both our sakes?" I was negotiating Old Street circle and it took me several minutes to grope under my seat belt and into my pocket for the Dictaphone. I switched the machine on and handed it to Saskia.

She held it awkwardly in front of her face. "I got off the bus at Hornsey Lane, and as I was walking down toward the pub I saw him come out with a couple of guys—police officers in suits."

"What does that mean?"

"They were coming out of the pub together. Two of them and Kevin. I could see Kevin was giving them the chat, just like he always did. Trying to slither his way out of something. And I could see they weren't buying it. They crossed the road together and I followed them." She took the bottle out of her pocket and took a mouthful of water. "I was going to jump out at him and embarrass him. I should have done. But I sort of got into the stalking thing, dodging behind cars, flattening myself against lampposts. It was so cold that night. And then it was too late." Her voice cracked.

"How did you know they were police officers if they were in suits?" I asked quickly.

"Frankie," she smiled at me, "you can always tell, you must know that."

"Even in the dark?"

"Yes. Almost better in the dark. It's their silhouettes, the way they move. You obviously haven't been arrested enough. Anyway, I could tell from their conversation. They were his old pals from Camden. The taller officer was saying, 'Come on, Kevin. It'll save so much trouble.' And then Kevin passed him some money. Which was ironic. In the days when Kevin worked in licensing, dealing with the vice problem, he was the one collecting money. From the clubs and stuff. Then he gets fired and ends up sticking post-cards in phone booths, and he's got to give sweeteners to the police, so they don't hassle the women.

"That was his girlfriend, you know. One of the women. He drove Margo crazy talking about her, how fantastic she was, all that stuff. He was such a bastard.

"So then they started talking about women. The tall one was getting at Kevin about someone he knew. Kind of, 'What's it to you? What's she ever done for you?' Then he started getting a bit threatening. 'Don't forget, we've got you on video using stolen cards.' "

"So they did know about P. J. Kramer," I murmured. "I suppose putting postcards in phone booths doesn't exactly allow for a lavish lifestyle."

"No," she said, "that's why he started buying credit cards."

We were in a line of traffic in Farringdon Road. She fell silent. I needed her to tell me what she knew about the credit cards, but she needed to finish her story.

"What happened?" I asked. "How come he's dead?"

"I don't know, it was all getting a bit tense. Something the tall one said made me think it might be Margo they were talking about. We had an expression in our family, in the old days, when he was being nice and jokey, and Margo was getting us all to sing, and we'd forget the words and she'd say, 'It's the singer not the song.' And the tall one said something about 'the singer' and laughed. Anyway, Kevin went ballistic and just lunged at him and all of a sudden the three of them were wrestling and kicking and then one of the cops fell over. Then Kevin fell over, and it was like a cartoon, arms and legs appearing and disappearing. Then there was a sort of horrible scream. I knew, I knew it was Kevin, I knew he was dead. And the two cops stood up and looked at each other. The shorter one had something in his hand. They were arguing and I couldn't really see that clearly, but it had to be a knife, because they grappled over it and it looked like the tall one of them was threatening the other one with it. I thought I was going to see another killing right there in front of me. I was terrified they'd see me and I'd be next.

"I was behind a car, praying someone would come along, would come back to their car, and they'd have to stop. Then there was a sound, a real crack, like someone had been slapped really hard across the face, and the knife fell on the ground. And I could hear one of them making a noise, like keening; I think he was crying. The taller one picked up the knife, wiped it on some grass and put it in a plastic bag—you know, like they have at the scene of a crime. And they stood there for a bit, discussing, and then the two of them lifted Kevin up and tipped him over the railings into the park. Something fell out of his jacket. It looked like a car license plate."

I sucked in air through my teeth.

"And they poked that through the railings beside him. Then the tall one bent down and put some notes into Kevin's pocket, which looked like the money he'd just taken from him. It all happened so fast. Then they walked away, just walked away. The tall one was brushing himself down as if he was about to go into an interview. Smoothing his hair back. They walked off around the corner. And then I went over to where they'd been. I wanted to see if I could do anything. I thought he might not be dead, even though I knew he was. When I got there, there wasn't much blood, you could hardly see where he'd been stabbed. The blood must have been soaking into his coat.

"I stretched my arm through the railings and his sleeve was all wet. It was awful, knowing that it was blood. It was like touching . . ."

"A murder victim?"

"Well, yeah. It was horrible. It wasn't Kevin any more. I felt his wrist for a pulse, but I couldn't feel a thing. I don't know if that was because I was shaking too much or because he was dead. Your shirt got covered in blood, I'm afraid. I was crouching there, waiting to calm down, to try again, and looking around for someone to tell, or to see if there was a phone, and the bastards drove past in their big shiny car. And slowed down.

"The tall one was driving; he looked over and saw me, and stared at me as they drove past. And I just freaked. When they'd gone around the bend in the road I stood up and ran down toward Archway, and then I hid in a garden. Dartmouth is so narrow I knew it would take them a little while to turn around. I stayed there for about an hour. Then I just got really scared and I . . . I left. I got the bus at Archway.

"No one deserves to die like that. I mean, I know Kevin was a complete bastard, but I was really upset."

"You would be," I said. "But why are you so anxious? He didn't know who you were, this officer, did he?"

"Well, I don't know for sure," she mused. "But he must have. Kevin was such a groupie. He loved hanging out with them, calling them his friends. And there was one night we were all out for a family thing and he insisted we went into a pub for a drink. I mean, it was Carley's seventh birthday, the girls didn't want to go into a pub, we were meant to be going to McDonald's. Anyway, surprise surprise, there were his buddies, and he was off for an hour talking to them, while we sat in the children's room with an orange juice and a bag of chips. And one of his chums sent a drink through for us, came to the door, raised his glass to us. I was pissed off but Margo played along, smiled, made the girls raise their glasses. I'm sure he was the one."

Saskia was nodding her head, her eyes fixed on the Dictaphone. I was wondering why, assuming that the men who killed Latimer were not about to confess, and bearing in mind that it was Saskia who had seen it all, *I* was the one who'd been arrested. Why not cut out the middle woman—me—and just arrest her? Of course there was no reason to arrest Saskia, and there was the small matter of the evidence against me.

"You didn't pick up one of the credit cards while you were beside Kevin, did you?"

"No. Kevin wouldn't give me the time of day." Her lip curled. "I never got a thing from him and I didn't want it either."

"Why did Kevin lose his job?" I said. "Your mom said he blamed you."

"Kevin was so full of shit. He reckoned I'd snitched on him. As if! I think it was his pals in the police force who did that. Kevin was probably getting greedy. There's a big sex trade in Camden. He was earning a lot of money from the clubs and the police weren't getting a big enough cut. I'm sure one of them put a word in someone's ear. He wouldn't believe it was them. Still thought they were his great buddies. You know that day I came to your apartment—"

"How many times did you come to my apartment? Before the fire."

"I only came once. That day after court. See, I think Kevin got his buddies to arrest me so that he wouldn't be charged with assaulting me."

"Did they really do that kind of stuff for him?" I asked. "Would they have broken into Kay's office?"

"What do you mean?"

"The night you were arrested, she was meant to meet me to give me the brief, but she was clearing up after a burglary."

"To see if I'd made a statement saying something incriminating? Oh, don't, he probably was behind it. I'm so sorry. And I was trying to protect you. Because you said someone at court had been asking about me. When you were on the phone it dawned on me that Kevin and a pal or two might have followed us to your apartment. I didn't want to get you involved. I just panicked and dashed out." She paused. "When else do you think I came?"

"The week before last. You left a card that said, 'Make love not sausages.' "

She laughed, and it made a sad fleeting sound in the car. "That's a good one, I like that card. I had a load of them in my bag when I was arrested, but I didn't leave one at your place."

"You said the apartment was easy to break into."

"Frankie, I would never do that. Not break in." She paused, struggling to be honest. "Well, if I did, I'd stay there till you got home. Prepare something delicious and healthy for you to eat when you got back after a hard day's work . . . Maybe something out of your freezer, one of those great desserts you used to have." Now she had relieved herself of her story, she was starting to relax.

"I thought you might have left one of Kevin's credit cards . . . for safe-keeping?"

"No," she said simply. It was dawning on me that she didn't know I had been arrested for the murder. But then, why would she? I hadn't told her and it appeared her mother hadn't either.

"When was this?" she asked.

I thought back. "I can't remember. Given everything that's happened it doesn't seem the most important thing. By the way, did Latimer chew gum?"

She turned her head to look at me as a cyclist overtook us in a dangerous maneuver. "Sometimes you can be quite weird, Frankie."

"Sugar-free gum?"

"Weirder and weirder."

"Did he have a date to meet you in Gino's the night he died?"

"No, but I was supposed to be having dinner there with Margo."

"Did you formalize that?"

"What do you mean?"

"Did she send you an invitation or anything?"

"Margo? No. I think she wrote it down on a scrap of paper, that's right, to remind me. But then I lost it, after I was arrested, and I thought he might have found it, and then I got a bit anxious about being in Islington. So the upshot was, we didn't go."

"Might he have heard you arranging that?"

"Mmm—maybe. He could have got it out of Margo."

"Didn't you go to the police about him? About his death?"

"No, who would I have told? Anyone I spoke to could have been one of his weird friends. I wouldn't have known who was involved. And they'd all try to protect each other, anyway. Or lay it on me."

There was a small click as the tape machine stopped. Saskia jumped.

"What does your mom think?"

"I haven't told her!" She sounded shocked. "She would be so scared, she'd do something stupid. Try and save me. Tell all the wrong people." She cleared her throat.

"Do you need a drink?"

"It's OK," she said, and pulled out the bottle of Evian water from her pocket. She took a mouthful. "It's the smoke inhalation."

"What do you think about that?" I asked. "The fire."

"I think someone was trying to get rid of me," she said in a small voice. "I mean, I didn't do anything, you know, knock over a candle or anything. I didn't think I was scared but one of the doctors looked just like that smarmy officer and it terrified the shit out of me. I think someone's after me."

I didn't want to push myself after that declaration, but I said, "Do you think I came into it at all? Do you think someone was trying to hurt me?"

She turned to me, her eyes wide with alarm. "Oh, Frankie, I hope not. That would be terrible. Terrible." She took a swig of water. "Especially after you drove all that way with Margo."

"WHAT!" A grimy white van narrowly missed having a stripe of Renault red on its passenger side.

"Well," she said uncertainly, "isn't that what happened? I can't remember much about that night. They said at the hospital it might be post-traumatic stress—"

"Picture the scene," I said, sharply. "She was dry and I was drowning in my own wet jacket."

"Oh," she said vaguely. "Oh, yes. But I thought that was what she told the police, that she came to the trailer with you. But that's all right, isn't it?"

"The police might think I was involved in the fire."

"You? No one would suspect *you* of arson—you're a barrister."

"Saskia, I'm a barrister who is suspected of murder. A little arson may well be considered par for the course." A chaser to quench my thirst for criminal excitement. Arson with intent to endanger life carries a maximum penalty of life. It seemed I was now at risk of two life sentences. If they ran concurrently I might be out in time to benefit from a free TV license.

She made choking noises of disbelief as I told her briefly

about my night in the cells following my arrest for Latimer's murder.

"I don't think Margo gave them your real name," she whispered in a horrified tone.

I hoped she had given them a bloody good name, and not the one I gave when we went to the hospital. This was all getting out of hand. I tried to think what Kay would say if she were here. First I put on the face. Then I said to Saskia, "Look, if these pals of Latimer's were police from Camden, wouldn't you be safe going to another station? You could even go to another borough—Hackney? Stoke Newington."

"Is that the station where you were arrested?"

"Well, you don't have to talk to Fletcher."

Saskia looked at me sharply. Then she said slowly, "Fletcher is the name of the man Kevin used to talk about. I never met him, but he was the main man that Kevin dealt with at Camden police station."

"Spooky coincidence. Two bastards called Fletcher."

"He's not at Camden any more," she said, "he was transferred somewhere. There was some trouble. They moved him out."

We were at the Museum of London and somehow I was stuck between two taxis in a two-lane stretch.

"But look, if they're accusing you of doing it, I've got to tell someone what I saw." Saskia was wringing the Dictaphone with both hands.

"We're both in trouble," I said. "We should think about this. The tape of you explaining what happened is a very good start. And now I've got to put it somewhere secure." The traffic was jostling up St. Martin's le Grand. "In case my apartment gets broken into again."

We turned past St. Paul's, around on to Ludgate Hill past the Old Bailey and into New Bridge Street. I suppose I should have asked her if she knew anything about any boyfriend of Margo's, but I couldn't bear the humiliation.

I smiled broadly at the warden in his little box at the back entrance to the Temple and swore I would only be five minutes because I was dropping something off. I parked wildly in the crowded car park, promised Saskia she would be safe and dashed into chambers. Shouting hello into the clerks' room, I ran down the corridor to my room, opened the bottom drawer of my desk and carefully put the Dictaphone and its precious contents under my copy of the Bar's *Professional Code of Conduct*. If anyone felt like rifling through my drawers they would be reminded that it was unprofessional behavior.

On my way out, I ducked into the clerks' room to say goodbye. It was getting toward the time when conferences happened and the chances were that there would be a solicitor in the room who would respond to a quick hello and a sweet smile by sending me a brief, but there were only clerks in the room. Gavin was making end of call noises on the phone and Jenna was reading the Warned list, standing in front of the vertical lines of T-shaped cards tucked into the board, checking the imminent Crown Court trials. As Gavin put the receiver down, Jenna laughed and said to me, "Is this anybody you know, Frankie? I've got a card here for a case at the Bailey: 'R *versus* Richmond F.' Is that a relative of yours? Hmm," she went on, reading, "it's a murder. You should do it, Frankie—that would be a laugh, wouldn't it?"

"Where did that come from?" Gavin had walked up to Jenna and snatched the T-card from her hand. He tore it up. "There isn't a case at the Bailey. There won't be a case at the Bailey."

Jenna looked at him in surprise. Then she looked at me. I was shaking. "Don't throw it away," she said to Gavin. "If that's someone's idea of a joke, we ought to find out who it is. I'm sorry, Frankie, I didn't think."

"Oh, Jenna, it doesn't matter," I said, backing out of the room. They were both looking at me with real concern. I couldn't bear it. "I'd better be off—things to do, places to go."

I went straight back to my room and snatched the machine out of my drawer. This was horrible. It couldn't have been Gavin. It was obvious from his reaction that he had known about my arrest, but he wouldn't have said anything to anybody and he had quite clearly known nothing about the T-card. I didn't think Tony would have mentioned anything because of the shame of it. No, someone in chambers had been talking to the police, probably someone who did prosecution work and who had contacts in the force. There weren't many people who prosecuted in our chambers, but I had a very strong suspicion who it might be and I wasn't going to leave the tape to be found by someone, possibly using my room for a conference, for whom the Bar's Professional Code of Conduct seemed to mean nothing. Someone whose own personal code of conduct didn't even seem to extend as far as behaving courteously toward other members of chambers.

I wasn't sure what any Code of Conduct meant to me at the moment, and, on that basis, I crossed out all names currently on my "Must Kill" list and mentally wrote "MARCUS, probably." I felt a little better.

Thinking about the foes out there waiting to be vanquished, I remembered that Saskia was sitting in my car in the car park alone. Shouting goodbye at the closed door to the clerks' room, I left the building.

The sky was a metallic grey and everything was sharp and clear—the cars, the trees, the lamp-posts—as we drove silently back to my flat. Saskia was silhouetted like a lightning conductor as she ran up the steps to the house, where I was relieved to find that my front door was still safely locked.

Because we hadn't had time for a proper lunch I cooked some pasta. As I proudly put the steaming bowl of fettuccini on the table I realized that I wasn't hungry. Saskia poured olive oil into the bowl, covered the pasta with ground black pepper and ate ravenously while I sat cradling a cup of tea.

I ran her a bath and as I added herbal essence to the water I had a sense that I had been here before—more déjà vu. I once read somewhere that too much déjà vu means you've got brain problems. That about summed up how I felt.

I needed fresh air, I needed to think, I needed to do something with the tape. I needed to go and see Kay.

"Before you go," Saskia said tentatively, "could you let me have something to wear? Something old, that you would have thrown out anyway. Did Margo return that lovely grey shirt of yours? I found it on Sunday. I remember giving it to her."

"She didn't give it to me," I said. "I think she had other things on her mind."

I went to the bag of Lena's thrift store clothes and pulled out a creased red shirt that I had never seen Lena wear and an old pair of stonewashed black denim trousers that I had advised her to stop wearing only a few months before.

"Perfect," Saskia said.

As she stood at the doorway of the bathroom, framed in the steam rising from the bath, she looked like a waif in an enchanted world. I wanted to look after her, keep her safe, put her in a tower away from harm, but instead I jotted down Kay's number and, as an afterthought, my cell number, on the pad by the phone. Then I cautioned her, "Keep the door locked and don't let anyone in. And don't answer the phone—unless it rings twice, then it'll be me. And call me if there are any problems."

"Yes, ma'am," she said, with a flicker of a smile.

She should have come with me, I thought as I went down the steps into the gathering evening mist.

Thirty-four

Wednesday Afternoon—Kay's Office

Kay was in the smart, brightly lit reception area of her office, talking quietly to the receptionist when I arrived. It was almost four o'clock. She looked at me with concern and ushered me into her room. "Are you looking after yourself?" she asked as I sat down in the seat reserved for clients.

"No," I said. "So, what have you got?"

Kay waited until the receptionist had put down two cups of tea and left the room. Then silently she handed me two sheets of A4 paper. It was a bad fax that at first glance looked like a huge barcode on a tin of beans. The rest of the paper was filled with blank spaces, really small handwritten words and a few yawningly large ones.

"What is it?" I asked, not wanting to read it.

"Have a look at it and tell me what you think."

Slowly I looked down at the letter and began to read what I could. It seemed to be dated three days earlier.

I can't take this any mœ This is not why I came into
the police force. Thingsharp want to blame anyone else,
but I need to explain myself
I have taken money for my actions. I have hurt since
Latimer.   I was with my

Here a word was scrubbed out hard. I held it up to the light but I could see nothing. I read on.

te home of an innocent pson I found dje incident in the High St
no official complainttbat offense at Stoke Newington police ht

htn only get worse He this dreadful treadmill. I am sorry for what I have done

wrong

"This is Rowland's suicide note, isn't it?" I said.

"I think so."

I began pacing around the large table in Kay's neat office. "This handwriting . . ." I said, ". . . you know where we've seen this before?"

Kay looked at me.

"It was on Saskia's card, the one in my apartment." I was having difficulty thinking straight. "The one she didn't leave."

"What?"

"Where is it—that card?"

Kay went to her filing cabinet. She drew out the card I had found in my apartment. She opened another drawer, rifled through and drew out a form. "This is an old application for Legal Aid for Saskia. She filled in her name and address herself." She laid all the papers on the table. We both stared at them. I noticed Saskia had given Margo's address.

"You do this more often than I do," I said, "but the capital letters on the card don't look like the capital letters on the Legal Aid form."

"She filled in the Legal Aid form in the office, so that's definitely her writing."

"But they do look, those small tight letters, quite like the handwriting on the fax."

"So this," Kay held up the card with the picture of the smiling pig, "appears to have been left by . . ."

". . . a member of Her Majesty's police force." I shivered with retrospective uneasiness. "Saskia was very clear that she didn't come to my apartment that night." I looked at the fax again. "He's talking about my apartment. He broke into my bloody apartment and left that credit card there, and then he has the nerve to leave a calling card, saying my security's not up to scratch."

"Which it obviously wasn't."

"Thank you, Kay. But they framed me. They framed me."

"It's not unheard of."

"I know," I said. "Just let me tell you, it feels a lot different when it's you and not a client." I peered at the fax. "So he's talking about Latimer, and what's he saying here? 'Incident in High Street . . . Stoke Newington police station . . .' That must be Margo—he stabbed Margo! The guy was crazy."

"If that's right, this is heavy stuff," Kay said.

"It's a death-bed confession, isn't it?" I said. "He wanted to get his affairs in order before he did the deed. Perhaps the parts we can't read say who was involved in Latimer's death."

"You hope," she said.

"Where did this come from?"

"It was here when I arrived in the office this morning. There's no indication where it came from."

"What time was it sent?" I asked, squinting at the top of the page. The time looked like 4:27 A.M. printed in small crunchy numerals, which could mean half past three or half past five, or even half past four, but anyway, it was an unsociable hour for office work. "Who do we know who would be sending faxes at that time of the morning? Who's at work at that time?"

"The police," we said together.

"Who, though?" I said. "What police officer would be helpful enough to send us this letter?" Especially if Saskia was right that it was police officers she had seen. "You'd better listen to my tape of Saskia." I pulled out my small Dictaphone.

"Extra points for organization," Kay commented.

We listened to the tape. The quality wasn't good and Saskia's voice was occasionally obscured by my shouting at other drivers.

As the tape ended Kay said, "If she's right, you and Saskia are both in trouble."

"But doesn't this get me off the hook?"

"Potentially, yes, but those officers are going to fight hard to stop Saskia's story getting out."

"If one of those officers was Rowland, he's not going to be doing much fighting, having carelessly committed suicide. So there's only one person to be worried about. And we've got the tape and now"—I picked up the fax from her desk—"we've got this." I walked around the room, smiling in triumph. "Take that, DCI Armani-suit Fletcher."

Kay picked up the Dictaphone and carefully took out the tape. I looked at her and the small tuft of hair in her dark bangs which stood out at right angles to her forehead. I had loved that little clump of hair, but she had spent a fortune on gels and mousse trying to flatten it into submission.

"The letter doesn't actually mention Fletcher," Kay reminded me. "And Saskia doesn't know for certain it was him."

"I know, but who else could it be?" I picked up the letter again. " '*I was with my . . .*' that crossed out word must be 'superior'. And Fletcher was his superior."

"It could be 'colleague'," Kay said.

"It could be 'mother'. Why would a colleague blackmail him? A colleague would have just as much to lose, he wouldn't have enough clout. Fletcher's involved in this, I know he is. It can only be Fletcher. This must mean I'm in the clear. What more could we want?" I was exultant. I read aloud, " '. . . *this dreadful treadmill* . . .' Don't you hate this confessional style of writing?"

"I don't regard literary criticism as part of my job," Kay said shortly, as one of her phones began to ring.

"Do you think he was religious?" I mused, as she barked "Yes?" down the phone. Then her voice softened and I threw a glance at her. "Oh, I know, I'm sorry, you did tell me. There's a new one in the closet in the hall. Yes, yes, I'll see you later. I shouldn't be at the office too late."

I tried to think of other things like murder charges and dangerous police officers on the loose but the intimate conversation and the sound of her voice being sweet and loving made a great longing rise up in me. I knew exactly what was kept in the closet in the hall. Vacuum cleaner bags.

She came off the phone struggling to keep a small smile from her face. "But just in case it is Fletcher, you've got to be on the lookout. He could start causing trouble for you."

"Start?"

"If Fletcher is the last in some awesome Fletcher–Rowland–Latimer trio, he's hardly the weakest link," she said grimly. "It's not going to stop him pursuing you for the murder."

"Who were you talking to on the phone?" I had blurted out the question before I could stop myself.

Kay's mouth moved into a straight line of distaste. All the bad things in our relationship flashed to the front of my memory.

"Never mind, never mind," I said.

"I'm having some building work done," she said.

"By Butch Builders of Bermondsey? No, no, it doesn't matter."

"Hackney, actually. Is there anything else you want to know before we get back to what some might consider the more important job at hand?"

"No," I said. "Yes, what are you having done?"

She sighed. "I'm having the two living rooms knocked into one."

"Oh yes?"

"I'm having new windows, wooden shutters and a new floor. Enough?"

"Paid for, no doubt, with the Legal Aid obtained from the suffering of those of us under the threat of criminal proceedings."

"I have probably earned about three hundred pounds out of you so far, which won't even pay for the new light fittings. Can we talk about Fletcher now? Or do you want to see some of the curtain samples?"

Deliberately I ran the words of the Millie Jackson song through my head about wasting too much time worrying. I felt calm. Calmer. It was a disadvantage that it was a seventies track. "Don't we just have to produce the tape and the fax?" I moaned.

"Frankie, get real: the tape is one person's version of what happened, which she could have made up to suit her own purposes or even to help you. The letter, certainly this version, proves nothing. It's almost illegible and could mean anything. We don't even know how it got here."

I sat down on a chair at the far side of the room.

"If it came from the police station it could possibly have come from Fletcher himself," she went on. "It's no threat to him."

"One of his little jokes, you mean. Of course," I groaned, "it must have been Fletcher who sent it. That's why he looked so terrible in court on Monday morning.

Rowland had killed himself and he was terrified what might come out. But then he saw Rowland's suicide note. And now he's faxed it to you to taunt us. But we shall have the last laugh." I hoped I sounded more convinced than I felt. My feelings of elation at being in the clear were fading. "Has anyone rung you about me and the fire?"

"No."

"I think they may not know I was there."

"At the moment that can only be a good thing."

"But why would I kill Kevin Latimer?" I wailed in exasperation.

"Drunken rage? You were drunk, weren't you? And angry. Plus you had the skills."

I looked at her.

"You did that pathetic self-defense class."

"Defense," I reminded her. "Not attack."

"If I was prosecuting this I could make a perfectly good case against you."

"Fortunately the police didn't live with me for six and a half years. They may not know my history of failed hobbies."

She put her hands flat on the table. "Seriously, Frankie, you've got to stop drinking. You really have."

She held me with her gaze. It was like being at a religious revival.

"All right, all right, I will," I said, before she could say it again. "If this all gets sorted out, I will give up drinking."

She made a move toward a drawer in her desk. I thought she was going to draw up a deed of commitment and make me sign it and seal it with a red blob of wax and a piece of green ribbon. Instead she took out a small cash box which she placed on the table. She took up a bunch of keys, unlocked the box and then ceremoniously folded the fax in two and put it inside.

"You'd better put in Saskia's tape as well," I said.

"She should come and see me to make a formal statement," she said as the tape dropped with a small click into the box. "Tonight," she said, turning the key, "this will go in the firm's safe."

"And is it?" I asked.

She looked up.

"Safe. Remember your office got broken into."

"If you're worried, I'll take the cash box home with me."

"Why bother? You could probably leave it outside the front door with a message saying 'Take Me', since it seems that none of it's going to do me any good." I felt desperate. "You said I had to find Saskia, I found her and now you say she's no use to me."

"Well, yes, you had to find her, but it doesn't mean she can solve the whole thing." She looked at my face. "But it's better than nothing," she said softly.

"I'd better get back." I stood up. At the door I hesitated. I remembered the last part of my conversation with Kay before I left the house. "What did you say Fletcher's first name was?"

She looked back into the file containing all the papers in my case. "Jack," she read.

"Oh, shit," I groaned. "It's him."

Thirty-five

Wednesday Evening

I drove home looking in the rear-view mirror all the time, watching out for lurking police officers, and nearly rear-ended a bus. Fletcher had been with Margo at the trailer. Was he the person who had gone to her apartment? Was it Fletcher she had been speaking to on the phone? What was the deal? To set me up? To set fire to the trailer? The implications of it all were too horrible to think about.

It was twenty past five and I hadn't collected my messages for the day so, sitting behind a bus on Stoke Newington Road, I rang chambers. The phone rang for a long time. It was the busiest time of the day and Jenna answered sounding harassed.

"You haven't got any messages," she said. "But things are getting sorted. Tony and Gavin are having a meeting with Marcus at the moment."

I'd almost forgotten about that. As I switched off the phone, I considered the knot in my stomach and yes, there was a part of it which was about who had been saying what to whom in chambers about my private business. And now Marcus was talking to Tony and Gavin. "Shit," I said. I wondered if Fletcher had rung Marcus or perhaps spoken to him at court the other morning? Had they discussed me and Latimer, my black eye, my life, sniggering together like school boys? Surely not. Probably.

The 243 pulled away from the bus stop. I sat motionless. Was this about me or Saskia? Saskia!

I realized I hadn't given her a thought for the last two hours and suddenly things that she was afraid of that might have happened to her while I was away filled my mind. I rang my own phone number. I let it ring twice and then rang again, as we had arranged. Saskia answered "Hello?" in a languorous voice.

"Nice bath?" I asked.

"Fine, wonderful," she said, "I've just had a nap. Oh, the phone rang."

"Who was it?" I asked.

"What?" she said in a voice that was hissy with static.

"Who was it?"

"Can't hear," she said.

A number 76 bus was hooting and revving behind me.

"Keep the door locked," I shouted. "I'm coming home now."

I drove as fast as I could, hooting at other drivers and people thoughtless enough to consider crossing the road, fuming at the lights against me. I screeched into Amhurst Road, parked the car at a hazardous angle and threw myself up the steps two at a time.

The flat was full of the warm smell of onions simmering softly in melting butter. Saskia was stretched out on the couch, looking lovely in the red shirt and the stonewashed denims, watching a program about shopping. "Hiya," she said, "I've cooked some vegetables for us. Are you hungry?" She swung her legs down and walked into the kitchen. The comforting sound of food bubbling in a pan filled the room as she took off the lid. "Sit down," she said. She moved around my kitchen as if she'd lived there for years.

"Can we have wine?" I asked.

"Yes, I would have opened some," she said, putting

plates on the table, "but I didn't know which cost £3.99 and which you'd paid £4,000 for."

"None of it cost £4,000, but thank you for your sensitivity," I said, bending down at the cabinet where my small but exquisite wine collection was kept. I opened a bottle of Morgon, wishing in a small but insistent way that Margo was there to share it. I poured out two glasses of wine and took a large mouthful. Its soft richness made me sit back in my chair and stretch my legs. Then I remembered the conversation we had started earlier. I put my glass on the table. "The phone rang?"

"It was your mom." Saskia was stirring the stew. "I answered it when she began to speak. She said you don't let her answer the phone either."

I didn't want to investigate how the two of them had got to that level of intimacy within the conversation.

"She wants to come up tomorrow. I said I thought that would be fine."

A small sound left my throat.

"Was that the wrong thing to say?"

"Different people have different relationships with their mothers," I said. "Did she say how long for?"

"No."

"I don't have a lot of room here," I said. "Where would she sleep?"

"I don't think she wants to stay. But I'm not staying. I can't stay, actually."

"Yes, you can," I said. "Certainly tonight. Where have you got to go anyway?"

"I've got to see my mom, talk to the group about the trailer. I've got so much to do." She sighed.

"It's too late to go anywhere tonight."

She looked at the clock. It was half past six. "OK," she said.

"Did you say to my mom that there might be a crazed

lunatic police officer on the doorstep waiting to take out anyone who steps in his path?"

"No, I didn't. I said you'd ring and confirm, so you can tell her not to come if you'd rather she didn't. But if you're worried about that, I ought to go now."

"It's not just you. Fletcher doesn't like me any more than he likes you."

The phone rang. We both froze. I let it ring and then the machine clicked on. A voice I recognized filled the room. "DCI Fletcher here. I was wondering if you had made any headway with your search for a new license plate. Or your friend. Did you see that Fairport Convention is appearing for one night only at Wembley Arena? Are you going? See you." The machine clicked off.

Saskia was watching me. Her face was pale. I wondered what Fletcher's game was. Saskia opened her mouth. "Let's not talk about it tonight," I said.

It was only ten o'clock when I made up the bed in the living room for Saskia. We had finished the wine and drunk a lot of tea and we hadn't talked about Kevin or Margo or DCI Fletcher or knives or burning trailers. We had talked about the old days and people we had both known and vegetarianism and hair cuts. I had decided not to mention my suspicions about Fletcher and the fire and her mother until the morning. Then I would tell her everything I knew. But tonight I wanted her to get a good night's sleep. Things were going to get gruelling. Tomorrow would be soon enough and then I would take her to see Kay.

At midnight I woke up and couldn't think why. I got up and went to the bathroom. The living-room door was open. The bed was empty. Saskia had gone. "That girl is the original Road Runner," I thought. "Roaming around." I was worried, but not that worried. She was a big girl.

I forgot that she didn't know half of what had been going on. I went back to bed.

Thirty-six

Thursday Morning

My mom arrived at ten o'clock the next morning. I had been up for three hours working on my Morris papers—being on the edge of disaster was concentrating my mind—so for once her arrival was a pleasant break.

She had brought treats and we sat in the kitchen, looking out at the garden, watching a cat prowling through the long grass, and drank coffee and chewed doughnuts.

After fifteen minutes I said, "Why are you here, Mom?"

She looked at me with a smile.

"Don't tell me," I said, "it's your boyfriend."

"We're going away for a few days."

"Ooh," I said, "registering under the name of Smith for a dirty weekend?"

"Where does this aspect of your personality come from, I wonder," Mom said. "Must be your father's side. We're not going to a hotel at all. Alan has a Winnebago." She said the word slowly as if she'd only just learned it.

"A camper van, in other words."

"Probably, but a bit fancier, I think. It should be very nice."

"Well, it is lovely to see you, Mom, but why have you come?"

"With Alan in Brighton and me in Colchester, you're a nice central position for us. But we're not going till this evening, after Alan finishes work, so I thought, since I have been visiting you rather more often than usual, I should pay for my keep."

"Oh, Mom—" I began.

"By doing some housework." She looked around the kitchen. "I don't think you're in a position to argue, are you?"

"OK," I said, with no reluctance at all. "I've got to get back to my paperwork. Can I leave you to it?"

For an hour my mom worked happily, humming the hits of Little Stevie Wonder. She began in the kitchen, putting on a load of laundry and cleaning the sink, then moved into the bathroom and finally, humming "Sweep it in the pan, pan, pan, harmonica man," she bustled past the door of the living room toward the bedroom. Then the singing stopped abruptly and she came back and stood dramatically in the doorway, waiting for me to notice her.

I was typing:

> No notice as to the date on which this appeal will be in the list for hearing will be given: it is the duty of solicitors to keep themselves informed as to the state of the lists . . .

It was the formal, last paragraph of the grounds of appeal. Reluctantly I dragged my eyes from the screen and looked at my mother.

Her mouth was pursed.

"That room is a disgrace. What have you been doing? No wonder you and Kay separated." She, like everyone else, had liked Kay and had mourned the end of our relationship probably more than I had.

"Mom, our differences were a little more complicated than that."

She shook her head in clear disagreement.

I went on carefully, "The bedroom is like that because I got very muddy the other day."

She gave me a piercing look. "And?"

"And nothing. Don't start, Mom. I'm going out to buy a *Guardian*."

"But I've got one."

"Yes, but I expect you've done the crossword, haven't you?"

"Well, not all of it, but I've started, yes."

"There you are, then."

With the security of the *Guardian* under my arm, when I got back to the flat I felt calmer. And then I walked into the living room. Mom was sitting on the sofa, surrounded by an old cardboard box which I recognized from under my sink, some markers, a roll of plastic wrap and other kitchen detritus.

"What are you doing, Mom?"

"I'm making you a license plate," she said.

"Sorry?"

"The phone rang a few moments ago and I didn't answer it, like you said but I couldn't help listening to the message and it was from—now where did I put my glasses? I wrote it down, on the back of the sports section . . . You don't read the sports section, do you? . . . Now, where are we? Let's see, ah yes, it was DCI Fletcher and he reminded you that you didn't have a license plate and he said did you want tickets. He sounded very nice. Is he married?"

"I have no idea," I said, tightly.

"So I thought I'd make you a temporary one. We can tie it on with this string. What's your registration number?"

Seeing her sitting there so earnestly with my best interests at heart I had to tell her.

"How are you getting on with Alan?" I said, to change the subject.

She sat up straight, with a glue stick in one hand and a box cutter in the other. "We're getting on all right. He's very nice." Then there was a pause. She bent over the license plate. "He wants us to get married, but I said, 'What's the point?' What do you think?"

"Whoa, Mom, that's a bit quick. I don't know what to say," I said. "You know me. You say marriage, and I say bourgeois method of social control. You say hearts and flowers and I say moral corruption and, ultimately, low chance of success. But don't let that stop you. What you want is the important thing. Do you need to get married? You're not pregnant, are you?"

"You're obsessed with my fertility," she said. "Would you have liked a little brother or sister?"

"That was a joke, Mom," I said. "I mean, do you want the security? Does he need it for his work, somehow? Is it a money thing?"

"He just wants us to get married," she said.

I could feel tears in my eyes. I obviously hadn't had enough proper food, recently. Perhaps the cold was coming back. "You might get some nice wedding presents," I said.

"Would you want to be a bridesmaid?" she asked.

I laughed. "Only if it was a theme wedding. All right, OK, you can get married as long as it's a sixties do. You could go as a Ronette. You could have your hair teased and wear a short, tight skirt."

"Who could Alan be?" she said.

"Phil Spector. And I could be the Wall of Sound."

"He's too tall to be Phil Spector," she said.

"OK, he could be Long John Baldry and you could be Julie Driscoll. And I could be the Steam Package, or just Rod Stewart. I could have a few more highlights put in my hair. I could have it cut short on top—of course I wouldn't be able to go to court for a couple of weeks till it grew out. But this is great. I could wear tight shiny white trousers.

And a tank top. Let's go and have lunch somewhere, to celebrate true love and the fact I've finished my appeal papers and make plans for the wedding of the year."

As we put on our coats we sang "Wheels on Fire," and as we walked down the steps to the street we did the wiggly arm movements. One of my neighbors from upstairs was putting garbage into a trash can. "Great song," he said.

"What nice neighbors you have," my mom said as, arm in arm, we walked down to Church Street.

Thirty-Seven

Thursday Evening

"Your answering machine is flashing," Mom said brightly and I dragged myself out of the bathroom where I had just turned on the taps. In the living room my mother was settling herself in the comfy armchair with the *Guardian*. She seemed completely unaffected by our afternoon's activities.

After lunch at Lorca, where we'd eaten a lot of tapas, she had decided we should go for a walk. She said it was a lovely day and I didn't look as if I was getting enough exercise. We made our way to Clissold Park and walked around it twice, with my mother encouraging me to breathe deeply. Obviously new love was releasing fresh energy in my mom, but after an hour, as dusk fell and mist was settling on the tops of the trees, I was cold and limping and I had pleaded with her to let us go home.

Weakly I switched on the machine. A quiet-sounding Saskia said, "Margo and I would like to take you out for supper. How about Gino's at seven thirty? If we don't hear from you, we'll assume you're coming."

"That's good," Mom said. "I'm glad you'll be doing something nice while we're setting out on our great adventure." Alan was coming to the flat at seven o'clock to pick her up.

I didn't want to go out, and this was not the dream

party list I would have chosen to share my thoughts about Fletcher, but Saskia needed to know. I added five drops of essence of geranium to the running bath water and was just painfully unlacing my damp, muddy boots when the phone rang. It was Gavin.

"Don't forget, the Morris papers have got to be in tomorrow."

"Yes," I said.

I sat on the sofa and took off my boots.

"Deeply held belief, finding of guilt," Mom said, looking at the paper. "Ten letters. First letter C, third letter N, fifth letter I, ninth letter O."

"No idea."

"Oh, conviction," she said casually, and my heart lurched as the phone rang again.

It was Kay. "This is just to remind you that we're due back at the police station at ten thirty tomorrow morning."

"Thank you," I said.

I limped back into the bathroom and was pulling off my sweater when the phone rang again.

"You are a popular person," my mom said. "Not that you deserve to be, with that face."

I grunted at her.

It was Lena. "Do you fancy a cup of tea?"

"Not really," I said.

"Oh, come on," she said, sounding hurt. "I've got to speak to you."

I looked longingly across at the steaming hot bath, running so warmly and invitingly, the essence of geraniums that smelled so sharply of roses filling the room. My bones ached, my muscles ached, my head ached. I yearned for the comforting velvety heat of a good deep bath. So I said, "Yes, Lena, I'd love a cup of tea." She was my friend. She was always there for me.

Wearily I put on my last pair of dry boots, the hard

pointed black ones that pinched my toes and chafed my ankles.

I looked in the mirror by the front door. My cheeks were pale and I had huge rings under my eyes. I looked like someone who was about to be charged with murder. I slapped my cheeks sharply and a small pink circle appeared in the right cheek. I looked like someone who had been slapped in the face.

I left the apartment and ran down the stairs trying to convince myself that I was full of energy. I slumped into the car, stupefied with fatigue, and fumblingly put the key into the ignition. The car wouldn't start.

I was meeting Lena at Fox's. I tried the car again. It did its best, whirring and turning, but it was obviously exhausted too. Unlike me, it had no ludicrous sense of duty so felt no obligation to perform. After thirty seconds it gave up the struggle altogether and we sat, the car and I, in silence. "I do love you," I said, speaking to the dashboard. "I just may have to trade you in for a new model."

I got out of the car and began to jog to Church Street. By now it was quite dark and a strong wind, filled with spits of rain, had replaced the gusts of the afternoon. By the time I passed the bookshop I had a huge blister on the back of my left heel and it had started to rain in earnest. By the time I got to Fox's, I had blisters on both heels and I was soaking. And Lena wasn't there.

Robby picked up a bottle of Lairg Whisky without my even asking and poured me a generous slug. I was almost too cold to say thank you and I grunted at him and carried the glass over to a table for four, near enough the door to watch for Lena and far enough away to avoid the draught.

Lena arrived, quivering with excitement. "Is she here yet?" she asked.

"Who?" The look on her face told me who. "If you mean Nicky, I don't think so," I said irritably. "I did a quick scout around for you when I arrived. I didn't know we were bringing partners."

"And who would you have brought?" she asked as she headed for the bar. A moment later she returned with two glasses of white wine and threw herself into the chair opposite me. "I don't know what to say, Frankie."

"Couldn't you have not known what to say on the phone?" I asked, realizing the second glass of wine was not for me.

"This is so wonderful and so . . . different. I can't eat, I can't sleep. I just want to be with her, more than I've ever wanted anything in my life."

I thought of the steaming therapeutic bath I had left behind. "I'm sure she's lovely," I said. "And I don't want to rain on your parade, but this evening is sort of the condemned woman having a last drink."

"Oh God, I'd forgotten!" She looked stricken. "Is there any more info that I should feed into the computer?" She patted her black bag, where I assumed the notebook was languishing.

I thought back over the last few days. I was too tired and too miserable to tell Lena that I had discovered Margo was Saskia's mom, or that Saskia had seen Latimer's death, or that we had a piece of paper that might be Rowland's suicide note. It didn't make any difference anyway. I just said, "No. So, when Nicky comes, I might just take off." I had an hour before I was due at Gino's, but I could jump into the bath, rub ointment into my heels, put on different shoes and even have time to staple fancy corners on to my grounds of appeal.

Her face fell. "I told Nicky you'd be here. She wants to meet you."

"Don't tell me, she's having trouble with her neighbors and she needs a lawyer," I said. "Sorry, sorry. I'll stay for ten minutes."

"I think your friend Fletcher is putting some pressure on her," Lena said. "I think it's to do with her work."

"Well, it would be. Unless she's murdered someone."

"I don't think so." Lena raised her eyebrow. "But I was thinking that you could compare notes and perhaps learn something to your advantage."

She took a sip of wine. "I've told Sophie," she said quietly.

"Told her what?"

"That I really want to try and make a go of this thing with Nicky."

I experienced the pang of loss you feel when people you want to stay together forever split up. "What does she think about that?"

"It was hard to tell," Lena said. "She shouted at me and stormed out of the room. I suppose I—here she is!" And I knew from the way her voice and face softened into a smile that she didn't mean Sophie.

Nicky came in. She was wearing a small blue denim jacket over a white T-shirt and black jeans. She looked about twenty-six. I recognized her from having seen her in the street with Fletcher. What I hadn't noticed were her dark eyes, which now flashed brightly around the room until they settled on Lena. Then she smiled and showed a mouth full of small perfect teeth. She moved quickly over to our table and hugged Lena fiercely. I could see the attraction.

Lena said, "This is Frankie."

"So you're Frankie," she said, sitting down next to Lena. She had a light, husky voice. "I've heard a lot about you."

"From Lena?"

She smiled and the diamond in her tooth flashed. Lena pushed the glass of wine in front of her and they said fond sweet things to each other for a few moments. Then Lena told us about the man in the flat upstairs listening in to her visitors through the intercom on the front door and Nicky and I looked at each other and agreed that now she should complain about him to the Housing Association.

Nicky groped in the pocket of her jacket. She spoke quietly. "I've also heard about you from a member of the police force," she said to me. "Although not the one you think. He thought you were quite nice." She handed me a folded-up piece of paper. "He wasn't happy about what was happening. He probably would want you to have this." It was a page torn out of a spiral notepad.

Slowly I unfolded it. It was a letter, the letter from Rowland. The original of the fax. "Did you know about this?" I asked Lena.

"I don't know what's going on," Lena said. "What is that?"

"It's a goodbye letter from a friend of mine," Nicky said. "A really sweet boy, who needed all the friends he could get."

Quickly I scanned the letter.

> *I can't take this any more. This is not why I*
> *came into the police force. Things have*
> *happened that shouldn't have, I've done things*
> *I shouldn't have. I've taken money. I don't want*
> *to blame anyone else, but I need to explain.*
>
> *I have allowed myself to be used. I have*
> *taken money for my actions. I have hurt innocent*
> *people.*
>
> *I killed Kevin Latimer. I was with my . . .*
> *[scrubbed-out word] . . . another officer when*
> *it happened. I stabbed an innocent woman,*
> *although there has been no official complaint*
> *of that offence at Stoke Newington police*
> *station. I did it on my own initiative. It was a*
> *warning to keep away. I could not think of*
> *another way. I have broken into the home of an*

*innocent person in an attempt to implicate and
to put her in fear.*

*He feels no guilt. Things can only get worse.
This is the only way I can think to take myself
off this dreadful treadmill. I am so sorry for what
I have done wrong.*

"How did you get this?" I said.

"His name was Ian," Nicky said. "He came down here because he thought the opportunities would be better. Of course he didn't know anyone." She took a mouthful of wine. "So Fletcher took him under his wing, and then he was just in it. He needed to do it, he had family up North he was supporting. I think he thought he owed it to Fletch as well. That's how I met him, my weekly meetings with Fletcher. When the money changed hands."

Sometimes people treat barristers like priests or doctors and tell you things they wouldn't tell anyone else, certainly not so early in the relationship. I could tell from her look of anguish that Lena hadn't known of Nicky's financial relationship with Fletcher.

"Ian used to drop around to my apartment, for a chat, for a cup of tea. To hear someone say his name."

Lena was struggling with the expression on her face.

"And then one morning when I got in from work I found this on the mat. About the same time as Fletcher showed up, frantic, beside himself. He was really upset."

"Oh yes?" I said.

"No, I think they really cared about each other. Ian was such a sweet kid." Her voice dropped. "He worshiped Fletcher and Fletcher treated him, well, like a younger brother."

"God help us," I said. "But you think this is true?" I held up the letter.

"Yes. Oh yes. Some of it Fletch had already told me anyway, hinted at it. Boasting."

"So it is definitely Fletcher he's talking about?"

"No question."

"You don't like Fletcher, do you?" I asked her. "Showing me this means big trouble for him."

She shrugged. "Ian gave it to me. He expected me to do the right thing with it."

"Perhaps he just wanted you to decide what to do with it," I said cynically.

"Well, this is my decision." She smiled at Lena.

"Can I keep it?" I asked, carefully folding the letter. "Kay Donaldson, my solicitor, has a rather bad fax of it."

"Didn't it come through?" Nicky said. "I paid good money to send that."

"You sent it? At that time of night? How come you knew who my solicitor was?"

"I went to that twenty-four-hour store on High Street. And I didn't know she was your solicitor, I just knew she was a solicitor. I thought someone legal should have it. And Kay was really good when I had to go to court." I felt Lena stiffen. Was this the reason Kay had left the Street Life group? A clash of professional and personal interests? "Don't worry, precious." Nicky turned to Lena. "She was always a bit too intense for my taste."

The implications of the letter were sinking in. "This is wonderful and terrible," I murmured. It fitted exactly with what Saskia had said. "Fletcher could be guilty of murder," I said. "Latimer was killed when Fletcher and Rowland were out together on illegal business. Look, I'm about to go and see Margo." I slid the letter into my back pocket. "Can I tell her? Should I tell her?"

"Margo?" Nicky said slowly. "Do you mean Margo, the night club singer? Lesley."

"Oh yes," said Lena. "That's who she means."

I ignored her. "Yes, Margo. Do you know her?" I asked.

"Not really. I knew her husband."

"Kevin," we both said together.

"That's how I met Fletch," she said.

"Is this a useful conversation?" Lena asked brightly.

"Yes," I said. "My God—" I turned to Nicky—"you're not the one Kevin ran off with?" My emotions were running up and down like a bad piano exercise. I thought of Margo's bare, shabby apartment.

"No," she said. "Well, he thought he was running off with me, but he'd misread the signs. He hadn't read them at all. He never listened to anyone, that was his problem. That was a big problem when he was trying to get one over on Fletcher. He was way out of his depth. Fletcher's a pig, but he's not stupid."

There was a question burning in my throat which I didn't want to ask, but I had to. "What do you know about Margo?"

"Not a lot. She took too much nonsense from Kevin. I'd have thrown him out years before, but then I haven't got children."

Lena said, "Do you want some more wine?"

"No thanks, sweetie," she said, and softly grazed Lena's cheek with her nails.

I took a deep breath. "Does Margo know Fletcher?"

"Oh, yeah. He's been sniffing around her for a long time. It was the one thing that Kevin had that Fletcher didn't have. I think he's quite sweet on her. He bought her some of those dresses she wears."

I pushed the image of the black sequined dress to the back of my mind and looked at Lena. "So Jack Fletcher has to be the same Jack who drove Margo to the trailer. What was she playing at, taking him there, putting her own daughter at risk?"

"If she knew," Lena said, reasonably. "She might not have known."

"She did know, she thinks Saskia killed Latimer. So to

take any police officer there was pretty bloody stupid. Plus I have this terrible and overwhelming feeling that it was Fletcher who set fire to the trailer."

"I don't know about that," Nicky said. "Although he was pretty shaken up by Ian's death. He really did care about him. He couldn't understand why Ian had done it. And 'cuz I was about the only person who ever spoke to the guy, he just kept on at me: When did I last see Ian? What did Ian say? Did I know Ian was thinking about killing himself . . ." Each time she said "Ian" it was as if she was lighting a small candle of remembrance.

"Did he know you had the letter?"

"I don't know. I may have said something to make him think I knew something he didn't know."

"Do you think you're in any danger from Fletcher?" I asked.

"Not with my tough gal around," she said, and put her arm around Lena's neck. "No, I'm no risk to Fletcher, I'm just a whore, aren't I? I'd be crucified in court by his defense lawyer, so I'm not in any danger. You might be, though," she said. "There's something funny going on. I don't know, some deal between him and Margo."

I remembered Margo hissing "We had a deal!" down the phone.

"Saskia saw the murder," I said. Lena gasped. "I think he knows."

"Oh, shit," Nicky said.

It was twenty past seven, time to go to Gino's. I had a feeling that someone other than Margo should play the part of mother to Saskia for a bit. Saying goodbye, I kissed Lena and on impulse I kissed Nicky. She smelled of the soft musky scent of Issey Miyake.

Thirty-eight

Thursday Night

I walked painfully back to the house, intending to order a cab to go to Gino's. I would have a quick shower, put on my grey heavy silk shirt and black gabardine trousers, wave off my mom and go out.

I ran up the stairs. As I groped for my house keys I felt the letter in the back pocket of my jeans. I would show it to Saskia. I was starting to feel quite positive. The letter proved I was innocent. Rowland had admitted it. And now that it was all in the open, Saskia had nothing more to fear.

Perhaps I didn't need to show her the letter, not with Margo there. Perhaps I should put it somewhere safe, in a plastic folder on a shelf in my living room at the very least.

I turned the key in my front door and I could hear voices in the kitchen which didn't sound like the radio. Mom! Oh my God, all that worry about Saskia and it was my mom I had to be concerned about. I slammed the door and barged into the kitchen.

Saskia was leaning against the table while my mom cleaned the stove. They looked at me in surprise.

"Hello," I said, breathlessly. I was getting too jumpy for

my own good. "I was just coming to see you," I said to Saskia. Her blonde hair was clean and fluffy. She was wearing a pale pink shirt and jeans and was looking better than I had seen her in a long while. "I assume you two have introduced yourselves."

"We spoke on the phone only the other day," Mom said. "You're a little late, I think?"

Sometimes my mom has only got to say four or five innocuous words and I want to parcel her up and send her to a thrift store. "Where's Margo?" I said, looking toward the living room, expecting to see her sitting on my couch, perhaps flicking through my record collection. What was I to think? She'd done the most stupid things, deceived me about Fletcher, taken him to the trailer, been married to Latimer. But someone had stabbed her. Suddenly I longed to see her.

"She said she was waiting for my aunty." Saskia looked at me helplessly. "To babysit, she said." Her voice trailed off. "It's nice to see you."

"Very nice to see you too. So where have you been?" I asked, watching her.

"Around. Here and there. At my mom's." She pulled at the sleeve of her shirt. She hadn't been this noncommunicative when she was in the cell at Highbury Magistrates' Court or when she was creeping around the pub thinking Fletcher was going to find her.

"She hasn't rung you then?" She looked at the clock. ". . . Margo."

"Did she say she would?" I was getting an empty feeling in my stomach.

"Well, yes."

"Before we met up at Gino's?"

My mom was looking at both of us with a concerned air. "Cup of tea?" she asked brightly.

"Yes please, Mom," I said. "We'll go into the living room while you make it."

Saskia went to leave the kitchen and we bumped into each other at the doorway. In the living room we both went to sit on the armchair. I moved over to the sofa as she sat on the chair. Everything seemed stiff and uneasy as if I didn't know her.

"She should have rung by now," she muttered. She tore at a fingernail on her left hand.

"Are you worried or just irritated?" I asked.

"I don't know—both."

"Is there anywhere we can ring?" I dragged the phone toward me and punched in Margo's number. The phone rang and no one answered. "She's not at home," I said, "so she's probably on her way to the restaurant. Don't bite your nails. Look, why don't we just go and meet her there? Or shall we wait here and get really irritated? Or worried."

"She won't be there," she said bitterly. "She hasn't rung because she doesn't want to deal with this."

"Deal with what? The trailer stuff?"

"What trailer stuff? No. This. You. You and her."

The room was suddenly silent and all the blood in my head had disappeared.

"Perhaps you should deal with it, then." Someone was using my voice to speak. I could hear my mom opening the fridge door for the milk.

"She was going to tell you that she couldn't do it."

"What?"

"Have a relationship with you."

"Why not?"

"I don't know. That's why she should have rung or come here herself. To explain. I can't do this." Her eyes swept the room. "I think, I think she's not here because she's embarrassed."

"About anything in particular?"

"I don't know. How she's behaved."

"Well, she does have a lot of questions to answer. With all that's been happening."

"She's useless under pressure. But what do you mean? What kind of questions has she got to answer?"

Now that the opportunity had come up I felt reluctant to speak. "I don't really want to have that conversation with you, Saskia. Not without her here. She's your mom." And she was stabbed.

"What? What questions?"

"Do you know how she got to the trailer on Sunday?"

"With you, wasn't it?" She had that vague look again. "Oh, no, that's right, you said. Who then?"

"I'm not exactly certain."

"But you think you know. Who?"

"Margo should tell you."

"But she's not here. She's left me to do the dirty work. She is so useless."

I couldn't tell her. "Perhaps she's having babysitting problems." It was dawning on me that there might be another reason she might not be here, but I didn't want to worry Saskia. "Perhaps she's gone to her sister's or your nan's," I suggested.

"Perhaps."

"Do they have a phone?"

"My nan does—but I haven't got her number."

My answering machine was flashing. "I think I've got a message," I said. My mother must have been singing so loud as she cleaned the kitchen that she hadn't heard it.

I listened to the message and then said, "Nothing. Just British Telecom reminding me to use their services. Look, I'll tell you what . . ." Being maternal felt peculiar. I had a desire to shelter her from what was about to happen. I had an idea, rightly as it turned out, that I was going to do something stupid. ". . . I'm just going to pop down to your mom's apartment, to see if we've missed each other in the process of all this. You can stay here with my mom, although you might have to watch something terrible on TV."

Mom walked in with three mugs of tea on a tray. "We'll have to drink these quickly because when Alan arrives we'll be off straight away."

I'd forgotten. "OK," I said to Saskia, "change of plan. You go to your auntie's to see if she's there, and I'll go straight to the apartment."

She took a mouthful of tea, then we said cheerio to my mom.

As I pulled open the front door I said to Saskia, "Did Margo actually say, in specific terms, that she was going to finish with me?"

"Yes," she said. "I'm sorry. But she actually did."

"Bastard," I muttered under my breath.

The car started. Sometimes they're worth every penny you pay for them.

I dropped Saskia off at the bottom of Cross Street where her relatives lived. I hadn't told her anything about Margo and Fletcher, or the letter from Rowland. I thought at the moment the less she knew, the better. At least she'd be safe at her auntie's apartment.

I watched her go into the building, saw her disappear and reappear as she climbed the stairs, watched her walk along the landing, knock on a door and finally disappear inside.

I turned the car, drove ten yards and then I made some calls.

Thirty-Nine

Late Thursday

I hadn't told Saskia what the message on my answering machine was because I was being motherly and protective. A husky voice had said, "Margo needs to see you." It was hard to say if it was a man or a woman. The voice gave Margo's address.

I didn't like it. And at the moment I liked Margo even less, but I knew I had to go.

Kay had made me promise I would tell her of any developments so I rang her first. She wasn't at home. "Probably out painting and decorating in some hot nightspot," I thought as her machine began. Her message said to try her at the office and gave her direct line number. I couldn't believe she was still at work this late on a Thursday night and I didn't agree with it if she was, so I left a message there and then. "Kay," I said, "it's Frankie. I'm going to Margo's."

I considered ringing the police, but my only contact was dead, and he'd been something of a double agent anyway.

I rang Lena. The answering machine snapped into action. "Oh, Lena," I said. The machine butted in, saying, "This is the message you have left," and my voice echoed back at me: "Oh, Lena—"

As I put down the phone I remembered that Kay didn't know where Margo lived.

The arrows on my mobile were low.

I rang my apartment to see if Margo had left a message there saying, "Ha, ha. It's all a joke, I'm on my way." Mom answered. I didn't even bother to reprimand her for picking up the phone. "Oh, Mom! Thank goodness. I thought you might have gone."

"Frankie?" she said. "Alan's just arrived and we're loading up."

"Has anyone rung?"

"Like who?"

"Like anyone."

"No, no. Are you all right? You sound strange. Is this to do with your license plate?"

"Possibly," I said. I was going to give her Margo's address and tell her to ring the police, or at least to ring Kay. But even as I formed the sentence in my mind it sounded ridiculous. *I* was ridiculous. Nothing was going to happen, I was just feeling melodramatic. "Have a good trip," I said.

I drove to Margo's, parked in front of her block and got out of the car. It was bitterly cold and I wished I'd worn my long coat. The sky was clear and dotted with stars. But on the ground where I was there was only old furniture and spilled plastic bags spilling household trash. I jumped as an empty tin can rolled along the pavement and rattled into the gutter. I tried not to remember that everyone in London is only ten feet away from a rat. Everything told me I shouldn't be here.

I shook my head and tried to think positive thoughts. The most positive I could get was that some people keep rats as pets.

I walked firmly up the stairs to Margo's landing and along to her apartment. As I lifted the knocker the door moved. Silently I released the knocker and pushed the door. It swung open.

I peered into the dark hall and called softly, "Margo? Margo?"

There was a small sound from the bedroom. I didn't know what to do. All sorts of embarrassing scenarios filled my mind. But someone had rung me, I was expected.

I crept down the hall, recognizing her smell of cigarettes and sweet mossy perfume. "Margo?" I tapped lightly on the bedroom door.

I gave it a gentle push. It moved and I pushed again. As the door opened in the dark room I was aware of flickering candles in saucers, I took in the bed with its soft, inviting comforter and then, at the foot of the bed, next to the mirror where I had seen her glance at herself before sinking into my arms, I saw Margo. My first instinct had been right. She wasn't alone. She was standing very close to DCI Fletcher.

They both stared at me in silence as I took two slow steps into the room.

Margo shook her head wearily. "Oh, Frankie," she said, "go away. It's very nice of you to come, but go now." The lyrics of the Moody Blues' song drifted through my head. I tried to remember how it ended for a pointer as to what to do. I wasn't quick enough.

Fletcher slid over to the door, behind me. "Oh no, Frankie, no." He shut the door. "Come in." I could smell something on his breath: alcohol.

"Don't be stupid, Fletch," Margo said.

"What's going on, Margo?" I asked.

"Nothing. Just go. This has nothing to do with you."

A mass of emotions rose up in me. She looked so lovely standing there in her soft blue cardigan and tight black skirt, her legs bare in her high-heel shoes, but half an hour ago she had finished our relationship, by proxy, and now she had called him Fletch. I shuddered.

"Are you trying to prevent me leaving, Fletcher?" I said. "That's an offense, isn't it?"

"That's the least of his worries," Margo said, with something like affection.

"Shut up," Fletcher said. There was the smell of stale sweat as he brushed against me, moving back to stand close to her. He looked wretched, like he had at court on Monday, his hair and clothes were a mess, the suit had been replaced by jeans and a rather bad green sweater.

"Just get out, Frankie," Margo said again.

"Your friend, DCI Fletcher, seems to want me to stay."

He leaned against a thin chest of drawers, looking relaxed. "I was wondering whether you wanted to come to that concert," he said.

Margo's head snapped around to stare at him.

"Thanks," I said, "but I'm busy that night. I have to wash my wig."

"They're good," he said.

"Yes, but they're not as good as they were."

"Well, Frankie, isn't that true for all of us?" Since when had he called me Frankie?

"What are you two talking about?" Margo asked suspiciously. "Since when have you called her Frankie?"

"Frankie and I share your love of music," Fletcher said. He bent his knees and, swaying to and fro, began humming "Meet on the Ledge." He had a good voice. Margo was still staring at him.

"Where's Saskia?" he asked pleasantly.

I thought Margo stiffened. "I don't know," I said.

"You've just been out to dinner with her," Fletcher said. "You must know where she is."

"Oh, please," I said.

"Why didn't you bring her with you?"

"For goodness' sake, why would I? Look, I dropped her off in town, and I have no idea where she might be now."

"Well, we're all going to have to wait till she comes then, aren't we?" Fletcher said. "It's only fair that she gets second refusal on those tickets."

"We could be waiting a really long time," I said. "You know what she's like. Anyway, I don't think she's into seventies music. What do you really want with Saskia?"

"He's going to try and get her out of this mess," Margo said. "He's going to help her get out of the country."

I stared at her. "Margo, for God's sake. The only mess Saskia's in is one that he's made for her." I had an idea that Fletcher's methods of getting Saskia out of the country might be fairly ultimate. "Why are you listening to this guy?"

"Margo and I go back a very long way," Fletcher said complacently. "A very long way. When she was just little Lesley Page, trying to break into the big time. I knew the clubs that would like Lesley. And Lesley knew what she liked, didn't you, Les?" His voice softened and I thought she swayed toward him. My stomach contracted with jealousy. Fletcher looked at me and a sickly smile covered his features. "We've had a very close relationship," he leered, "very close. Really close. I was fucking her, you know."

"Yes, all right," I said. "I get your point. We've all had to make sacrifices to get to where we are. I'm sure you'd have gone to a Sweet concert if you'd thought it would look good on your résumé."

"Oh, but you don't understand." He smiled. "We still fuck. Sorry, is that language a bit strong for you? We make love—that's what you feminists like to say, isn't it? We made love last Friday, as a matter of fact."

Margo looked over at me. "Frankie . . ." There was a catch in her voice. Her eyes swept over my face and I remembered being with her myself, in this room, three nights before. "He's Saskia's best chance," she said.

"Of what?" I exploded. "Margo, what are you doing? This is the man who drove you to Saskia's trailer when it burst into flames."

"Yes."

"And then what happened?"

"You dragged her out."

"Yes, OK, but before that."

"He went to get help."

"Right. Margo, he's a bloody policeman. He could have got help in two minutes if he'd wanted. Where did he go?"

She looked at me helplessly.

"Ask him. Ask him."

She was silent.

"I'll tell you where he went: he went and sat beside the M11 for half an hour."

Fletcher was listening with interest. "And what other bright theories have you got? As far as anyone knows, I wasn't even there. But you were, as your friend Margo made clear. Under an assumed name, it would appear from the file."

"What has he told you, Margo?" I asked.

Her head drooped. "He didn't have to tell me," she whispered. "I've known all along Saskia killed Kevin."

I was speechless with outrage. "Margo! It was not Saskia! He knows it wasn't Saskia."

"Shut the fuck up," Fletcher said quietly.

"Frankie, I know it wasn't you, I do know it wasn't you," Margo said. "But he said it was the best way. You're a barrister, you wouldn't be convicted, and then Saskia would be off the hook. That way everyone wins."

"No they don't, Margo. My career is ruined and Saskia could still be in the frame. If there's any evidence against her. Which, as far as I know, there isn't."

"Well, that depends, Frankie," Fletcher said smoothly. "There is your bloodstained shirt. *Your* shirt, covered with Latimer's blood. And I have it. Courtesy of your friend Margo. You say you lent it to Saskia Baron. Perhaps you did. Perhaps you didn't. I don't really care, one way or the other."

My stomach contracted. This was very bad news.

"Fletcher, you're a bastard," I said. He had my license plate and now he had my shirt, the shirt Saskia had been wearing as she reached out to say a last farewell to Latimer. And got covered in his blood. I could be convicted of murder. Or she could.

"I washed it," Margo said. "I washed the shirt. I did it for Saskia."

Fletcher's arm shot out and cracked across her face. She staggered against the bed and he grasped her arm to stop her from falling. "You stupid bitch."

"Don't do that!" I said.

He laughed knowingly. "She likes it."

"Jack!" she exclaimed.

"I'm sorry, I've had enough of this, I'm leaving. Margo, are you coming?" I had to get the police. Some other police.

"No, it's OK. It's OK." She fingered her face.

"I wouldn't go yet, if I were you," Fletcher said to me.

"Oh, drop it, Fletch," she sighed. "Let her go and we'll just wait for Saskia."

"Margo, you've got to come with me," I pleaded. "He can't do anything for Saskia. He was the one who set fire to the trailer."

She looked at me blankly. I wasn't getting through to her.

"Someone stabbed you, remember. It could have been you they wanted, or even me, but it was probably Saskia."

"That was nothing to do with me," Fletcher said.

"Fuck off, Fletcher," I said. "Margo, he tried to kill your daughter. Your daughter. And do you know why? Because he killed Kevin."

"I did not kill Kevin," he said. His hand still circled Margo's arm.

"And she saw him," I went on. "She told me everything that happened. She sat in my car, shivering with fear, and told me how she saw him do it." Margo's eyes gazed into mine. "She tried to help Kevin," I said, "that's how she got covered in blood. In my shirt."

"Is this true, Fletch? Is it true?" She tried to pull her arm away, to face him. He wouldn't let her go. She began to struggle. "Is it true? Tell me, is it true?" Her eyes sparkled with tears.

"What do you think?" he drawled.

She wrenched her arm away from him. "Tell me, tell me!"

"Come with me, Margo," I said. "He's waiting for Saskia so he can try again. He wants her out of the way. He'll say she died resisting arrest or some nonsense like that."

Margo stood between the two of us. If I stretched out my arm I could touch her. She looked at him in anguish. He was smiling at her, a loving, possessive, cruel smile. "Let's just wait for Saskia, shall we?" he said.

She took a step toward me and the door.

"Not yet," said Fletcher. In one movement he pulled Margo back in front of him and slid the other hand into the pocket of his jeans, then with a slow, cool flick he produced a knife. The blade was about six inches long and flashed in the candlelight. Margo gasped and her body quivered as slowly, caressingly, he lifted the knife to her throat.

Now I had a dilemma. For all I knew it was the knife that had killed Latimer. He could use it now to hurt Margo, I'd jump at him to stop him—possibly—my fingerprints would be on it and then, bingo, I've got myself implicated in another serious offense.

The room was silent. It began to dawn on me that if he was that desperate, desperate for Saskia to come, thinking her presence was the answer to all his problems, he obviously didn't know that he had a much bigger problem to deal with: Rowland's note. I could use it to barter with him. It was the only thing which stood between me and

Saskia and a conviction for murder, the only objective piece of evidence in this whole affair, and it was currently nestling three feet away from Fletcher in the pocket of my jeans. If he got hold of it either Saskia or I would be doomed. "I have a letter," I said desperately.

He raised his eyes with a look of insolence. "Interesting. Would that be a French letter? A love letter? A chain letter?"

"I have your colleague's suicide note," I said, watching his face. "Your little protégé has spoken from the other side of the grave. And put you in the center of the frame. He says it was you, Fletcher."

"Is that true?" Margo gasped.

Fletcher said nothing.

"And, Fletcher, I must tell you that my solicitor has the only copy of that letter. Locked securely in her safe," I added. I stopped myself checking to see if it was still in my back pocket.

"There is no letter," he said.

"Now, how did it go . . . ?" I began, " 'I have allowed myself to be used. I was with my superior officer. We killed Latimer. Since then he has blackmailed me. I stabbed an innocent woman, I broke into the home of another woman . . .' Does that remind you of what you and Rowland have been up to?"

An expression like fear passed across his face, but it could have been anger or even grief.

Margo saw it. "Dear God," she said. "Oh, dear God."

Then Fletcher said, "Well, you'd better get the letter, hadn't you?"

"I might, repeat, *might,* get it for you," I said, affecting a jaunty confidence, "but only on the understanding that you let Margo go and all possible charges against me and Saskia are dropped."

"Get it," he said. He hitched the knife up and angled it close to Margo's jugular.

"OK," I said. "But I shall need to use my phone." I put my hand in the pocket of my jacket. "I'm getting out my cell phone," I said, carefully drawing it out, then pressing the numbers of Kay's direct line. I spoke into the phone. "Hi . . . Yeah, I'm fine . . . It's about the letter. Can you bring it to—" Abruptly Fletcher leaned across and snatched the phone from my hand and put it to his ear.

"Hello?" he said. "Liar!" he shouted. "She's not there." Skillfully he jabbed at the off button and threw the phone on the bed. "You haven't got the letter, have you? There is no letter."

I looked at my watch. "According to my calculations, she should be with us in about five minutes and then you'll find out."

"Well, if it's not in my hand in the next five minutes, you'd better start thinking about stain remover. Blood-stains." As if to prove his point he nicked the skin at Margo's throat.

Her hand flew to her neck and her eyes widened as she looked at the smear of blood on her fingers.

"And when, or should I say *if* she gets here," Fletcher's confidence was returning, "I'm afraid she will find herself assisting you on an assault charge, assaulting Lesley Latimer," he enunciated. "Whether that's ABH or GBH depends on how well behaved everyone is. Let's hope she remembers the Legal Aid forms."

Actual Bodily Harm carries a maximum sentence of five years, Grievous Bodily Harm could carry life. It all depends on the severity of the assault. What exactly was he planning?

My phone rang. I dived for it. The number on the screen was not a number I recognized. "Hello?" I murmured.

"Hi, it's Saskia. I wondered if you'd found her." Her bright tone was tinged with anxiety.

"Oh, hi," I said, "How are you? Everything's fine. Can't

talk right at the moment." I didn't want her coming to the apartment.

"That's her, isn't it?" Fletcher reached out again, but I jumped back in time and fell on to the bed.

"Frankie? Are you all right?" Saskia asked.

Fletcher shouted, "Saskia, we need you. Your mother needs you."

"Who was that?" Saskia's voice quivered. "Are you at the apartment? I'm coming over."

"No need, Lena," I said, "it's just some drunk."

"I'm coming now," Saskia said. The line went dead.

In the room the candles sputtered and flickered. Margo stood frozen in Fletcher's embrace. Saskia was on her way.

The letter burned in my pocket. Should I give it to Fletcher, to stop him wounding Margo? Or should I keep it, and watch him cut her, in order to safeguard the evidence which would clear Saskia? And me. I knew Margo would want to save Saskia, so in that sense I knew she wouldn't want me to give him the letter. But would giving it to him save her anyway? He seemed to have lost any sense of logic. He was inflicting serious injury on a woman he desired, for whom he had bought sexy, expensive dresses. But then that was the behavior of many of the men in my cases. I could hardly say he had taken leave of his senses.

"Fletch," Margo murmured.

He grazed the knife against her throat again and her legs buckled. Blood was soaking into the neck of her cardigan. In the thick warm silence, as my hand slid toward my back pocket, there was a rap on the front door. Everyone froze.

Fletcher's eyes darted from Margo to the door and back. He kept the knife at Margo's throat as the sound of tapping on each door in the hallway echoed in the bedroom.

"Margo?" It was Saskia's voice. "Margo?"

I looked at Margo and she looked at me. In one second we shared a silent conversation.

For goodness' sake, Margo.

I know.

How could you?

Oh, don't.

Saskia's blonde head was peering into the room and outside the building the sounds of wailing sirens grew louder as simultaneously Margo stamped very hard on Fletcher's foot and I, with a roar, leapt for the wrist of the hand holding the knife. Fletcher howled and dropped the knife. He lost his balance and Margo and I shoved him to the floor and fell on to his chest. With a startled look, Saskia came and sat on his legs. Outside there was a screech of brakes.

My cell phone rang. With one hand I reached across the bed for it. "Kay!" I said, reading the name on the screen. "At last. Where are you? I can hardly hear you."

"Outside with the police," she said. "What have you been up to?"

I looked around the room. "You'd better come in and find out."

Forty

Friday Evening—The Club

Lena and I were sitting at a small round table at the club. A few people were dancing on the podium to the sound of the Pointer Sisters. On the table sat a shiny stainless-steel ice bucket, filled with ice, water and a half-empty bottle of Laurent Perrier champagne which Lena had bought. Lena, dressed in a long navy coat, was glowing with good cheer. I was wearing my great leather jacket and black jeans, I had been asleep most of the day, I was fresh, I was clean. And I felt completely and utterly miserable.

"Think of it this way," Lena said, "it was great fun, but it was just one of those things."

"If you're going to speak to me in platitudes," I said, "it would help if they were a bit more specific."

"You mean like, Margo was a nice girl, but she would stir her tea with her finger?"

"That sort of thing," I moaned.

"Here, misery." Lena fished round in her backpack. She slid a small, flat plastic bag across the table.

"What's this?"

"Thank Nicky. She knows someone who knows someone who's got a record shop."

I opened the bag and pulled out an old 45. It was the Sir Douglas Quintet singing "She's About a Mover."

"Oh my God, Lena, you're right, she is wonderful! Let's

have a toast." We raised our glasses. "To my best friend, for remembering."

"To my best friend," said Lena, "for being cleared of all suspicion." We both took a large mouthful of champagne.

"To me," Lena went on, "for helping to save the day." My mom had been so worried about my phone call to her that she had found Lena's number in my phone book and rung her and they'd agreed that I sounded as if I needed help. So Lena had telephoned Nicky to get Kay's number and then she rang Kay who had Saskia's address which she gave to the police. We drank more champagne.

"To me, for being instructed in an inquiry that will last three months." I had dashed into chambers that morning with my Grounds of Appeal and Gavin, with a smile on his face, had told me the great news. He'd also told me there was an emergency management committee meeting tonight to discuss Marcus's position in chambers, which he said I could attend if I wanted to but they would understand if I didn't.

"Three months!" Lena crowed. "Think of the money— you'll be living in clover. You can get a new car. We'll be able to go out for really good meals." We emptied our glasses.

Lena took hold of the bottle and filled my glass to the brim. "Do another one," she said. "Go on."

"To Mom and Alan and their future happiness." My mom had arrived at Margo's apartment at the same time as the police, while we were still sitting on Fletcher. "If this is all to do with a missing license plate, I think it's getting a little out of hand," she had said in her best school teacher voice. Then we had to wait for Alan, who was trying to find somewhere to park the Winnebago. And after Fletcher was led away I had stood with a small group of interested young boys to wave them off on their weekend adventure.

"A final toast," Lena concluded, "to true love. Wherever we may find it." We poured champagne down our throats.

Kay appeared at the doorway.

"What's she doing here?" Lena asked with a sigh.

"She said she might drop in when she rang me to say I didn't have to go back to the police station." Apparently the police were very grateful for PC Rowland's suicide note. I raised a hand in greeting.

But Kay was looking toward the bar where Ash was polishing glasses. She walked across the room and said something to Ash. Ash put a bottle on the bar and then pointed toward our table.

Kay came over and slid another bottle of champagne into the bucket. She put two glasses on the table. "Ash is going to join us in a minute for a quick glass of champagne. To celebrate our victory."

"Oh yes?" I said.

"Stoke Newington police rang this afternoon. They've interviewed Saskia, and now they're saying that Rowland suffered a breakdown and flipped. They may need to interview you about the fire, but they seem to be working on the basis it was an accident."

"And where does Fletcher come into their theory?"

"Not sure. But people like him. They say he's a good policeman. There's no independent evidence about the other stuff in Rowland's letter. Your friend Margo doesn't want to press charges . . ."

Ash strolled over to the table. I opened Kay's bottle of champagne and poured her a glass.

"Congratulations," she said, raising her glass to me. She put a tin of tobacco on the table and began to roll a cigarette. As she licked the paper the stud in her tongue flashed and I thought of Margo. I was surrounded by reminders of my lack of social success.

Kay was delving into her handbag. She drew out a long thin envelope which she handed to Ash. "I am paying Ash for the work she has just completed on the house," she said clearly. She raised her glass. "To purely business trans-actions," she said.

I looked at her suspiciously.

"Saskia rang," Kay went on. We had left Saskia and Margo in an ambulance sticking Band-Aids on the small cuts on Margo's neck, talking. "She said she might come tonight, but only so long as Margo's not singing."

Saskia obviously felt as screwed over by Margo as I did.

The MC leapt on to the stage and set up a microphone. "We didn't think she'd make it!" she announced. "But she's here, back by popular demand! Please clear the floor and give a big hand to Margo Baron!"

The small crowd in the bar applauded and someone whooped. Lena threw an anxious look at me as Margo stepped on to the stage dressed in the tight red dress and the red high-heeled shoes. The pianist played the first notes of "Stand By Me."

Carefully I put my new single on the table, pushed back my chair and walked over to the edge of the stage.